Georgia Walks

Georgia Walks

**Discovery Hikes
Through the Peach
State's Natural and
Human History**

Ren and Helen Davis

PEACHTREE
ATLANTA

Ω

Published by
PEACHTREE PUBLISHERS, LTD.
1700 Chattahoochee Avenue
Atlanta, Georgia 30318-2112
www.peachtree-online.com

Maps by Ortelius Design
Design by Loraine M. Balcsik
Composition by Robin Sherman

First Edition
10 9 8 7 6 5 4 3 2 1

Manufactured in the United States of America

Library of Congress Cataloging in Publication Data
Davis, Ren, 1951–
    Georgia walks : discovery hikes through the peach state's natural and human history /
    written by Ren and Helen Davis. – 1st ed.
        p. cm.
    Includes bibliographical references.
    ISBN 1-56145-212-2
    1. Georgia—Tours. 2. Georgia—History, Local. 3. Historic Sites—Georgia—Guidebooks.
4. Parks—Georgia—Guidebooks. 5. Natural History—Georgia—Guidebooks. 6.
Walking—Georgia—Guidebooks. 7. Hiking—Georgia—Guidebooks. I. Davis, Helen,
1951– II. Title.

F284.3 .D38 2001
917.5804'44–dc21
                                                                    2001021093

CONTENTS

NORTHWESTERN MOUNTAINS (HUB CITY: ROME)

Rugged river canyon on the western
slope of Lookout Mountain. Scenic
views, ancient geological formations,
and dramatic waterfalls.

Pastoral valley between mountain
ridges. Site of one of the pivotal battles
of the Civil War.

Mountain and woodland trails with
scenic views of ridges and valleys.
Pocket campground was the site of a
Civilian Conservation Corps camp
(1938–42).

An ancient stone wall, dating back over
1500 years, is the centerpiece of this picturesque state park high in the Cohutta
Mountains.

A broad, open plain near the banks of
New Town Creek was the site of the historic last capital of the Cherokee Nation.
The Cherokees' removal to Oklahoma
on the Trail of Tears began here. Reconstructed buildings and woodland trails.

Situated at the confluence of three rivers
(the Oostanaula, Etowah, and Coosa)
and surrounded by rolling hills, Rome

has been the commercial hub of northwestern Georgia for over a century. The downtown business district and surrounding neighborhoods are a treasure of Victorian architecture.

Located just north of Rome, Berry College occupies a rolling and wooded, 28,000-acre campus nestled in the Appalachian foothills.

Footpaths lead to earthen mounds built by Native Americans more than a thousand years ago.

NORTHEASTERN MOUNTAINS (HUB CITY: GAINESVILLE)

Located in the foothills of the Appalachians, Dahlonega was the site of the nation's first gold rush. Historic buildings around the town square and the nearby campus of North Georgia College and State University are highlights.

U.S. Forest Service area features picturesque waterfalls and a legend of the Spanish explorer Hernando de Soto.

This stretch of the National Scenic and Historic Trail captures the rugged flavor of the unbroken footpath between Georgia and Maine. (This is a linear hike; a second vehicle or shuttle is recommended.)

Scenic trails offer a glimpse at the rugged mountains that inspired native poet Byron Herbert Reece. Vogel is the state's second oldest park and several facilities were constructed by the Civilian Conservation Corps in the 1930s.

Majestic Anna Ruby Falls springs forth from mountains that were heavily logged a century ago. The Smith Creek Trail winds through highland ridges and cove forests of the Southern Appalachians, connecting the falls area with Unicoi State Park. (This is a linear hike; we recommend a second vehicle or shuttle.)

On this meandering loop trail along the ridges of geologically diverse Black Rock Mountain, there is evidence of early 20th-century logging and forest restoration. Watch for the rock fall caused by the last Ice Age.

CHATTAHOOCHEE VALLEY (HUB CITY: COLUMBUS)

HEART OF GEORGIA (HUB CITY: MACON)

Once a major business hub in the heart of Georgia's "Cotton Kingdom," Americus may be best known today as the world headquarters for Habitat for Humanity. The downtown business district is a treasure of well-preserved Victorian buildings anchored by the elegant Windsor Hotel.

The major commercial center for southern Georgia, Valdosta is rich with Victorian architecture. The walk includes a visit to the Spanish Mission–style campus of Valdosta State University.

CLASSIC GEORGIA (HUB CITY: AUGUSTA)

Established in the 1730s by General James Oglethorpe as a frontier outpost on the Savannah River, Augusta has grown to be the state's second-largest city. The city is filled with historic buildings, churches, and houses (including the boyhood home of President Woodrow Wilson). The Riverwalk is a popular gathering place.

Dug by immigrant and slave labor during the 1840s, the Augusta Canal was built so that barges could bypass dangerous river shoals as they delivered cotton to Augusta's mills. Today the canal towpath is a popular linear park for walking and biking. (We recommend a second vehicle or shuttle.)

Washington is a place rich in Revolutionary War and Civil War history. Established as Fort Washington in 1780, it was the first community in the nation to bear the future president's name. Eighty-five years later, Confederate President Jefferson Davis held the last meeting of his cabinet here. The city is filled with historic homes and buildings. The 1779 battle of Kettle Creek took place a few miles outside Washington.

Established in the early 19th century on the bluffs above the Oconee River, Athens grew up around the campus of the University of Georgia, the oldest land-grant college in the nation. Explore historic downtown, nearby Prince Street, and the campus of Old College.

xi

Georgia's Many Treasures

From the rugged peaks of the Southern Appalachians and the rolling hills of the Piedmont Plateau, to the broad Chattahoochee River Valley and the ancient Coastal Plain, Georgia offers the traveler a rich and diverse treasure of natural beauty and human history.

Learn about our geologic past revealed in the walls of Cloudland Canyon, on the face of Black Rock Mountain, and in the shifting dunes of Cumberland Island. Marvel at the mysterious legacies of our native ancestors atop Fort Mountain, and at Etowah, Ocmulgee, and Kolomoki Mounds. Share the excitement of pioneers who founded a colony and built a state as you stroll through Savannah, Brunswick, Washington, Augusta, Milledgeville, Dahlonega, Columbus, Macon, Athens, and other historic communities. Experience the tragedies of the Civil War at the battlefields of Chickamauga, Pickett's Mill, and Atlanta, and ponder its enormous human cost when you visit Andersonville. And enjoy scenic beauty at Vogel and Unicoi State Parks, along the rugged Appalachian Trail, by the shores of the mighty Chattooga River,

at Callaway Gardens and Pine Mountain, and along the coast at historic Melon Bluff.

In *Georgia Walks*, a companion to our *Atlanta Walks* guide, we invite readers to experience on foot some of the very best the state has to offer. The fifty-nine walks in the fifty-two chapters cover more than three hundred miles of the state's most beautiful and historic landscapes. Hike to scenic forest summits; pause to read battlefield monuments; stroll through vibrant small towns and historic districts, marveling at the varied architecture; and feel salt breezes spinning through seaside dunes—all at your own pace.

From the original idea to the finished manuscript, this guide was more than a decade in the making. Many people lent us encouragement, shared ideas about their favorite destinations, and generously offered shuttle rides, an occasional meal, or an overnight stay as we crisscrossed the state seeking new places to walk. Even as this guide goes to press, we continue to search for other destinations to explore by foot.

While it would be impossible to recognize the many persons in local historical societies and visitor centers who helped us along the way, we are truly grateful to Margaret Quinlin, Kathy Landwehr, Vicky Holifield, Loraine Balcsik, Melanie McMahon, Amy Sproull (now at the American Cancer Society), and the other creative staff at Peachtree Publishers who encouraged us to keep exploring and writing. A special thank-you goes also to our editor, Marian Gordin, who never ceased finding ways to trim a lengthy manuscript without sacrificing the flavor of each destination and its story.

For more than a dozen years, we have been blessed to have the opportunity to explore Atlanta and Georgia through the eyes of our son, Nelson, watching him grow in understanding and appreciation for the rich heritage of his home state. As with *Atlanta Walks*, this guide is dedicated in part to him.

It is also dedicated to Virlyn B. Moore Jr., a native Georgian, lawyer, banker, and historian, past president of the Atlanta Historical Society, master storyteller, and longtime family friend who, as he passes his ninetieth birthday, continues to share his contagious enthusiasm for Georgia's colorful history. He, too, is one of Georgia's many treasures.

Ren and Helen Davis
Atlanta, Georgia
February 2001

Discovery Hikes Through Georgia's Natural and Human History

The path of Georgia's history begins high in the Appalachian Mountains. The oldest range on Earth, the Appalachian peaks once stood taller than the Himalayas. Worn down by the winds and rains of almost a half-billion years, the jagged summits now gently curve along nearly unbroken ridges stretching from northwestern Georgia to Canada.

A hike on any trail in north Georgia will offer a glimpse into the distant geologic past, but some of the best spots for exploring include the sandstone and limestone formations of **Cloudland Canyon State Park** [chap. 1] on the western side of Lookout Mountain; along the shaded **Appalachian National Scenic Trail** chap. 11]; and atop **Black Rock Mountain** [chap. 14], where large boulders were sheared from the side of the mountain during the last Ice Age.

The massive amount of rock eroded from these mountains washed toward the sea over many hundreds of millions of years, eventually forming the rolling hills of the Piedmont and the sandy soils of the Coastal Plain. The **State Botanical Garden of Georgia** [chap. 46] and **Little Ocmulgee State Park** [chap. 38] are excellent places to explore these younger, but still ancient, landscapes. The state's newest and most fragile natural areas, having been formed in only the past few thousand years, are the string of coastal marshes and barrier islands, including **Melon Bluff Natural Heritage Preserve** [chap. 49] and **Cumberland Island National Seashore** [chap. 52].

While the subject of how man reached the North American continent remains under debate, archaeological evidence indicates that humans arrived in Georgia at least 12,000 years ago. The earliest inhabitants, the Paleo-Indians (10,000–8,000 B.C.E.), were nomadic hunter-gatherers who left behind few artifacts and little evidence of their existence. Spear points and stone tools from these ancient peoples have been found in various locations along the Savannah and Flint Rivers, near Lake Allatoona, and at **Ocmulgee National Monument** [chap. 34]. Ocmulgee, an extraordinarily significant site on the banks of the Ocmulgee River, was occupied almost continuously from 8,000 B.C. to 1700 A.D. Another ancient site, possibly dating from the Archaic-Indian Period (8,000–1,000 B.C.E.), is **Fort Mountain [chap. 4]**, a location that remains shrouded in mystery. Just beneath the summit of this peak, high in the Cohutta Range of northwestern Georgia, sits a man-made stone wall of ancient and unknown origin. Today the wall is the centerpiece of a popular state park.

The most dramatic examples of the Native-American presence in Georgia are the temple and burial mounds constructed beginning more than a thousand years ago by Mississippian Period Indians (800–1540 C.E.). In addition to the mounds at Ocmulgee, two other major sites have been preserved. Along the banks of the Etowah River at **Etowah Mounds State Historic Site [chap. 8]** are three mounds constructed by a prosperous Indian community that lived and farmed here for more than 500 years. Further south, a few miles from the Chattahoochee River below Columbus, is **Kolomoki Mounds State Historic Park [chap. 30]** preserving seven different mounds ranging from 1000 to 2000 years old. The park's museum displays evidence of Indian cultures at the site dating back more than 6,000 years.

The Spanish were the first Europeans to explore and settle parts of Georgia. In 1540, Hernando de Soto and his conquistadores traveled north through the Chattahoochee Valley searching for gold and plundering Creek villages, including the town of Ulibahali near present day Rome. Much of de Soto's exact route is unknown, but myths of his presence abound. **DeSoto Falls Scenic Recreation Area [chap. 10]**, high in the Appalachians, draws its name from a bit of what some believed was Spanish armor found near the falls many years ago. While it may be unlikely that de Soto ever saw his namesake falls, it does not detract from their natural beauty. A few years after de Soto's expedition, Spanish priests traveling north from Florida, established several missions along the coastal barrier islands. The reluctance of the native Guale Indians to convert to Christianity, combined with pressure from the English in the Carolinas, finally forced the Spanish to abandon these colonization efforts.

The modern history of Georgia truly began with the arrival of General James Edward Oglethorpe and the first English colonists to Yamacraw Bluff above the Savannah River in February 1733. Their earliest settlement, laid out in a precise pattern of streets and squares became the prosperous city of **Savannah [chap. 48]**, which is still recognized as one of the most historic and masterfully planned cities in North America. While the colony of Georgia was established for commercial purposes, it had great military importance as well, serving as a buffer between Spanish enemies in Florida and the prosperous English plantations of South Carolina.

Only a short time after his arrival, Oglethorpe sought to solidify the English presence by building a series of military outposts. Several forts were built south of Savannah to protect the colony from the Spanish. These were located at Sunbury near Midway, at Fort King George east of Darien, and at Fort Frederica on St. Simons Island. Another fort, built to protect Savannah from hostile natives, was located up the Savannah River at **Augusta [chap. 42]**.

The coastal settlement of **Brunswick [chap. 50]** was established in 1771 and grew to become one of the major shipbuilding and fishing ports in the nation. In the forty-four years between the settlement of the colony and the outbreak of the Revolution, settlers pushed into the interior and established isolated forts and farming villages. One of the most historic towns is **Washington [chap. 44]**, established as Fort Heard in the early 1770s, and renamed to honor General George Washington in 1780.

At the outbreak of the American Revolution in 1775, few colonies were as bitterly divided between patriot and Royalist supporters as Georgia. Families were torn apart and neighbors fought a guerilla war so brutal

that one British officer described the colony as a "hornet's nest." For most of the war, Savannah and Augusta remained under British control, while the rugged interior, made up mostly of self-reliant frontiersmen, was decidedly pro-patriot. The two sides clashed in the pivotal Battle of Kettle Creek outside Washington in 1779. The British were badly beaten in what patriot General Andrew Pickens called the "severest check and chastisement the Tories (loyalists) ever received in South Carolina or Georgia."

Only a few years after winning independence, Georgia became the site of another revolution with profound and far-reaching consequences. New Englander Eli Whitney, serving as a teacher for the Greene family at Mulberry Grove Plantation near Savannah, observed slaves tediously pulling cotton fiber from its seed. He believed he could build a machine to do the job more efficiently. After a few weeks of work, he demonstrated his first cotton engine [gin]. Farmers quickly realized that they could separate nearly ten times as much cotton per day with the machine than by hand. Almost overnight, cotton went from a marginal crop to the agricultural staple for central Georgia and much of the South. However, cotton planting and harvesting remained enormously labor intensive, requiring plantation owners to add many thousands of slaves to do the work.

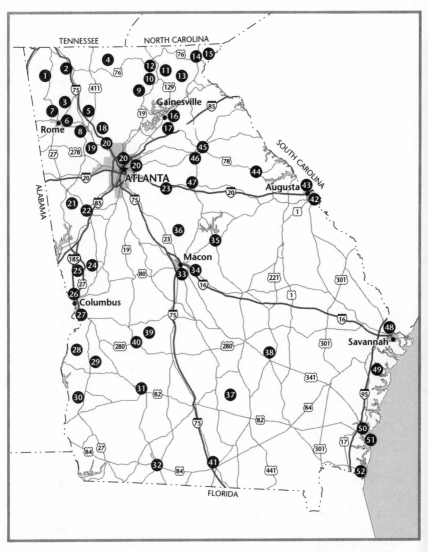

Numbers in black circles correspond to chapter numbers.

By the early years of the nineteenth century, cotton had become the South's major agricultural product, and slavery was so entrenched it would only be ended in a bloody civil war.

In the first quarter of the century, the Creek and Cherokee were forced to cede more of their ancestral lands as settlers moved even further into the interior. With the shift in population, the state capital was moved to Louisville in 1796, and then again to the new village of **Milledgeville [chap. 35]** in 1803. The capital would remain here until the final relocation to Atlanta in 1868. Across the central part of the state older settlements grew, new communities were established, and railway lines were built to support the expanding cotton trade. Some of the best preserved of these antebellum towns include **Macon [chap. 33]**, on the banks of the Ocmulgee River, **Columbus [chap. 26]** on the Chattahoochee, **Madison [chap. 47]**, **Covington/Oxford [chap. 23]**, **Newnan [chap. 22]** and **Athens [chap. 45]**, which was also home to the fledgling **University of Georgia [chap. 45]**. The living-history village of **Westville [chap. 29]**, near Lumpkin, captures the atmosphere of a typical small Georgia town of 1850.

In addition to railroads, waterways were used to transport cotton. The **Augusta Canal [chap. 43]** was completed in the late 1840s to permit cotton-laden barges to bypass treach-

erous shoals on the Savannah River above Augusta. Built mostly with slave and immigrant Irish laborers, the canal was an engineering marvel of its day.

In the late 1820s, the discovery of gold on Cherokee lands near present-day **Dahlonega [chap. 9]** brought scores of prospectors into north Georgia and heightened demands for the removal of the Indians from the state. From their capital at **New Echota [chap. 5]** the Cherokee used all available legal means to prevent eviction, but failed. A decade after the discovery of gold on their land, the Cherokee were forced from Georgia on the infamous Trail of Tears. A few years earlier, the Cherokee's chief rivals, the Creeks, had been forced through a series of treaties to forfeit their ancestral lands in Georgia and relocate to the west. The final treaty, signed at Indian Springs in 1825, led to the assassination, by fellow Creeks, of Chief William McIntosh on the grounds of **McIntosh Reserve [chap. 21]**, his plantation on the banks of the Chattahoochee River.

As the nation expanded westward, tensions between slave-holding Southern states and free Northern states worsened. After the failure of the Great Compromise of 1850, guerilla warfare over the slavery issue broke out in the new territories of Kansas and Nebraska. The blood shed there would be only a precursor of the horrors to come. The election of anti-slavery candidate Abraham Lincoln to the presidency in November 1860 forced many Southern slave owners to seriously consider secession from the United States. South Carolina was the first state to leave the Union, seceding only a month after the election. In February 1861, the Confederate States of America was established at Montgomery, Alabama. By spring, nearly a dozen states, including Georgia, had followed South Carolina into secession.

On April 12, 1861, the hostilities that many considered inevitable finally broke out when Confederate artillery shelled Fort Sumter in Charleston harbor. Four years of civil war lay ahead and, by its end in April 1865, more than 600,000 soldiers would die on battlefields throughout the North and South.

Because Georgia was the breadbasket of the Confederacy, and Atlanta the hub of its transportation network, Confederate military forces sought to protect the state's vital resources. Shortly after secession, Rebel troops captured Fort Pulaski located on the river approach to the port of Savannah. They held the masonry fort until the spring of 1862 when it was heavily damaged by U.S. Navy warships armed with new and powerful rifled-cannon.

A year later, in September 1863, the conflict reached Georgia in earnest when Union and Rebel forces fought one of the bloodiest battles of the war at **Chickamauga [chap. 2]**, just south of Chattanooga. The following spring, the Federal army commanded by Maj. Gen. William T. Sherman began an invasion of Georgia with the goal of capturing Atlanta and marching on to the sea.

The Rebel commander, Maj. Gen. Joseph E. Johnston tried in vain to stall the invasion, fighting battles at Resaca, Cassville, and New Hope Church, as he slowly retreated southward. At **Pickett's Mill State Historic Site [chap. 19]**, the Rebels tried a rare night attack to slow the Union advance. Finally, Johnston's weary troops retreated to the heights of Kennesaw Mountain and the defenses of Atlanta, engaging Sherman's troops in the **Battles for Atlanta [chap. 20]** throughout the months of June and July 1864. Faced with capture by overwhelming forces, the Rebel army abandoned Atlanta in early September and the city fell into Union hands. By Christmas, Sherman's troops had carved a 60-mile wide swath through the state and offered the city of Savannah as a Christmas present to the newly reelected President Lincoln. Four months later, the bloodiest war in American history was over.

The assassination of President Lincoln, only days after the South's defeat, spurred an anger in the North that was soon fueled by revelations of horrible conditions and alleged atrocities committed on Union soldiers at the terribly overcrowded Confederate prisoner-of-war camp at **Andersonville [chap. 39]**. In an act of vengeance by the victors, camp commander Henry Wirz was the only Confederate official hung for "war crimes."

Despite the harshness of Reconstruction, Georgia's economy rebuilt and expanded. By the 1880s the state, with its moderate climate and rich natural resources, was growing both as a commercial center and a resort destination. Towns like **Valdosta [chap. 41]** in the south and **Rome [chap. 6]** in the north prospered as regional economic centers, while **Thomasville [chap. 32]** became a winter vacation retreat for wealthy northern businessmen. Some of America's most prominent families, including the Rockefellers, Cranes, Macys, and Morgans, also chose Georgia as their vacation destination, establishing the exclusive **Jekyll Island Club [chap. 51]** on that pristine barrier island in the 1880s. Today the historic island village offers a glimpse into that opulent, gilded age.

A migration of a different kind occurred in the pine hills of central Georgia in the 1890s, when northern newspaper publisher Philander Fitzgerald purchased 50,000 acres of land and created a deep South colony for Union veterans. By 1895, nearly 3,000 people had moved to the new town of **Fitzgerald [chap. 37]**. While most locals welcomed their former enemies, others still referred to the town as a "nest of Yankees" well into the next century.

The early years of the twentieth century saw continued growth as expanding railroads and roadways linked communities throughout the state. Cities like **Gainesville [chap. 16]** and **Albany [chap. 31]** became regional hubs for business, transportation and education. The U.S. Army turned **Ft. Benning [chap. 27]** near Columbus into a major center for training infantry and paratroopers who would fight the nation's battles from Normandy to the Persian Gulf.

Beginning in the early 1800s, a century of poor agricultural practices depleted the soil and caused massive erosion in some areas of the state. Interestingly, these practices led to the creation of geologically unique **Providence Canyon [chap. 28]**. Crop failures and boll weevils plunged Georgia into a post–World War I recession and, only a few years later, the state was further damaged by the catastrophic effects of the Great Depression. Near his home in Warm Springs, future president Franklin D. Roosevelt saw this devastation first hand and used his land on Pine Mountain as a model farm demonstrating soil-saving techniques. Textile executive Cason Callaway, owner of land near Roosevelt's farm, collaborated in these efforts. Later, portions of Roosevelt's land became **Franklin D. Roosevelt State Park** [**chap. 24**], and Callaway's property the world renowned **Callaway Gardens** [**chap. 25**].

The New Deal programs developed by President Roosevelt proved helpful in providing meaningful work for many unemployed. An especially popular program, the Civilian Conservation Corps (CCC) was responsible for a wide variety of soil conservation, forest restoration, and parks development projects across the state. We may still see the legacy of their work in many places including the **Pocket Recreation Area** [**chap. 3**] in the Chattahoochee National Forest, **Piedmont National Wildlife Refuge** [**chap. 36**] in the Oconee National Forest, and at **Vogel** [**chap. 12**], **Little Ocmulgee**, and **Roosevelt State Parks**.

During the latter half of the century, the explosive growth in Georgia's population placed even greater emphasis on preserving the state's rich natural legacy for everyone's enjoyment. Today, city dwellers flock to places like **Anna Ruby Falls** and **Unicoi State Park** [**chap. 13**] near Helen, the **Chattooga River Trail** [**chap. 15**] outside Clayton, **Elachee Nature Center** [**chap. 17**] in Gainesville, **Red Top Mountain State Park** [**chap. 18**] east of Cartersville, and **Melon Bluff Natural Heritage Preserve** [**chap. 48**] south of Savannah, where they may relax and renew a kinship with the natural world that began with those first Georgians so many centuries ago.

Oak Hill, in Rome, the lifelong home of educator Martha Berry

Cherokee Chieftain Vann's Tavern at New Echota

The stone observation tower atop Fort Mountain

European-style dairy buildings on the Berry College campus at Rome

NORTHWESTERN MOUNTAINS

FROM THE AIR, the mountains of northwestern Georgia appear as long fingers stretching southwestward from Tennessee into Alabama. This is the Ridge and Valley region of the Southern Appalachians, an area very different from the mountains in northeastern Georgia. Here, the slopes and summits are sedimentary, not volcanic in origin, composed of countless layers of sand, mud, and organic materials deposited on the floor of ancient seas and marshes for hundreds of millions of years.

Northwestern Georgia's human history is no less fascinating. The wide river valleys between the ridges were village sites and natural trade routes more than 2,000 years ago. Mysterious reminders of lost civilizations exist along with evidence of the Cherokee Nation, including their final capital city at New Echota, abandoned when they were forced west on the infamous Trail of Tears in the 1830s. A decade later the first railroad line was constructed through the region to connect the new city of Atlanta with the settlement of Ross's Landing (Chattanooga). Federal and Confederate armies clashed in these remote mountains during the Civil War.

Northwestern Georgia's natural beauty remained a well-kept secret until the coming of the automobile and construction of reliable roads into the region in the early 20th century. Today, the area is easily reached from interstate highways and a network of state and county roads, making the state parks, scenic areas, small towns, and historic cities popular destinations for day and weekend explorations.

CHAPTER 1

Cloudland Canyon State Park

LOCATION

✚ The park is about 15 miles northwest of LaFayette on GA 136. LaFayette is about 27 miles northwest of I-75 (exit 133) where GA 136 intersects with U.S. 27. *Information:* (706) 657-4050.

PARKING

🚗 There is a large parking area adjacent to the picnic grounds, near the East Rim Trail. A daily parking fee is charged.

BACKGROUND

📖 A two-hour drive from Atlanta, Cloudland Canyon is 1,800 feet above sea level along the spine of Lookout Mountain. For millennia, the cascading waters of Daniel and Bear Creeks have carved deep gorges as they flow—uncharacteristically—northward through Sitton Gulch. At its extreme, the resulting Y-shaped Cloudland Canyon is more than 1,000 feet deep. Look down the walls and you travel back in time more than 300 million years, to a world before dinosaurs roamed the Earth, when this region was beneath a shallow, primordial sea.

The Cumberland Plateau is marked by almost flat-topped mountains, formed during the Paleozoic era (580–200 million years ago). For more than 70 million years, shifting tides, rising and falling waters, rain, and wind deposited countless layers of sand in an inland ocean. Surrounding lands were marsh forests not unlike those in the present-day Okefenokee Swamp.

The youngest rock is the hard sandstone on the summit, while the oldest is the limestone that makes up the wide base of Lookout Valley. The East and West Rim Trails provide an excellent overview of the canyon's geologic history, with each chapter carefully detailed in the steep descents to the two spectacular waterfalls on Daniel Creek.

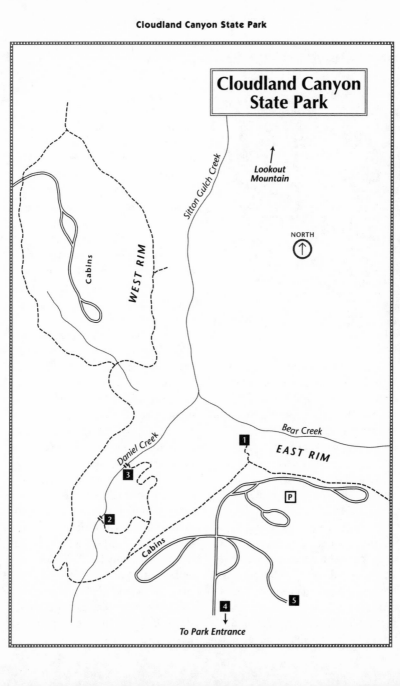

Cloudland Canyon
State Park

Cloudland Canyon

Over countless centuries, as sediment fell over sediment, each was compressed and, under tremendous pressure, hardened into solid rock. As the Earth alternately warmed and cooled, the waters expanded and contracted many times causing layers to be of varying thicknesses and producing sediments composed of different materials.

Beneath these layers, near the bottom of the canyon, are sediments of dark gray-brown shale. Unlike the sea-deposited sand, the thin and easily broken shale is hardened clay from a wide river delta and marsh that existed before warmer climatic conditions enlarged the inland ocean. Much of the material seen in the cliffs at this level was laid down during the Pennsylvanian period about 280–325 million years ago.

At the bottom of the canyon, visible in only a few places in Lookout Valley, are thick layers of soft, porous limestone created from the remains of sea plants and creatures that lived in an earlier Mississippian period ocean about 325–340 million years ago. The presence of limestone is the geologic indicator that this is cavern country. In the vernacular of spelunkers, or cavers, the area is simply called "TAG" (Tennessee, Alabama, Georgia) and is noted for its many underground chambers.

While human beings have inhabited this area for many centuries, the rugged terrain made travel difficult. Cherokee hunters wandered the hills in search of game but established no permanent villages. After the removal of the Indians in the 1830s, settlers began to move in, most living on remote farms. The village of Trenton, the seat of Dade County, was accessible only through Tennessee and Alabama until completion of GA 136 in the late 1930s. Isolation made the mountain folk so fiercely independent that Dade County left the Union and declared itself the "Free State of Dade" late in 1860, weeks before the rest of Georgia seceded. The county did not "formally" rejoin the Union until *July 4, 1945.*

In the mid-1930s, the U.S. Forest Service established a Civilian Conservation Corps work camp near the site of the present-day state park, and work crews undertook reforestation projects in the surrounding Chattahoochee National Forest, which had been extensively logged. Acknowledging the magnificent scenery and unique geology of the area, Georgia created Cloudland Canyon State Park in 1938. Today, the park comprises more than 2,100 acres of rugged mountain land, filled with majestic panoramas, cascading waterfalls, and a variety of camping, lodging, picnicking, and recreational facilities. In a human lifetime little will change here, but the canyon's evolution continues.

WALK DISTANCE AND TERRAIN

Hiking at Cloudland Canyon runs to extremes. The .25-mile *East Rim Trail* is easy and affords some of the most spectacular views of the weathered sandstone cliffs and Sitton Gulch. The optional descents to the Upper (.3 miles) and Lower (.5 miles) Falls on Daniel Creek offer fascinating, close-up looks at the eroded gorge and the diverse flora found at different elevations. The Upper Falls is particularly breathtaking as it leaps over a 100-ft. cataract to a large boulder-strewn pool. The steepness of these trails makes this a short but strenuous hike.

The 5.2-mile *West Rim Trail* crosses a wooden bridge and climbs out of the canyon as it follows the rim northward. Several overlooks give an excellent perspective of Daniel and Bear Creek Canyons, Sitton Gulch, and the long valley and spine of Lookout Mountain. On an especially clear day, it is possible to see hanggliders soaring above the western slopes of the mountain. At its midpoint, the trail turns away from the rim and returns through a mixed hardwood forest, thick with oak, pine, hickory, and lush stands of rhododendron and mountain laurel.

In addition to the rim trails, the park also has a strenuous 7-mile backpacking trail that traces a loop through Bear Creek Canyon. Two primitive campsites are located on this trail. Overnight hikers are required to register at park headquarters.

Due to the rugged terrain and the proximity to steep cliffs, caution should be exercised when hiking with children on any of the park trails. The difficult terrain of the *West Rim Trail* may make it unsuitable for small children.

SIGHTS ALONG THE WAY

1. Sitton Gulch Overlook— An observation platform atop the sandstone cliffs provides a spectacular view of the Lookout Valley.

2. Upper Daniel Creek Falls— The falls drop 100 feet over a sheer cliff.

5

3. Lower Daniel Creek Falls—
Deeper into the depths of the canyon, this cataract carves into the shale and limestone bedrock.

4. Park Headquarters and Visitor Center—Staff here assist with park information and registration for camping, lodging, and backcountry hiking. *Hours:* 8 A.M.–5 P.M., daily. (706) 657-4050.

5. Park Recreation Area— Recreation facilities include a swimming pool, tennis courts, and open meadow.

NOTES

Chickamauga Battlefield

LOCATION

Chickamauga Battlefield, a part of Chickamauga and Chattanooga National Military Park, is located in Ft. Oglethorpe about 60 miles north of Rome via U.S. 27. The park may also be reached from I-75 by exiting on GA 2 (exit 350, Battlefield Parkway) and following signs to the visitor center. *Information:* (706) 866-9241; www.nps.gov/chch.

PARKING

There is a large lot at the visitor center and smaller ones at various locations throughout the park.

BACKGROUND

 The legacy of the Cherokee lingers in this land of rugged hills, wide valleys, and meandering waterways. Here names such as Chattanooga, Oostanaula, and Etowah, both melodic to the ear and descriptive in meaning, remain as a tangible link to the Cherokee people who lived here for centuries. Nestled in a wide valley between low ridges is a small, slow-moving stream the Cherokee called, almost prophetically, "Chickamauga"—*River of Death.* One can only wonder if they did not have a vision of the carnage that would occur along its course during three hellish days in September 1863.

Except for the excitement caused by the "Great Locomotive Chase" in April 1862 (when Federal raiders stole a railroad engine near Marietta and attempted to destroy the railway lines connecting Atlanta and Chattanooga), northwestern Georgia had remained far from the battlefields of the Civil War. Despite the superficial appearance of normalcy, however, the people knew the threat of Union invasion was real and growing. By early 1863, Nashville, Tenn. was occupied by Federal troops, and everyone knew that the next campaign would focus on nearby Chattanooga.

Anticipating action, the Confederate Army of Tennessee under command of Maj. Gen. Braxton Bragg, heavily fortified the town nestled on the Tennessee River below Lookout Mountain. In early September, the Union Army of the Cumberland, commanded by Maj. Gen. William Rosecrans, made its move and, in a brilliant tactical maneuver, flanked Bragg's army, forcing a Confederate retreat from Chattanooga without a fight. Rosecrans, mistakenly thinking the Rebels were in full retreat, divided his forces into three corps to search them out in the rugged, mountainous country of northwestern Georgia.

In reality, Bragg had fallen back with his entire army to LaFayette, Ga., about 20 miles south of Chattanooga and was awaiting the advancing Federals. By September 9, Union Maj. Gen. Alexander McCook's 20th Corps reached as far south as Summerville; Maj. Gen. George Thomas's troops of the 14th Corps were in the vicinity of LaFayette; and the 21st Corps, under Maj. Gen. Thomas Crittenden, was marching south from Chattanooga. At this point the Federal troops were spread far apart in terrain that was so difficult it would have been virtually impossible for them to support each other in the event of an attack.

Just as historians have considered Rosecrans foolish for dividing his forces in the face of an unseen enemy, they have been equally unkind to Bragg and his subordinate generals, Leonidas Polk, D. H. Hill, and Thomas

Hindman, for failing to appreciate the Federal blunder and vigorously taking advantage of the situation. For three days, until September 12, the armies shadowboxed in the dense woods and rugged hills southwest of Chattanooga. Finally, Bragg, realizing the enormity of his opportunity, prepared to attack elements of Thomas's Corps at McLemore's Cove west of LaFayette. Delays caused this chance to be lost, but served to alert Rosecrans to his army's predicament. He quickly issued orders for McCook's and Thomas's men to quick-march north toward Crittenden along the west bank of Chickamauga Creek.

Seeing a chance to recapture Chattanooga, Bragg also force-marched his troops northward along the east bank of the creek in an effort to position his men between the Federals and the town, hoping to attack them before they could regroup. On September 18, elements of the two armies clashed at Alexander's and Reed's bridges as Confederate infantry, under the command of Ohioan-turned-Rebel Gen. Bushrod Johnson, and cavalry, commanded by Gen. Nathan Bedford Forrest, sought to get a foothold on the west bank Chickamauga Creek. Johnson crossed easily at Reed's Bridge while, at Alexander's Bridge, Forrest ran into stern opposition from Col. Robert Minty's Union cavalry and a Federal artillery battery commanded by Capt. Eli Lilly, a young

Chickamauga Battlefield

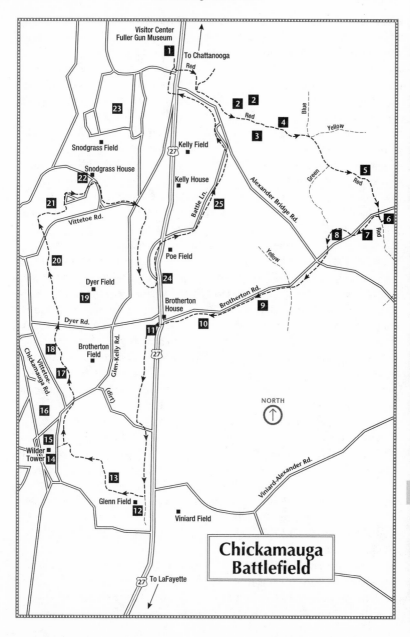

druggist-turned-soldier. Forrest's cavalry eventually forced a crossing of the creek and gained a second foothold. By evening, both armies faced each other in the thick woods near the Kelly Farm; Rosecrans and Bragg both worked feverishly to position their forces for the massive, inevitable battle the next day.

Early in the morning of September 19, Gen. Thomas dispatched Gen. John Brannan's Brigade to seek out and attack the Confederate north flank east of the Winfrey farm and near Jay's Mill. These troops clashed at midmorning and, within a short time, fighting spread south along the line. The dense woods made tactical troop movements almost impossible and most of the combat was fought between small bands of soldiers with neither side able to gain an advantage.

Around 3:00 P.M., Confederate Gen. A. P. Stewart's troops found a weakness in the Federal center and drove across the LaFayette Rd. near the Brotherton farm, threatening to split the Union army in half. Only a withering fire from Gen. Joseph Reynolds's artillery batteries (Capt. Lilly again) prevented a breakthrough, and the Rebels were ultimately forced back with heavy casualties. By nightfall, the two armies remained opposite one another in the thick woods east of the LaFayette Rd., uneasily separated only by an old wagon trail (now Battle Line Rd.).

Advance elements of nearly 10,000 reinforcements, sent from Confederate Gen. Robert E. Lee's Army of Northern Virginia and under the command of Lieut. Gen. James Longstreet, arrived by rail at nearby Catoosa Station in Ringgold late on September 18, reaching the battlefield in time to take part in the afternoon fighting on the 19th. The main body, including Gen. Longstreet, de-trained near midnight and arrived at Chickamauga a few hours before dawn. Longstreet's rank entitled him to high command and Bragg realigned his command, assigning Longstreet to his left wing and Gen. Polk to his right. Historians have long criticized Bragg for making such changes in his army in the middle of a battle. It ultimately proved to be a tactical error that created confusion in the chain of command, and cost the Confederates precious opportunities in the fighting on September 20.

Bragg's battle plan called for a dawn attack by Polk against Gen. Thomas and the Union left flank, with an attack against the Federal center by Longstreet's fresh troops later in the day. For unexplained reasons, Polk delayed his assault for nearly five hours and was not fully engaged until midmorning. When the attack finally commenced, one of the first casualties was Confederate Brig. Gen. Benjamin H. Helm, a favorite brother-in-law of Pres. Abraham Lincoln. (Lincoln

10

mourned the loss and was widely condemned when he permitted Helm's widow, Mary Todd Lincoln's half-sister Emilie, to visit the White House.)

Gen. Thomas, fearful of a Confederate breakthrough, sent Capt. Sanford Kellogg down the Glenn-Kelly Rd. to Rosecrans's headquarters with an urgent request for reinforcements. Along the way, he passed behind infantry in the thick woods east of the road. Along one stretch Kellogg saw no troops and was concerned that the line might be vulnerable at that point. When he found the commanding general (Rosecrans had moved his headquarters from the Widow Glenn house to a low ridge west of the Brotherton cabin to be closer to the fighting), he submitted the request for reinforcements and shared his observation of an apparent gap in the Federal line, in the deep woods separating the divisions commanded by Generals Reynolds and Wood.

Fearing that a dangerous hole existed in his line, Rosecrans, without sending a scout to verify the report, dispatched Adjutant Gen. Lyne Starling with an order for Wood to immediately pull out from his position and "close up on Reynolds, as fast as possible, and support him." Knowing that Gen. Brannan's troops were already in this position, Wood questioned the courier about the order but nonetheless chose to obey it, an act for which he would long be criticized. (Wood had recently been reprimanded by Rosecrans and some historians believe he followed the order, calling it "the fatal order of the day," knowing it would be disastrous for both the army and Rosecrans.)

Ironically, Rosecrans's misguided order created the gap he had sought to close and, just as the last elements of Wood's division pulled out of the line near the Brotherton cabin, Longstreet launched his attack, spearheaded by Bushrod Johnson's division of Hood's Corps. Within minutes, five Confederate divisions poured across the LaFayette Rd., overwhelmed the Union right wing, and nearly succeeded in destroying the entire army. Rosecrans's headquarters was only a short distance behind the line and was quickly overrun, he and his staff narrowly averting capture as they fled north to the outskirts of Chattanooga. (In an interesting footnote to history, Rosecrans's adjutant at Chickamauga was Gen. James A. Garfield, later the 20th President of the United States.)

Remaining in the field and desperately attempting to protect the Federal line of retreat, Gen. Thomas grudgingly gave ground against the Rebel onslaught. Longstreet urged Bragg to bring up more troops and press the attack against Thomas, but Bragg failed to grasp the enormity of Longstreet's achievement and the opportunity it presented to annihilate the Union army. He delayed the call

11

for additional men, giving Thomas time to fortify his defensive position along the crest of Horseshoe Ridge and adjacent Snodgrass Hill. Here his vastly outnumbered troops, reinforced by soldiers from Gen. Gordon Granger's Reserve Corps at Rossville, held out against multiple Rebel assaults, often fighting hand-to-hand. They bought time for the remnants of the Union army to retreat and regroup. Finally, under cover of darkness, Thomas and his weary survivors withdrew to Chattanooga. Longstreet's troops were too exhausted to pursue them. For his heroic stand at Snodgrass Hill, George Thomas would forever be remembered as the "Rock of Chickamauga."

Despite Longstreet's pleadings, Bragg did not vigorously pursue the Federals, allowing Rosecrans's shattered army to slip back into the safety of the heavily fortified city. The Rebels occupied the heights above Chattanooga with plans to lay siege to the city and starve the Federals into submission.

In November, the Union army, now under the command of Maj. Gen. Ulysses Grant (Rosecrans had been relieved after the humiliating retreat from Chickamauga), broke the siege with a stunning victory in the fighting at Lookout Mountain and Missionary Ridge. The Confederates were driven south to Dalton, where Bragg was removed from command

and replaced by Maj. Gen. Joseph E. Johnston. Pres. Abraham Lincoln summoned Grant to Washington to take command of all Federal armies, and his successor in Chattanooga, Maj. Gen. William Tecumseh Sherman, prepared for the invasion of Georgia in the spring of 1864.

Created by an act of Congress in 1890 and dedicated during an emotional ceremony attended by thousands of Union and Confederate veterans in 1895, Chickamauga and Chattanooga National Military Park was the first Civil War battlefield so preserved. Placement of more than 1,400 markers and monuments around the battlefield was the culmination of the work of hundreds of veterans from both sides who walked the battlefield, pointing out significant landmarks and providing "eyewitness" accounts of the events as they unfolded along the River of Death (these informational tablets still dot the battlefield with Union information in blue text, Confederate in red).

For many years after it was set aside, the park was under the jurisdiction of the U.S. Army and was used primarily as a place for military officers to study field tactics. Two other National Battlefields, Shiloh and Gettysburg, were also established for this purpose. During World War I, troops from nearby Ft. Oglethorpe carried out training maneuvers in the park, and the meadow beneath Wilder Tower served as a temporary airfield. Though the Army's use of the park ceased with the closure of the fort in 1946, military officers in training continue to tour the battlefield on "staff rides."

In the park we enjoy today, the paved roads, foot trails, landscaping, and the Greek Revival–style visitor center were constructed by the Civilian Conservation Corps in the 1930s. Interestingly, the two companies that carried out much of the project, Cos. 1464 and 2402 of Camp Booker T. Washington, were made up of the first African-American CCC workers in the state of Georgia.

Work is under way to construct a bypass along the western boundary of the park. When this is completed, the present U.S. 27 (the old LaFayette Rd.) will be limited to park traffic only.

WALK DISTANCE AND TERRAIN

There are more than 40 miles of marked trails crisscrossing the park, and a trail map is available from the visitor center. The 11-mile hike profiled here combines portions of several of these trails with lightly traveled park roads. The route was selected to capture the beauty of the land, as well as the ebb and flow of the epic battle. For the most part, the terrain is level, with some gently rolling hills, and is a blend of open meadows and deep forest.

Given the length of the walk, combined with the many sites to see along

the way, you should plan an entire day to tour the battlefield. Sturdy walking shoes or boots are strongly recommended. *You should also carry water as there are no facilities available outside the visitor center.*

SIGHTS ALONG THE WAY

The blend of field and forest draws naturalists to the park to enjoy its physical beauty, while students of American history are attracted for a different reason. Here a great battlefield remains preserved much as it was nearly a century and a half ago. Numerous historical markers, monuments, and artifacts provide an excellent account of the conflict. Sites of particular interest include:

1. Park Visitor Center (1930s, expanded 1995)—McFarland Gap Rd. and U.S. 27. Built in a style reminiscent of an antebellum plantation house, the renovated and greatly expanded complex houses exhibit areas, bookstore, and a new 150-seat theater. Particularly noteworthy is the Fuller Collection of American Military Firearms. *Hours:* 8 A.M.–5:45 P.M. (summer); 8 A.M.–4:45 P.M. (winter). (706) 866-9241.

2. Colquitt and Helm Death Monuments—In the woods east of the Alexander Bridge Rd. Stacked cannonballs mark the death sites of key Confederate officers killed during the battle. These two monuments, only a few yards apart, mark the places where

13

Col. Peyton Colquitt (commander of the 46th Georgia Battalion) was killed storming Federal breastworks less than an hour after Gen. Helm had been killed attempting to do the same.

3. Lieut. Gen. Daniel H. Hill's Field Headquarters, September 19–20

On the right of the Red Trail. At the outset of the Battle of Chickamauga, Hill was in command of one corps and Polk the other. When Longstreet arrived and Bragg reorganized his army into a left and right wing, Hill was passed over in favor of Polk for command of the right wing. Fuming at this slight, Hill was slow to carry out Polk's attack order on the morning of September 20.

4. Lieut. Gen. Leonidas Polk's Headquarters, September 20

On the Red Trail. Called the "Fighting Bishop," Polk was a friend and West Point classmate of Confederate Pres. Jefferson Davis. He forsook a military career for the clergy, becoming an Episcopal priest and later bishop of Louisiana. With the outbreak of the Civil War, Polk returned to service in the Confederate army, rising to the rank of lieutenant general. His strained relationship with Gen. Bragg contributed much to the confusion and missed opportunities the Confederates experienced at Chickamauga.

5. Indiana Monument

Left of the Red Trail. This stone marker was erected by Indiana as a tribute to the soldiers of its 74th Infantry.

6. Gen. Braxton Bragg's Headquarters

South of the Brotherton Rd. A short spur trail leads to the spot of Bragg's headquarters on the night of September 19. It was from here that he reorganized his army into two wings, and issued the attack orders for the morning of September 20.

7. Capt. E. P. Howell's Georgia Battery

South of the Brotherton Rd. During the afternoon and night of September 19, Howell's artillery battery was located here to support the night attack across the Winfrey farm fields by Gen. Patrick Cleburne's troops. Howell, grandson of Atlanta mill owner Clark Howell, went on to become editor and publisher of the *Atlanta Constitution* newspaper.

8. Winfrey Field

Both sides of the Brotherton Rd. During the late afternoon and evening of September 19, Gen. Patrick Cleburne led a rare night attack against the Federals in what was described as "one of the most confused incidents of the battle." In the dark, soldiers could not tell friend from foe. The stacked cannonballs at the northwestern edge of the field mark the site where Union Col. Philemon Baldwin was killed.

9. Brock Field

South of the Brotherton Rd. During the afternoon of September 19, Confederates under command of Gens. Strahl and Maney battled Hazen, Dodge, and Willich's Federals in repeated attacks across this field. Over the long afternoon, the

Brotherton Cabin, Chickamauga Battlefield

Rebels were pushed back to the woods southeast of the field.

10. Brig. Gen. Bushrod Johnson Marker—South of the Brotherton Rd. This recent marker rests on the spot where Johnson's division formed for the attack across the LaFayette Rd. near the Brotherton cabin in the late morning of September 20. These troops led the breakthrough of the Union line caused by Gen. Wood's withdrawal from the woods northwest of the cabin.

11. Brotherton Cabin (1850s)— Dyer Rd. at U.S. 27. Standing today as it did in 1863, this rough-hewn log structure survived fierce fighting. On September 19, just south of the cabin, Gen. A. P. Stewart's Confederates broke through the Federal line almost dividing the Union army before being forced back by heavy artillery fire. The following day, Gen. Wood's Federals occupied the woods just west of the cabin until they received the ill-fated order to pull out. Longstreet's Rebels rushed from the trees east of the LaFayette Rd. (U.S. 27), pushed past the cabin, and drove through the gap in the Union lines.

12. Brig. Gen. Hans Heg Death Monument—West of the LaFayette Rd. This Norwegian-born, Wisconsin farmer was considered one of the most gifted volunteer officers in the Union Army of the Cumberland. He was mortally wounded on the afternoon of September 19 while leading his Wisconsin troops (many were fellow Scandinavians) in a counterattack across the LaFayette Rd. against Gen. John Bell Hood's forces.

13. Glenn Field—Through the trees on the west side of the LaFayette

15

Rd. This field and the adjacent Viniard family fields across the LaFayette Rd. were the scene of intense fighting as both armies sought to turn the other's flank during the midafternoon of September 19. Union troops under Gen. Thomas Crittenden pushed across the LaFayette Rd., but a counterattack by Hood's troops forced the Federals back into the Glenn field (where Gen. Heg was killed). They were on the verge of turning the Union right flank when Col. John T. Wilder's 39th Indiana Brigade of mounted infantry fired repeated volleys into the oncoming enemy with their new Spencer repeating rifles (a rifle the Rebels called "that damned Yankee gun you loaded on Sunday and fired all week!"). Although outnumbered, Wilder's troops forced the Confederates back to the woods east of the road.

14. Wilder Tower (1903)—Less than 24 hours after forcing the Rebel retreat described above, Wilder's 2,000 infantrymen were cut off from the main body of the Union army by Longstreet's breakthrough at the Brotherton cabin. Again using their superior firepower and again outnumbered, Wilder's men held off advancing Confederates while other Federal troops retreated north to Snodgrass Hill or back toward Rossville. Their gallantry prevented the wholesale rout of the army and

earned them the nickname, "the Lightning Brigade." The 85-ft.-high stone tower marks the spot where Wilder's men held the enemy at bay until the sheer weight of numbers forced them to retreat. The observation area atop the tower offers a panoramic view of the surrounding battlefield.

15. Site of Widow Glenn House—Adjacent to Wilder Tower. An historical marker just north of the tower identifies the location of the Widow Glenn's cabin, which served as Gen. Rosecrans's headquarters until the early morning of September 20.

16. Site of Bloody Pond—Side trail west of Glenn-Kelly Rd. A shallow cattle pond was located in a small depression in these woods. The weather had been unseasonably dry, and thousands of men converged on this tiny pond for the only drinking water available to Union soldiers.

17. Brig. Gen. William Lytle Death Monument—On the Red Trail north of the Glenn-Kelly Rd. Called the "poet-general," William Lytle was both a well-respected military officer and a renowned author and poet whose works were widely read before the war. A veteran of the Mexican War, Lytle had many friends in both the Union and Confederate armies.

During the confusion following the Confederate breakthrough on September 20, Gen. Rosecrans ordered Gen. Philip Sheridan to bring two brigades forward from the area of the Widow Glenn house to fill the expanding gap in the Union center. Lytle's brigade came across the ridge from the southwest and attacked the Confederates near the Glenn-Kelly Rd. Outnumbered and outflanked, Lytle's men gave ground grudgingly. Lytle urged his men on until he was mortally wounded just beneath the crest of the hill.

18. Rosecrans's Headquarters, September 20—The large stone marker notes the location where Rosecrans issued the controversial order for Gen. Wood to pull his troops from the line, thus clearing the way for Longstreet's breakthrough. The Confederate advance overran this position, and Rosecrans and his staff (including future Pres. James A. Garfield) narrowly escaped capture.

19. Dyer Field—North side of the Dyer Rd. On September 20, thousands of Rebel troops exploited the gap west of the Brotherton cabin. They turned north and rushed across the Dyer field in pursuit of the Federals who were fleeing to the heights of nearby Horseshoe Ridge and Snodgrass Hill.

20. Landrum Death Memorial— On the Red Trail between the Dyer Rd. and Horseshoe Ridge. This small memorial was erected by the family of Lt. George Landrum of the 20th Ohio Regiment's Signal Corps. Attached to the staff of Gen. George Thomas, Landrum was killed on September 20

while carrying an urgent message to Gen. Rosecrans.

21. Horseshoe Ridge and Snodgrass Hill—At the intersection of the Red and Yellow Trails. Following the breakthrough at the Brotherton cabin, Longstreet's forces turned north to drive the remnants of the Union army from the field. However, Gen. Thomas rallied the Federal left wing and quickly put up a strong defensive position along these heights. Throughout the afternoon of September 20, repeated Rebel assaults could not take this ground, and Thomas moved among the troops to offer direction and encouragement. His valor earned him lasting fame as the "Rock of Chickamauga."

At one point, the Federals were about to be overrun when Gen. Gordon Granger arrived with nearly 7,000 fresh troops who had been stationed near Rossville. Without orders but sensing trouble in the distance, Granger marched south to "the sound of the guns."

As you walk among the numerous markers, note how the Union and Confederate memorials are intermingled—a testament to the ferocity and closeness of the fighting here. Two monuments are especially symbolic. The Tennessee Monument is topped by a weary Rebel soldier carrying a rifle with the stock broken off—a sign that it had been used as a club in hand-to-hand combat, while the memorial to the 2nd Minnesota Infantry is crowned by three soldiers, each with an expression of grim determination, supporting each other and the U.S. flag.

22. Snodgrass Cabin (c. 1850s)—This rough log structure was used as a field hospital during the desperate fighting on the afternoon and evening of September 20. Gen. Thomas maintained his headquarters in the field just north of the house. Like the nearby Brotherton cabin, this structure remarkably survived the battle.

23. South Post (c. 1940s)—Glenn-Kelly Rd. north of Snodgrass Hill Rd. This area, now used as a group camp, was developed as a Women's Auxiliary Corps (WAC) training base during World War II.

24. Georgia Monument—Poe Rd. at the LaFayette Rd. This monument's column is topped by a soldier bearing the Confederate flag, while the base is flanked by sculpted figures representing the three branches of the army—the infantry, the artillery, and the cavalry.

25. Battle Line Road—East of the LaFayette Rd. This narrow lane follows the route of an old farm road that meandered through thick woods east of the Kelly field. On the night of September 19, the main components of the two armies rested uneasily in the woods on the opposite sides of this road anticipating the fierce battle to come. The proximity of the markers along the road—Union to the west and Confederate to the east—reflects the armies poised for combat.

NOTES

Johns Mountain, Keown Falls, and Pocket Recreation Area

LOCATION

The Johns Mountain–Keown Falls and Pocket Recreation Areas are located about 40 miles north of Rome and about 18 miles west of I-75 at Resaca. From the interstate, follow GA 136 (exit 320) west for 14 miles. Just before the community of Villanow, turn south on Pocket Rd. and look for the U.S. Forest Service signs for the Johns Mountain Trail and Keown Falls. The entrance to the Pocket Recreation Area is a short distance further south on Pocket Rd. *Information:* (706) 638-1085.

PARKING

There is a small parking area at the top of the gravel road to the summit of Johns Mountain and a larger parking lot at the Keown Falls trailhead. A separate parking lot is adjacent to the Pocket Recreation Area's picnic ground.

BACKGROUND

For hundreds of years, Native Americans lived in these valleys, and their trade routes followed meandering waterways such as the Armuchee and the Oostanaula Rivers. Pioneers who moved in after the forced removal of the Cherokee in the late 1830s used these same paths when they established settlements at Summerville, LaFayette, Villanow, Rome, Dalton, and other nearby communities.

During the Civil War, Union Maj. Gen. William T. Sherman used his extensive knowledge of this rugged terrain (gained from his travels there as a young lieutenant in the 1840s) to formulate his strategy for the invasion of the state. At that time, the route of the Western and Atlantic Railroad followed the valley east of Rocky Face Ridge outside Dalton before turning northwest at Tunnel Hill and proceeding to Chattanooga. From his headquarters in Dalton, Maj. Gen. Joseph E. Johnston positioned his

19

Confederate defenders atop Rocky Face to gain a commanding view of the surrounding valley and to protect this railway lifeline.

Sherman knew that frontal assaults against these heavily fortified positions would be suicidal, so he chose to use the terrain to his advantage by feinting against the main Confederate position while sending Gen. James B. McPherson's army on a southwestern path. Screened by Taylor's Ridge, McPherson moved toward LaFayette and Villanow, through Snake Creek Gap, and on to the small town of Resaca. If undetected, McPherson would be in the Confederate rear with an opportunity to capture the railroad and force the surrender of Johnston's army without a pitched battle.

McPherson was successful in reaching Resaca undetected with his army of 25,000 men, but the small garrison of 4,000 Rebel defenders put up such fierce resistance that McPherson hesitated. Fearful that his movements had been anticipated, and that Johnston's entire army was in front of him, McPherson retreated to Snake Creek to plan his next move. This delay gave the Confederates the time needed to reinforce Resaca and retreat from Rocky Face Ridge and Dalton. Needless to say, Sherman was furious over McPherson's failure to attack and considered it a major tactical blunder. From the overlook atop Johns Mountain, you have a spectac-ular view of the valley and can gain a better understanding of how Sherman used this terrain so effectively.

In the mid-1930s, the Federal Government purchased many acres of land in the area for the new Chattahoochee National Forest. From 1938 to 1942, a Civilian Conservation Corps camp was located in the Pocket (so named because it is a small valley surrounded on three sides by mountains), where they carried out forest conservation work, carved trails, built a now-gone fire tower atop Johns Mountain, and constructed some of the early visitor facilities for the Pocket Recreation Area. When the camp closed, most of the buildings were dismantled or razed by the Army, and the site is now part of the Recreation Area campground and picnic area.

Today, the natural beauty of this region is its main attraction. The trail along the narrow spine of Johns Mountain, the trail descending to Keown Falls, and the Pocket Trail, which meanders past mountain streams and beneath towering hills, all carry you through an oasis of wilderness filled with panoramic vistas, cascading water, lush vegetation, and secretive wildlife.

WALK DISTANCE AND TERRAIN

The Johns Mountain Trail is a 3-mile loop from the mountaintop parking area, while the Keown

Johns Mountain, Keown Falls, and Pocket Recreation Area

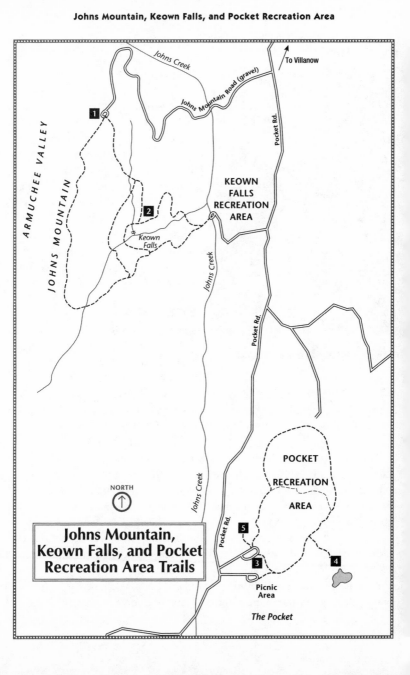

Johns Creek

To Villanow

Johns Mountain Road (gravel)

Pocket Rd.

ARMUCHEE VALLEY

JOHNS MOUNTAIN

KEOWN FALLS RECREATION AREA

Keown Falls

Johns Creek

Pocket Rd.

Johns Creek

POCKET RECREATION AREA

Pocket Rd.

NORTH

Johns Mountain, Keown Falls, and Pocket Recreation Area Trails

Picnic Area

The Pocket

Johns Mountain

Falls Trail is a 2-mile round-trip from its picnic-area trailhead. Combining the trails makes a challenging 5-mile walk.

The hike along Johns Mountain is gently rolling as it follows the narrow spine of the ridge. Several places along the route offer vistas of the Armuchee Valley and Taylor's Ridge to the west. As the trail circles northward through thick woods filled with oaks, hickories, sourwoods, yellow poplars, and evergreens, it descends slightly and follows the lower eastern slope of the

ridge to the Keown Falls overlook. A moderate ascent returns you to the parking area.

The trail from the Keown Falls trailhead is a winding ascent to the overlook with a return along several switchbacks to the parking area.

The 2.5-mile Pocket Trail leaves the Recreation Area's picnic ground and winds along the banks of several small streams beneath the surrounding hills. The canopy of hardwood trees offers summer shade and brilliant fall golds and yellows. Stands of rhododendron, mountain laurel, and wild azaleas provide a splash of vivid spring colors.

SIGHTS ALONG THE WAY

1. Scenic Overlook—Atop Johns Mountain. From this vantage point, you have a panoramic view of the scenic and historic Armuchee Valley and the parallel rise of Taylor's Ridge. To the north is the spine of Lookout Mountain.

2. Scenic Overlook—Above Keown Falls. Perched on the rocks above the falls, a platform offers a good view of the falls and the surrounding woodlands.

3. Site of CCC Camp—Pocket Recreation Area picnic area. Concrete building foundations are all that remain of the Civilian Conservation Corps camp. When occupied, the camp was home to nearly 250 men, including workers, military officers, and Forest Service supervisory staff.

4. Aquatic Wildlife Observation Area—Pocket Trail. A platform at the end of a short side trail overlooks a small pond.

5. Fowler Cemetery—Adjacent to the Pocket picnic area. This old burial ground contains the remains of many early pioneer families.

NOTES

CHAPTER 4

Fort Mountain State Park

LOCATION

The park is located about 22 miles east of Dalton. From I-75, follow GA 52/U.S. 76 (exit 333) toward Chatsworth. When the highways fork, continue on GA 52 through Chatsworth. The park is about 8 miles east of Chatsworth. *Information:* (706) 695-2621.

PARKING

There are large parking areas at the Summit trailhead, at the day-use area by the lake, and at a picnic area adjacent to the Big Rock Nature Trail. There is a daily parking fee.

BACKGROUND

Deep in the Cohutta Range of the Southern Appalachians lies a mystery that has long baffled archaeologists and historians. Just east of Chatsworth rests a mildly undulating stone wall, nestled beneath two peaks, one aptly named "Fort Mountain." Stretching 885 feet across the southern face of the mountain, the low wall follows the contours of the rolling hillside. Spaced at irregular intervals are shallow pits outlined by coarse rocks. Since their rediscovery over a century ago, the inevitable questions have been posed: Who built the wall? When? and Why? Myths and theories abound.

One theory asserts that the wall was built by the Cherokees for some unrecorded purpose. The Cherokees' own legends, however, attribute construction to a light-skinned, "moon-eyed" people of unknown origin and even more obscure demise. Some historians have interpreted the Cherokee stories as references to a legendary 12th-century Welsh prince, Madoc, who was said to have landed with a band of followers on the Alabama coast and marched northward into the mountains.

Another theory asserts that the wall was built by Hernando de Soto and his Spanish conquistadores as a defense against hostile natives. Two concerns have cast this theory into disfavor. First,

Fort Mountain State Park

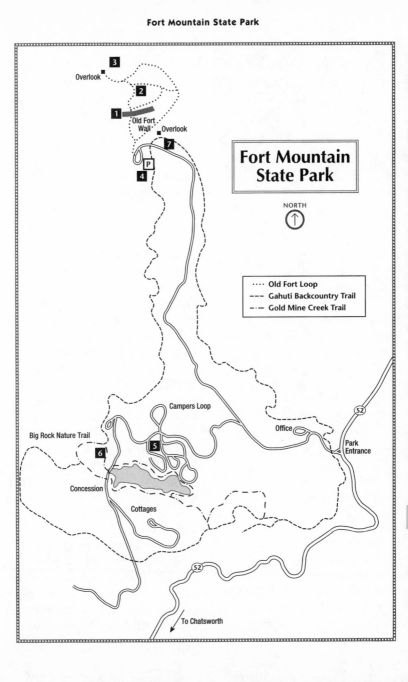

The ancient stone wall, Fort Mountain

there is no record of the wall in existing journals of de Soto's expedition; and second, the Spanish were in this area for far too short a time to carry out such a massive project.

Most scholars now firmly believe that the wall was the work of Woodland-era natives who constructed it about 1,500 years ago. Its exact purpose remains a mystery, but its east-west alignment supports the belief that it may have been used in sun-worship ceremonies.

Today, the ancient wall is the centerpiece of a popular state park that features a 105-site campground, 21 rustic cabins, picnic shelters, miles of foot and horse trails, and a lake for swimming, boating, and fishing. While a visit to the park may not reveal the origins of the ancient wall, its rugged beauty has the power to draw you back again and again.

WALK DISTANCE AND TERRAIN

The park has nearly 50 miles of day-hiking, backpacking, and equestrian trails to explore.

The Summit Trails

Combining the Tower, Stonewall, and North Face Trails produces a round-trip of about 2 miles. From the trailhead, the red-blazed Tower Trail ascends by a graded path, with stone steps, to the wall. The blue-blazed Stonewall Trail follows the east-west course, crosses the wall, and climbs again to the stone observation tower. Going west from the tower, the trail descends, at some places steeply, to a panoramic overlook. The yellow-blazed North Face Trail forks away and traces an undulating route below the ridgeline as it loops back along the eastern side of the summit and returns to the parking area.

The Lake Loop, Gold Mine, and Big Rock Nature Trails

These paths combine to make a walk of about 4 miles. The blue-blazed Lake Loop winds around the lake on a route that is fairly level with a few moderate hills along the southern bank. It takes you through the popular day-use areas around the beach house and miniature golf course. On the southern side of the lake, a red-blazed spur leads to the white-blazed Gold Mine Trail that forms a gentle loop along Gold Mine Creek. The yellow-blazed Big Rock Trail begins across the road from the dam and almost immediately descends, fairly steeply, to an outcropping of rocks between two fast-running streams. Short side trails lead to overlooks. The path ascends briefly before descending by wooden steps to a level path beside a waterfall. The trail then climbs upward, parallel to the stream, and returns to the road just north of the starting point.

Gahuti Trail

While this orange-blazed, 8.2-mile loop is the main access trail to the park's backcountry campsites, it is also a strenuous, but rewarding, day hike. The path follows ridges and coves as it climbs northward toward the crest of Fort Mountain. Along the way, the hiker is treated to outstanding views to the east of the rugged Cohutta Mountain Wilderness and to the south of Chatsworth Valley and distant Rocky Face Ridge. At its southern end, the Gahuti Trail intersects with the Gold Mine and the Big Rock Nature Trails.

SIGHTS ALONG THE WAY

Along the Summit Trail

 1. The Stone Wall (c. 500 C.E.) —The origin of the stone wall remains a mystery.

2. Observation Tower (1930s)— The tower, and the steps leading up to the trail, were built by workers from the Civilian Conservation Corps. Just above the window on the east-facing wall is a heart-shaped stone with a story. It was carved and placed there by CCC foreman and stonemason Arnold Bailey as an

expression of love for his fiancee, Margaret, who lived nearby in Ellijay.

3. Overlook Platform—The platform offers a spectacular westward view of the valley, the town of Chatsworth, and the mountain ridges to the west.

4. Picnic Pavilions (c. 1930s)— Rustic log pavilions with stacked-stone fireplaces were constructed by the CCC.

The Lake Loop, Gold Mine, and Big Rock Trails

5. Day-Use Area—Found here are the beach house, miniature golf course, boat dock, picnic area, and playground. The beach concession and golf course are open from Memorial Day through Labor Day.

6. Waterfall—The waters of Gold Mine Creek cascade over rocks on their journey to the valley below.

Gahuti Trail

7. Cohutta Overlook—Adjacent to the trail just south of the Summit Trail parking area, a short, paved, handicapped-accessible path leads to a platform with a spectacular view eastward.

27

CHAPTER 5

New Echota State Historic Site

LOCATION

New Echota is located just east of I-75 near Calhoun. Take GA 225 (exit 317) and follow the signs to the park entrance. *Hours:* 9 A.M.–5 P.M., Tues.–Sat.; 2–5:30 P.M., Sun. and holiday Mondays. (706) 624-1321.

PARKING

There is a large parking area adjacent to the visitor center.

BACKGROUND

In the decade before their forced removal to Oklahoma on the "Trail of Tears," the Cherokee made enormous efforts to assimilate the ways of the white settlers in a fervent hope that, by adapting, they might peacefully coexist. Nowhere were these efforts more evident than at New Echota, the last capital of the Cherokee Nation.

While boundaries fluctuated following conflicts with neighboring nations—most notably the Creeks—the Cherokee lands encompassed much of present-day northern Georgia, western North Carolina, eastern Tennessee, and northeastern Alabama. In the first century following European settlement along the Georgia coast, this land of rugged mountains and narrow valleys had little allure for white settlers because the difficult terrain and isolation made the region unsuitable for their agricultural economy.

Having served as allies of the United States during the war against the British in 1812, Cherokee leaders learned about the federal system of government and adapted it for their own use. They divided their nation into eight districts (states), which each elected four delegates to the National Council (House of Representatives). The council, in turn, elected twelve of its members to the National Committee (Senate), and this body selected the principal chief, assistant chief, and the treasurer.

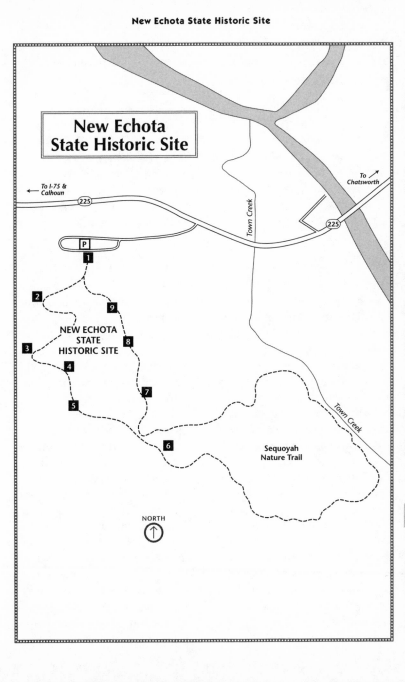

By 1819, the meeting place for the council was established at a small, centrally located village called New Town. In 1825 the National Council enacted legislation establishing a national capital at New Town and changed its name to New Echota to honor the ancient Cherokee village of Chota (located in eastern Tennessee). New government buildings, businesses, and homes were built and, by the late 1820s, New Echota was a thriving community of several thousand people.

From his print shop at New Echota, Cherokee leader Sequoyah published a newspaper, the *Phoenix*, printed in both Cherokee and English. After years of experimentation, Sequoyah had created a written syllabary of the Cherokee language. The 78 characters of the "alphabet" represented vocal sounds. By memorizing the characters, the Cherokee could communicate in a written language —something unique among Native Americans of the day. The paper made its debut in 1828 and existed for six years.

Among the settlers at New Echota was the Rev. Samuel Worcester, a white missionary from New England. Worcester arrived at the capital in 1827 and built his home on a small rise just southeast of town. In addition to preaching, Worcester wrote articles for the *Phoenix* and operated a mission school in his home. Today,

the Worcester house is the only original building still standing at New Echota.

Treaties with the Federal Government assured the sovereignty of the Cherokee Nation and prohibited white settlement within its boundaries. However, with the discovery of gold on Cherokee lands near present-day Dahlonega in 1828, prospectors defied the law and streamed across the borders. Despite Cherokee demands that the treaties be enforced, Federal troops were ineffective in stemming the rising tide of white settlement. At the same time, there was increasing support in the state government for legitimizing the settlers' claims. In 1829, the Georgia legislature, ignoring the Federal treaties, enacted a law giving itself jurisdiction over all Cherokee lands within the state's boundaries.

Native American appeals to Federal authorities continued to fall on deaf ears as the administration of Pres. Andrew Jackson had already established itself as anti-Indian and pro-settlement. Finally, to avoid bloodshed and possible annihilation, Cherokee leaders Major Ridge, John Ridge, Elias Boudinot, and others, in the face of strong opposition, reluctantly signed a new treaty in 1835. Prophetically, Ridge commented, as he signed, that he was "signing his death warrant." Within four years, he and several other treaty signers would be assassinated by fellow Cherokees.

30

By its terms, the Cherokee were paid $5 million for their eastern lands and given new lands in Oklahoma on which to resettle. The removal west began in late 1838, and New Echota was a gathering place for those preparing for the difficult journey. The trek to Oklahoma took place during the bitter winter of 1838–39. Along the way, thousands of Cherokees died from exposure, disease, and starvation. One of the most tragic events in American history, this exodus of the Cherokees from their homeland has become forever known as the Trail of Tears.

As the years passed, New Echota fell into disuse, and the land was turned back to farming. By 1900, only the Worcester house remained to mark the town's location. In the 1950s citizens of nearby Calhoun, recognizing its significance, began efforts to excavate the site. Eventually, 200 acres were acquired and presented to the State of Georgia as a historic site. Archaeologists and historians worked to identify notable features and building locations. Using old records, they reconstructed selected buildings important to understanding the significance of New Echota. Today, a number of buildings have been reproduced or relocated here, the Worcester house has been restored, and other building sites are identified by markers. New Echota stands as a reminder of a remarkable race of people and a memorial to the injustices they endured.

WALK DISTANCE AND TERRAIN

The round-trip from the modern visitor center to the Worcester House, including the Sequoyah Nature Trail, is about 1.2 miles. From the visitor center to the Vann Tavern is open, level ground. Stands of shade trees mark the approach to the Worcester House, and the Nature Trail snakes its way along rolling hills through dense forest. A small booklet identifying selected plant life along the trail is available at the visitor center. Park staff conduct guided tours of the historic area several times daily.

SIGHTS ALONG THE WAY

1. Visitor Center/Museum—The center houses a variety of exhibits pertaining to life at, and the history of, New Echota. Among them are a diorama depicting New Echota at its peak and an audio interpretation of the Cherokee alphabet. *Hours:* 9 A.M.–5 P.M., Tues.–Sat.; 2–5:30 P.M., Sun. and holiday Mondays.

2. Old Farm (c. 1830s)—This small complex of buildings represents a typical Cherokee farm of the early 1800s. The farmhouse was relocated to the park in 1983. It is notable that the Cherokee chose to adapt to the Euro-Americans' style of construction for most of the buildings that stood here.

3. Boudinot House Site—Elias Boudinot, editor of the *Phoenix*, lived in a house on this site from 1827 to 1837. Although a full-blooded

31

Log cabin on the Cherokee farm

6. Worcester House (1828)—The only original standing structure from New Echota, this house was built by Samuel Worcester and used as a church, school, and post office. Forced from the home in 1834, Worcester went west with the Cherokee and spent the rest of his life in Oklahoma ministering to his chosen people.

Cherokee, Boudinot had been educated at an American Board of Foreign Missions school in Connecticut and had received a degree from Andover Theological Seminary. Boudinot was a signer of the Treaty of New Echota in 1835 and was assassinated in 1839 shortly after relocating to Oklahoma with his family.

4. The *Phoenix* Printing Office—This building is a reproduction of the shop where the 4-page weekly was printed in both Cherokee and English. The paper was distributed throughout the Cherokee Nation.

5. Vann's Tavern (1800)—This original Cherokee structure was built by Chief James Vann, whose home, built in 1804, still stands just west of Chatsworth. The tavern, originally near Gainesville, was relocated here in the 1950s to save it from inundation by the waters of newly created Lake Sidney Lanier.

7. Rogers House Site—A simple log structure built by a white settler, John Rogers, for his Cherokee family, is thought to have occupied this site.

8. Supreme Court Building—This simple, 2-story white frame building is a reproduction of the original Cherokee Supreme Court House built in 1829. Note the elevated judges' bench, which accommodated three justices.

9. Council House—This building is a recently completed reproduction of the Cherokee capitol building, reconstructed according to historical records that indicate it was a 2-story structure made of hewn logs. The identical floors probably served as chambers for the National Council and the National Committee.

Rome

LOCATION

Rome is midway between Chatta-nooga and Atlanta in the Appa-lachian foothills. Downtown Rome is about 30 miles west of I-75 via U.S. 411/GA 20 (exit 290). From U.S. 411/GA 20, follow U.S. 27/GA 20 (Turner McCall Blvd.) north to Broad St. and turn left. The walk begins at City Hall. *Information:* Greater Rome Convention and Visitors Bureau, (800) 444-1834; w.romegeorgia.com.

PARKING

 There is ample parking along Broad St., and commercial lots are available on side streets.

BACKGROUND

This picturesque land of rolling hills at the conflu-ence of three rivers—the Etowah, the Oostanaula, and the Coosa—was home to generations of native cul-tures. Journals kept by soldiers trav-eling with Spanish explorer Hernando de Soto in 1540 described impris-oning the great Creek chief Coosa at a village called "Ulibahali." Scholars be-lieve that a site excavated west of Rome in the early 1970s may have been this walled village.

Following de Soto's departure, the Creeks remained virtually undis-turbed for another two centuries until they fought and lost a war with the Cherokees. The Creeks retreated south of the Chattahoochee River, and all their lands in northern Georgia be-came a part of the Cherokee Nation. Less than a century later, the Chero-kees would fall victim to the white man's lust for gold and be forced west.

In asserting its claims to the land, the Georgia legislature created several counties, including Floyd, which was established in 1832. Within a few years, a new community of farmers, merchants, and traders grew up along the rivers, and in 1838, the small town of Rome was selected as the county seat. Despite the mythical parallels be-tween the seven hills of Rome, Italy, and the seven hills of Rome, Ga., the town actually got its name from a list of choices drawn from a hat!

Rome became the economic center of northwestern Georgia. Keelboats and barges navigated the three rivers, and a railway spur connected Rome with the main line running from Atlanta to Chattanooga, Tenn. Mills and factories were built along the waterways, and merchants set up shop to trade in both raw and finished goods. Although the city escaped wholesale destruction during the Civil War, much of its industry, most notably the Noble Iron Works, was wrecked and burned when Union troops captured the city and moved to eliminate Confederate supply sources. Following the war, Rome's renewed importance as a regional transportation and manufacturing center fostered a steady return to prosperity. Fine examples of Victorian commercial structures and elegant houses remain as tangible links to this era of rebirth.

At this time two men who would later gain national prominence were working in Rome. One was Henry W. Grady, a promising young journalist who would later move to Atlanta and become editor of the *Atlanta Constitution*. Within a few years he traveled the nation on behalf of rebuilding the "New South." The other was a young attorney named Woodrow Wilson, who was practicing law and courting his future wife, Ellen Axson, daughter of the pastor of the local Presbyterian church. Wilson's career led him to the presidency of Princeton University and, in 1912, to the presidency of the United States.

WALK DISTANCE AND TERRAIN

The loop through the heart of downtown is mostly level. There are moderately steep ascents to the summit of Myrtle Hill and Clock Tower Hill. The total walk distance is about 3.5 miles. There are good sidewalks in the commercial district and an abundance of shade trees along Clock Tower Hill.

SIGHTS ALONG THE WAY

1. City Hall (1916)— 601 Broad St. This building, which also houses the Rome City Auditorium, was designed in the Classical Revival style by Atlanta architect A. Ten Eyck Brown. The statue at the front entrance depicting the Capitoline Wolf with Romulus and Remus was a gift to the city from Italian dictator Benito Mussolini in 1929 (it was removed during World War II to prevent its being vandalized). Adjacent to City Hall is the Carnegie Library (1911), one of the many libraries established by philanthropist Andrew Carnegie.

2. Nemophila (1867)—603 W. First St. This small Greek Revival house was a wedding gift from Confederate Col. Wade Cothran to his daughter. The unusual name comes

Rome

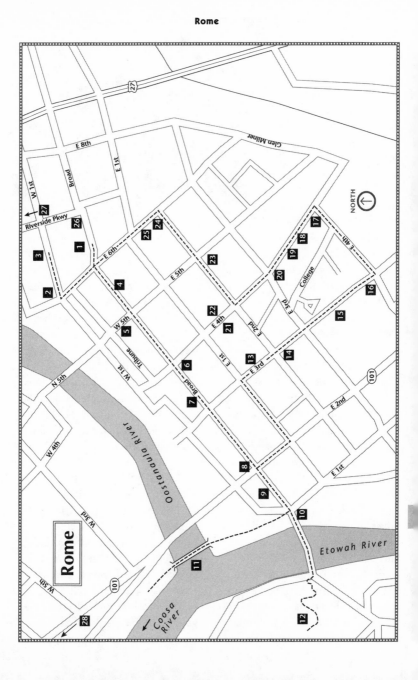

from the Greek and means "for love of pastured woodlands."

3. Omberg House (c. 1850)—615 W. First St. Tucked away on a hillside above First St., this brick home, with its white-columned portico, survived the Union occupation of the city in 1864 though its owner did not. Nicholas Omberg was killed by soldiers when he tried to stop the lynching of a friend. Dr. Robert Battey performed the world's first successful oophorectomy (removal of the ovaries) on the kitchen table. The patient, Julia Omberg, survived the emergency operation and lived into her eighties.

Masonic Temple on Broad Street

4. DeSoto Theatre (1929)—528 Broad St. This Classical-style movie house was the first in the South to be designed for "talkies" (movies with sound). Today, it is home to the Rome Little Theater Company.

5. Floyd County Courthouse (1892)—101 W. Fifth Ave. Long a downtown landmark, this Romanesque Victorian red-brick building is noted for its distinctive clock and bell tower. Inside is a gallery providing exhibit space for local artists. *NR*

6. Masonic Temple (1877)—336 Broad St. This excellent Gothic Revival building replaced the original temple burned by Union troops in 1864. After the war, many Union vet-

erans who were also Masons sent contributions to rebuild the temple.

7. Rome Area History Museum (1880s)—305 Broad St. Exhibits in this restored retail store trace the colorful history of Rome and Northwest Georgia. *Hours:* 10 A.M.–5 P.M., Tues.–Sat.; 1–5 P.M., Sun. (706) 235-8051.

8. Old First National Bank (1880)—200 Broad St. Noted for its finely detailed lobby and bank vault, this building now houses a popular restaurant.

9. Cotton Block (1870s–90s)—Along Broad St. from Second Ave. to the Etowah River Bridge. The heart of Rome's post–Civil War textile factoring and shipping business, this block of fine Victorian commercial buildings is now home to a variety of retail businesses and restaurants.

10. Site of the Noble Iron Works Foundry (1850s)—Broad St. at E. First Ave. The iron works located here, which produced cannon for the Confederacy, was destroyed by Union troops in 1864.

11. Robert Redden Memorial Bridge (1900s)—Situated at the confluence of the Coosa, Etowah, and Oostanaula Rivers, this old railroad bridge is now a pedestrian walkway to nearby Heritage Park and its extensive system of levee trails.

12. Myrtle Hill Cemetery (1857) —Branham Ave. above the Etowah River. Rome's oldest burial ground is the final resting place for early pioneers, Civil War soldiers, and prominent citizens (including First Lady Ellen Axson Wilson). The summit's Confederate Monument offers a panoramic view of the entire city. *NR*

13. First Presbyterian Church (1854)—101 E. Third Ave. In this beautiful brick Gothic Revival–style church, Woodrow Wilson met and married Ellen Axson, daughter of the pastor, the Rev. Samuel Axson.

14. First Methodist Church (1884)—202 E. Third Ave. The tower of the Victorian Greek Renaissance–style church is especially notable, as is the beautiful mahogany interior woodwork.

15. Hillyer House (1885)—316 E. Third Ave. This well-proportioned Queen Anne–style house was built by Dr. Eben Hillyer.

16. Fahy House (1893)—320 E. Third Ave. Thomas Fahy built this rambling residence for his wife and eleven children. *Gone with the Wind* author Margaret Mitchell, a close friend of his daughter Agnes, was a frequent visitor. The Queen Anne–style home remained in the Fahy family until 1985.

17. Judge Kelly House (1905)— 316 E. Fourth Ave. Judge James F. Kelly was the third owner of this house. By the stipulations of the sale, the previous owners, the Printup sisters, were permitted to live in the upstairs rooms until their deaths. According to local lore, the ghosts of the spinster sisters still inhabit the upper floor of the house.

18. Site of Sherman's Headquarters —312 E. Fourth Ave. The house that previously occupied this site served as the headquarters of Union Maj. Gen. William T. Sherman during his brief stay in Rome in 1864. The present Greek Revival structure, completed in 1911, is modeled after the Gordon-Lee House in Chickamauga, Ga.

19. Rev. Samuel Axson House (1867)—304 E. Fourth Ave. This grand Greek Revival–style house was once owned by Rev. Axson, pastor of First Presbyterian Church and father-in-law of Pres. Woodrow Wilson.

20. Bass House (1879)—302 E. Fourth Ave. This modest house was originally constructed as a slave cabin in 1860. It was remodeled and expanded by Rome merchant Charles Bass. His wife died in the house during childbirth and, following a fire

37

many years later, workers removing a mirror from a wall discovered the un-charred silhouette of a mother and child hidden behind it.

21. First Baptist Church (1958)—100 E. Fourth Ave. The original church on this site was completed in 1855 and served as a hospital during the Civil War. Union troops stabled their horses in the basement, and the pews were removed to be used in building a bridge over the nearby river. A new church was built in 1883 and was used until construction of the present sanctuary.

22. St. Peter's Episcopal Church (1898)—101 E. Fourth Ave. The first services were held in the present church on Christmas Day 1898. The stained-glass window over the altar, an 1867 gift of John Noble, owner of the Noble Iron Works, was brought from the original structure.

23. Clock Tower And Museum (1871)—E. Second St. at E. Fifth Ave. Perched atop one of Rome's highest hills, the tower doubled as a pumping station for the city's first reservoir. The water system was designed by John Noble, and the clock was de-signed by the E. Howard Clock Co. of Waltham, Mass. Today, the tower houses a museum. *Information:* (706) 236-4416. NR

24. St. Paul African-Methodist-Episcopal Church (1852)—106 E. Sixth Ave. Built on land donated to the Methodist Church by Col. Daniel Mitchell, one of the city's founders, this church served the Methodist con-gregation for many years (and as a stable for Union horses during the Civil War). In 1884 when the new Methodist church on Third Ave. was completed, the building was acquired by St. Paul's, one of Rome's oldest pre-dominantly African-American con-gregations. The original bricks have been covered with stucco.

25. Methodist Parsonage (1856)—104 E. Sixth Ave. This frame, 2-story house served as the residence of the Methodist minister from 1856 to 1888. It was later used as a boarding house, law offices, and a radio station.

26. Metropolitan United Methodist Church (1867)—700 Broad St. This Gothic-style, brick church is one of the oldest in Rome.

27. Rome Visitor Center (1901)—402 Civic Center Dr. Housed in a former railroad depot, the center pro-vides information on attractions, ac-tivities, and accommodations in Rome and Floyd County. Also on the grounds are an 1847 lathe from the Noble Iron Works, a pioneer cabin, and a cotton gin. *Hours:* 9 A.M.– 5 P.M., Mon.–Fri.; 10 A.M.–3 P.M., Sat.; 12–3 P.M., Sun. (800) 295-5576.

28. Riverview And Heritage Parks—Second Ave. These popular recreation areas include boat ramps, nature trails, and picnic areas.

CHAPTER 7

Berry College Campus

LOCATION

✣ Berry College is located on Martha Berry Blvd. (U.S. 27) about 1.5 miles north of downtown Rome. From I-75, travel west on U.S. 411/GA 20 (exit 290) for about 30 miles. Turn right on GA 1 (Veterans Memorial Hwy.) and follow it to the intersection with U.S. 27. Turn right and the college's main entrance will be ahead on the left. *Information*: (706) 236-0226; www.berry.edu.

PARKING

🚗 On the main campus, visitor parking is available at the Krannert Center, Hermann Hall, Ford Complex, and several other locations. Parking on the mountain campus is available at the WinShape Center and at Frost Memorial Chapel.

BACKGROUND

📖 Martha Berry epitomized the heritage of Southern planter aristocracy. The eldest daughter of Thomas Berry, she was born at the family plantation, Oak Hill, in 1866. Her father, with unwavering perseverance, rebuilt his fortune from the devastation of the Civil War. From her early childhood experience, she learned the enduring principles of determination, self-reliance, and dedication to service that would forge her life's mission.

Martha had the benefits of an education from the finest schools and could have settled easily into a comfortable social life; instead, she chose a different path. As a young adult she had seen, firsthand, the impoverished existence of so many children from the surrounding area, and she firmly believed that the way out of poverty was through hard work and education. Providing children with an education became her life's work and passion.

Martha started modestly in the late 1890s. She read Bible stories to small groups of children in a cabin-classroom at Oak Hill. Before long, more children, and a few adults, began attending Miss Berry's Sunday school. In 1900, she was forced to

39

find larger quarters, acquiring an old church building in a small community nearby and converting it to a school. Soon it was full of people who came from across the region to take instruction from the "Sunday Lady of Possum Trot."

As word of the school continued to spread, Martha faced a dilemma. There were now too many students for her to teach effectively alone, and she knew the school must be expanded. Despite opposition from family and friends, she purchased 80 acres of land near Oak Hill, constructed simple wooden buildings, and, in 1902, opened the Berry Industrial School.

Originally intended to serve as a high school and vocational school for boys, the institution grew steadily and became coeducational in 1910. By this point, the first rustic buildings, most built by the students, had reached capacity and Martha tirelessly traveled across northwestern Georgia seeking funds for continued expansion of the campus and its programs dedicated to the "education of the head, the heart, and the hands."

Word of the school's success brought Pres. Theodore Roosevelt to Berry in 1910, and within a few years, Miss Berry's efforts had garnered millions of dollars in contributions. When Martha Berry died in 1942, she was mourned by students, alumni, and educational leaders nationwide. Her

grave, a campus landmark, is located next to her beloved Berry Chapel.

As Berry grew, educational offerings also expanded. With the main campus increasingly devoted to college-level academics, the high school relocated to an area about 3 miles west, near what is now known as Mount Berry. Mount Berry Academy operated until the early 1980s, when the high school curriculum was phased out. The mountain campus is now home to the WinShape Center, a residential and recreational complex housing students attending Berry on scholarships awarded by the Chick-fil-A Company. Today, Berry encompasses more than 28,000 acres, much of it a wooded wildlife refuge, making it one of the largest academic campuses in the world. Enrollment numbers around 2,000, and nearly all students are involved in campus work programs, from farming and cattle-raising to office and administrative duties. As the college approaches its centennial celebration, Martha Berry's guiding principle, "Not to be ministered unto, but to minister," remains its educational foundation.

WALK DISTANCE AND TERRAIN

The 3-mile loop around the main campus follows gently rolling, shaded terrain. There are some sidewalks. The mountain campus loop is a 3.3-mile path that

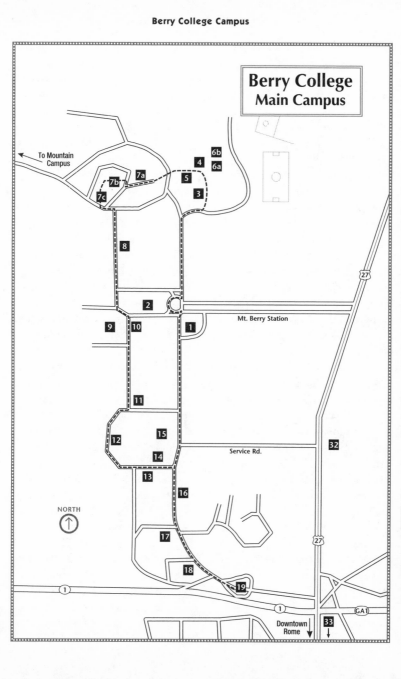

Berry College
Main Campus

To Mountain Campus

Mt. Berry Station

Service Rd.

NORTH

Downtown Rome

passes rustic academic buildings, serene Frost Chapel, and a European–style dairy complex as it meanders through the heavily wooded foothills.

SIGHTS ALONG THE WAY

Main Campus

1. Krannert Center (1969)— A gift of Mr. and Mrs. Herman Krannert, this Georgian-style building houses the cafeteria, bookstore, and other student services.

2. Hermann Hall (1964)—In the 1930s, Martha Berry picked this site for the school's Administration Building. In her typical way, she had a road built leading to the vacant lot in hope of spurring donations. Unfortunately the Depression and World War II brought the project to a halt. However, in 1962, Chicago businessman Grover Hermann made a generous contribution that led to the building's construction.

3. Ford Auditorium (1928)— A focal point of the English Gothic–style buildings of the Ford Complex, this building is notable for its needle spire and large clock tower. The 500-seat assembly hall features an ornate wooden balcony. For all of the Ford buildings, Henry Ford personally selected the architects and brought stone masons from Italy to construct them.

4. Ford Dining Hall (1925)— The dining hall has large stained-glass windows and is modeled after the dining hall at Christ College of Oxford, England. A special vantage point for viewing this building is across the beautifully landscaped grounds and reflecting pools.

5. The Archway (1925)— Separating the classroom buildings and Clara Hall, a women's dormitory named for Mrs. Ford, the carved stone archway architecturally ties the complex together. Note its cathedral-style dome with depictions of domestic and wild animals. Visitors should also watch for the scriptural and literary sayings that adorn the entrances to many of the buildings.

6. Other Ford Complex Buildings
A. Mary Hall (1931)—Named for Henry Ford's mother.

B. Ford Gymnasium (1928)— According to campus legend, when Miss Berry asked the Fords to build this "recreation building," Mr. Ford thought she requested a "recitation building." So they gave the school both buildings! The school's soccer and baseball fields are adjacent to the gymnasium.

7. Log Cabin Buildings (1910–19) —This small complex of rustic log buildings is the original site of the Martha Berry School for Girls. Today, the buildings are used as student residences. Especially notable are:

A. Barnwell Chapel (1911)— Named for Capt. John Barnwell,

42

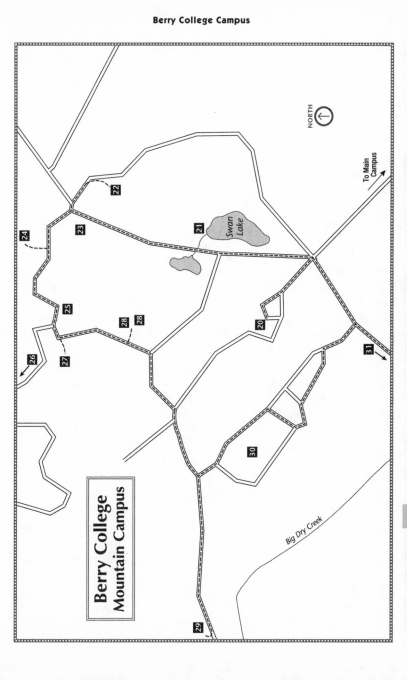

designer of many of the rustic structures, this simple and warm church building has long served as a chapel, recital hall, and classroom.

B. *Atlanta Hall (1910)*—Built with funds raised by the Martha Berry Circle of Atlanta, the building originally served as a dining hall and residence. Today it serves as a laboratory day care center for students studying child development.

C. *Faith Cottage (c. 1910)*—Built as a home for orphan children cared for by Miss Berry, the building now houses campus offices.

8. Cabin in the Pines (1860s)—Nestled in the woods between Hermann Hall and the Log Cabin area, this rough-hewn cabin is one of the oldest buildings on the campus. Originally a "tenant house" for workers at Oak Hill plantation, the cabin has served a variety of uses through the years.

9. Ladd Center (1967)—Built with funds contributed by Mr. and Mrs. Walter Ladd, the building houses the campus infirmary, security department, and other administrative offices.

10. Roanie's Grave—A large stone marker across from Ladd Center marks the burial spot of Martha Berry's favorite pony, which died at the age of 35.

11. Cook Building (1937)—Classrooms for the science and agriculture departments. It was constructed by student labor.

12. Berry College Chapel (1915)—Designed to resemble Christ Church in Alexandria, Va., it was constructed by students under the guidance of architect Harry Carlson. Martha Berry's grave is just south of the chapel.

13. Thomas Berry Hall (1931)—Named for Martha Berry's father, the building serves as a men's dormitory. It was built with funds donated by Henry Ford.

14. Memorial Library (1920, additions 1970, 1976, 1988)—The original contributor to the construction of this building, Kate Macy Ladd, provided the funds as a memorial to her sister-in-law Edith Macy.

15. Green Hall (1922)—Now housing classrooms for business administration and science, it is one of the oldest academic buildings on the campus. Note the inscription above the colonnade: "Whether at work or play do you best."

16. Morton–Lemly Hall (1921, 1953)—Lemly Hall is the oldest brick dormitory on campus.

17. Memorial Gymnasium (1937)—Constructed by students to replace Pentecost Gymnasium built in 1911. Funds were raised as a memorial to James Kidder, who died following an accident in the old gym.

18. Roosevelt Cabin (1902)—Designed by Capt. Barnwell, the rustic log structure is one of the oldest buildings on the main campus. It

Ford Dining Hall, Berry College Campus

served as a guest cottage and social-center demonstration building highlighting the philosophy that "a home may be simple and inexpensive and at the same time in good taste and even beautiful." Miss Berry lived in the cabin for four years, and it became a center for campus social life. During his 1910 visit to the campus, former Pres. Theodore Roosevelt was enter-

tained here. The cabin is now a small museum.

19. Hoge Building (1905)—This attractive 2-story frame building is one of the earliest constructed on the main campus and the oldest still in active use. It is named for E. F. Hoge, Berry College's first controller. Designed to serve as a classroom space, it later served as an administration building until completion of Hermann Hall. Today the building houses weavers' studios and a small gift shop.

Mountain Campus

20. WinShape Building (1931)—Originally built as barns for the Berry College farm, the structure was later converted to maintenance shops, industrial arts classrooms, and a gymnasium for Berry Academy. It is now headquarters of the WinShape Center.

21. Swan Lake and Mirror Lake—These quiet spots for reading or relaxing were constructed by students.

22. Frost Memorial Chapel (1937)—For many years, atop this hillside stood a small wooden cross marked with the words "Chapel needed." Mr. and Mrs. Howard Frost, while visiting the campus from Los Angeles, saw the sign and decided to give the funds for a chapel in memory of their son, John L. Frost. The building was designed in the Gothic Revival style by Samuel I. Cooper and built by student labor. It is an especially popular location for weddings.

23. Barstow Memorial Library (1940)—Built with funds donated by the family of George E. Barstow, the rustic wood and stone building served for many years as the Berry Academy's library. It remains today a study area for WinShape students.

24. Hill Dining Hall (1923)—Built by students, the wooden building is notable for its cathedral ceiling and massive stone fireplace. The building is named for Clifford Hill, a 1916 Berry graduate who returned in 1920 to "help" the school for a few weeks and remained for the rest of his life.

25. Friendship Hall (1926)—The building has served as a combination classroom and dormitory. Its notable features include a 2-story common room with beamed ceiling and leaded casement windows.

26. Road to House O' Dreams—This dirt road ascends 6 miles to the top of Lavender Mountain where, in 1926, staff and students built a retreat cottage for Miss Berry in honor of the school's 25th anniversary. The home is opened for special occasions.

27. Meacham Hall (1921)—Built with funds donated by Cincinnati businessman D. B. Meacham as a memorial to his son, Robert, the hall has served as residence facilities for students and campus guests.

28. Cherokee Lodge (1920) and **Pine Lodge (1916)**—The two oldest structures on the mountain campus, these rustic log buildings have had many uses through the years.

29. Old Mill (1930)—Set in beautiful wooded surroundings, the 42-ft.-diameter overshot waterwheel is one of the largest in the world. For many years, the mill was used to grind Berry-grown corn into meal and grits for serving in the campus dining hall.

30. Normandy Apartments and Dairy (1931–37)—Designed in the style of a French country estate, the hilltop complex includes student housing as well as dairy barns for the school's registered Jersey and Holstein herds.

31. Possum Trot (1850)—The old church building that was the "Cradle of Berry College" was used for classes until 1954. It is open for special occasions and by appointment.

Near the campus

32. Berry President's Home (1940)—Built as a private home, it was acquired by the college as the executive residence in 1956.

33. Oak Hill (1847) and the Martha Berry Museum and Art Gallery (1972)—U.S. 27 at GA 1. Oak Hill was purchased by Capt. Berry in 1859 and was only slightly damaged during the Civil War. However, an 1890 fire destroyed the rear of the house. Following her parents' deaths, Martha Berry became the matron of Oak Hill and lived here until her she died in 1942. Guided tours of the home are conducted by Berry students.

The museum and art gallery are housed in a Greek Revival–style building that features an extensive collection of Miss Berry's personal artifacts, as well as items tracing the history of the school. The film *Miracle in the Mountains*, which depicts Martha Berry's life, is shown on a regular basis. Behind the museum is the "Walkway of Life" paved with stones from Lavender Mountain and featuring plaques with Miss Berry's favorite sayings and scriptural passages. There is a small fee for touring the museum and Oak Hill.

A short distance from the museum is the 1877 cabin built by Capt. Berry as a playhouse for his children. It was later Martha's study and became the first classroom where she taught the mountain children.

Hours: 10 A.M.–5 P.M., Mon.–Sat.; 1–5 P.M., Sun. (800) 220-5504; www. berry.edu/oakhill.

NOTES

47

CHAPTER 8

Etowah Mounds State Historic Site

LOCATION

Etowah Mounds State Historic Site is 3 miles south of Cartersville on Etowah Dr. From Atlanta, follow I-75 north to GA 113 (exit 288). Take GA 113 through downtown Cartersville to Etowah Dr. *Hours:* 9 A.M.–5 P.M., Tues.–Sat.; 2–5:30 P.M., Sun.; closed Mondays (except legal holidays). There is a nominal admission charge. *Information:* (770) 387-3747.

PARKING

There is parking at the visitor center.

BACKGROUND

 A small group of men struggled against the undergrowth as they made their way through the forest. Entering a clearing, the leader abruptly stopped and gazed upward in amazement. Standing before him, shrouded in drifting mist from the nearby river, were the ancient mounds of Etowah. In his published account of this 1817 expedition, the Rev. Elias Cornelius posed the questions that puzzled historians and archaeologists into the next century. Who built these mounds? When and for what purpose? What happened to the people?

Serious archaeological work at the site did not begin until the 1880s when the Smithsonian Institution's Bureau of American Ethnology began excavations at the site. The extraction of artifacts and scientific study continued on and off until the 1920s. Three decades later, in 1953, the land was acquired by the state and set aside for restoration and preservation as a historic site. Scholars now believe that much of the story of Etowah can finally be told.

The origin of the mound-building era dates to a culture called the Hopewell that arose in the Ohio Valley around 100 B.C.E. Characteristics of Hopewell villages such as river access, large ceremonial grounds, and earthen mounds were all features later found at

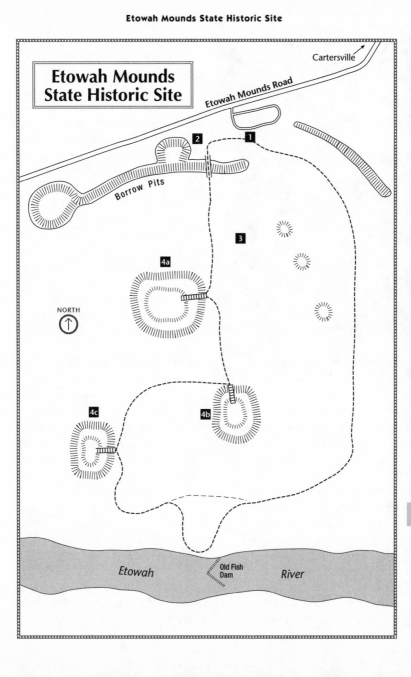

Etowah Mounds

and over the course of five centuries (700–1200 C.E.) expanded its influence throughout the region.

As the culture flourished, populations expanded and new villages were settled, one on the banks of the Etowah River around 1000 C.E. These mound builders now included fortifications such as ditches or wooden walls in their village configurations. Their artistic abilities advanced, with greater use of ceramics and sophisticated engravings and painting.

The mounds were a fundamental part of the culture's emphasis on a tightly knit social and religious structure. They were the focal point of religious ceremonies, and temple buildings once occupied their summits. The mounds also served as burial places for village chiefs.

The village was central to life throughout the river valley and, based on excavation, this community had trade contacts with numerous other cultures in the region. At its peak, the population of the village and surrounding area may have been as high as 2,000 people.

For reasons still not fully understood, the Mississippian culture faded, and by the time the first European explorers entered the region, it had vanished. Their descendants, the Creeks and Cherokees, provided little in their own traditions to explain their ancestors' demise.

Etowah. Also notable within the Hopewellian culture were the presence of agriculture and the existence of trade routes extending from the Rocky Mountains to the Atlantic Coast.

Around 500 C.E., this culture faded due in large part, scholars believe, to a breakdown in trade. As a result, geographically separate cultures, Hopewellian in their roots, evolved independently. One such culture, the Mississippian, established a center in the Mississippi River Valley near present-day Memphis, Tenn.,

Today, when so much is known about our history, the lingering mystery of the peoples of Etowah draws visitors to explore the grounds, pause, and wonder.

WALK DISTANCE AND TERRAIN

 This 1-mile walk begins and ends at the visitor center. The ground is nearly level for the entire distance with the exception of the fairly steep ascents of the three mounds. The site is mostly open fields with an abundance of shade trees nestled along the banks of the Etowah River and around the visitor center.

SIGHTS ALONG THE WAY

1. Visitor Center And Museum—This facility houses an excellent museum depicting the culture of the people who lived here.

2. The Ditch—Adjacent to the center, this long, deep cut was the source of the earth used to construct the mounds. It may also have served as a defensive moat around the northern part of the settlement.

3. Ceremonial Plaza—The large, open, level area around the mounds was the focal point of religious rituals and secular activities.

4. The Mounds—The three principal Mounds (A, B, and C) were used for a variety of purposes including burials of prominent priests or chiefs,

religious ceremonies, and defensive lookouts. Mound A (the largest at just over 60 ft. in height) and Mound B once had temple buildings atop their summits. Neither has been excavated. Mound C has been completely excavated and found to be primarily a burial site with more than 500 interments. The artifacts unearthed have given archaeologists many clues about the culture and lifestyle of the Mississippian peoples.

Steps have been constructed on the side of each mound to encourage visitors to explore them and gain a new perspective of the village site and the natural beauty of the Etowah River Valley.

NOTES

51

NORTHWESTERN MOUNTAINS ANNUAL EVENTS

March
◆ Artifact Identification Day
(Etowah Mounds)

April
◆ Native American Tools and
Weapons Demonstrations
(Etowah Mounds)

May
◆ Crafts in the Clouds
(Cloudland Canyon)
◆ New Salem Mountain Festival
(Rising Fawn)
◆ Spring Wildflower Hikes
(Fort Mountain)
◆ Mayfest on the Rivers (Rome)
◆ Coosa Valley Arts and Crafts Fair
(Rome)
◆ Prater's Mill Country Fair (Dalton)

July
◆ Independence Day Concert
(Chickamauga Battlefield)
◆ Salute to America Festival (Rome)
◆ Homespun Festival (Rockmart)

August
◆ Fort Mountain Mysteries
(Fort Mountain)

September
◆ Possum Trot Homecoming
(Berry College)
◆ Battle Anniversary
Commemoration
(Chickamauga Battlefield)
◆ Fort Mountain Crafts Fair
(Fort Mountain)

October
◆ New Salem Mountain Festival
(Rising Fawn)
◆ Frontier Days (New Echota)
◆ Heritage Holidays (Rome)
◆ Chiaha Harvest Fair (Rome)
◆ Mountains Day (Berry College)
◆ Skills of the Past (Etowah Mounds)
◆ Prater's Mill Country Fair (Dalton)
◆ Georgia Marble Festival (Jasper)
◆ Georgia Apple Festival (Ellijay)

November
◆ Artifacts Identification Day
(Etowah Mounds)

December
◆ Holiday Candlelight Tours
(New Echota)
◆ Coosa River Boat Parade and
Classic Christmas Festival
(Rome)
◆ Berry Christmas (Berry College)

Hiker along the Appalachian Trail, which has its southern terminus at Springer Mountain

Walasi-Yi Center at Neels Gap—the only building through which the Appalachian Trail passes

The Old Courthouse, home to Dahlonega's Gold Museum

The rugged mountains of northeastern Georgia are slightly younger (by about 100 million years) than their counterparts to the west and vastly different in origin. While Georgia's western mountains were built up slowly through eons of sedimentation, the eastern summits, part of the Blue Ridge range, were created through the enormous pressures of continental drift and plate tectonics.

The Blue Ridge Mountains and the northern Appalachians were formed more than 200 million years ago when the North American, European, and African continents collided. As the plates pushed together, heat and pressure vented through volcanoes that deposited vast quantities of molten rock on the landscape. This hardened stone, mostly schists and gneisses, eventually reached over five miles in height (higher than the present-day Mount Everest and surrounding Himalayan range in Asia), before eons of climactic change, winds, and rain eroded the slopes and summits to their present heights and rounded appearance. Nearly all of the land in North America east of the Appalachians, including the underwater continental shelf, was formed from the erosion of this mighty chain of jagged peaks.

Unlike the long, straight ridges and wide valleys of northwestern Georgia, the topography of northeastern Georgia is a jumble of steep slopes and narrow coves. Before the arrival of white settlers in the late 18th century, the area had been fought over by ancestors of the Creeks and Cherokees. One epic battle was said to have taken place many centuries ago on the slopes of what is now known as Blood Mountain near a place appropriately called Slaughter Gap. In the early years of the 19th century, this remote land, part of the

Cherokee Nation, was considered worthless by whites because of its thin, rocky soil, and lack of access to roads and navigable waterways.

Then, in the late 1820s, prospectors discovered traces of gold in the waters of some mountain streams and the nation's first "gold rush" was on. Despite protests by the Cherokees, prospectors poured in by the thousands, and the natives were eventually forced from their lands by the Treaty of New Echota in 1835.

Today, the mountains of northeastern Georgia are a premier tourist destination where visitors flock to enjoy cool summer evenings, spectacular fall foliage, dustings of snows in winter, and explosions of wildflowers in spring. Much of the region is contained within the boundaries of the Chattahoochee National Forest and is home to several state parks. Also found here is the southern terminus of the Appalachian National Scenic Trail, a 2,100-mile footpath stretching from Georgia to Maine.

A tranquil footbridge in Unicoi State Park

Dahlonega

LOCATION

✦ To reach Dahlonega from Atlanta, travel north on GA 400 to GA 60. Follow GA 60 north for about 5 miles to the town square. *Information:* Dahlonega–Lumpkin County Chamber of Commerce, (800) 231-5543, www.dahlonega.org.

PARKING

🚗 There is parking around the square and along adjacent side streets. There is also a public parking lot at N. Park and Warwick Sts.

BACKGROUND

📖 *Gold.* Its allure has drawn people to all corners of the globe in search of riches, from the gold of the Pharaohs in Egypt to the legendary Mayan "Cities of Gold." U.S. history is filled with facts and fables surrounding the famous California Gold Rush in 1849 and the race to the Alaskan Klondike at the turn of century. The country's first gold rush, however, occurred in northern Georgia. Although the exact date of discovery is obscure, the precious metal was found in the mid-1820s deep within the Cherokee Nation. Despite treaties prohibiting white settlement, waves of illegal squatters began to exert pressure on the state government to take the land from the Cherokees.

In December 1829, the legislature defied Federal treaties and enacted laws giving the state jurisdiction over Native American lands within its borders. This led, in 1832, to the subdivision of more than one million acres into 40-acre "gold lots." In October of that year, drawings for these lots were held at the state capitol in Milledgeville, and more than 130,000 people applied for the 35,000 available parcels. Eventually the Cherokee people were forced west along the tragic Trail of Tears.

Even before the exile, prospectors had established a small settlement along a ridge above the Chestatee River. By the early 1830s the town, dubbed "Auraria" (Latin for "gold mine") was home to several saloons, a hotel, post office, and a few attorneys and merchants. Law and order were virtually nonexistent in the frontier town. With the creation of Lumpkin County in 1832, the citizens sought to build a courthouse and instill some order in this rough-and-tumble territory. Due to title disputes on land in Auraria it was decided to construct the courthouse about five miles north of town. A simple log structure served until 1836, when it was replaced by the imposing brick structure which still stands. A town grew up around the courthouse as new settlers came into the country and businesses relocated from Auraria. The new town's name, "Dahlonega," came from the Cherokee word for gold.

Prospectors panned in streambeds to find the precious nuggets, and eventually, dug tunnels to seek out rich veins hidden within the mountains. Most investors were fortunate if they earned back their stake, but a lucky few made fortunes. The gold was plentiful enough that the U.S. government authorized $50,000 for construction of a branch mint in Dahlonega to turn the raw metal into coins and bars. Built on ten acres of land atop a hill just outside town, the mint opened for business in February 1838.

Dahlonega thrived through the 1840s until the discovery of gold at Sutter's Mill in California. Though some prospectors stayed, many others could not resist the lure of adventure in California. When Georgia seceded from the Union in January 1861, the Federal government quickly shut down the mint and removed most of the gold before it could be seized by the Rebels. At war's end, mining resumed in the area. For the remainder of the 19th and well into the 20th century, mining and the businesses that supported it remained Dahlonega's main industry.

Despite the continued excavation of high-grade ore, the mint was not reopened, and when the government fixed the price of gold at $35 an ounce, most of the mines around Dahlonega became unprofitable and shut down. The small town entered an era of quiet, slow decline marked only by the notoriety gained when the State Capitol dome in Atlanta was gilded with Dahlonega gold in 1960 (it was regilded in 1980 and touched up in 1996 for the Olympic Games).

In the early 1970s, tourists began to stream into the county to enjoy the nearby mountains, explore the old buildings around the square, and learn a little of the region's colorful history. With the help of faculty and students from the University of Georgia's School of Environmental Design, a plan was developed to

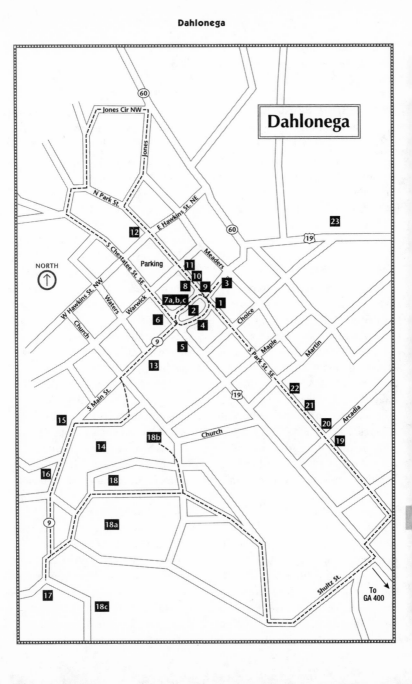

Dahlonega

NORTH
↑

Parking

restore the buildings and revitalize the town. Today, Dahlonega is enjoying a second "gold rush" of tourist dollars.

WALK DISTANCE AND TERRAIN

 The 2.5-mile route begins and ends on the square. There are good sidewalks in the center of town and an abundance of shade trees throughout the trail. The terrain ascends toward Crown Mountain in the northwest and descends gradually toward the southeast.

SIGHTS ALONG THE WAY

1. Dahlonega Chamber of Commerce and Welcome Center—13 Park St. This modern facility is staffed by volunteers ready to share information on activities in Dahlonega and the surrounding mountains. *Hours:* 9 A.M.–5:30 P.M. daily. (800) 231-5543.

2. Dahlonega Gold Museum State Historic Site (1836)—Town Square. This imposing brick structure built in the Federal style is the oldest public building in northern Georgia. Constructed by Ephraim Clayton, the building served as county courthouse, offices, and marketplace for nearly 130 years. In 1965, Lumpkin County donated the building to the State for use as a museum. It contains exhibits on the gold rush and the history of Dahlonega. *Hours:* 9 A.M.–5 P.M., Tues.–Sat.; 2–5:30 P.M., Sun. Closed on

Mondays (except legal holidays). (706) 864-2257. *NR*

3. Rev. Goodman Hughes House (c. 1860s)—E. Main and Derrick Streets. This timeworn frame structure was built by an early Dahlonega clergyman. In the late 1800s, it served as a general store. It now houses several specialty shops.

4. W. P. Price Building (1897)—S. Town Square. A prominent citizen and U.S. congressman, Price constructed this Italianate-style building to house his law office on the second floor, while his son operated a general store below. It later housed the town's first movie theater and is now a popular Christmas shop.

5. Smith House (1899)—84 S. Chestatee Street. This large house was built by Frank Hall when his family outgrew its residence across the square. It was purchased by Henry and Bessie Smith in 1922 and expanded into an inn and restaurant that has become a regional landmark for Southern cooking. Diners may browse in the country store or pan for gold as they wait for a table.

6. C. H. Jones House (c. 1885)—W. Town Square and N. Chestatee St. This large Victorian-style home was constructed by a local physician as home and office. In 1909, Jones had the building next door constructed to serve as a drug store. Both buildings now house shops.

7. Hall's Block (1880s)—W. Town Square. Frank W. Hall came to Dahlonega in 1868 at the age of 23 to supervise operations at a local mine and mill. Later, he started several business, became one of the town's wealthiest citizens, and served as postmaster and mayor. He constructed the buildings along this block for his home, office, and mercantile business.

John Moore purchased the block from Hall's widow in 1919 and continued to operate several retail businesses here. All the buildings along Hall's Block continue to bustle with thriving shops.

A. The Hall Building (1883)—This 3-story building housed Hall's mercantile business.

B. Hall's Office (1884)—Hall built this small office adjacent to his home. It was later converted to the first home of the Bank of Dahlonega and eventually became a shoe store owned by Alec Housley, the "father" of poultry farming in Lumpkin County.

C. Hall House (1881)—The Hall family lived here until 1899. The second floor continues to serve as residential apartments.

8. Sargent Building (1910)—W. Town Square. This rambling 2-story building with its second-story open porch was built by Lumpkin County Sheriff John F. Sargent to serve as the Dahlonega Hotel. It was purchased by Dr. Homer Head in

Shops around Dahlonega's square

1925. He maintained his office on the ground floor and rented upstairs apartments to students at North Georgia College. Today the ground floor houses a variety of shops and the second floor is a restaurant.

9. Meaders Brothers Building (1914)—N. Town Square. Built by Frank and R. C. Meaders for the Bank of Lumpkin County and U.S. Post Office, the building still contains many original features including hardwood floors and pressed tin ceilings. It now houses shops and a real estate office.

10. Nix Grocery Store (c. 1858)—
N. Town Square. Thought to have
been built by early settler John Parker,
this frame building was operated by
N. A. Nix as a grocery from 1936 to
1983. Dahlonega's oldest existing
commercial building, it now houses
Appalachian Outfitters, an outdoor
equipment retailer and outfitter for
float trips on the nearby Chestatee
River. *Information:* (706) 864-7117.

11. Crawford House (1880)—
N. Park at Warwick Sts. The building
may have been constructed by local
businessman Hiram Gurley. The
name comes from Bruce Crawford, a
relative of Gurley's and the cashier of
the Bank of Dahlonega, who had his
family residence on the second floor.
The building has been remodeled several times.

**12. Dahlonega Women's Club
(c. 1930s)—**N. Park and Hawkins
Sts. This attractive building was constructed of locally quarried stone.
Today it is used as a community
events facility.

13. Holly Theater (1948)—
W. Main at Waters Sts. Recently restored and reopened as a nonprofit
community theater featuring both
films and live productions, this old-
time cinema is a slice of 1950s small
town life.

**14. W. P. Price Memorial Hall
(1880)—**College Cir. and W. Main St.
This stately Victorian-style brick
building, topped with a gilded spire, is
named in honor of U.S. Rep. Price
who secured the land and buildings to
start North Georgia College. Built on
the foundation of the U.S. Mint,
which was constructed in 1838 and
destroyed by fire in 1878, Price Hall is
the Administration Building of North
Georgia College and State University,
one of only four senior military colleges in the nation. *NR*

15. Worley Homestead (c. 1845)—
410 W. Main St. Pioneer citizen W. J.
Worley built this rambling, frame
house not long after the town was established. The home is now operated
as a bed-and-breakfast inn. *Information:* (706) 864-7002.

16. Vickery House (1909)—
W. Main Street across from Price Hall.
This attractively restored frame house
was once the home of long-time
North Georgia College Professor E. B.
Vickery. The building is owned by the
school and is used as a special events
facility. *NR*

**17. Mount Hope Cemetery
(1830s)—**W. Main Street. Dahlonega's
oldest burial ground was set aside as a
cemetery even before the territory was
ceded by the Cherokees. Pioneer families, Confederate soldiers, and even a
few Revolutionary War veterans are
interred here.

**18. North Georgia College and
State University Campus (founded
1870)—**Between W. Main Street and
S. Chestatee Sts. From humble beginnings shortly after the end of the Civil

War, the university now has an enrollment of more than 2,000 students. Points of interest include:

A. Parade Grounds—This large grassy plain serves as both drill grounds for military students and athletic fields.

B. Hoag Student Center—Located in the center is the campus bookstore, dining room, student lounge, art gallery, a small museum, and the office of the university president. The center is named for Dr. Merritt Hoag, president of the college from 1949 to 1970.

C. Planetarium—Sunset Dr. Public shows are presented on Friday evenings. *Information:* (706) 864-1511.

19. Hedden Hall (1883)—237 Park St. W. P. Price built this house for his daughter Carrie. It was later purchased and remodeled by North Georgia College and named for Pres. W. A. Hedden.

20. Mattie Craig House (1888)—225 Park St. Price built this house for his daughter Beverline, who married D. S. Craig. Mattie was their daughter.

21. Two Bells (1890)—192 Park St. Price built this house for his daughter Belle. She married William Charters, a one-time law partner of Price.

22. Seven Oaks (1875)—177 Park St. This beautiful mansion was built by Price as his family home. It replaced a structure that burned in 1874. *NR*

23. Old Jail (1884)—E. Main at Hill Sts. The red-brick building has not held a prisoner for many years, but the bars are still on the windows. Today it houses offices of the Lumpkin County Historical Society.

NOTES

63

CHAPTER 10

DeSoto Falls Scenic Recreation Area

LOCATION

✦ This U.S. Forest Service Recreation Area is located on U.S. 19/129 about 22 miles south of Blairsville and 40 miles north of Gainesville. To reach the area from Atlanta, go north on I-85 and I-985 to U.S. 129/GA 11 (exit 22). Travel on U.S. 129/GA 11 north through Gainesville and Cleveland, and past the intersection of U.S. 19 at Turner's Corners. The recreation area is about 6 miles ahead on the slopes of Blood Mountain. *Information:* Chattahoochee National Forest, Chestatee Ranger District, (706) 864-6173.

PARKING

🚗 The trails are open year round, but the parking area at the trailhead is open only from spring through fall. At other times you may park along the road outside the gate and walk the short distance to the trailhead.

BACKGROUND

📖 Nestled beneath the towering summits of Cedar and Blood Mountains is a meandering trail that leads to three beautiful, yet distinctly different waterfalls. Known simply as the Lower, Middle, and Upper Falls, their collective name honors the memory of Spanish explorer Hernando de Soto. Legends persist that de Soto and his Conquistadors passed through this area during their travels from Florida into western North Carolina in the 1540s.

The Recreation Area is part of the surrounding Chattahoochee National Forest and contains a campground (open spring to fall), picnic area, and trails.

WALK DISTANCE AND TERRAIN

🚶‍♀️🚶 All of the trails begin at the campground by the wooden bridge across Frogtown Creek. The walk distance between the three trails is about 2.5 miles and a round-trip hike is about 5.4 miles. The trails are open year round.

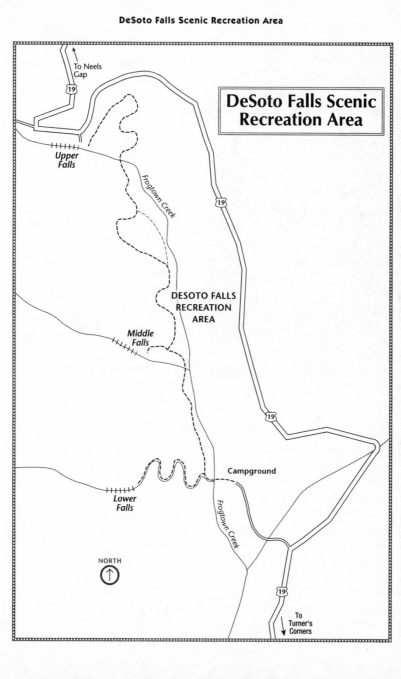

DeSoto Falls Scenic
Recreation Area

To Neels
Gap

19

Upper
Falls

Frogtown Creek

19

DESOTO FALLS
RECREATION
AREA

Middle
Falls

19

Lower
Falls

Campground

Frogtown Creek

NORTH

19

To
Turner's
Corners

Forest ferns along Frogtown Creek, DeSoto Falls

Lower Falls

These falls are .25 miles south of the bridge along a series of switch-backs which moderately ascend to the vista point.

66

Middle Falls

Heading north of the bridge for .7 miles, walkers reach the Middle Falls by a wide, mostly level path that parallels the creek for most of its length. The Middle Falls, actually a series of three waterfalls, spring from far up the hillside.

Upper Falls

An additional 1.5 miles beyond the Middle Falls, the Upper Falls overlook is reached by a moderately strenuous ascent including two short stream crossings. The Upper Falls are also accessible from a less difficult .5-mile trail from a parking area on U.S. 19/129.

Warning: Signs located near each of the falls, remind visitors of the slippery rocks and the dangers associated with approaching too close.

SIGHTS ALONG THE WAY

The luxuriant greenery along the creek and the mix of hardwoods and evergreens on the mountainsides assure a colorful and scenically beautiful hike at any season of the year. Be alert for deer, raccoon, or even a wild turkey while exploring the trails.

CHAPTER 11

Appalachian National Scenic Trail— Neel's Gap to Tesnatee Gap

(404) 634-6495; Appalachian Trail Conference, (304) 535-6331; www. atconf.org.

PARKING

On U.S. 19/129 there is limited parking at the Walasi-Yi Center (a camping supply store), and an overflow lot a short distance further north. At Tesnatee Gap there is a small unpaved parking area for a shuttle car.

BACKGROUND

Stretching unbroken for more than 2,000 miles from the rhododendron-shaded hills of northern Georgia to the rugged forests of central Maine, the Appalachian National Scenic Trail affords the hiker an opportunity to explore a thin ribbon of wilderness near urban America. This trail, following the ridges and valleys of the Eastern mountains, was the vision of Benton MacKaye, a pioneer naturalist and urban planner. MacKaye first proposed the idea for a trail in his article, "An Appalachian Trail: A Project in Regional Planning," published in a 1921 issue of the *Journal of the American Institute of Architects.* Over the next 16 years, trail clubs were formed and countless volunteers slowly carved a footpath from

LOCATION

The trail crosses Neel's Gap on U.S. 19/129 about 40 miles north of Gainesville. Gainesville is about 50 miles north of Atlanta via I-85 and I-985. From the interstate, travel north on U.S. 129/GA 11 (exit 22) through Gainesville and Cleveland. Continue north, past the intersection of U.S. 19 at Turner's Corners and climb to Neel's Gap. To reach Tesnatee Gap, continue north on U.S. 19/129 past Vogel State Park. Turn right on GA 180 and, after one mile, turn right on GA 348. Follow this road for about 9 miles to the small unpaved parking area just off the road on the right.
Information: Chattahoochee National Forest, Supervisor's Office, (770) 536-0541; Georgia Appalachian Trail Club,

67

Trees in winter along the Appalachian Trail

popular book, *Walking with Spring*. The idea caught on and today several thousand travelers, from children to retirees, have earned the privilege of being called "thru-hikers." Persons planning a hike of the entire trail in a single season often begin at Springer Mountain (near Amicalola Falls State Park) in March and follow warm weather northward, arriving at Maine's Mt. Katahdin in October. In the summer of 1998, Schaefer repeated his trip to the acclaim of the media and hundreds of other hikers who came out along the way to walk with him.

the rugged mountains. At the time, no one envisioned a single footpath to be hiked end to end, but rather a series of connected trails suitable for day trips and weekend camp-outs.

It was not until 1947 that anyone chose to hike the entire length of the trail in a single trip. That year, Eric Schaefer, a recently returned World War II veteran, hiked from Georgia to Maine, chronicling his adventure in a

While only a handful of hikers can "drop out" for six months to hike the A.T. in a single trip, others with the dream to "thru-hike" do so over the course of several years. Most people, though, are content to explore trail sections close to their homes. If the allure of the trail draws you and you wish to experience a portion, the section from Neel's Gap to Tesnatee Gap is an excellent introduction to the

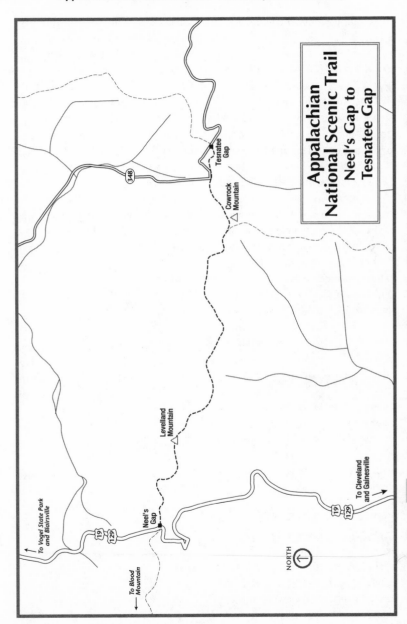

Appalachian National Scenic Trail Neel's Gap to Tesnatee Gap

trail's rugged beauty and enduring character.

WALK DISTANCE AND TERRAIN

This 6.5-mile section of the trail begins behind the Walasi-Yi Center at Neel's Gap and immediately ascends along a series of switchbacks to the summit of Levelland Mountain. From this vantage point, on a clear day, look for the distinctive silhouette of the observation tower atop Brasstown Bald about 20 miles away. To the southwest, the narrow steep valleys hide the rushing waters of DeSoto Falls. The trail continues to follow the ridgeline for another 4 miles ascending to the top of Cowrock Mountain, which offers a breathtaking southern-facing vista. (Some folks claim that on very clear winter days they can see the skyline of Atlanta 100 miles away.) From this point, the trail proceeds steadily, and sometimes steeply, downward to Tesnatee Gap.

For a day hike, wear sturdy walking shoes or boots, pack a jacket or windbreaker (even in summer), and carry ample water for the trip.

SIGHTS ALONG THE WAY

This section of the Appalachian Trail provides all of the finer characteristics of the trail as it is found in Georgia—lush foliage, thick forest, breathtaking views, glimpses of wildlife, and an opportunity to enjoy a small slice of wilderness. Amidst the natural beauty, the rustic stone Walasi-Yi Center is noteworthy. Constructed by the Civilian Conservation Corps during the 1930s, the center is a welcome sight for many weary backpackers. The stone archway connecting the center's two buildings is the only place in the A.T.'s 2,000-mile length where it passes through a building.

Today the center continues to serve travelers by selling camping supplies and equipment, clothing, books, and regional crafts.

NOTES

Vogel State Park— Bear Hair Trail

LOCATION

Vogel State Park is located on U.S. 19/129 about 42 miles north of Gainesville. It is about 110 miles north of Atlanta, via I-85 and I-985 to U.S. 129/GA 11 (exit 22). Travel north through Gainesville and Cleveland; at the intersection with U.S. 19 at Turner's Corners, continue on 19/129 and climb over Neel's Gap. The park is on the left about a mile north of Neel's Gap. *Information*: (706) 745-2628.

PARKING

There is a large parking area at the visitor center, which is just a short distance from the trailhead. A daily parking fee is charged.

BACKGROUND

Located in a narrow cove below 4,458-ft. Blood Mountain, Vogel State Park has long been one of the most popular travel destinations in the mountains of northern Georgia. Whether you come to enjoy the spectacular scenery and mountain air, to participate in the varied selection of outdoor activities, or to learn more about Indian and mountain folklore, Vogel is an excellent point to begin your explorations.

Vogel is Georgia's second-oldest state park (Indian Springs is the oldest), having been established in 1928 on land donated by businessman Fred Vogel. During the Great Depression, Civilian Conservation Corps workers built many of the park's attractions, including 20-acre Lake Trahlyta (named for a Cherokee princess whose grave, according to legend, is marked by a cairn of stones at the intersection of U.S. 19 and GA 60), rental cottages (some of which are still in use), a campground, and hiking trails. The park welcomes the "Boys of the CCC" back to a reunion each spring.

For hikers, the trailheads for the .7-mile Byron H. Reece Nature Walk, the 12.7-mile Coosa Backcountry Trail, and the 4-mile Bear Hair Trail are located just behind the cabin area a short distance from the visitor center. The Reece trail, named for the renowned Georgia poet who grew up in these mountains in the 1920s, is an excellent choice for a short stroll through the forest, while the Coosa Trail is a challenging backpacker's route deep into the mountains. The Bear Hair Trail offers a moderately strenuous day hike into the wooded hills. Another path, the Lake Trahlyta Trail, begins at the picnic area and follows the shore of the lake in a 1-mile loop.

WALK DISTANCE AND TERRAIN

The 4-mile Bear Hair Trail (orange blazes) climbs quickly up from the trailhead before leveling out and paralleling fast-flowing Burnett Branch. After crossing an old logging road, the Coosa Trail (yellow blazes) diverges to the right and the Bear Hair ascends fairly steeply on long switchbacks to a point high above the park. (A .5-mile-long side trail leads to a scenic overlook of the park and Lake Trahlyta.)

The latter half of Bear Hair follows a downward course, with one particularly steep descent, before passing through an area that was heavily logged during the early years of the century (look for the telltale remains of rotting stumps). The trail closes the loop just above Burnett Branch before returning to the trailhead.

Lake Trahlyta in Vogel State Park

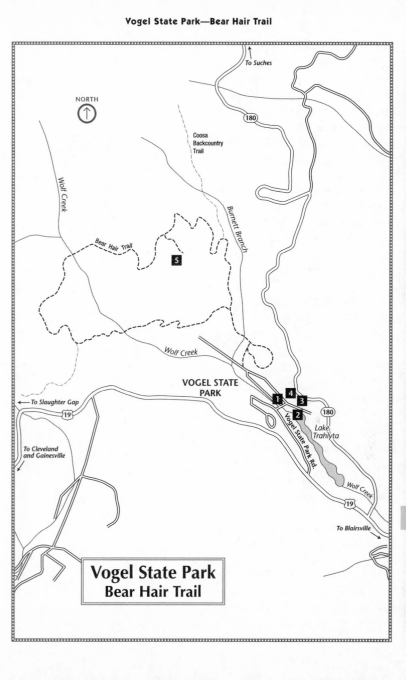

Vogel State Park
Bear Hair Trail

SIGHTS ALONG THE WAY

The Bear Hair Trail provides an excellent hike into the hills of the Southern Appalachians. Here you may enjoy luxuriant foliage and spectacular seasonal colors while perhaps capturing a glimpse of varied wildlife. Sights on the trail and in the park include:

1. Park Visitor Center (1930s, renovated 1970s)—The building houses park headquarters, lodging/camping registration, miniature golf equipment rental, gifts, and groceries. *Hours:* 8 A.M.–5 P.M. (later in summer).

2. Lake Trahlyta Pavilion (1930s; 1970s)—The CCC built a wooden pavilion that was replaced by the present concrete structure. During summer, the pavilion offers paddle-boat rentals, fishing supplies, and refreshments.

3. CCC Museum (1930s)—Located in a converted snack bar, the museum features many artifacts and photographs depicting life in the Civilian Conservation Corps and the work done at Vogel State Park. Hours vary.

4. CCC-Built Cottages (1930s)—The cabins constructed of rough-hewn logs were built by CCC workers.

5. Lake Trahlyta Overlook—This point on a short side trail provides a panoramic view of the park, lake, and surrounding mountains.

NOTES

74

Unicoi State Park—Anna Ruby Falls

LOCATION

✦ Anna Ruby Falls is located on a spur road off of GA 356. From Atlanta travel north on I-85 and I-985 to Gainesville. Follow U.S. 129/GA 11 (exit 22) north through Gainesville to Cleveland; then travel north on GA 75 past Helen to GA 356. *Information:* Chattahoochee National Forest, Chattooga Ranger District, (706) 878-3574; Unicoi State Park, (800) 864-7275; Helen–White County Convention and Visitors Bureau, (800) 858-8027.

PARKING

🚗 There is a large parking facility adjacent to the Falls visitor center and another, smaller area across from the Unicoi State Park trailhead. There is a daily charge for parking in the state park.

BACKGROUND

📖 Confederate veteran Col. John H. Nichols purchased the falls and several thousand acres of adjoining land for farming and timber harvesting. He frequently brought his daughter, Anna Ruby, up to the falls to picnic and enjoy the scenery and named them for her. Nichols died in 1898 and, a short time later, the falls and surrounding property were purchased by the Byrd-Matthews Lumber Company, which began logging the area in earnest. At one time, a narrow-gauge cart track snaked down Smith Creek from the falls to get cut trees to the mills more quickly. Track remnants may still be seen in the debris at the bottom of the falls. In 1925, the U.S. Forest Service, in the process of establishing the Cherokee (and later the Chattahoochee) National Forest, purchased this land. The Anna Ruby Falls Scenic Area was set aside for preservation in 1964.

To complement the National Forest preserve, Unicoi was created in 1954. From the Cherokee, Unicoi means "New Way" and, in a real sense,

75

the park has long served as the site for state-sponsored experiments in recreation. From the "squirrel's nest" group camps to the beautiful Lodge and Conference Center, the park has developed facilities and activities of wide popular appeal.

The meandering Smith Creek Trail connects Anna Ruby Falls with Unicoi State Park. Beginning just below the falls, the path winds along heavily forested ridges and narrow creek bottoms on its 5-mile route down to the Little Brook Campground adjacent to Unicoi Lake.

Anna Ruby Falls, Unicoi State Park

WALK DISTANCE AND TERRAIN

From the Anna Ruby Falls visitor center it is a .5-mile, sometimes steep, ascent to the base of the falls. This path is paved and passes through lush forest as it parallels Smith Creek. From the base of the falls, the blue-blazed Smith Creek Falls Trail winds along away from the creek as it clings to the western slopes of Hickory Nut Ridge. It moderately descends on a meandering 4.5-mile path to Unicoi State Park's Little Creek Campground. The walk is lined with ferns, trilliums, flame azaleas, and stands of rhododendron and mountain laurel that combine to make a rich palette of

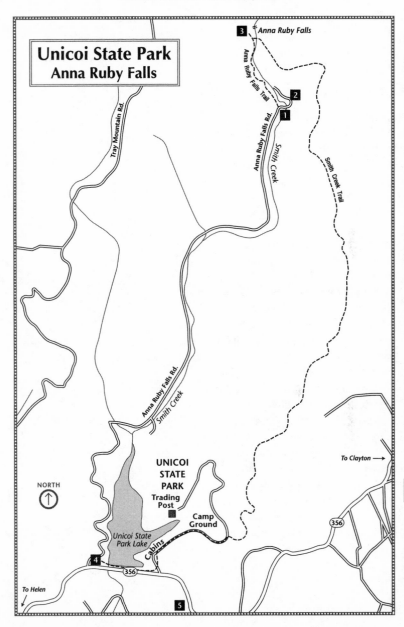

Unicoi State Park
Anna Ruby Falls

Anna Ruby Falls

Anna Ruby Falls Trail

Anna Ruby Falls Rd.

Tray Mountain Rd.

Smith Creek

Smith Creek Trail

Smith Creek

To Clayton →

UNICOI
STATE
PARK

Trading
Post

Camp
Ground

NORTH
↑

Unicoi State
Park Lake

Cabins

356

356

To Helen

color in spring. Watch for lingering reminders of the logging operations as you pass through this regenerating Appalachian Cove forest.

SIGHTS ALONG THE WAY

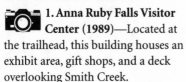 **1. Anna Ruby Falls Visitor Center (1989)**—Located at the trailhead, this building houses an exhibit area, gift shops, and a deck overlooking Smith Creek.

2. Lion Eyes Trail—This short loop trail from the visitor center parking area follows the course of Smith Creek. It is wheelchair accessible and features braille markers for the visually impaired.

3. Anna Ruby Falls Overlook Platform—At the base of the twin falls, the deck provides an excellent vantage point to view the cascading waters.

4. Unicoi State Park Information Center—GA 356 at Unicoi Lake Dam. This rustic wooden building provides information about the park and nearby attractions.

5. Unicoi Lodge and Conference Center (1973)—GA 356 east of Unicoi Lake. The comfortable complex, designed to complement its rugged surroundings, provides 100 rooms, meeting facilities, gift shop, restaurant, and lighted tennis courts.

NOTES

Black Rock Mountain State Park— Tennessee Rock Trail

LOCATION

From Atlanta travel north on I-85 and I-985 to Gainesville. Continue north on I-985, which merges into U.S. 441 near Clarkesville. About 3 miles north of Clayton, turn left off of U.S. 441 on Black Rock Mountain Rd. and follow the signs to the park visitor center. *Information:* (706) 746-2141.

PARKING

There is a small parking area at the trailhead and additional roadside parking along the road between the visitor center and the park cottages. A daily parking fee is charged.

BACKGROUND

Nestled in the heart of northeastern Georgia's Appalachian Mountains, Black Rock Mountain State Park is the highest park in the state. The Eastern Continental Divide follows the high ridges across Black Rock Mountain, which draws its name from the sheer outcrop of dark stone cliffs that dominate its southern face. The bare rock is clearly visible from Clayton and throughout the valley to the south. Explorers in these surroundings will find fascinating evidence of what took place here eons ago as well as signs of the impact of logging from the last century.

A detailed guide to the Tennessee Rock Trail, with descriptions keyed to numbered markers along the trail, is available for purchase at the visitor center.

WALK DISTANCE AND TERRAIN

79

The 2.2-mile loop Tennessee Rock Trail makes a short ascent from the parking area before descending, at times steeply, to an old logging road. After climbing a gentle grade through a pine forest, the path ascends steeply to the summit of Black Rock Mountain before its steady descent back to the trailhead. For its entire length, the trail is above 3,000 ft. in elevation and provides an excellent opportunity to explore the botanical wonders of an Appalachian mixed forest.

SIGHTS ALONG THE WAY

 1. Boulder Field—A short side trail leads to this botanically and geologically significant area.

Morning clouds seen from Black Rock Mountain

The Southern Appalachians were beyond the farthest reach of the glacial ice sheet, but the epoch's cold, harsh climate still kept this area shrouded in ice and snow for much of the year. The constant freezing and thawing action, over many centuries, weakened these rocks, causing them to crack and tumble from high above to here where they have remained undisturbed for millennia.

2. Stand of White Pines—This area of evergreen depicts a forest in transition caused by the logging of hardwoods on the hillsides earlier in this century. Over time, the pines will once again give way to the deciduous trees that are better suited to sur-

80

viving in the upper elevations.

3. Black Rock Mountain Summit—The park's highest point rests 3,640 ft. above sea level and is astride the Eastern Continental Divide.

4. Tennessee Rock Overlook—The trail draws its name from this granite outcrop that provides a panoramic view into the valley below and on to the distant northern mountains of Tennessee and North Carolina.

5. Park Visitor Center—Situated on the southern face of the mountain, the center features exhibits on the plants and animals that occupy park habitats. An observation deck offers a magnificent view of the town of Clayton and the mountains to the south and east. *Hours:* 8 A.M.–5 P.M., daily. (706) 746-2141.

6. Ada Hi Falls Trail—Ada Hi in the Cherokee language means "forest," and this short .2-mile path descends through hardwoods and thick stands of rhododendron to a cove of tulip poplars surrounding a deck that overlooks the falls.

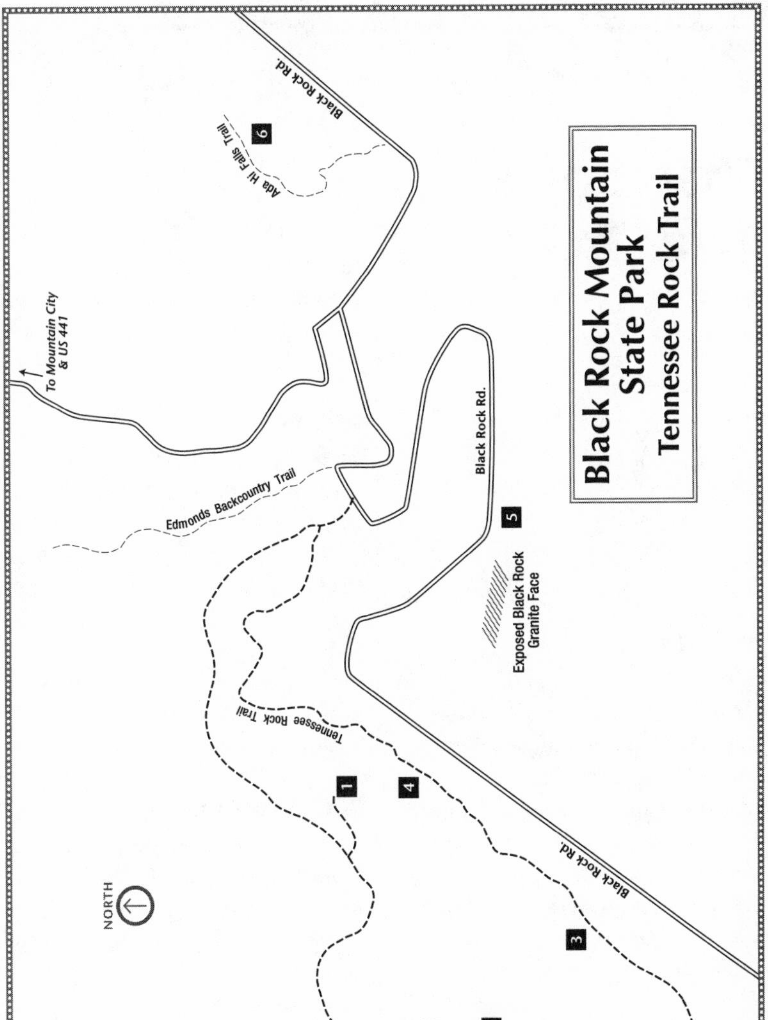

Black Rock Mountain
State Park
Tennessee Rock Trail

NORTH

To Mountain City
& US 441

Black Rock Rd.

Ada Hi Falls Trail

Edmonds Backcountry Trail

Tennessee Rock Trail

Black Rock Rd.

Exposed Black Rock
Granite Face

Black Rock Rd.

Tennessee Rock Trail

Old Logging Rd.

Chattooga River Trail

LOCATION

The northern end of this section of the 20-mile-long Chattooga River Trail is located about 9.5 miles east of Clayton. Follow Warwoman Rd. about 6 miles to Antioch Church (watch for the sign). Turn right on unpaved Sandy Ford Rd. (Dick's Creek Rd.) and travel about 3.5 miles. After crossing a shallow ford of Dick's Creek, look for the small parking area. Nearby, an engraved boulder marks the crossing of the Bartram Trail. A short distance east on the Bartram Trail is the point where the Chattooga and Bartram Trails fork. The southern trailhead is located about 8 miles east of Clayton, on the western side of the

U.S. 76 bridge. The trail is reached from Atlanta by traveling north on I-85 and I-985 to U.S 441 to Clayton, then following the directions above. *Information:* Chattahoochee National Forest, Tallulah Ranger District, (706) 782-3320.

PARKING

There is a small parking area at the northern trailhead. It is on the left, just past the Dick's Creek ford. A larger, gravel parking area is located at the bridge where the trail intersects U.S. 76. Because this is not a loop trail, it is necessary to have two cars or to make arrangements for someone to drop you off at the trailhead or pick you up at the end of the hike.

BACKGROUND

Rabun County is a walker's paradise, with foot trails for people of nearly any skill level or physical condition to explore. An especially scenic path is the Chattooga River Trail along the banks of the waterway that carves the northeastern boundary between Georgia and South Carolina. Made famous by the James Dickey novel and 1972 movie *Deliverance*, the challenging river annually draws thousands of white-water

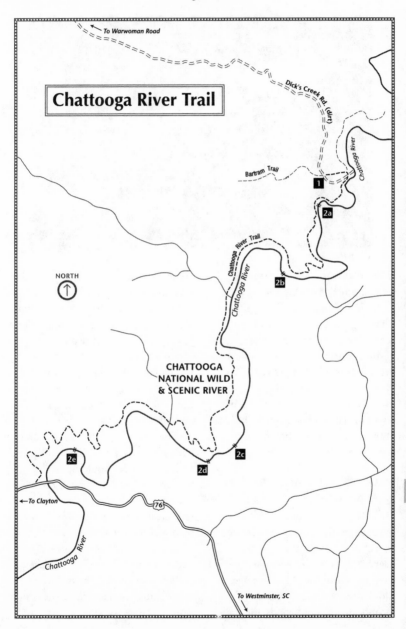

Chattooga River Trail

Along the Chattooga River Trail

enthusiasts who come to test themselves against its world-class rapids.

In 1974, Congress designated the Chattooga as a National Wild and Scenic River and protected the river's 57-mile course from its headwaters beneath North Carolina's Whiteside Mountain to its end in Georgia's Tugaloo Lake. The designation also preserves the land corridor on both sides of the river, assuring that the ecosystem remains relatively undisturbed.

WALK DISTANCE AND TERRAIN

The moderately strenuous 10.7-mile section of the Chattooga River Trail described here begins at its fork with the Bartram Trail near Sandy Ford and ends on the Georgia side of the U.S. 76 bridge. Along its way through a forest of second-growth hardwoods, the trail climbs over several steep ridges and descends at times to follow the river bank. There are several excellent spots for picnicking, swimming, and fishing (Georgia fishing license and trout stamp required), as well as for watching people "shooting" the rapids. Also, watch for white-tailed deer, wild turkeys, raccoons, hawks, and other wildlife as you walk.

The Chattooga River Trail is both a beautiful and a physically challenging path that hikers should not tackle unprepared. Wear sturdy hiking boots and carry food, water (always filter or chemically treat river or stream water before drinking), rain gear, and a flashlight. While the trail is marked with diamond-shaped white blazes, old logging roads, game trails, and other paths can make the route confusing at times. Be sure to carry an

84

up-to-date trail map (available from the U.S. Forest Service or at camping and outdoor equipment retailers) that will help you safely navigate and fully enjoy your visit to this wild and special place.

At the Bartram Trail fork, the Chattooga River Trail heads to the right. For a short distance it parallels Sandy Ford Rd. (which leads to a scenic picnic area on the river), then crosses it and climbs over a ridge above the river. After about a mile, the trail bends close to the river and its spectacular rapids.

The trail then climbs several hundred feet above and away from the river into the hardwood forest for another mile before returning to hug the river bank for the next 1.6 miles. This section offers several spots for soaking your feet, taking a swim, casting your fly-rod for a trophy rainbow or brown trout, or relaxing with a snack and a drink. For the next several miles the trail angles along the steep ridges above the river, at times following old logging roads that predate the creation of the protected corridor. Watch for stands of white pines that mark the transition areas where the hardwood forest is slowly healing itself from the extensive logging of the first half of the 20th century.

Nearing its southern end, the path descends along switchbacks to a point close to the river near the powerful Bull Sluice rapid. You will know you are close to it, not by sight, but by the sounds of the white water and the screams of excitement from rafters preparing to go through it. Continuing along the trail, you will cross a wooden footbridge above Pole Creek and climb over a final ridge before making a steep descent to the gravel parking area along U.S. 76. To view Bull Sluice, take the short path north out of the parking area along the river bank.

SIGHTS ALONG THE WAY

1. Bartram Trail Marker— At the intersection of the trail and Sandy Ford Rd. This brass plaque marks the route of naturalist William Bartram, who walked through the South in 1775–76 to collect botanical specimens.

2. Rapids—From several vantage points you can see some of the class III–V rapids that make the Chattooga River so popular with white-water enthusiasts.

A. Second Ledge (III)
B. Eye of the Needle (III)
C. Roller Coaster (III)
D. Painted Rock (IV)
E. Bull Sluice (V)

85

CHAPTER 16

Gainesville

LOCATION

✝ Gainesville is located about 50 miles northeast of Atlanta via I-85 and I-985. To reach the starting point of the walk, follow U.S. 129/GA 11 from I-985 (exit 22) and travel about a mile northwest to Jesse Jewell Pkwy. Turn left, and the Gainesville municipal complex (city hall and county courthouse) will be on the right.

Information: Greater Hall Convention and Visitors Bureau, (770) 536-5209; www.ghcc.com.

PARKING

🚗 In downtown Gainesville there are both metered parking spaces and commercial parking decks.

86

BACKGROUND

📖 For many centuries, the native Creek people gathered for festivals and ceremonies near a natural spring in the Appalachian Mountain foothills east of the Chattahoochee River. In the early years of the 19th century, white traders camped at the site to barter with the natives, and the area came to be known as Mule Camp Springs.

Through a series of treaties brought about by unrelenting pressure for white settlement, the Creeks were forced to cede much of their ancestral land in Georgia to the state. In 1818, Hall County (named for Lyman Hall, a Georgia signer of the Declaration of Independence) was established along the northern border of the former Creek Nation, and in 1821, the state legislature granted a charter for a new settlement to be called Gainesville in honor of Gen. Edmund P. Gaines, a hero of the War of 1812 and of the Creek and Seminole Wars. The site chosen for the village was the area around the old Mule Camp Springs.

Gainesville grew slowly until the discovery of gold on Cherokee lands to the north. Despite prohibitions against white settlement in the area, gold-seekers rushed into the region, and the

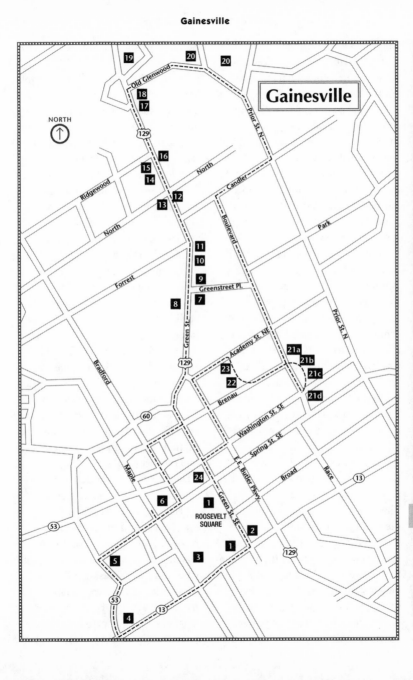

Gainesville

Cherokees were eventually forced from Georgia. Gainesville, the largest and closest permanent settlement to the gold fields, prospered as an important supply and trade center for the miners. After the gold rush, Gainesville remained the gateway to the rugged and remote northern Georgia mountains.

With the outbreak of the Civil War in 1861, Gainesville and the entire region became a tense and dangerous place. Few mountain people owned slaves, and many were staunch Unionists who wanted nothing to do with secession and the Confederacy. Families were torn apart as, ironically, the mountain counties provided a nearly equal number of men to both armies. Marauding and murder were commonplace. In November 1864, Confederate sympathizers captured several men who were leaving to enlist in the Union army and brought them to Gainesville, where they were publicly executed as an example to others.

Tensions eased after the war, and Gainesville prospered again with the arrival of the railroad in the 1870s. The improved access, combined with the cool mountain climate, made Gainesville a popular summer resort during the latter years of the 19th century. The elegant Piedmont Hotel (no longer standing) was constructed to house the tourists, and in 1889, the completion of a municipal power plant made Gainesville the first city

south of Baltimore, Md., to have electric street lights.

Cotton fields lined the nearby hills, and merchants offered the latest goods to local citizens and to the mountain people who came to town by wagon and, later, by automobile. The wealth of this period is reflected in the grand homes that still line Green Street, a popular residential area developed on a ridge above the downtown commercial district.

The city's prosperity was suddenly shattered on the morning of April 16, 1936, when severe thunderstorms rolled through the mountains. Without warning, a massive tornado (believed to have been one of the largest ever recorded) touched down just west of downtown Gainesville. In minutes, the twister cut a mile-wide, 8-mile-long swath of utter destruction that included the heart of the city's business district. More than 170 people were killed and more than a thousand injured; 992 structures were destroyed and property losses were staggering. In a few horrifying seconds, downtown Gainesville nearly ceased to exist.

Help came immediately from many sources as the city sought to recover. Within a few months, the city and county governments, in collaboration with President Franklin Roosevelt's Works Progress Administration (WPA), a Depression-era relief agency, had spent more than $3 million in repairing, restoring, and rebuilding downtown Gainesville. A new city hall, county courthouse, and municipal complex were completed in 1937 and Roosevelt spoke at the rededication ceremony.

Gainesville became an educational center with the founding in 1878 of the Georgia Baptist Female Seminary. Now Brenau University, the campus is located just east of the central business district and is a treasure of Victorian architecture.

Over the years, as cotton declined in importance, it was replaced by poultry farms producing chickens and eggs for local, and eventually, regional consumption. Today, Gainesville proudly boasts of being the "Poultry Capital of the World."

In the mid-1950s, the Army Corps of Engineers undertook the construction of a massive reservoir near Gainesville to serve the water needs of thirsty Atlanta and communities further south. They acquired land along the shores of the Chattahoochee River west of the city and built a massive dam near Buford. In 1957, when the waters filled the 38,000-acre reservoir, now named Lake Sidney Lanier to honor the 19th-century Georgia poet, Gainesville became the gateway to one of the largest and busiest recreational lakes in the United States.

WALK DISTANCE AND TERRAIN

The loop through downtown, along Green Street, and past

Brenau University is about 2.5 miles. The business district is level with a moderate rise to the ridgeline that follows Green Street northward. From the Civic Center, the route descends through City Park before a short climb to Boulevard and a turn south toward Brenau. There are good sidewalks and abundant shade throughout the route.

SIGHTS ALONG THE WAY

 1. Gainesville Government Complex (1937)—300 Green St. The marble-faced, Art Deco–style City Hall and County Courthouse were built with support from the Works Progress Administration (WPA) to replace the government buildings destroyed in the 1936 tornado. The green space between the buildings is Roosevelt Square, named to honor Pres. Franklin D. Roosevelt, who spoke at the ceremony dedicating the buildings in 1937. *NR*

2. Georgia Mountains Museum (1940s)—311 Green St. Designated as a Smithsonian Museum, this former retail building now houses an extensive collection of historical artifacts tracing the history of Gainesville and the mountains of northeastern Georgia. Two exhibits are especially notable. The first traces the life and career of the late Ed Dodd, creator of the popular comic strip, "Mark Trail," which still appears in newspapers around the

89

country. The second exhibit profiles the life of Gen. James Longstreet, who was the second in command to Gen. Robert E. Lee in the Confederate Army of Northern Virginia. Longstreet spent the last years of his life in Gainesville and is buried at the city's Alta Vista Cemetery. *Hours:* 10 A.M.–5 P.M., Tues.–Fri.; 10 A.M.–3 P.M., Sat. (770) 536-0889.

3. Georgia Mountains Center (1980s)—301 Main St. With auditorium, trade-show, and meeting spaces, the center is the largest facility of its type in northeastern Georgia. It is used for a wide variety of musical and theatrical productions, conventions, and other events.

4. Railroad Museum—Jesse Jewell Pkwy. at W. Academy St. Affiliated with the nearby Georgia Mountains Museum, this attraction traces the importance of railroads in Gainesville's history through exhibits housed in a restored baggage car. Also on site are the Gainesville-Midland R.R.'s massive steam locomotive #209, the last commercial steam engine to operate in Georgia, and a working miniature railroad display. *Hours:* 10 A.M.–3 P.M., Thurs.–Sat. (770) 536-0889.

5. Arts Council Depot (1910s)—331 Spring St. The restored railroad depot now houses gallery space, banquet and meeting facilities, an auditorium, and a sculpture garden. *Hours:* 8:30 A.M.–5P.M., Mon.–Fri. (770) 534-2787.

6. Downtown Commercial District and Gainesville Square (c. 1900)—Main St. between Spring St. and Brenau Ave. This area has been the heart of Gainesville's business district for more than a century. Mountain farmers used to travel by wagon to sell their goods on the square. This area was extensively damaged by the 1936 tornado, and the repairs are evident in the different colors of bricks that are visible in many of the buildings.

7. Boone-Garner-Norton House (1885)—380 Green St. Built by Joseph Boone as a simple 4-room cottage, the house was subsequently remodeled with rich Victorian exterior and interior detailing. It is now a law office.

8. Matthews-Norton House (1933)—393 Green St. The adaptive reuse of this attractive Tudor Revival–style house as a real estate office in 1967 marked the beginning of the preservation and restoration of a number of the older homes along Green Street.

9. Lathem-Barnett-Moore House (c. 1880)—404 Green St. One of the earliest residences constructed on Green Street, it was built for businessman George Lathem. The house originally had a verandah that was removed many years ago. Today, the house serves as a dental office.

10. Nalley-Martin House (1937)—434 Green St. One of the last homes built on Green Street, this elegant

Brenau University campus, Gainesville

Georgian Revival–style residence was commissioned by C. V. Nalley and designed by architect Norman Stambaugh. A writer of the period called it "the finest house ever constructed outside Atlanta." The house was later owned by Mrs. J. H. Martin, who bequeathed it to Brenau College for use as the president's home. It was later sold and now houses offices.

11. Smith-Palmour House (1886)—446 Green St. An excellent example of the Queen Anne style, this rambling home, built for James Whitfield Smith, is notable for its elaborate Victorian porch and turret.

12. Quinlan Art Center (1963)—514 Green St. This center, built on the site of an earlier estate, provides gallery space for works by local and regional artists. The Redwine House (1887) located next door at 502 Green St. now serves as additional gallery and meeting space. *Hours:* 9 A.M.–5 P.M., Mon.–Fri.; 10 A.M.–4 P.M., Sat.; 1–4 P.M., Sun. (770) 536-2575.

13. Pruitt-Wheeler House (1909)—539 Green St. This imposing Classical Revival house was built for merchant J. C. Pruitt and was later owned by Judge A. C. Wheeler. Today, it houses law offices.

14. Col. W. A. Charters House (1906)—625 Green St. This large 2-story house with elegant portico remains unaltered since it was built by Charters, a prominent attorney from Dahlonega. The house remained in the family for many years.

15. The Dunlap House (1912)—635 Green St. This 2-story Neoclassical structure was built by Samuel Dunlap as a wedding gift to his son. In 1986 it was adapted for use as a bed-and-breakfast inn. (800) 276-2935.

16. Rudolph House (1916)—700 Green St. Designed by Mrs. John Rudolph as a residence for her mother, Mrs. Annie Dixon, the Tudor–style

91

home was noted for its beautifully landscaped grounds. Today it is a popular restaurant. (770) 534-2226.

17. Longstreet-Newton House (1910s)—746 Green St. This frame house was once owned by Helen Dortches Longstreet, second wife of Confederate Gen. James Longstreet. Mrs. Longstreet was one of Georgia's first environmentalists and ardently opposed the fledgling Georgia Power Company's plans to dam the Tallulah River and destroy the world-famous Tallulah Falls. She established Gainesville's first Roman Catholic congregation in the basement of this house.

18. Miller-Banks House (1912)—756 Green St. This monumental Neoclassical-style house was built for the Miller family by designer Levi Prater. The structure is notable for its 2-story, four-columned portico above a wide, ground-floor porch.

19. Gainesville Civic Center (1970s)—830 Green St. With a low profile and classical styling, the civic center was designed to complement the beautiful older homes that surround it. The center offers meeting rooms and banquet facilities that make it a popular location for a variety of events from business seminars to wedding receptions.

20. Gainesville City Park—Green St. at Prior St. This 43-acre city park offers tennis facilities, recreation fields, and picnic areas. The Gainesville High

School football and baseball stadiums are also located in the park.

21. Brenau University (1878)—Boulevard between Academy and Spring Sts. Founded in 1878 as the Georgia Baptist Female Seminary, a private educational institution for women (that was never directly affiliated with the Baptist church), the school's name was changed to Brenau College in 1900. Over the years, the college expanded its educational curriculum, earning university status in 1992. While there are approximately 1,500 female students attending classes on the main campus, the university has initiated a successful program of evening and weekend classes for both men and women. From its earliest days, Brenau has been an important part of the Gainesville community. Notable buildings on the National Historic Register campus include:

A. Wilkes Hall (c. 1900s)—This Greek temple–like structure is noted for its cone-shaped dome.

B. Bailey Hall (c. 1880s)—The oldest building on campus, this 4-story, Second Empire–style structure is one of the most distinctive academic buildings in Georgia. Adjacent to the central tower is century-old Pearce Auditorium, one of the most beautiful facilities of its type in the nation. It was completely restored and modernized in 1983.

C. Simmons Memorial Hall (1905)—The office of the university president is located here as are the classrooms and studios of the school's highly regarded visual arts program and the Sellars Art Gallery, which exhibits works by faculty, student, local, and regional artists. During exhibitions, gallery hours are: 10 A.M.–4 P.M., Mon.–Fri., and 2–5 P.M., Sun. (770) 534-6263.

D. Wheeler House (1900s)— Boulevard at Washington St. Formerly the residence of the president, the facility now houses administrative offices.

22. Whitepath Cabin (c. 1780)— 403 Brenau Ave. One of the oldest structures in Hall County, this cabin was built by Cherokee Chief Whitepath. One room has been restored to display the furnishings found in a typical Cherokee home. Chief Whitepath died during the Cherokee Removal to Oklahoma on the Trail of Tears. The house was relocated here from its original site and restored as a museum. *Hours:* 10 A.M.–5 P.M., Mon.–Sat.; 1–5 P.M., Sun. (770) 536-0889.

23. Bete Todd Wages and Princess Luci Shirazi Clothing Collection— 406 Academy St. A frame bungalow houses this extensive collection of clothing spanning styles from the 18th through the 20th centuries.

24. Gainesville Federal Building (c. 1930s)—126 Washington St. This stately building was constructed shortly after the devastating tornado that ripped through downtown Gainesville. A notable interior feature is the large mural *Morgan's Raiders*, a New Deal project painted by Daniel Boza in 1936. *NR.*

NOTES

CHAPTER 17

Elachee Nature Science Center

LOCATION

The Elachee Nature Center, located adjacent to the Chicopee Woods Nature Preserve, may be reached by exiting I-985 at the Oakwood Exit (exit 16). Travel west, then north on Frontage Rd. to Atlanta Hwy. (GA 13). Turn left and go about a mile. Turn right at the sign for Chicopee Woods/Elachee Nature Center and, crossing over I-985, follow the road to the center's parking area. *Information:* (770) 535-1976; www.elachee.net.

PARKING

There is a large parking area adjacent to the interpretive center.

BACKGROUND

The Elachee Nature Science Center was established in 1978 as an environmental education component of the 1,200-acre Chicopee Woods Nature Preserve. Elachee is Cherokee for "new green earth." Located within the city limits of Gainesville and less than 4 miles from the heart of downtown, it is one of the largest urban parks in the eastern United States. More than 50,000 visitors a year, many of them students, tour the museum exhibits, participate in classes, or hike the trails that crisscross the property. The adjacent Chicopee Woods Nature Preserve maintains an extensive network of mountain bike trails for recreation and competition.

WALK DISTANCE AND TERRAIN

Four trails wind through the center's property. The trails are free and open to the public from 8 A.M. to dusk, daily.

The Ed Dodd Trail (red blazes) traces a 1-mile loop as it descends east of the interpretive center to the banks of Walnut Creek. It climbs through thick stands of hardwoods to join the Boulevard Trail on a return to the center.

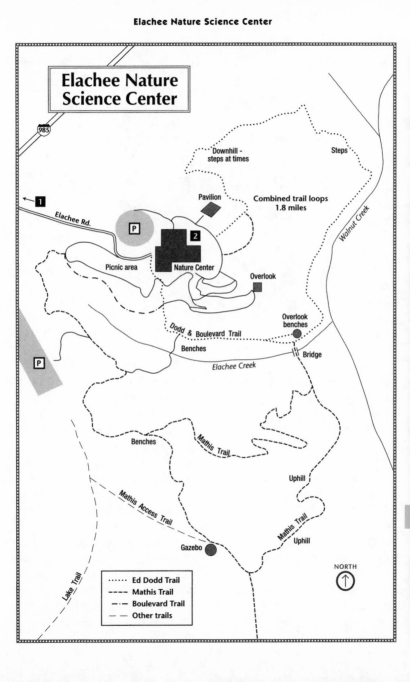

Elachee Nature Science Center

985

Elachee Rd.

1

P

Picnic area

Nature Center

2

Pavilion

Downhill - steps at times

Steps

Combined trail loops 1.8 miles

Walnut Creek

Overlook

Overlook benches

Dodd & Boulevard Trail

Benches

Bridge

Elachee Creek

P

Benches

Mathis Trail

Mathis Access Trail

Uphill

Mathis Trail

Uphill

Gazebo

Lake Trail

NORTH
↑

········· Ed Dodd Trail
– – – Mathis Trail
–·–·– Boulevard Trail
——— Other trails

The Mathis Trail (blue blazes) proceeds west from the interpretive center, also on a 1-mile descending loop toward Walnut Creek. It climbs over several ridges and past Elachee Creek before it connects with the Boulevard Trail.

The Boulevard Trail (yellow blazes) is a .25-mile trail connecting the Dodd and Mathis Trails. Adjacent to the Boulevard is a handicapped accessible, graded cement pathway that winds through the woods between the center and the picnic area.

The Lake Trail (blue blazes) descends, steeply at times, on a winding 2.5-mile path to the waters of Chicopee Lake. Along the way, the trail crosses over Vulture, Redwine, and Walnut Creeks. The route offers excellent views of the changing forest as you descend from the upland ridges to the creek valleys and flood plain. If you prefer not to climb the steep trail back to the center (an additional 2.5 miles), you may park a second vehicle at Calvary Church near the eastern end of the trail.

Elachee Nature Center

SIGHTS ALONG THE WAY

1. Chicopee Mill Village (c. 1920s)—GA 13 at the entrance to Chicopee Woods Nature Preserve. Beneath stately shade trees, the orderly rows of solid, red-brick homes were once part of the mill village of the Chicopee Manufacturing Company. The company closed in the early 1960s, and the houses were sold to private owners.

2. Elachee Nature Science Center (1984, with expansions)—2125 Elachee Dr. This rambling, 2-story building is extensively used for student and adult education programs and houses exhibits, class and meeting rooms, and a small gift shop. *Hours:* 10 A.M.–5 P.M., Mon.–Sat. (770) 535-1976; www.elachee.net.

3. Chicopee Lake Aquatic Studies Center (1999)—Calvary Church Rd. at Chicopee Lake. This wetlands education facility includes trails and a boardwalk, as well as a pavilion and teaching pier overlooking a 13-acre lake.

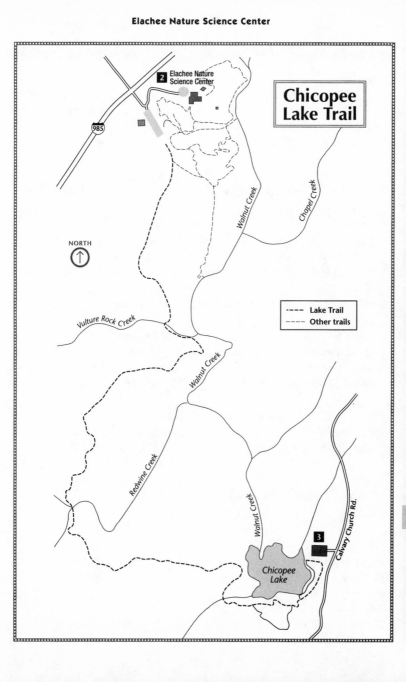

NORTHEASTERN MOUNTAINS ANNUAL EVENTS

January
◆ Fasching Karnival (Helen)

February
◆ Fasching Karnival (Helen)

April
◆ Bear on the Square Mountain
   Festival (Dahlonega)
◆ Wildflower Walks
   (Vogel and Unicoi State Parks)
◆ Alpine Volksmarch (Helen)
◆ Georgia Country Music Arts Festival
   (Gainesville)
◆ Earth Day (Elachee Nature Center)

May
◆ CCC Reunion (Vogel State Park)
◆ Mayfest in the Mountains (Helen)
◆ Chattahoochee Trout Festival
   (Helen)
◆ Hot-Air Balloon Festival (Helen)
◆ Wildflower Walks
   (Black Rock Mountain State Park)

June
◆ Blue Grass Festival (Dahlonega)
◆ The Reach of Song (Young Harris)

July
◆ July Fourth Celebration (Dahlonega)
◆ Float the Fourth Tube Parade and
   Fireworks (Helen)
◆ The Reach of Song (Young Harris)
◆ Appalachian Music Festival
   (Unicoi State Park)

August
◆ Old Times Day (Vogel State Park)
◆ Georgia Mountains Fair
   (Hiawassee)
◆ The Reach of Song (Young Harris)

September
◆ Sorghum Festival (Blairsville)

October
◆ Gold Rush Days (Dahlonega)
◆ Oktoberfest (Helen)
◆ Mule Camp Market (Gainesville)
◆ Great Pumpkin Arts and Crafts
   Festival (Gainesville)

November
◆ Magical Alpine Christmas (Helen)
◆ Christmas Lighting Around the
   Square (Dahlonega)

December
◆ Old Fashioned Christmas
   (Dahlonega)
◆ Magical Alpine Christmas (Helen)
◆ Festival of Trees and Christmas
   in Hall (Gainesville)
◆ First Night Celebration
   (Gainesville)

Atlanta's skyline seen from the site of Fort Walker in Grant Park

*The Trading Post at Red
Top Mountain State Park*

*Confederate Lion monument at
Oakland Cemetery in Atlanta*

*Neal-Patterson House
in Covington*

GREATER ATLANTA

While metropolitan Atlanta is home to more than 3 million people, there are unspoiled woodlands, scenic mountains, historic areas, and quaint Southern towns nearby that are a delight to explore. Within an hour's drive of Atlanta, you may find yourself trekking on a mountain trail, gazing at antebellum houses, or tracing the unfolding events of a Civil War battle.

Today, Atlanta is the largest city in the Southeast, but little more than and a century and a half ago it was a rough railroad town on the line that connected Georgia's interior with its important coastal cities. In the decades before the Civil War, towns like Madison, Covington, and Newnan rivaled Atlanta in importance, as these communities were major supply centers for surrounding cotton plantations. By the time of the war, Atlanta had become the hub of a network of railroads that extended north into Tennessee, west into Alabama, south toward Macon and Savannah, and east to Augusta and Charleston, S.C. Atlanta's value to the Confederacy as a transportation center made it an important strategic target for Maj. Gen. William T. Sherman's invading Union army in 1864, and led to a series of battles at places like Pickett's Mill, Kennesaw Mountain, and Peachtree Creek, before the climactic Battle for Atlanta in July 1864. While Atlanta was burned, several surrounding communities were spared, leaving a lasting legacy of antebellum architectural treasures that provide a tangible link to the past.

CHAPTER 18

Red Top Mountain State Park

LOCATION

✴ The park is about 40 miles north of Atlanta via I-75. Exit on Red Top Mountain Rd. (exit 285) and travel east about one mile to the park entrance and visitor center.

PARKING

🚗 There is a parking area at the trading post/visitor center, which is adjacent to the Sweetgum and Homestead Trails. There is also a large parking lot at the Red Top Mountain Lodge. A daily parking fee is charged. *Information:* (770) 975-0055.

BACKGROUND

📖 Occupying a 1,950-acre peninsula jutting into the deep blue-green waters of Allatoona Lake, Red Top Mountain State Park offers a wide assortment of recreational opportunities for families, boaters, anglers, and hikers. Miles of clearly marked trails meander through creek bottoms, along the banks of the lake, and over the rolling, heavily wooded Appalachian foothills. Blessed with good forage and abundant water, the park is an excellent place for viewing wildlife.

From the mid-19th century through the early years of the 20th century, the area was a center for iron mining, and the name "Red Top" is believed to refer to the rust color of the area's mineral-rich soil. Even today, it is not uncommon to come across old mine sites while exploring the park and surrounding lands. Portions of the park were once part of an extensive iron foundry established at Allatoona Pass in the early 1840s. During the Civil War, the works produced arms and equipment for the Confederate army, and the factory's yard engine, *Yonah*, played an important role in the famous Great Locomotive Chase in April 1862. Today, a ruined blast furnace, located at the Cooper's Furnace Recreation Area south of the park, is all that remains of the once bustling factory.

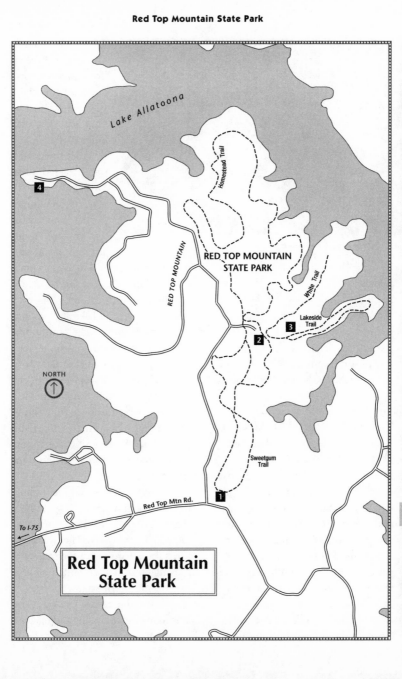

Red Top Mountain State Park

Homestead Trail, Red Top Mountain

Lake Allatoona itself is the oldest Army Corps of Engineers lake in the Southeast. Long a popular destination for Atlantans, it was constructed in the 1950s. The state park, established a short time later, preserves the scenic and historic landscape and offers easy access to the lake's many recreational opportunities.

WALK DISTANCE AND TERRAIN

The network of trails at Red Top Mountain is one of the most extensive in Georgia's state park system. There are four marked trails: Homestead, Sweetgum, White Tail, and Lakeside. Shorter paths lead to the campground and picnic shelters. The White Tail and Lakeside Trails start near Red Top Mountain Lodge and are each about a mile in length. Lakeside is paved and graded for access by the mobility impaired. The 5.5-mile Homestead Trail and the

3.5-mile Sweetgum Trail begin at the visitor center and form a rough figure eight with the crossing point just west of the lodge parking lot.

From the starting point, the red-blazed Sweetgum Trail gently descends on a northerly course to a fern-covered creek valley and meanders through an Appalachian cove forest shaded by pines, oaks, hickories, and of course, sweetgum trees. It ascends along a finger of Allatoona Lake and past the lodge area before winding southward on its return to the trailhead.

The yellow-blazed Homestead Trail follows a similar route through the woods from the visitor center before crossing the lodge road and meandering along a many-fingered peninsula, following ridge tops and descending, sometimes steeply, to the lakeshore. In winter, the expanse of the lake is visible beyond the leafless trees, while in summer, the path is shaded beneath a thick canopy of pines and hardwoods. The trail returns southward across the road to its starting point. The combination of the two trails forms a moderately strenuous 6-mile hike. The lodge sits at roughly the midpoint and makes a great place for a lunch break.

Note the sign on the trail just south of the lodge road pointing out that parts of the forest were heavily damaged by winds from Hurricane Opal in October 1995.

SIGHTS ALONG THE WAY

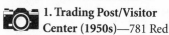 **1. Trading Post/Visitor Center (1950s)**—781 Red Top Mountain Rd. Located in a rustic wooden building with the feel of an old "general store," the trading post/visitor center is the first stop for most park visitors. Staff provide maps and park information, and handle campground registration. Snacks, drinks, and souvenirs are also available. *Information:* (770) 975-4203.

2. Red Top Mountain Lodge (1989)—Red Top State Park Rd. Perched on a hillside above Allatoona Lake, the lodge features a 33-room hotel, conference rooms, gift shop, swimming pool, and the full-service Mountain Cove Restaurant. *Information:* (770) 975-0055 or (800) 864-PARK (7275).

3. Old Homestead (1860s)—Lakeside Trail near the lodge. This old log cabin, depicting frontier life in the Georgia mountains, was relocated to the park and restored in 1996.

4. Red Top Marina—Red Top State Park Rd. This full-service facility provides ramps and docking space, boat rentals, repairs, and fuel.

NOTES

105

Pickett's Mill Battlefield State Historic Site

LOCATION

The site is located about 30 miles northwest of Atlanta via I-75. Exit on GA 92 (exit 277) and follow it south across U.S. 41 to Ga 381. Continue south on GA 381 for about two miles to Mt. Tabor Rd. The entrance will be on the left. *Hours*: 9 A.M.–5 P.M., Tues.–Sat.; 12–5 P.M., Sun; closed on Mondays. There is a small admission fee. *Information:* (770) 443-1115.

PARKING

 There is a large parking area adjacent to the visitor center.

BACKGROUND

The battlefields of the Civil War's Georgia Campaign have long been described in the memoirs of participants and the works of historians. Places like Rocky Face Ridge, Resaca, New Hope Church, and Kennesaw Mountain are familiar to anyone who has studied Union Maj. Gen. William Tecumseh Sherman's March to the Sea.

Interestingly, the battle site at Pickett's Mill was, for many years, conspicuously absent from most of the literature, including Sherman's personal memoirs, despite its description by Union Gen. William Hazen as the "most fierce, bloody, and persistent assault by our troops in the Atlanta Campaign…."

Situated between Dallas and Kennesaw, the battlefield was a thickly wooded area of steep ridges and narrow valleys coursed by the flow of Pumpkinvine Creek (now called Pickett's Mill Creek). At the time of the battle, portions of the area had been cleared for wheat and corn by the Pickett family, and a small grist mill stood along the banks of the creek.

Near Dallas, at the Battle of New Hope Church on May 25, 1864, Union forces under command of Gen. Joseph Hooker had been fiercely repulsed by Gen. John B. Hood's Confederates.

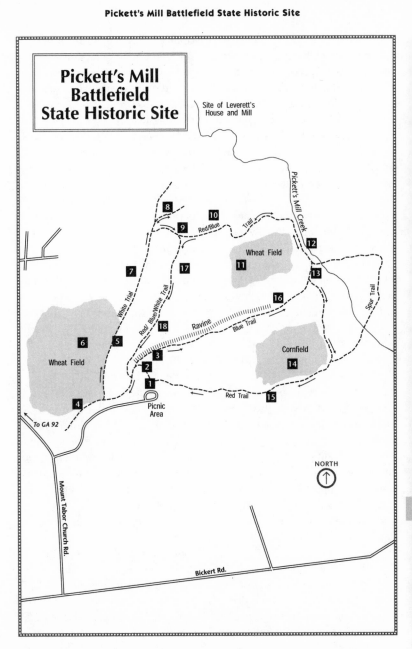

Pickett's Mill
Battlefield
State Historic Site

Site of Leverett's
House and Mill

Pickett's Mill Creek

Red/Blue Trail

8

10

9

Wheat Field

11

12

13

Spur Trail

7

17

White Trail

Red/Blue/White Trail

16

18

Ravine

Blue Trail

Cornfield

6

5

14

Wheat Field

3

2

15

1

Red Trail

4

Picnic
Area

To GA 92

Mount Tabor Church Rd.

NORTH

Bickert Rd.

After resting the night, the Federals sought to extend their lines eastward until they could locate and encircle the extreme right flank of the Rebel's defensive position. Once found, they would attack in force in an attempt to trap and destroy the defenders.

All day on May 26 and into the afternoon of May 27, Union troops of Gen. Thomas Wood's division of Maj. Gen. O. O. Howard's 4th Corps of the Army of the Cumberland maneuvered through almost impenetrable woods in search of the Rebel flank. All the time, Confederate commander Maj. Gen. Joseph Johnston was observing these movements and repositioning troops eastward to extend his own lines.

On the afternoon of May 26, Johnston ordered Gen. Thomas Hindman's division to move from New Hope Church to a position on the Confederate Army of Tennessee's extreme right flank. Gen. Patrick Cleburne's troops were also ordered to move and occupy positions east of Hindman. Additional troops were quick-marched to the area to provide additional support to the rapidly entrenching defenders. All of these movements were hidden by the rugged terrain and went unobserved by Federal scouts.

In the early afternoon of May 27, Col. Robert Kimberly's troops of Hazen's Union Brigade were ordered to march southeastward and attack the enemy when found. After several confusing hours in the thick forest (including a near attack on other Federals), the men reached the vicinity of Pickett's Mill around 3:00 P.M. and encountered a strong Rebel force directly in their front.

With his troops gathering in position, Gen. Howard dispatched the following message to Maj. Gen. George Thomas, Commander of the Army of the Cumberland: "I am on the ridge beyond the hill that we were looking at this morning. No person can appreciate the difficulty in moving over this ground unless he can see it. I am now turning the enemy's right flank, I think." Without time for detailed reconnaissance, Howard prepared to send his men into battle over rough and unknown terrain.

By the time Gen. Wood's men formed for battle, it was late afternoon and they were near exhaustion from their all-day march. Wood's plan called for an attack by three brigades in column (one after another) almost like a battering ram. In this manner he would concentrate his force in a small area, breach the Confederate line, and wheel in behind it.

However, at some point this plan changed and Wood decided to send Hazen's troops alone against the Rebels and see how they fared before committing more men to the assault. On Hazen's staff was the noted writer Ambrose Bierce, who wrote of Hazen's acceptance of this order,

"Only by a look which I know how to read, did he betray his sense of the criminal blunder." Under a darkening sky, Hazen's 1,500 men formed two lines for the attack while 11,000 others watched and waited.

Gen. Patrick Cleburne's Confederates had spent the day establishing a strong defensive portion on a high ridge above a narrow ravine and artillery had been brought up to pour shot and shell into the valley. Gen. John Kelly's dismounted cavalrymen also were stationed on a rocky hillside above Pickett's Mill.

At 4:30 P.M. Hazen's men moved slowly forward, through thick brush, toward an overgrown ravine that they did not know was there. As they approached, the air exploded with Rebel gunfire. Within moments, Hazen's force was decimated, his first line trapped at the bottom of the ravine and the second driven to the left toward a small cornfield where, ironically, the Rebel position was weakest. However, before the advantage could be exploited, Confederate Gen. Daniel Govan's Brigade was quickly dispatched to reinforce the line. After intense fighting in the open field, the Federals were pushed back.

To support the Union assault, a small force commanded by Col. Benjamin Scribner had been sent along the banks of Pumpkinvine Creek to protect Hazen's flank. These men ran headlong into Kelly's cavalrymen near the mill and were pinned down, preventing them from reaching Hazen's desperate troops.

Despite the gravity of the situation and Hazen's repeated calls for help, Wood chose not to immediately dispatch additional troops to the fighting. Near dark, Hazen's men were told to withdraw, an almost impossible order given their exposed position.

Around 6:00 P.M. after much confusion and delay, Wood ordered Col. William Gibson's Brigade to attack and cover Hazen's retreat. However, the Rebel troops, by this time strengthened and resupplied, poured murderous fire into the approaching reinforcements. Soon, Hazen's rescuers were themselves trapped in the ravine, pinned down by incessant rifle and artillery fire.

As darkness closed in, Wood realized the assaults had miserably failed and ordered his remaining brigade, commanded by Col. Frederick Knefler, to move forward, not to assault the enemy but to support the ravaged troops long enough to cover a withdrawal and recovery of their wounded. As they inched through the woods, they were joined by the remnants of Scribner's force which had finally succeeded in driving Kelly's men from the area around the mill. Within moments, the ground erupted with withering fire and Knefler's column was pinned down along with their predecessors.

109

The shelling continued for nearly four hours until around 10 P.M. when, in a rare night attack, Gen. Hiram Granbury's Confederates, shrieking a "Rebel Yell," charged down from their positions into the huddled Federals at the bottom of the ravine.

Hazen's and Gibson's men fled in terror while Knefler's relatively fresh troops held their ground, preventing a rout of Wood's entire command. By midnight, the Rebel assault was spent and Knefler's survivors were able to safely withdraw.

Early the next morning, Lieut. R. M. Collins of Granbury's Brigade viewed the carnage and wrote in his journal, "...dead men strewn among blooming wildflowers. What is man and his destiny to do such a strange thing?"

It has often been said that the history of war is written by its winners, and so the relative obscurity of the fierce Union assault at Pickett's Mill may be due, in large part, to its conspicuous failure in a campaign filled with victories.

Today, the Pickett's Mill State Historic Site is considered one of the best-preserved Civil War battlefields of the Georgia Campaign and in the nation. For serious students of the conflict it is a place to analyze tactics and terrain, while for many others it is simply a place to enjoy a peaceful walk in the woods.

WALK DISTANCE AND TERRAIN

The White, Red, and Blue Trails at Pickett's Mill are arranged in three interconnected loops, each focusing on a different aspect of the battle. For an excellent overview of the engagement, follow this 3-mile route that combines parts of all the trails:

Walk west from the visitor center on the *White Trail*. You will pass in front of positions held by Confederate generals Govan, Granbury, and Walthall. Turn right and follow the wide path that was once a road leading to the pre–Civil War Leverett farm and mill, where Maj. Gen. O. O. Howard had his headquarters. On your left is an open wheat field where Federal troops were pinned down by heavy fire.

Beyond the field, you will pass through woods where Hazen's, Scribner's, and Knefler's Federals formed for their attacks. Bear right (east) until you reach the intersection with the *Red and Blue Trails*. Continue straight ahead on the *Red/Blue Trail* and descend toward Pickett's Mill Creek. Along the way, you may view the fading remains of trenches hastily dug by Union troops. On your right will be the wheat field through which Hazen's troops marched as they descended toward the ravine.

After crossing a footbridge over a small stream, you will reach the banks of Pickett's Mill Creek. A short distance ahead is the site of the Pickett family mill where there was intense fighting between Scribner's Federals and Kelly's Confederates. As you ascend past the the mill site you will see the remains of the Pickett family's cabin. The family operated the mill at the time of the battle, and the cabin was probably damaged or destroyed during the fighting. When the *Red* and *Blue Trails* diverge, continue southeast on the *Red Trail*. The *Red Trail* climbs to the ridgeline where the Rebel troops were dug in and waiting for Hazen's attack. (For an extended hike follow the side trail that leads left into the woods on the eastern side of Pickett's Mill Creek. After about a half-mile, this trail reconnects with the *Red Trail* at the top of the ridge.) Along the ridgeline, you will see what a commanding defensive position the Confederates enjoyed as they poured deadly fire on the Union troops trapped below in the ravine. Watch for signs of trenches dug by Lowrey's Confederates. Follow the *Red Trail* west along the ridge to where it intersects again with the *Blue Trail*. Turn right (north) on the *Blue Trail* and begin to descend through the ravine where the Federal troops were trapped. A glance at the terrain clearly shows how ill-fated was the Union attack.

Retrace your steps past Pickett's Mill and follow the *Blue Trail* west beyond the wheat field until you reach the intersection of all three trails. Turn left (south) on what is now the *Red/Blue/White Trail*. This route roughly traces the line of the Federal attack as troops moved from the woods to the north, toward the ravine to your left. The thickness of the woods and underbrush in this area reveals how difficult it must have been to fight a battle here. As you walk south you ascend toward the ridgeline. It was from this area that the Rebel defenders charged, screaming the "Rebel Yell," on the vicious night attack. The trail ends near the visitor center.

Notable points of interest are identified throughout the battlefield by wooden markers with color-coded numbers. Detailed trail guides to each loop are available at the visitor center.

SIGHTS ALONG THE WAY

1. Visitor Center (1990)— The center features a small theater where an audiovisual program about the battle is regularly shown. An exhibit area contains historical information about the battle and excellent displays of artifacts excavated from the site. (Note: The use of metal-detecting equipment and the removal of artifacts from the historic site is strictly prohibited.) There is a picnic area across the parking lot from the center.

111

2. Ravine Overlook—Behind the visitor center, this wooden platform overlooks the old Pickett's Mill Rd., the ridge, and the ravine beyond.

3. Original Pickett's Mill Road—Now a footpath, this rutted road led to the mill.

4. Govan's Earthworks—This series of trenches was hastily dug by Rebel troops before the battle and strengthened afterward. At one time they were part of a 5-mile-long defensive line stretching toward New Hope Church.

5. Leverett's Mill Road—This road was erroneously followed by Howard's Federals, who thought they would turn the Confederate right flank.

6. Wheat Field—Now an open meadow, at the time of the battle it was ripe with wheat and covered ground on both sides of the trail. Govan's artillery poured shells onto the Union troops moving through the woods north and east of the field.

7. Gen. Howard's Reconnaissance —Howard rode forward to this point north of the wheat field and saw Rebel troops moving in the distance. From this brief observation, he believed he had found the Confederate right flank and ordered the attack.

8. Union Artillery Fortifications— A short side trail leads to several

Civil War reenactors at Pickett's Mill Battlefield

horseshoe-shaped earthen mounds. These were dug during the night of May 27 to protect cannons brought up to support the Federal withdrawal from the ravine.

9. Union Line of Attack—It was in this area that Hazen's Federals formed for their attack late on the afternoon of May 27.

10. Union Rifle Pits—Along the hillside above Pickett's Mill Creek, these shallow trenches were hastily dug by Federal soldiers on the night of May 27.

11. Wheat Field—Scribner's Union troops moved through this small field in an effort to support Hazen's flank. They were soon pinned down by heavy fire from Kelly's Rebels positioned in the hills east of Pickett's Mill Creek.

12. Site of Pickett's Mill—All that remains of the mill that gave the battlefield its name are a few stacked foundation stones above the riverbank.

13. Site of Pickett Family Residence—Foundation stones and an old well mark the location of the home of the family that operated the nearby mill. Historians believe that the house was destroyed during the battle.

14. Cornfield—Hazen's troops reached this field before being repulsed by Confederate troops, who had been rapidly deployed to extend the Rebel right flank. They drove the Federals back down toward the ravine. Hazen's advance through this field was the "high tide" of the Union attack on this day.

15. Confederate Right Flank—This path follows the position of the extended Confederate line. The reinforcement of this line forced Hazen's men—and most of the Union troops that followed—into the narrow ravine.

16. Confederate Rifle Pits—The shallow trenches here were dug by Kelly's dismounted cavalry. It was from this area that they attacked Scribner's troops on Hazen's left flank.

17. Hazen's Troops Split—Near this site, elements of Hazen's attacking force got lost in the thick woods and did not follow the troops in front of them toward the ravine. Instead, they moved left and crossed the cornfield. By sheer accident, they nearly achieved the objective of flanking the Rebel line before Confederate troops were hastily marched to the area and drove them back.

18. The Ravine—From this vantage point you can clearly see the impossible terrain that the Federal troops faced. Thousands of men were trapped at the base of the ravine and faced murderous rifle and artillery fire from above. The Rebel night attack came from the hills directly ahead of you.

NOTES

113

CHAPTER 20

The Civil War Battlefields of Atlanta

LOCATION

✛ Routes through three battlefields are profiled in this chapter. Each comprises a half to a full day to explore. They are listed in chronological sequence as the campaign for Atlanta unfolded. The first is Kennesaw Mountain National Battlefield Park located on Old U.S. 41 south of Barrett Parkway and I-75 (exit 269). The second is the battlefield at Peachtree Creek, now part of an Atlanta residential area located north of I-75 at Northside Dr. (exit 252A) The third site is the ground on which the Battle of Atlanta was fought on July 22, 1864. The focal point of the battlefield is in the heart of the Victorian neighborhood of Inman Park, about 2 miles east of downtown Atlanta via Edgewood and Euclid Aves. The area may also be reached from I-20 by traveling east to Moreland Ave. (exit 60), then turning left and going about 2 miles north on Moreland to Euclid Ave.

PARKING

🚗 At Kennesaw Mountain National Battlefield Park there is ample parking at the visitor center, at the summit, at Cheatham Hill, and adjacent to the Kolb Farm. Parking for the battlefield at Peachtree Creek is at Tanyard Creek Park on Collier Rd. or along adjacent side streets. Street parking is also available in Inman Park for touring the Battle of Atlanta Trail.

BACKGROUND

📖 During the Civil War, Atlanta played unwilling host to an army of visitors from up North. Unlike today's tourists, these guests came bearing arms, not cameras, and under the watchful eye of Maj. Gen. William T. Sherman, they spent their time not just seeing the sights, but destroying them.

Today, most of the battle sites, with the notable exception of Kennesaw Mountain, have given way to a century of commercial and residential

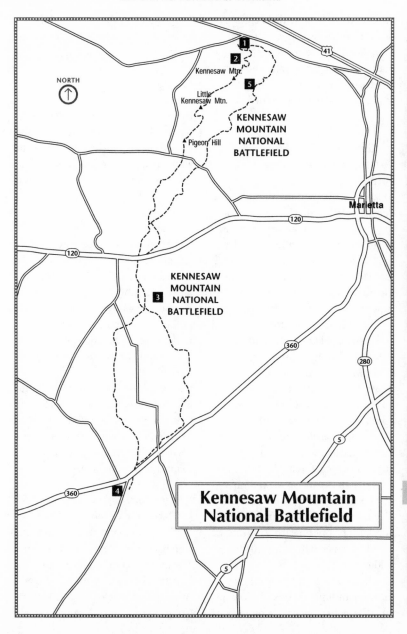

Kennesaw Mtn.

Little
Kennesaw Mtn.

Pigeon Hill

KENNESAW
MOUNTAIN
NATIONAL
BATTLEFIELD

NORTH

Marietta

KENNESAW
MOUNTAIN
NATIONAL
BATTLEFIELD

Kennesaw Mountain
National Battlefield

development. Despite these changes, one can still explore these areas on foot, taking time to read the historical markers, study the terrain, and gain a greater understanding of this dramatic campaign as it unfolded.

The Battle of Kennesaw Mountain

Like a sentinel guarding the northern approach to Atlanta, Kennesaw Mountain offered a formidable defensive position, while presenting the attacking Sherman with a serious dilemma. Should he attempt to flank the Confederates or unleash a frontal assault on the mountain fortress that threatened his army and its fragile supply lines?

Sherman chose the former strategy and dispatched troops around the Rebel's left flank toward the rail line below Marietta. Anticipating this move, 11,000 Confederate troops quick-marched to bolster their southern flank. In the fierce fighting that ensued, the Rebels were badly mauled, but they succeeded in thwarting Sherman's plan, forcing him now to consider an assault on the mountain.

Sherman's new plan called for two diversionary attacks to pin down the Southern troops on each flank and a central strike with nearly 60,000 soldiers.

The attacks began early on the morning of June 27, 1864. Following an artillery barrage on the mountain,

Union soldiers emerged from the woods and literally ran up the steep, rocky slopes toward strong Rebel fortifications held by veteran troops. The Confederate guns remained eerily silent as wave upon wave of bluecoats dashed from their cover. Then, with the first Federals only yards from their objective, the Rebels opened up with all the rifles and artillery they had. Like freshly hewn wheat, hundreds of Yanks fell, killed outright or grievously wounded.

Within moments, the attack turned into a massacre. After only a few hours filled with terrible carnage, it was clear that Sherman's plan had failed miserably.

Following three days of regrouping, Federal troops pulled out under cover of darkness. With blankets wrapped around wagon wheels to muffle the sound, Union forces moved southward toward the Chattahoochee River near Smyrna. His rear now threatened, Johnston was forced to abandon his position and retreat to his defensive river line. The fighting at Kennesaw Mountain was over.

The Battle of Peachtree Creek

Only two weeks after forcing Johnston back from Kennesaw Mountain, Sherman had crossed the Chattahoochee River and was threatening Atlanta's inner defenses. McPherson's troops were sent to Decatur to capture

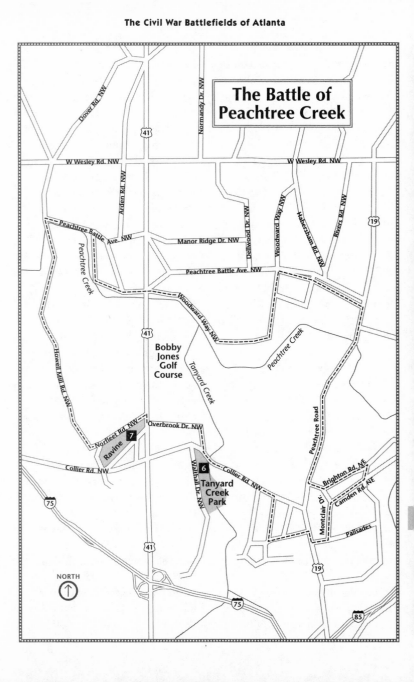

The Battle of Peachtree Creek

the eastbound railway, while the remainder of the army stretched on an almost unbroken line from Bolton to what is now the residential neighborhood of Virginia-Highland.

On July 17, 1864, Gen. Johnston had his Rebel troops dig in along a line just south of Peachtree Creek and await a move by his opponent. That evening, Johnston received a telegram from Confederate Pres. Jefferson Davis. Davis, frustrated by Johnston's failure to stop Sherman's advance, relieved him of command and replaced him with the more aggressive Gen. John B. Hood. Union Gens. McPherson and Schofield, classmates of Hood's at West Point, called him a fighter and quickly warned Sherman to expect a drastic change in Rebel strategy.

Early on July 20, Union Maj. Gen. George Thomas dispatched troops of the Army of the Cumberland's 4th Corps down the Peachtree Rd., across Peachtree Creek, and upwards toward the wooded summit on the far side (the present site of Piedmont Hospital). Throughout the morning, he solidified this position—apparently unaware of a 3-mile-wide gap between his left flank and a portion of the 4th Corps that had been dispatched to Gen. Schofield.

Hood had detected the gap and planned to boldly attack there—and, in a westward movement, roll down

the Union line and drive it back to the banks of the Chattahoochee River. This plan had merit but Hood encountered numerous delays in getting orders to his commanders and troops in position. The attack was set for noon but did not begin until 4 P.M., a delay that would cost the Confederates dearly.

When finally ready, the Rebels advanced through dense woods and struck the Union left flank at Clear Creek. Here, near what is now Brighton Rd. in the neighborhood of Brookwood Hills, troops of Confederate Gen. William Bate attacked the position held by Union Gen. John M. Newton's division. Just to the west, Gen. W. H. T. Walker's troops struck Newton's right flank astride the Peachtree Rd.

Newton's line briefly faltered, and Rebels commanded by Gen. George Maney attempted to breach the line between Newton and Gen. John Geary, whose men held positions to the west along the Collier Rd. Seeing this weakness, Gen. William T. Ward's Federals rushed up from their positions on the north side of Peachtree Creek to reinforce the line and halt the enemy advance.To the west, Southerners under command of Gens. W. W. Loring and Ed C. Walthall pressed the attack against Geary and Ward. A massed assault north from the Mt. Zion Church (site of present-day Northside Park Baptist Church on Howell Mill Rd. at

Cannon atop Little Kennesaw Mountain

I-75) drove Geary's men from the high ground near Northside Dr. and Collier Rd. and pushed them back to the present site of the Bitsy Grant Tennis Center and Bobby Jones Golf Course. This success was short-lived. Union reinforcements forced the Rebels back on a murderous retreat through a deep ravine.

For more than two hours, the fighting raged around Andrew Jackson Collier's mill on the Tanyard Branch of Peachtree Creek. By nightfall, Hood, badly beaten in his first engagement, withdrew his troops from the field. As a footnote to history, one of the Union officers engaged in the fighting that day was Col. Benjamin Harrison. In 1889, Harrison would be elected as the 23rd President of the United States.

The Battle of Atlanta

Within hours after his troops withdrew from the battlefield at Peachtree Creek, Hood was hard at work developing a bold plan to strike again. On July 21, he ordered Lt. Gen. William J. Hardee's Corps to march southward under cover of darkness, through Atlanta and then northeast toward Decatur. If all went according to design, Hardee would be in position to launch a surprise attack on the rear of Gen. McPherson's Army of the Tennessee at dawn on July 22. At the same time, Gen. Benjamin Cheatham's veteran troops would assault McPherson's front, squeezing the Federals in a pincer movement.

Unfortunately, Hood did not anticipate the time nor the difficulties

119

Hardee's already weary men would encounter, and they were not in position until nearly noon. As a result, the attack struck the Union flank at Legget's Hill (near the present intersection of I-20 and Moreland Ave.) instead of the rear. After some initial success, the Rebels were pushed back with heavy casualties.

When the attack began, McPherson was having lunch with his staff. On hearing the firing, he mounted his horse and rode through the woods to the sound of the guns. Moments later, he was killed by Confederate skirmishers. Today, a granite memorial marks this spot at the intersection of McPherson and Monument Avenues. Another key officer killed early in the battle was Confederate Gen. W. H. T. Walker. Ft. Walker in Grant Park is named in his memory.

Delays continued to plague Hood as Cheatham's assault on the Federal front did not commence until after 3 P.M. Once under way though, his troops attacked along an almost unbroken line stretching from Legget's Hill to the Georgia Railroad line. Spearheading the advance was Brig. Gen. Arthur Manigault's Brigade, which overran Capt. Francis DeGress's Union artillery posted near the unfinished Troup-Hurt house. Masses of Rebels poured through a widening breach in the Federal line and, despite its problems, Hood's plan appeared on the threshold of success.

Sherman saw the Confederate breakthrough from his vantage point at the Augustus Hurt house on Copenhill (now the site of the Carter Presidential Center). He immediately ordered Schofield's artillery to direct their guns at the oncoming enemy. At the same time, Maj. Gen. "Black Jack" Logan, in temporary command of the Army of the Tennessee following McPherson's death, brought up reinforcements and re-formed his lines. It is this precise moment in the battle that is vividly captured in the famous painting at the Cyclorama in Grant Park.

Whether Hood anticipated the counterattack or not, he issued the order for his men to withdraw to their lines and, by nightfall, both armies were in the positions they had occupied when the battle began. Once again, Hood had gambled and failed to loosen Sherman's tightening grip on Atlanta. Within days, the Federal artillery bombardment of Atlanta began and the city's fate was virtually sealed.

WALK DISTANCE AND TERRAIN

🚶🚶 Kennesaw Mountain

The National Park Service maintains a network of foot trails throughout the Kennesaw Mountain National Battlefield Park. The trails trace a 16-mile loop from the visitor center to the Kolb Farm and back, winding over the summits of Kennesaw Mountain, Little Kennesaw

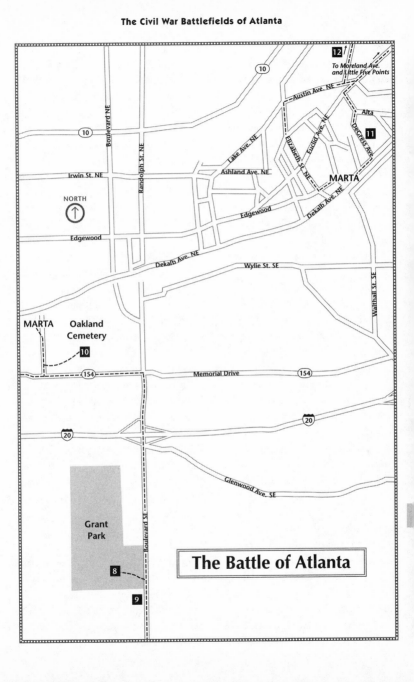

The Battle of Atlanta

Mountain, and Pigeon Hill. The path meanders through open meadows, marshy creek bottoms, and thick stands of woods that look much the same as they did in June 1864.

A day hike of the entire loop is a strenuous trip and advance planning is advised. Trail maps are available and the staff at the visitor center offer guidance on planning long or short walks in the park. *Hours:* The park is open dawn to dusk, daily. The visitor center is open 8:30 A.M.–5 P.M., daily. (770) 427-4686; www.nps.gov/kemo.

The Battle of Peachtree Creek

This 5-mile walk begins at Peachtree Rd. and Peachtree Battle Ave. and proceeds southward, retracing the steps taken by Newton's Federals as they moved into position early on July 20. The path follows Brighton Rd. through Brookwood Hills, where the men of Bate's Rebel division waited in the woods to strike. From Peachtree, the path descends along Collier Rd. to Tanyard Creek Park. This green space marks the point of some of the fiercest fighting in the battle. Following Overbrook Dr., the path crosses Northside Dr. at the ravine through which Geary's men retreated and where many Rebels died in the Union counterattack. Climb to the crest of the ridge and continue north on Howell Mill Rd. Turn right on Peachtree Battle and meander along the banks of the creek that the Federals crossed on July 19 and 20.

Imagine the masses of soldiers gathered on the banks awaiting their turn to cross. Return along Woodward Way to the starting point on Peachtree Battle Ave.

The Battle of Atlanta

This 4-mile trail combines a walk in Grant Park with a short drive (or ride on MARTA) to the residential neighborhood of Inman Park. Begin on the hill behind the Cyclorama, glancing southward to the crest of the hill. This is Ft. Walker, and the remains of an earthen fortification mark the site of a Rebel artillery battery during the battle. Walk north on Boulevard through the restored Victorian neighborhood surrounding the park and cross the bridge over I-20. Turn left and walk four blocks to Oakland Ave. Turn north and enter the grounds of Oakland Cemetery. Within the cemetery are the graves of several thousand Confederate (and a few Union) soldiers who died in Atlanta's Civil War hospitals. Near the northern boundary of the cemetery, a historical marker notes the spot where Gen. Hood watched the battle of Atlanta unfold. Return to Oakland Ave., turn right and go the King Center MARTA station. Board the eastbound train and get off at the Inman Park–Reynoldstown station. Follow DeKalb Ave. east to DeGress Ave. and turn left. A short distance ahead on the right a historical marker identifies the location of the

Troup-Hurt house. A little further, another marker rests on the spot of the DeGress artillery battery. Continue down DeGress and left on Alta to Euclid Ave. Follow Euclid toward the Little Five Points commercial district and turn left on Colquitt Ave. Cross Highland Ave. and enter the grounds of the Carter Center, where Sherman had his headquarters. Return south on Highland to Washita Ave. and then west on Austin Ave. to Elizabeth St. Travel south on Elizabeth, past several superbly restored 19th-century houses, to Edgewood Ave. A short distance to the left is the MARTA station.

SIGHTS ALONG THE WAY
Kennesaw Mountain

 1. Visitor Center (1999)— Stilesboro Rd. at Old U.S. 41. The newly expanded visitor center offers audiovisual programs about the battle, a museum, and a well-stocked bookstore. Staff are available to offer assistance. On weekends, a free shuttle bus to the summit of Kennesaw Mountain departs from the parking area behind the center. *Hours:* 8:30 A.M.–5 P.M., daily. (770) 427-4686.

2. Kennesaw Mountain Summit— A line of restored cannons marks the site of the Rebel batteries that once menaced the Union army located in the open ground to the north.

3. Cheatham Hill—Cheatham Hill Dr. off Dallas Hwy. The large monument erected by Illinois veterans

stands in front of the preserved Confederate breastworks manned by Cheatham's Confederates. It was here that some of the fiercest fighting of the entire battle took place.

4. Kolb Farm (1836)—Cheatham Hill Rd. at Powder Springs Rd. Built by pioneer settler Peter Kolb, the house was occupied by his son's widow at the time of the battle. Federal sharpshooters were located in the house during the fighting. Today, the restored cabin is used as staff housing and is not open to the public.

5. Site of Civilian Conservation Corps (CCC) Camp (1939)—East of Kennesaw Mountain summit. The CCC was a New Deal program initiated by Pres. Franklin D. Roosevelt to provide work to many unemployed young men. Much of the early work in the park was carried out by men from this camp, only faint traces of which remain.

The Battle of Peachtree Creek

6. Tanyard Creek Park—Collier Rd. at Overbrook Dr. Historical markers describe the furious fighting that encircled Andrew Jackson Collier's mill on the banks of Tanyard Branch, just north of Collier Rd.

7. The Ravine—Northside Dr. between Springlake and Norfleet Drs. This deep, narrow ravine was the site of heavy fighting as troops from both sides battled for the high ground along the Collier Rd.

123

The Battle of Atlanta

8. Cyclorama (1921)—Next to Zoo Atlanta on Cherokee Ave. in Grant Park. This building houses the massive circular painting (400 ft. in circumference) of the Battle of Atlanta completed in 1888. In the 1930s, foreground figures were added to provide a three-dimensional depiction of the fighting. The building also houses a museum of Civil War artifacts including the locomotive *Texas*, famous for its role in the 1862 "Great Locomotive Chase." *Hours:* 9:30 A.M.–4:30 P.M., daily (open until 5:30 in summer). (404) 624-1071.

9. Fort Walker (1864)—Grant Park west of Boulevard. An eroded earthen fortification marks the site of a Rebel artillery battery that fired shells on Union troops engaged in the battle to the northeast.

10. Oakland Cemetery (c. 1850)—Memorial Dr. at Oakland Ave. Atlanta's oldest burial ground is a treasure of Victorian funerary art. In addition to the graves of thousands of Civil War soldiers surrounding a tall granite monument, the cemetery is the final resting place for many notable Atlantans including legendary golfer Bobby Jones and *Gone with the Wind* author Margaret Mitchell. Cemetery maps are available from the sexton's office. *Information:* (404) 658-6019.

11. Site of Troup-Hurt House (c. 1864)—DeGress Ave. A historical marker notes the site of the unfinished house that became the focal point of the Confederate breakthrough during the battle.

12. Carter Presidential Center (1985)—One Copenhill. The center, which includes the Carter Presidential Library, a museum, and offices of the Carter Center, occupies the site of the Augustus Hurt house, where Sherman had his headquarters during the battle. *Hours:* 9 A.M.–4:45 P.M., Mon.–Sat.; 12–4:45 P.M., Sun. (404) 331-0296; www.emory.edu/CARTER_CENTER.

NOTES

McIntosh Reserve

LOCATION

McIntosh Reserve is located about 40 miles west of Atlanta off I-20 at GA 5 (exit 34). Travel south on GA 5 about 20 miles to U.S. 27 and the community of Whitesburg. Cross the highway and continue south about 2 miles. The reserve will be on the left. *Information:* (770) 830-5879.

PARKING

There is ample parking at the visitor center, by the ponds, and at numerous other locations along park roads.

BACKGROUND

The McIntosh Reserve, with its rolling woodlands, rock-strewn hillsides, and wide bottomlands along the banks of the Chattahoochee River, is a site rich in both scenic beauty and human history.

In the earliest days of the Paleo-Indians in Georgia (10,000–1,000 B.C.E.), hunter-gatherers traveled through this bountiful area and paused here near the river. During the Woodland period (1,000 B.C.E.–800 C.E.), a permanent village stood on the site. By the peak of the Mississippian Culture (900–1,500 C.E.), the era of the "mound-builders" who erected the great pyramid-like structures at Etowah, Kolomoki, and Ocmulgee, the reserve was part of a network of trading paths that crisscrossed the region from the Mississippi River to the Atlantic coast.

When the first Europeans arrived in the new English colony of Georgia in 1733, this was the site of Chattahoochee Old Town, a principal village in the Lower Creek Nation. By the time of the American Revolution, many of the Lower Creeks, concerned about westward expansion of white settlements, sided with the English, who had promised the Indians sovereignty over their lands under British rule. Not surprisingly, within a few years after winning independence from England, the U.S. government began demanding Creek lands for settlement. A number of treaties ceding land followed, nearly all with the promise that it would be the last.

In an effort to survive on their ancestral lands, many of the Lower Creeks adopted the ways of the white settlers. They built log homes, farmed, raised cattle, wore American-style clothing, and even owned slaves. There were a number of mixed marriages between white men and Creek women. Probably the most notable was the union between William McIntosh and Sejoyah, the daughter of a prominent Creek family of the Wind Clan. McIntosh was the son of a Scots Highlander, John McIntosh, who had arrived in Georgia with Gen. Oglethorpe and received a grant for a large tract of land in what would later be Alabama.

One of William and Sejoyah's six children was a boy they named William, who grew to become a courageous soldier and a chief of the Lower Creeks. During his life he dined with presidents, fought alongside Andrew Jackson in a war against the Upper Creeks, and sought continually to bridge the two cultures. These efforts eventually cost him his life.

In 1800, William McIntosh was chosen as chief of Coweta Town (near present-day Columbus), a principal town of the Lower Creek Federation. With his background, McIntosh was the ideal person to lead the Lower Creeks, a people determined to adopt the ways of the white settlers and assimilate as much as possible into their culture—while still retaining their sovereignty.

Their neighbors, the Upper Creeks, were nearly polar opposites. They resisted every advance from white settlers and refused to adopt new customs or assimilate, preferring to cling to old ways despite mounting pressures. Brutal fighting took place between the Indian nations, often involving American soldiers and settlers on the side of the Lower Creeks and, during the War of 1812, the British, who allied with the Upper Creeks. Following the massacre in 1813 of more than 500 white settlers, soldiers, and friendly Creeks at Ft. Mims (near present-day Mobile, Ala.), the U.S. government deployed 3,000 troops under the command of Maj. Gen. Andrew Jackson to subdue the hostile Indians. Joined by warriors led by McIntosh, this force attacked and crushed the Upper Creeks at the Battle of Horseshoe Bend near Alexander City, Ala. For his heroism in the Creek and Seminole Indian Wars, McIntosh was made a brigadier general in the army, and his influence grew. In 1821, McIntosh convened a meeting of Creek and Cherokee chiefs at his home to establish a clear boundary between the lands of the two nations. The Treaty of Council

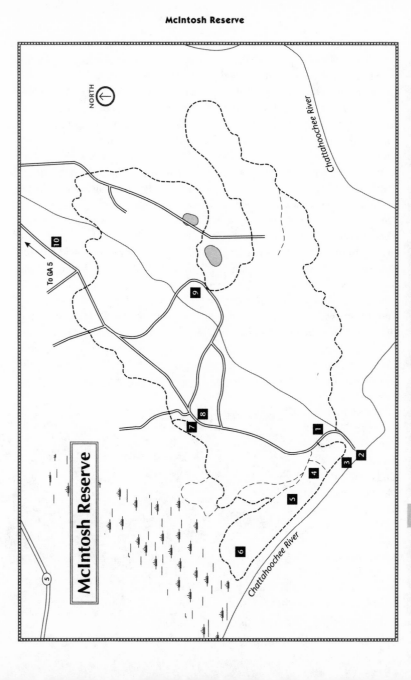

Bluffs set the Chattahoochee as the boundary, with the Cherokees occupying the lands to the north, while the Creeks retained their ancestral lands to the south of the river. Even as the tribal leaders departed from the council, they knew that pressures from whites for continued expansion would place their lands in continuing jeopardy.

Four years later, Governor George Troup was running for reelection on a platform calling for the removal of all Indians from Georgia, by purchasing their lands if possible, or by force if necessary. McIntosh, who was Troup's cousin, knew that armed resistance to this pressure was futile, and, as a principal Creek chief, he signed additional treaties ceding more land, always with a promise from the state that no more treaties would be necessary. Finally, on February 12, 1825, he signed the Treaty of Indian Springs ceding the final parcels of Creek lands in Georgia. McIntosh expressed the futility of Indian resistance when he said, "The White Man ... wants our lands. He will buy them now, but by and by he will take them and the little band of our people will be left to wander without homes, poor, despised, and beaten like dogs...." For his service in negotiating the treaty, McIntosh retained ownership of three large parcels of land in Georgia: one at Indian Springs, one near Macon, and an upper reserve that included the plantation on the bluffs above the Chattahoochee River. At this last property, he operated a ferry, two taverns, a trading post, and a stagecoach inn. It was here that a large group of Upper Creeks got their final revenge on Chief McIntosh, by dragging him from his home and murdering him on the night of May 1, 1825. A short time later, these Creek militants were finally forced from the last of their lands east of the Mississippi, just as McIntosh had prophesied.

After the assassination, much of the land along the river became part

Council Bluffs at McIntosh Reserve

of newly formed Carroll County. A small settlement grew around the ferry, but the discovery of gold in the northern part of the county in 1830 and the coming of the railroads a few years later shifted the county's population growth away from the river. The old McIntosh Reserve remained a rugged, sparsely settled land.

Early in the 20th century, the Georgia Power and Railway Company purchased lands including the McIntosh Reserve with plans to dam the river to produce electricity. The reservoir was never built, but Georgia Power retained ownership of the land for more than 70 years. Finally, in 1978, the company donated the historic McIntosh Reserve lands to Carroll County for use as a park for community recreation and education. The park opened in 1984.

WALK DISTANCE AND TERRAIN

There are approximately 12 miles of foot and horse trails crisscrossing the 527-acre park. Most of the land is a mixture of rolling, wooded ridges, valleys, meadows, and open fields for recreational activities. The highlighted unblazed trail is a 7-mile loop from the park's ranger station. It traces an especially scenic route along the Chattahoochee past the old river ferry site and Council Bluffs, before turning inland and crossing the edge of a large open field

and ascending into the low hills. It then follows heavily forested slopes, passing close to a re-creation of Chief McIntosh's house, before continuing northward. After crossing the park's main road, the trail descends past an old, primitive camping area to an open meadow and two small ponds. Just south of a restroom building and parking area, the trail bends northward again, climbing for about a half-mile before turning southward on a steady, slow descent back to its starting point.

SIGHTS ALONG THE WAY

 1. Park Ranger Station (1984)—This wood-frame building houses offices of the park staff. An exhibit area traces the life of Chief McIntosh and a history of the reserve. *Hours:* 9 A.M.–6 P.M. (later in summer). (770) 830-5879.

2. Old Ferry Site (c. 1820s)—The old dirt road just east of the ranger station leads to the likely site of McIntosh's ferry, which was once one of the few crossing points of the Chattahoochee River for miles in either direction.

3. Outdoor Amphitheater and River Overlook—A hillside amphitheater hosts a variety of educational programs. On the crest of the hill, the overlook platform offers a panoramic view of a bend in the river, where the ferry crossed.

129

4. Council Bluffs—These ancient rock outcrops on a hillside above the river were a gathering place for Native Americans from prehistoric times until the leaders of the Creek and Cherokee Nations met in 1821 to reach agreement on the boundaries between the two tribes.

5. Recreation Fields and Picnic Area—Picnic tables offer a view of both the river and fields for soccer, softball, and other outdoor sports.

6. Meadows—During the years that McIntosh operated a plantation here, his slaves cultivated crops here along the river floodplain.

7. Old Log House (c. 1839)—This typical dog-trot house resembles the home of William McIntosh that sat on this site until it was burned in 1825. This building, constructed as the Acorn Bluff Inn and Tavern in Centre, Ala., was relocated to the reserve in 1987.

8. Grave of William Mcintosh (c. 1825)—Large boulders beneath the shade of an ancient oak tree reputedly mark the final resting place of McIntosh, though some versions of the story of his assassination indicate that his body may have been thrown in the river.

9. Ponds and Recreation Area (c. 1984)—This area features two small ponds, a playground, restroom building, parking spaces, and picnic areas.

10. Pioneer Cemetery (c. 1840s)—On a small rise just east of the park road, weatherworn markers note the locations of the graves of several of Carroll County's pioneer settlers.

NOTES

130

Newnan

LOCATION

✦ Newnan is located about 35 miles southwest of Atlanta via I-85. Exit on Bullsboro Rd. (exit 47) and travel west about 2 miles and turn onto Jackson St., which is one-way, south-bound. Go four blocks to the courthouse square. *Information:* Coweta County Convention and Visitors Bureau, (800) 826-9382; www.coweta.ga. us/Resources/welcomecenter.

PARKING

🚗 There is curbside parking around the square. Parking is also permitted on side streets unless otherwise posted.

BACKGROUND

📖 When Chief William McIntosh (see previous walk) signed the Treaty of Indian Springs, ceding Lower Creek lands, one of the original counties created by Georgia was Coweta. Named for Coweta Town, the last capital of the Lower Creek Nation, the county was chartered by the legislature on June 9, 1825. The first county seat was the small village of Bullsboro, established in 1827. As the village grew, citizens chose to rename their town for Gen. Daniel Newnan, a Georgia congressman and military hero of the War of 1812.

Many early settlers acquired large tracts of land for growing cotton and became wealthy planters. Newnan prospered as a commercial center providing goods and supplies for these surrounding farms and plantations. Planters and local business owners constructed large town-homes around the bustling square to enjoy the educational and social life of the community. By the 1850s, wagon roads and railway lines had replaced Indian trails, and Newnan was developing strong bonds with the rapidly growing business and transportation center of

131

Atlanta, 35 miles to the north. These links would soon define Newnan's role in the impending Civil War.

Early in the war, Georgia was far removed from the battle. Atlanta's network of rail lines carried supplies out to armies at the front and brought back thousands of casualties. In the spring of 1864, war finally came to Georgia in earnest. In preparation for Atlanta's defense, Dr. Samuel Stout, medical director for the Army of Tennessee, began relocating the wounded from the city to outlying areas. Many were transferred to large hospitals established in Newnan. These hospitals, Bragg, Buckner, College Temple, Coweta House, Foard, Gamble, and Pinson's Springs, would eventually provide care to more than 10,000 patients. Following Atlanta's surrender, the hospitals continued to operate under Union supervision, treating wounded from both armies. The failure of one Union foray into the area, combined with the presence of the hospitals, may have saved Newnan from eventual devastation at the hands of Maj. Gen. William T. Sherman's invading army. As a result, many of Newnan's most notable antebellum houses survived.

By the turn of the 20th century, Newnan was once again a thriving agricultural and commercial center of western Georgia. Prosperous merchants and business executives remodeled the older houses or constructed large Victorian homes along the shaded streets surrounding the busy commercial district. The centerpiece of this architectural boom was the grand, neo–Greek Revival Coweta County Courthouse completed in 1904. This courthouse was the scene of one of Georgia's most sensational murder trials, the case of John Wallace. Wallace was the richest and most powerful landowner in nearby Meriwether County (his plantation was called "the Kingdom"). After a car chase, he murdered one of his tenant farmers at a gas station just inside Coweta County. Despite intense political pressure, Lamar Potts, Coweta County's longtime sheriff, arrested Wallace. In 1948 he was tried and convicted in the ornate second-floor courtroom. The case was profiled in Margaret Anne Barnes's bestselling book, *Murder in Coweta County*, which was made into a 1982 movie starring Andy Griffith and Johnny Cash.

Today, Newnan prospers as the "City of Homes," a community offering both history and hospitality just a short distance from Atlanta.

WALK DISTANCE AND TERRAIN

The 3.5-mile route loops through the heart of the historic commercial district and along nearby residential streets. The terrain is shaded and gently rolling with sidewalks along most of the route.

132

Newnan

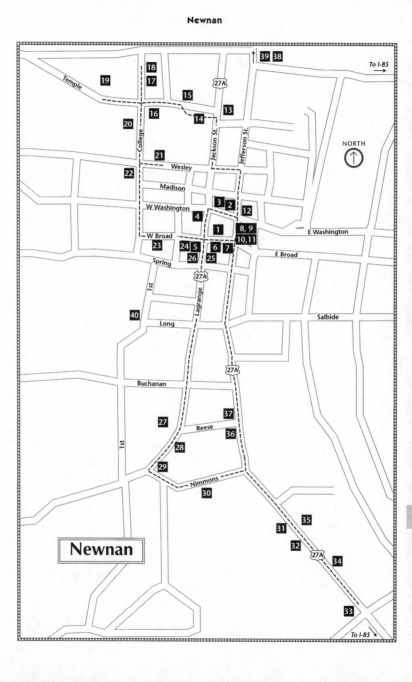

SIGHTS ALONG THE WAY

1. Coweta County Courthouse (1904)—E. Washington and Jackson Sts. One of the most photographed courthouses in Georgia, this elegant neo–Greek Revival structure was designed by James W. Golucke and constructed for $58,000. Notable architectural features include the large copper dome and expansive columned porticos on both the east and west sides of the building. This building replaced the original 1829 courthouse that had served as one of Newnan's many hospitals during the Civil War. *NR*

2. Newnan Bank and Trust Building (1894)—N. Court Square at Jefferson St. Constructed as a bank and drugstore, the building has also housed a clothing store and a radio station. Today it is used as a restaurant. Note the date "1894" above the second-story windows.

3. Meyer Building (1894)—N. Court Square. This building has had many retail functions. In 1997, it was completely renovated and is now a restaurant.

4. Alamo Theater (1890)—W. Court Square at Washington St. Originally constructed as a general store, the building was converted for use as a movie theater in 1925. It continued to be an entertainment mecca for locals until it closed in 1986. Today the building houses a home and garden shop.

5. Carnegie Library (1903)—Jackson and Court Sts. This large sandstone-brick building was constructed with funds donated by philanthropist Andrew Carnegie. It served as the main library until a modern facility was built in 1988. Today the building houses government offices.

6. Reynolds Building (1914)—S. Court Square. Operated as a furniture store for more than 80 years, the building now houses law offices. During Prohibition, a speakeasy was located behind a secret door on the building's second floor.

7. Old Opera House (1883)—S. Court Square at Jefferson St. This Romanesque-style 3-story building was constructed by Dr. J. T. Reese, a local druggist, as an opera house. Through the years it has served a variety of uses and is now a bank.

8. Cole Building (1889)—E. Court Square at E. Broad St. Madison Cole had this building constructed as an investment property, and it remained in his family until 1990. For many years it was the local Woolworth's department store. Note the inscription, "18 Cole 89," above the second story.

9. Cuttino Building (1866)—E. Court Square. Hidden behind a modern facade, this is one of the oldest buildings on the square. For many years it served as a department store. Today, it houses an office supply company.

Culpepper-Barge-McKoon house, Newnan

10. First National Bank Building (1871)—E. Court Square. This building served as a bank from 1871 until 1955. Today, it is part of a retail shop.

11. Arnall Building (1900)— E. Court Square at Washington St. Arnall Merchandise, a farm supply store, operated here from 1900 until 1922. It housed Kessler's Department Store from 1927 to 1993. Today, the renovated building serves as a popular local restaurant.

12. Virginia House (1868)— E. Washington and Jefferson Sts. Built to replace the original hotel that burned in 1866, this painted brick building was known for many years for the fine food in its dining room. Former Confederate Pres. Jefferson Davis gave a speech from the balcony of the building during a postwar visit

to Newnan. The building now houses law offices.

13. Sargent-Estanich House (c. 1840)—47 Jackson St. This house, built for factory owner Harrison Sargent, is an excellent example of the Greek Revival style.

14. Veterans Memorial Park— Jackson St. and Temple Ave. This pleasant green space with its fountain is a memorial to all Coweta County military veterans.

15. Welch-Parrott House (1843)— 9 Temple Ave. Built by James Welch, a founder of the *Newnan Herald*, this cottage originally faced Jackson St.

16. Male Academy Museum (1829, 1883)—30 Temple Ave. Founded in 1829 as a private boys' school, the academy served the wealthy families of Newnan for nearly 60 years. This building was originally constructed as a church. In 1883, it was adapted for use as the Newnan Male Academy. The academy closed in 1888, and the building was moved and converted to a private residence. In 1976, the structure was returned to its original site and restored as headquarters for the Newnan-Coweta Historical Society, including a museum with exhibits on local history. *Hours:* 10 A.M.–12 P.M. and 1–3 P.M., Tues.–Thurs.; 2–5 P.M., Sat. and Sun. (770) 251-0207.

17. College Temple—Smith House (c. 1853)—73 College St. Once part of College Temple, a private academy for girls that operated from 1853 to 1888 (except when the buildings were used as a hospital during the Civil War), this hexagonally shaped building was the college's science laboratory and reputedly housed the first printing press at a Southern school.

18. College Temple Building (1853)—75 College St. This structure housed the school library. All three of College Temple's buildings were designed by the school's founder, Prof. M. P. Kellogg. After the academy closed, the buildings were used as public schools. In 1904, Arcade Hall was demolished, and these two remaining structures were converted to private residences.

19. Dent-Scott House (1851)—43 Temple Ave. Situated on the crest of a tree-shaded hill, this house was built by U.S. Congressman William Barton Wade Dent and expanded by Dent's descendants in 1905.

20. Dent-Walls House (1854)—52 College St. This well-proportioned Greek Revival house was built by Ephraim Dent, brother of William Dent. The structure is notable for its four large Doric columns, second-floor balcony, and four exterior chimneys.

21. Culpepper-Barge-McKoon House (c. 1880s)—19 Wesley St. Designed for John Culpepper by a German architect, the house's style seems more European than American. Note the unusual central portico with a small second-story balcony.

22. Arnold-Arnall-Shapiro House (c. 1835)—34 College St. Built as a Plantation Plain–style farmhouse, the roof was raised and columns and balcony added in 1850. For more than 50 years, it was the home of Henry C. Arnall, president of the Wahoo Mfg. Co. and father of Ellis Arnall, Georgia's governor from 1943 to 1947.

23. Brewster-Barnett House (c. 1860s)—20 W. Broad St. This small, single-story house was constructed especially for Maj. Penn Brewster, a Confederate veteran who lost a leg in battle. Wide doorways and halls and large bedrooms accommodated his wheelchair.

24. Central Baptist Church (c. 1900s)—W. Broad and Brown Sts. Constructed of rough-hewn marble, this imposing sanctuary is Tudor-Gothic style.

25. Wall Mural of Coweta County History (1998)—Scott Furniture Bldg. at Court and LaGrange Sts. Artist Ans Steenmeijer created this large mural depicting significant places and people in Coweta County history. Included in the painting are the late humorist Lewis Grizzard and Governors Arnall and William Atkinson (1894–98).

26. Old Coca-Cola Sign (c. 1910s)—Coweta Co. Shopper Building at Lagrange and Spring Sts. A rare, early Coca-Cola sign fills the south-facing wall of this 1-story building.

27. Storey-Buchanan-Glover House (1830)—87 LaGrange St. Originally a small cottage constructed by Edward Storey, the house was purchased and expanded in 1850 by Storey's brother-in-law Hugh Buchanan, a prominent local judge and U.S. congressman. Buchanan called his home "Buena Vista" (Beautiful View), for its hilltop view of the surrounding countryside. During the Civil War Battle of Brown's Mill, the house served as headquarters for Confederate cavalry commander Gen. Joe Wheeler. The old log servants' quarters still stands behind the house.

28. I. N. Orr House (1905)—89 LaGrange St. Orr, a prominent business owner and Newnan mayor, built this large Neoclassical-style

house. It features a large central portico supported by two Ionic columns.

29. Orr-Thornton House (c. 1850s)—94 LaGrange St. Originally a country farmhouse, this structure was moved to the northern corner of this block in the late 1800s. It was moved a second time by I. N. Orr to make room for construction of his large house (see # 28).

30. Storey-Hollis House (c. 1850)—32 Nimmons St. Built as the main house of William Storey's plantation, the building was dismantled and moved to this location in 1866. According to local lore, the elderly Mrs. Mary Storey refused to leave her country home, so her family moved the house to town.

31. Lee-Hackney-Banks House (1850)—123 Greenville St. This 1-story house was built by Sanders Lee. It was remodeled in the Victorian style in the 1870s.

32. North-Young-Rosenzweig House (1852)—141 Greenville St. This large Greek Revival house is notable for its large Ionic-columned portico and nine-over-nine, first-floor windows. It was once the home of Dr. Abraham North, a surgeon in the Confederate Army.

33. Parrott-Camp-Soucy House (c. 1840s)—155 Greenville St. Once a simple frame house constructed by an early settler, this house was remodeled in 1885 by Charles Parrott, president of the Newnan National Bank, in a

137

remarkably eclectic blend of Eastern Stick, Eastlake, and Second Empire styles. This extraordinary structure received a Georgia Trust for Historic Preservation restoration award in 1987. In recent years, it served as a bed-and-breakfast inn.

34. Hackney-Passolt-Cox House (1860)—148 Greenville St. Originally built closer to the street, this house was moved deeper in the lot and enlarged around 1900.

35. Orr-Whatley-Bassett House (1850)—134 Greenville St. This symmetrical house features a twin-gabled portico supported by six small columns.

36. Reese-Umberger House (1856)—85 Greenville St. Originally a simple, 1-story house built by Dr. J. T. Reese, the second story and rooftop dormer were added in the 1880s. The columns were a 20th-century addition. The first telephone in Newnan connected Dr. Reese with his downtown drugstore.

37. Owens-Banks–St. John House (c. 1850s)—Built by Davis Owens, the house was acquired by Samuel Banks in 1905 and remained in his family for 75 years. It is now a special events facility. *Information:* (770) 251-1206.

38. Willcoxon-Arnold House (1852)—1 Bullsboro Dr. Constructed of handmade bricks, this large Greek Revival structure was once the main house of John Willcoxon's plantation,

"Shadowlawn." It is now Hillcrest Funeral Chapel.

39. Oak Hill Cemetery (c. 1840s)—Bullsboro Rd. at Jefferson St. Newnan's oldest public burial ground contains the graves of hundreds of Confederate soldiers who died in Newnan's hospitals. In 1997, the remains of Confederate hero William T. Overby, called the "Nathan Hale of the Confederacy" for his refusal to divulge secrets in exchange for his life, were reinterred here from a cemetery in Virginia.

40. Manget Brannon Center for the Arts (1909)—First Ave. at Long Pl. Housed in a 1909 warehouse, the center provides studio and gallery space for a variety of local arts organizations, including the Newnan Community Theatre Company. *Information:* (770) 251-4848.

NOTES

CHAPTER 23

Covington and Oxford College

LOCATION

Covington is about 30 miles east of Atlanta via I-20 and U.S. 278 (exit 90). From U.S. 278, travel south on Pace Street to the town square. To reach Oxford College, turn north from U.S. 278 onto Emory Street and travel about a mile. The campus will be on the left. *Information:* Coweta/Newton County Convention and Visitors Bureau, (800) 616-8626; Oxford College of Emory University, (770) 784-8888; www.emory.edu/OXFORD.

PARKING

In Covington, there is ample on-street parking around the town square and on adjacent side streets. Oxford College's visitor parking lot is located behind Humanities Hall at the corner of W. Hammil St. and Haygood Ave.

BACKGROUND

This area was opened to settlers in the early 1820s when Georgia forced the Creek Indians to give up their lands. The earliest settlers founded the primitive settlement of Winton at the crossroads of the Charleston–New Orleans and Milledgeville-Ruckersville wagon roads. However, inadequate water sources limited growth, and most settlers moved a few miles away and established a new community called Newtonboro. In late 1822, the town's name was changed to Covington to honor Revolutionary War hero Gen. Leonard Covington. Within a few years it became the Newton County seat and a regular stop on the new Milledgeville–Stone Mountain stage road. The town prospered with the construction of a railroad line connecting the Savannah River port of Augusta with the new, fast-growing city of Atlanta.

By the time of the Civil War, Covington was an agricultural and trade center with many fine homes constructed by the owners of the

139

surrounding plantations. The war brought great deprivation, and during the 1864 Union invasion, Federal cavalry burned bridges over the nearby Alcovy and Yellow Rivers, cut communication lines, and destroyed miles of railway. Fortunately, the town itself was spared, and the many antebellum structures in Covington provide a tangible link to the city's past. In recent years, Covington's small-town atmosphere and well-preserved downtown contributed to its selection as the site for the popular television series *In the Heat of the Night*, starring Carroll O'Connor.

Within a few years of Covington's founding, the Methodist Church established a manual labor school in the town for training young men in agriculture and the building trades. In 1836, the school's mission was broadened to encompass a more academic and pre-professional curriculum and, at the same time, it was renamed Emory College to honor Bishop John Emory, president of the North Georgia Conference of the Methodist Church.

In 1837, the Methodist Church purchased nearly 1,500 acres of land just north of Covington and, on 330 acres, Edward L. Thomas, a minister and surveyor from Columbus, Ga., laid out the plan for a new town and campus to be called "Oxford" after the English alma mater of Methodism's founders, John and Charles Wesley.

Emory College grew in size and prestige until the outbreak of the Civil War in 1861. The ranks of the faculty and student body were thinned by the call to Confederate military service, and classes were suspended in 1862. In 1863, several campus buildings were converted for use as hospitals to care for the wounded.

Oxford and the campus buildings, like those in nearby Covington, escaped destruction, and, in late 1865, Emory College resumed classes. During the postwar period, under the guidance of Pres. Atticus G. Haygood (1875–84), enrollment increased, a new administration building (Seney Hall) was completed, and the school's endowment topped $100,000. In 1881, from the pulpit of Oxford's Methodist Church, the Rev. Haygood preached an impassioned sermon on the importance of casting out the hatreds of the Civil War, seeking reconciliation, and building a vision for a "New South." Haygood's message was eloquently embraced and carried across the nation by journalist and *Atlanta Constitution* editor Henry Grady. A tangible result of this message was a $130,000 contribution to Emory by New York businessman George Seney, for whom the administration building was named.

The selection in 1888 of the Rev. Warren A. Candler as the college's third president ultimately propelled Emory into the status of an

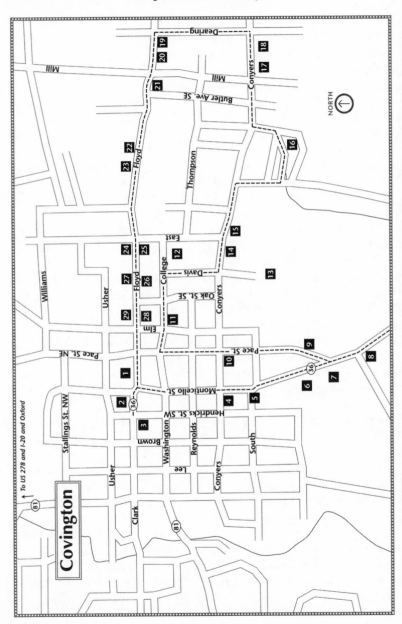

internationally renowned university. In 1898, he relinquished the presidency when he was appointed a bishop in the Methodist Church, and a few years later, he chaired a commission considering the establishment of a Methodist university east of the Mississippi River. Candler's brother, Asa G. Candler, founder and president of The Coca-Cola Company, offered the church $1 million and land in the newly developed Druid Hills area of Atlanta if the church would relocate Emory College there. The proposal was readily accepted.

With Bishop Candler as its chancellor, Emory University was chartered in 1915, and ground was broken for the first buildings on the Atlanta campus. World War I delayed completion, but the college relocated in 1919 to join the graduate schools of theology, law, and medicine that had opened a short time before.

With the move to Atlanta, the Oxford campus was not abandoned. Since 1929, "Emory at Oxford" has served as the university's junior college. Here, amidst a quiet, pastoral setting, a small group of students (enrollment is around 600) enjoy an academic atmosphere with great emphasis on teaching and faculty-student interaction.

Like the majestic, centuries-old "Yarbrough Oak" in the heart of town, Emory's limbs have stretched out to touch the world, but its historic

roots remain firmly rooted in Oxford's soil.

WALK DISTANCE AND TERRAIN

The 3-mile loop through Covington is gently rolling. It starts and ends in front of the Newton County Courthouse. There are many shade trees and good sidewalks along much of the route. Academy Springs Park—with benches, water fountain, picnic tables, and a playground—is at the midpoint of the walk.

The route through Oxford is also about 3 miles and includes a loop along the Lucy Candler Hearn Nature Trail on the Oxford College campus. The terrain, like Covington, is rolling with an abundance of shade trees.

SIGHTS ALONG THE WAY

Covington

1. Newton County Courthouse (1884)—North side of the square. This building, designed by the firm Bruce and Morgan, is an excellent example of the Asymmetrical Victorian style. The off-center clock tower is especially notable. *NR*

2. Bank of Covington (c. 1837)—West of the courthouse. Built originally as a hotel in Oxford, the structure was dismantled in 1855 and transported by ox team to this location to serve as a bank.

3. Presbyterian Church (1926)—1169 Clark St. Noted Scottish-born

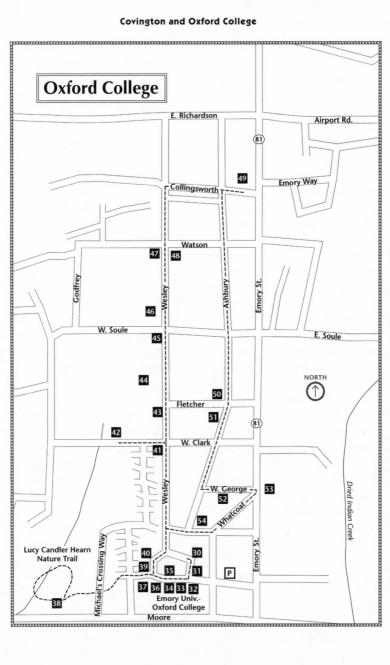

Oxford College

clergyman Peter Marshall once served as pastor here. He later went on to serve as chaplain of the U.S. Senate. Portions of his film biography, *A Man Called Peter*, were filmed in Covington in 1955.

4. Edwards House (c. 1830s)—1184 Monticello St. This somewhat plain clapboard house with small, square columns is one of the town's oldest structures.

5. Bates-Terrell House (1845)—2108 Monticello St. Built by Dr. Horace Bates, one of the first physicians to settle in Newtonboro, the house has been extensively remodeled through the years.

6. Whitehall (c. 1830s)—2176 Monticello St. The town house of John Harris, a prominent plantation owner and judge, is a classic example of Greek Revival architecture. Local legends describe the house as "haunted."

7. Regency Hall (1897)—2204 Monticello St. The home of E. D. Lee, who lived here with his wife and eight children. The home has features of the Roman Classical style.

8. Dixie Manor (c. 1830s)—3114 Pennington St. This is the only brick, 2-story antebellum house still standing in Covington. It was built by Judge Thomas Jones and contains elements of the English Regency and Italianate styles.

9. Dewald-Elliott-Pratt House (1850)—2171 Church St. This house is called the "Home of the Honest Man" for Solomon Dewald who, despite terrific hardships, paid off all his debts after the Civil War. The home was once owned by Robert Wood, a Confederate quartermaster who was involved in the mysterious disappearance of the Confederate gold after Pres. Jefferson Davis's capture outside Irwinville, Ga., in 1865.

10. First United Methodist Church (1854)—1113 Congress St. This imposing white brick church, in the Greek Revival style, was used as a hospital during the Civil War. The stained-glass windows were an 1897 addition.

11. Callaway House (c. 1900)—1144 College Ave. Built by Thomas Callaway, the home was occupied for many years by his son Thomas, Jr., a state senator, and his daughter-in-law Martha, granddaughter of Coca-Cola Company founder Asa Candler.

12. The President's Home (c. 1830)—1123 Davis St. With features from both the Georgian and Greek Revival styles, this house was constructed for the president of the Southern Masonic College. The now-defunct school once stood across the street on the site of the present city hall.

13. Confederate Cemetery (1864)—End of Davis St. in South View Cemetery. A historical marker notes the final resting place of several Confederate soldiers.

The President's Home, Covington

14. Greer Apartments (c. 1900)— 2126 Conyers St. The columns for this building came from a hotel that once stood on the town square.

15. Lee-Porter House (c. 1913)— 2146 Conyers St. This house is an excellent example of Greek Revival style.

16. Magnolia Terrace (c. 1846)— 3140 Academy Springs Cir. Designed in the Dutch Colonial style, this home was remodeled in the 1920s.

17. Ginn House (1941)— 3188 Conyers St. This house is built on the site of the antebellum William Anderson home, which locals called "Poverty Hill" for the financial devastation Anderson suffered as a result of the Civil War.

18. Camp-Pratt House (1859)— 4158 Conyers St. The house was built by Dr. Archibald Camp, an early settler in Covington. A local legend tells of Confederate soldiers hidden in a secret room to avoid capture.

19. Dearing House (1845)— 4182 Floyd St. Relocated to this site, the house was built by Dr. John Dearing as part of his large plantation.

20. Rheburgh-Sockwell-Hardman House (c. 1845)— 3190 Floyd St. This simple cottage was remodeled in the Williamsburg style by recent owners.

21. Henry-Mobley House (c. 1858)— 3166 Floyd St. This Victorian cottage was constructed by local dentist Dr. Henry T. Henry, reputed to be a descendant of the Colonial patriot Patrick Henry.

22. Cook-Adams-Williams House (1904)— 2173 Floyd St. Called "The Cedars," this house is believed to have been remodeled in the style of the home of Confederate general and Georgia governor John B. Gordon.

23. Neal-Patterson House (c. 1855)— 2149 Floyd St. Simply known as "The Cottage," this house was built by McCormick Neal. The house's appearance, with its large front porch and steps leading to the second-story entrance, has remained unaltered since its construction.

24. Usher House (c. 1845)— 1187 Floyd St. Built by Robert O. Usher, brother-in-law of Judge John Floyd, the house is a fine example of the Greek Revival style.

25. Floyd House (c. 1830)—1184 Floyd St. This was the home of pioneer Covington resident Judge John Floyd (for whom the street was named). His niece, Rebecca Latimer Felton, was the first woman to serve in the U.S. Senate. Note that the columns on the front of the house are not identical.

26. Swanscombe (1828)—1164 Floyd St. Believed to be the first clapboard house built in Covington, it was constructed by pioneer citizen Cary Wood. It was later owned by T. C. Swann, who named the house "Swanscombe" for his ancestral house in England. This is the oldest house still standing in Covington.

27. Graham-Simms House (1850)—1155 Floyd St. This was the boyhood home of Confederate general James P. Simms. The fanlight over the entrance is especially notable.

28. Porter-Rogers-Tuck House (1903)—1146 Floyd St. Built by James Porter, an owner of Porterdale Mills, the house is designed in the Neoclassical style.

29. First Baptist Church (1909)—1135 Floyd St. This impressive structure is in the Graeco-Roman style.

Oxford College

30. Few Hall (1852)—Northeast corner of Quadrangle. Named in honor of Emory's first president, Ignatius Few, this Greek Revival structure was built to house the Few Society, a literary and debating club.

31. Humanities Hall (1875)—East side of Quadrangle at W. Hammill St. Originally called Science Hall and later History Hall, this building continues to serve as classrooms and faculty offices.

32. Candler Hall (1897)— Southeast side of Quadrangle at W. Hammill St. Designed in the Neo-Roman style and named in honor of Bishop Warren Candler, the building originally served as the library. Today, it houses offices, bookstore, and student center.

33. Language Hall (1874)—South side of Quadrangle on W. Hammill St. This is one of the first classroom buildings built in the expansion years after the Civil War.

34. Seney Hall (1881)—South side of Quadrangle on W. Hammill St. This magnificent 3-story brick building designed in the Victorian Gothic style sits on the foundation of the original administration building constructed in 1852. The bell in the tower was an 1855 gift to Emory faculty member Dr. Alexander Means from England's Queen Victoria.

35. Few Memorial (1855)—On the Quadrangle north of Seney Hall. This marble monument was erected to honor the memory of Dr. Few.

36. Hopkins Hall (1885)— Southwest side of Quadrangle at W. Hammill St. Constructed to serve as the Technology Department during the tenure of Pres. Isaac Hopkins, it was converted to a gymnasium when Hopkins left Emory to assume the presidency of Georgia Tech. Today, the building serves as the Admissions Office and campus welcome center.

37. Williams Gymnasium (1907)— Southwest side of Quadrangle on W. Hammill St. Virtually unchanged since its construction, the building houses one of the oldest basketball courts in existence. The Woodruff addition came in 1975.

38. Soldiers' Cemetery (1863)—In the woods behind Williams Gymnasium. This small plot is the final resting place for 25 Confederate and 6 Union soldiers who died in the nearby hospital.

39. Prayer Chapel (1875)—West side of Quadrangle. A simple, 1-story brick structure built for campus worship services. It was renovated in 1988.

40. Phi Gamma Hall (1851)—North side of Quadrangle. An outstanding example of the Greek Revival literary society "temple" style of academic building typical of the period. The hall was used as a hospital building during the Civil War and is the oldest remaining academic building on the campus.

41. Haygood House (1894)—Wesley and W. Clarke Sts. The home of Bishop Atticus Haygood after his retirement as college president. It was built using contributions by friends and former students.

42. Florida Hall (c. 1840s)—W. Clarke St. This weathered clapboard house has been completely modernized.

43. Old Methodist Church (1841)—Wesley and W. Fletcher Sts. The focal point of the ties between the community of Oxford, Emory College, and Methodism. Simple in design and constructed of whitewashed clapboard, the church was expanded with the addition of the two wings in 1880.

44. Site of Kitty's Cottage (c. 1840s)—Wesley St. The small home of Kitty, a mulatto slave willed to Bishop James O. Andrews, an Emory Trustee, once occupied this site. In 1845, Andrews granted her freedom and offered to pay her passage to Liberia. She chose to remain in Oxford and, with the bishop's aid, she helped organize the Methodist Episcopal Church, South. The cottage was moved to a nearby church campground in 1938.

45. Isaac Hopkins House (1850)—Wesley and W. Soule Sts. This antebellum house was Dr. Hopkins's residence when he served on the Emory faculty.

46. Emory College President's Home (1837)—Wesley and W. Soule Sts. Only a small frame structure when first occupied by Dr. Ignatius Few, the house was expanded and remodeled several times through the years. When the college relocated to Atlanta, this became the official residence of the Dean of Oxford College.

147

47. Branham House (c. 1840)—Wesley and W. Watson Sts. Built in the Greek Revival style, this was one of several private homes in Oxford where students boarded during the college's early years. Dormitories were considered "facilities for mischief," and the first was not built until 1912.

48. Stone House (c. 1840)—W. Watson and Wesley Sts. Occupying the highest point in Oxford, this house was built by the town's surveyor, Edward L. Thomas. In 1854, the house was purchased by Emory professor George Stone, who lived here until his death in 1889.

49. Oxford Cemetery (c. 1837)—W. Collingsworth and Asbury Sts. Called the "Westminster of Georgia Methodism," this burial ground holds the remains of eight Emory presidents, three of whom were Methodist bishops.

50. Capers Dickson House (c. 1840)—Asbury and W. Fletcher Sts. Another private home where students once boarded. Dickson was a student at Emory during the early post–Civil War period.

51. Zora Fair Cottage (c. 1850)—Asbury St. between W. Fletcher and W. Clarke Sts. Dark-complexioned Zora Fair came to Oxford from Charleston, S.C., in 1864 and attempted to slip into Union-occupied Atlanta as a freed slave. Captured by Federal pickets and threatened with execution as a Confederate spy, she was ultimately sent back to Oxford and lived in this house.

52. The Yarbrough Oak (1700s)—Between W. George and W. Clarke Sts. This massive 250-year-old tree was so admired by the Rev. John Yarbrough (Dr. Haygood's father-in-law) that he acquired it to save it from destruction. It was later given to the town, and in 1929, the Oxford city government deeded the tree and a small plot of land around it to "itself" in order to ensure its continued survival.

53. Means House (c. 1820s)—W. Clarke and Emory Sts. Once a rude cabin built by a pioneer settler, this house was acquired by Dr. Alexander Means around 1834. Means was superintendent of the manual labor school in Covington and was instrumental in the founding of Emory College in 1837. He served on the faculty and was the college's president in 1854–55. Means called his home "Orna Villa" (Beautiful Home). *NR*

54. Allen Memorial Methodist Church (1910)—Whatcoat and W. Pierce Sts. This attractive sandstone brick church is named for the Rev. Young J. Allen, a Methodist missionary to China from 1860 until 1907.

April
- Dogwood Days—
  Red Top Mountain State Park
- A Taste of Newnan
- Newnan-Coweta Historical Society
  Tour of Homes
- Oxford Day—Oxford College of
  Emory University

June
- Living History Encampment—
  Pickett's Mill State Historic Site
- Magnolia Blossom Festival—
  Newnan

July
- Independence Day Parade and
  Fireworks Extravaganza—Newnan

September
- Fall Festival—McIntosh Reserve
- Powers Crossroads Country Fair
  and Arts Festival—Newnan
- Coweta County Fair—Newnan
- Downtown Arts and Crafts Show—
  Covington

October
- Halloween Hayride—
  Red Top Mountain State Park
- Battlefield Candle-Lantern Tours—
  Pickett's Mill State Historic Site
- Trick-or-Treating on the Square—
  Newnan
- Autumn in Covington

November
- Holiday Open House—Newnan

December
- Homestead Christmas
  Celebration—
  Red Top Mountain State Park
- Christmas Parade—Newnan
- Holiday Candlelight Tour of
  Homes—Newnan
- Covington Christmas Parade

Old Infantry School,
Ft. Benning

A tree-lined downtown street
in Thomasville

CHATTAHOOCHEE VALLEY

With its headwaters high in the Blue Ridge Mountains, the Chattahoochee River traces a winding course through the state before emptying into Lake Seminole in the southwestern corner. Since prehistoric times, the river and its surrounding lands have been the lifeblood for rich and varied civilizations. Remarkable evidence for a highly sophisticated society stands just a short distance east of the river at Kolomoki Mounds State Historic Park, where large ceremonial mounds, built more than a thousand years ago, are vivid reminders of life in Georgia long before the arrival of European settlers in the 17th century.

In the era of the modern Indians, two nations—the Creek and Cherokee—were bitter rivals for the lands around the Chattahoochee, and many battles were fought for control of the river and its tributaries. Because of unrelenting pressures for settlement in the 19th century, however, both tribes were eventually forced to cede all their lands to the state and relocate west of the Mississippi River. The cession of the last Creek and Cherokee lands opened up the interior of Georgia to settlement, and within a few years, the Chattahoochee Valley was one of the richest agricultural regions in the South.

This was a land of vast cotton plantations, tilled by tens of thousands of slaves, and of towns like Columbus, Albany, and Thomasville that prospered through manufacturing or supplying agricultural goods and equipment. While most of the region was spared the physical devastation of the Civil War, the slavery-based economic system was abolished, creating a period of social chaos in the years after the war. Nonetheless, the soil was still fertile, and systems of sharecropping and tenant farming brought back some prosperity, although racially uneven, by the turn of the 20th century.

Evidence of this wealth remains in the many elegant Victorian homes preserved throughout the region.

Eventually, poor agricultural practices, most notably reliance on soil-depleting cotton as the main crop, contributed to a deep recession following the boll weevil blights of the mid-1920s. Farms were worn out and farmers flat broke. Through Depression-era programs, lands were restored and modern agricultural practices put in place, while mobilization for World War II bolstered local economies through the military buildup at Ft. Benning and other locations. The communities of the Chattahoochee Valley continue to benefit from a growing mix of agriculture and industry.

From the eroded sandstone walls of Providence Canyon to the stunning beauty of Callaway Gardens, from the fascinating living-history village of Westville to elegant winter homes of wealthy northern visitors, the Chattahoochee Valley is an area rich in Georgia's natural and human history.

Ida Cason Callaway
Memorial Chapel at
Callaway Gardens

Franklin D. Roosevelt State Park— Pine Mountain Trail

LOCATION

The state park is located about 20 miles north of Columbus via U.S. 27 and GA 190. It may also be reached by traveling about 7 miles south on I-185 from I-85, exiting on U.S. 27 (exit 42), and going south through Pine Mountain to GA 190. Travel east on GA 190 to the visitor center on the summit of Pine Mountain. *Information:* (706) 663-4858.

The Pine Mountain Trail, 95 percent of which lies within the boundaries of the state park, is considered one of the finest hiking paths in the state and is supported and maintained by hundreds of dedicated volunteers. The trail is conveniently accessible with several trail crossings and parking areas along GA 190 and GA 85, making it an excellent choice for day hiking.

PARKING

There is a large parking area at the visitor center, at the campground, and at Dowdell's Knob. There are smaller parking lots at trail and road crossings and at the eastern and western Pine Mountain trailheads. A daily fee is charged.

BACKGROUND

Like the spines of giant serpents, Pine Mountain and several surrounding, lower mountains stretch more than 20 miles along the rolling Piedmont Plateau. Pine Mountain climbs nearly a thousand feet above the surrounding landscape. A classic example of nature's erosive forces at work, this geological oddity is an outcrop of hard quartzite that has resisted weathering far better than the surrounding softer rock. When hiking in areas where the rock is exposed, watch for the whitish crystals of quartz that make up nearly 90 percent of the ridge.

This area of small farms, deep in the heart of the rural South, was little known until the 1920s when New

153

York Gov. Franklin D. Roosevelt learned of the therapeutic qualities of the water at nearby Warm Springs. Stricken by polio in his late thirties, the once-athletic Roosevelt sought any cure that might restore some function to his withered legs, so he came to the Warm Springs Institute for lengthy sessions of physical therapy. Over the years, Roosevelt came to love the natural beauty and hard-working people of the region.

FDR purchased land for a farm and built a modest retreat just outside Warm Springs on the northern slope of Pine Mountain. During his long tenure as U.S. president (1933–45), the residence—the only house he ever owned—came to be known as the "Little White House." Here he escaped the relentless pressure of Washington to relax, think, meet with military and civilian leaders, and plan the strategies that brought the nation back from the brink of economic ruin and, later, to victory in World War II. Between sessions of therapy, Roosevelt took frequent automobile trips through the pastoral valleys and along the mountain ridge, often picnicking with friends at a promontory called Dowdell's Knob.

When the country was hit by the Great Depression, Roosevelt created a number of Federal agencies to help revive the nation's economy. At Pine Mountain, the Federal Land Program assisted farmers in developing better land-use techniques, utilizing Roosevelt's own landholdings and farm as a demonstration site, and assisted in setting aside lands for nonagricultural uses such as outdoor recreation. The summit and slopes of Pine Mountain were acquired by the state and set aside as a Recreation Demonstration Area. Workers from the Civilian Conservation Corps and later from the Works Progress Administration constructed the Roosevelt Inn and Cottages (now the state park visitor center), swimming pool, recreation lakes, and group camps to attract tourists to the area. The buildings were constructed of native Pine Mountain fieldstone and contributed to the park's distinctive architecture. Pine Mountain State Park opened to the public in the late 1930s, and FDR visited the park many times and took an active interest in the area up until his death at the Little White House in 1945.

After World War II, much of Roosevelt's land was acquired by the state and added to the park, which was renamed as a lasting memorial to the late president.

Through the years, numerous footpaths crisscrossed Pine Mountain, but there was no coordinated trail system for hikers to enjoy the rugged terrain and scenic panoramas from the mountain's ridges. In 1975, the nonprofit Pine Mountain Trail Association was established to create a

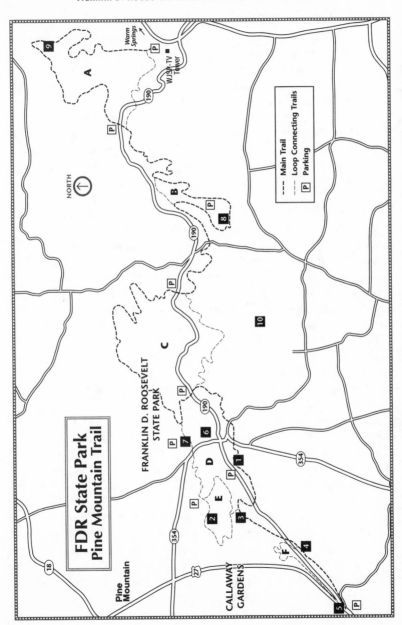

continuous foot-trail connecting the eastern and western ends of the mountain, opening up the natural beauty of the Piedmont's rolling foothills. One of the trail's founders imagined a "one hundred mile trail," linking Pine Mountain with Indian Springs State Park, but that vision died because of the overwhelming complexities of carving a footpath over many miles of private property.

WALK DISTANCE AND TERRAIN

The blue-blazed Pine Mountain Trail (PMT) follows a winding 23-mile route from its eastern terminus beneath the WJSP-TV tower on GA 85 to its western end on U.S. 27, across from the Callaway Gardens Country Store. Along the way, it meanders across the mountain's summit, ridges, and valleys, crisscrossing GA 190 several times and offering hikers multiple entry points to the trail.

Several connecting trails have been blazed that connect to the main trail and create six loops (with more planned for the future) ranging in distance from 3.2 to 7.8 miles in length. Each is ideally suited for exploring the varied natural and historic features of the mountain on either a day trip or overnight hike.

The main Pine Mountain Trail is marked by blue blazes, and connecting trails are marked with white blazes. The state park's Mountain

Creek Nature Trail is identified with red blazes. Four of the loops have backcountry campsites that may be reserved through Roosevelt State Park: (800) 864-PARK or (706) 663-4858.

Note that double blazes indicate either a change in trail direction or an approaching intersection. Detailed topographical maps of the trail network are available for purchase at the visitor center, at local outdoor equipment stores, or directly from the Pine Mountain Trail Association (P.O. Box 5, Columbus, GA 31902; www.ch-graphics.com/customer/pmta)

Warning: All water drawn from streams and other sources along the trails should be purified before drinking.

A. Wolfden Loop (6.7 miles)

Encompassing many acres that were once part of the Roosevelt farm, this section begins at the roadside park just north of the intersection of GA 190 and 85. The loop combines the 1.7-mile, white-blazed Beaver Pond connecting trail and the blue-blazed main trail. From the trailhead, the Beaver Pond Trail meanders nearly due west, descending through a narrow valley before climbing over the mountain ridge and crossing GA 190. From a vantage point just south of the highway, winter hikers are treated to a panoramic view of Dowdell's Knob about 3 miles distant.

Rocky Point marks the intersection of the Beaver Pond with the Pine Mountain Trail which, after crossing the highway again (there is a parking area), ascends through thick woods and past the Sassafras Hill backcountry camp. A steep climb over Hogback Mountain leads down the other side to the site of an old sawmill and along Wolfden Branch, which flows over Cascade, Slippery Rock, Big Rock, and Csonka Falls. The trail passes Mr. Roosevelt's fishing ponds on its return to the starting point.

B. Dowdell's Knob Loop (4.3 miles)

This loop begins at the picnic area located at the end of the Dowdell's Knob spur road from GA 190. One of the park's most popular destinations, the knob offers a spectacular view of the Pine Mountain valley. The trail follows the contour of the knob just beneath the summit following a gently undulating northerly route past Castle Rock before joining the 1.3-mile white-blazed Boottop connecting trail. From gently ascending Boottop, the section of the Pine Mountain Trail in this loop winds southward past Hornet Knob, Brown Dog Bluff, and then back to Dowdell's Knob. At several points along the way, the woods open up to reveal a panorama of the broad valley and the ridges of smaller Oak Mountain to the south.

C. Big Poplar Loop (7.8 miles)

From the Fox Den parking area on GA 190, east of GA 354, the trail descends northward through Fox Den Cove, past the intersection with the Pool Trail, and steeply ascends over Indian Mountain. The loop then winds down past the Big Knot and Beech Bottom backcountry camps before a climb beside the waters of Beech Branch and beneath Rattlesnake Bluff. After some distance along a ridge, the trail passes Big Poplar Creek before climbing steadily back to the road. Just south of the highway, follow the 2.7-mile, white-blazed Sawtooth connecting trail as it winds just below a ridge, past the Grindstone Gap campsite, and beneath the summit of L'il Butt Knob with its view of the park's group camp and Lake Franklin. After a short distance along a series of switchbacks, the loop returns to its starting point.

D. Long Leaf Loop (6.9 miles)

From the Pine Mountain Trail about .3 miles west of GA 190 at the Fox Den Cove parking area, follow the white-blazed Pool connecting trail as it winds westward toward the park campground, crossing the park swimming pool area and GA 354 along the way. At the intersection with the red-blazed Mountain Creek Nature Trail, follow the southern fork of the

157

Mountain Creek Trail until it reconnects with the PMT.

Before walking east on the Pine Mountain Trail, travel a short distance to the west to see a series of fish hatchery ponds built by the CCC during the 1930s. Beyond those, along the path to the western terminus of the Pine Mountain Trail, are several vista points offering spectacular views of nearby Callaway Gardens.

To complete the loop, return east on the Pine Mountain Trail and then south as it ascends over the summit ridge and crosses GA 190 before reaching an observation point at Buzzard's Roost. Continue east past the park headquarters as the trail follows a path just beneath the summit on its course back to the starting point.

E. Mountain Creek Nature Trail (3.2 miles)

This is an easy valley trail that winds through the park campground area and along the shores of Lake Delano. The variety of plant life, from moisture-loving rhododendrons and ferns to hardy mosses and aromatic galax, makes it a popular route for hikes led by park naturalists. The red-blazed loop begins and ends behind the Trading Post on the north side of the lake.

F. Overlook Loop (3.4 miles)

This section begins at the Gardens Overlook on GA 190 and meanders

westward following the steadily descending, white-blazed Chestnut Oak connecting trail along the northern slope of Pine Mountain. From the intersection of GA 190 and U.S. 27 at the Callaway Gardens Country Store, follow the blue-blazed Pine Mountain Trail on a steady 1.3-mile ascent along the southern slope of the mountain back to the intersection with GA 190 at Gardens Overlook.

SIGHTS ALONG THE WAY

 1. FDR State Park Visitor Center (c. 1930s)—GA 190. Located on the Pine Mountain Trail, this grand, 2-story fieldstone building was constructed by the CCC to serve as an inn. The center sits astride the summit of Pine Mountain with a commanding view of the valley to the south. Adjacent to the center is an outdoor amphitheater, also constructed of native fieldstone. The interior of the building features displays on the CCC and the history of the park. One historically significant architectural detail is an unsupported stone stairway that, according to historians, was designed in part by Pres. Roosevelt. *Hours:* 8 A.M.–5 P.M., daily. (706) 663-4858.

2. Campground, Cabins, and Lake Delano (c. 1930s)—Mountain Creek and Long Leaf Loops. The lake, campground, and several rustic log cabins were constructed by CCC workers. The original cabins were built in what came to be known as the "National Park Rustic" style, an architectural design intended to give the visitor the sense of living in a pioneer log cabin.

3. CCC Fish Hatchery Ponds (c. 1930s)—Located on the Main Trail. As part of the reforestation work carried out by the CCC workers, these ponds were utilized to grow and stock the fish populations of the park's lakes as well as replenish worn-out local streams.

4. Callaway Gardens Overlook—Gardens Overlook Trail. This opening in the trees provides a panoramic view of the lake, golf course, and landscaped grounds of nearby Callaway Gardens.

5. Callaway Gardens Country Store (1970s)—U.S. 27 at GA 190.

Adjacent to the western terminus of the Pine Mountain Trail, the store sells a variety of products from the Callaway orchards and vegetable gardens, as well as local crafts. The store's Country Kitchen Restaurant serves breakfast and lunch daily.

6. Franklin D. Roosevelt Memorial Bridge (c. 1930s)—North of Pine Mountain Trail (Long Leaf Loop) on GA 190 at GA 354. Spanning King's Gap, a narrow sag in the Pine Mountain ridge, this fieldstone bridge displays the design quality and characteristically rustic style of many CCC-built structures.

7. FDR State Park Swimming Pool (c. 1930s)—GA 354, north of GA 190, where Pool Trail crosses the highway. Historians believe that Pres. Roosevelt

View from Dowdell's Knob, FDR State Park

influenced the unique "Liberty Bell" shape of the large pool.

8. Dowdell's Knob—Southern end of Dowdell's Knob Spur Rd. off GA 190, on the Dowdell's Knob Loop Trail. This distinctive ridge that juts out to the south from the summit of Pine Mountain offers a spectacular panoramic view of Pine Mountain Valley. This site was Pres. Roosevelt's favorite picnic area, and he traveled here frequently when staying at the Little White House. The small fieldstone grill located here (now sealed up) was built by Roosevelt for cookouts.

9. Site of Old Sawmill (c. 1900s)—Wolfden Loop. A century ago, a sawmill operated in this clearing near Wolfden Creek. The mill produced lumber from the rich stands of loblolly pines that covered the hillsides. By the time of the Great Depression, most of the timber had been harvested, leaving eroded hills.

10. FDR State Park Stables, Group Camps, and Lake Franklin (c. 1930s)—South of main trail, off GA 190 and GA 354. The lake and group camp buildings were constructed by workers of the WPA.

Callaway Gardens

LOCATION

Located in Pine Mountain, a town about 35 miles north of Columbus, Callaway Gardens may be reached by traveling on I-185 to U.S. 27/ GA 1 (exit 42). Travel east about 10 miles, through Pine Mountain to GA 18/354. Travel west on GA 18, past the cottages entrance, to the new main entrance to the Gardens. The gate is open 7 A.M.–6 P.M., daily. A daily admission fee ($10) is charged. Multiday packages and annual "Friends of the Gardens" memberships are available. *Information:* (800) 225-5292; www.callawaygardens.com.

PARKING

Parking is permitted in designated areas. These are located at trailheads and at all Gardens attractions.

BACKGROUND

When Cason Callaway first visited this area in the 1930s from his home in nearby LaGrange, he found worn-out, eroded fields and rutted hillsides, the results of more than a century of one-crop (cotton) agriculture. Despite the poor condition of the land, Callaway discovered areas of natural beauty that drew him back for return visits. As the story goes, on one particular trip he came across a beautiful and rare wildflower that he asked his wife, Virginia, to identify. She told him that it was a plum azalea (*Azalea prunifolia*), a plant found only in this small area. Determined to preserve the fragile flower and its habitat, Callaway purchased nearly 4,000 acres of land around a hillside spring and built a summer cabin and a lake on what his family would call "Blue Springs Farm."

During those first few years, Callaway became a close friend to another visitor, Franklin D. Roosevelt, who traveled to nearby Warm Springs for polio therapy. Both men shared a deep love and respect for the land and the people of the region, and an unquenchable desire to restore and preserve the area's natural beauty.

In 1938, Callaway's desire to revitalize this land became so strong that

161

he turned over control of the family business, Callaway Mills, to his brother, Fuller, so that he could devote all of his energies to the farm. He began by purchasing 30,000 more acres of land and bringing in earth-movers to fill in gullies and to drain silt-laden bottomlands. He planted hybrid, fast-growing pine trees on hillsides and filled vast pasturelands with seed crops and hay.

Callaway experimented with a wide variety of cash crops and even dammed several streams to create well-stocked fishponds. His goal was to demonstrate to local farmers that, with a little ingenuity and a better understanding of the principles of crop rotation and soil conservation, even those with limited resources could return their lands to fruitful production. Callaway even used his strong influence to persuade local banks to offer farmers long-term loans so that they might have the capital needed to undertake those changes. When New York Gov. and, later, Pres. Roosevelt was in Warm Springs, the two men would often meet to discuss agricultural ideas and innovations. (Roosevelt also practiced new ways of managing the land at his Warm Springs retreat that came to be known as the "Little White House.")

Eventually, Callaway realized that the very best way to share the fruits of his years of labor was to establish a place for all to enjoy. With renewed inspiration he set about creating a magnificent garden, for both recreation and education, that would be a lasting tribute to his mother, Ida, and his wife, Virginia.

Beginning in 1949, an army of landscapers and gardeners planted azaleas, laurels, hollies, magnolias, dogwoods, and a diverse selection of wildflowers by the thousands. By the mid-1950s, the staff was establishing more than 20,000 new plants annually, with varieties chosen to provide color and beauty during any season of the year.

Since its opening, Callaway Gardens has continued to expand its horizons. Because Cason Callaway firmly believed in the joys of strolling through the gardens he loved, there is a perfect path for meandering, no matter your schedule or physical condition. From the half-mile-long Laurel Springs Trail to the 1.6-mile Azalea Trail, there are more than 7 miles of dedicated footpaths in the gardens.

WALK DISTANCE AND TERRAIN

From short nature walks to the nearly 10-mile-long bicycle path, more than 17 miles of trails have been carefully developed to offer visitors an opportunity to experience the beauty of the landscape and the diversity of plant life throughout the Gardens. Detailed maps are available at the Discovery Center and at other locations in the park. A schedule of

Callaway Gardens

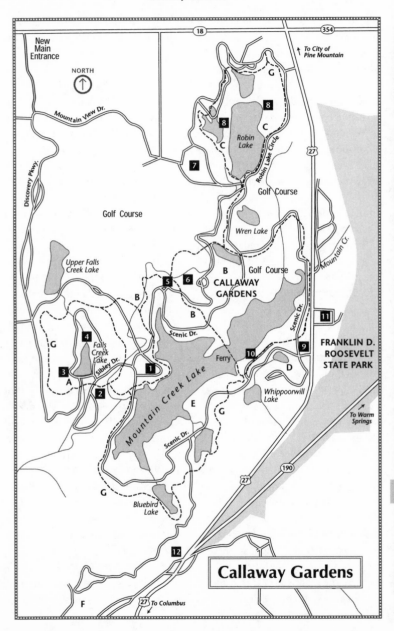

guided walks is also available at the Discovery Center.

Beginning just north of the Discovery Center, the trail systems are:

A. Callaway Brothers Azalea Bowl Trail

Winding along the shores of Mirror Pond and on the rolling hillside above, this 1.2-mile trail meanders through the world's largest azalea garden.

B. Meadowlark Gardens Area Trails

Three trails wind through this area near the Pioneer Cabin and the Butterfly Center.

Wildflower Trail. Located in the wooded area north of the Pioneer Cabin, this .6-mile trail contains specimens of several native Georgia plants, including the flame azalea, the symbol for Callaway Gardens. Features along the path include a gazebo, waterfall, and rustic footbridge overlooking Mountain Creek Lake.

Holly Trail. Featuring one of the nation's largest collection of hollies from Asia, Europe, and the Americas, this .8-mile trail is located west of the Butterfly Center parking area. Along the trail are a picnic area and gazebo.

Rhododendron Trail. The rich evergreen leaves and bright spring colors of several species of rhododendron are the highlight of this .6-mile trail located south of the Butterfly

Center. Seating areas along the path offer a chance to observe waterfowl on Hummingbird Lake.

C. Robin Lake Trail

A 2-mile paved, handicapped-accessible trail traces a loop around the shore of Robin Lake, a focal point for many summer activities.

D. Overlook Azalea Garden Trails

Located a short distance south of the Gardens Restaurant, this area held the world's largest collection of azaleas from its development in 1971 until creation of the Azalea Bowl in 1999. (Only at Callaway Gardens could a site of such beauty be second-best!) Two trails wind along the hillside and the shores of two small lakes.

Azalea Trail. Quite possibly the most-trodden trail in the Gardens, this 1.6-mile path has delighted thousands of azalea watchers who make a pilgrimage to Callaway each spring. Along the trail are several picnic areas and a large hillside overlook pavilion.

Whippoorwill Lake Trail. This .5-mile trail along the shores of a small pond offers opportunities for close-up observation of native waterfowl and other wildlife.

E. Mountain Creek Lake Trail

Following the shores of the lake from the boathouse to a road crossing south of the Sibley Center, this 1.5-mile trail winds through floodplain areas filled with native plants and shrubs. Two gazebos along the lakefront offer opportunities to rest and observe wildlife. This is a linear trail, and you may return to the starting point by retracing your steps or by following the Discovery Bicycle Trail for about 2 miles back to the boathouse.

F. Laurel Springs Trail

Situated on the slopes of Pine Mountain at the end of Laurel Springs Rd., this remote trail winds beneath the canopy of an Appalachian hardwood forest, filled with oak and hickory trees, and through a thicket of mountain laurel on a .5-mile loop from a roadside parking area. This scenic area was popular with local residents for many years before the Gardens were developed.

G. Discovery Bicycle Trail

Developed to provide bicyclists a place to ride free of automobile traffic, the trail opened in 1989. Walkers and joggers are welcome to use the paved, handicapped-accessible, 10-mile path that circles throughout the Gardens and connects nearly all major attractions and lodging areas. A small ferry offers bicyclists and walkers a shortcut across Mountain Creek Lake. Visitors may bring their own bicycles or rent them.

SIGHTS ALONG THE WAY

Note: Unless otherwise noted, attractions are open daily from 8 A.M. to 6:30 P.M.

1. Virginia Hand Callaway Discovery Center (2000)—Scenic Dr. Located at the end of a 2.5-mile scenic byway, the Discovery Center sits nestled on the shores of Mountain Creek Lake. The modern complex, carefully designed to blend with the surrounding landscape, is the starting point for exploring the Gardens' nearly 14,000 acres of natural beauty. The film *Time & the Garden* chronicles Cason and Virginia Callaway's vision. There are exhibits on the history of the Gardens, an exceptional collection of art works by Athos Menaboni, and a sculpture garden.

2. John A. Sibley Horticulture Center (1987)—Sibley Dr. This state-of-the-art greenhouse and garden complex provides more than 5 acres of spectacular greenery in every season.

3. Callaway Brothers Azalea Bowl (1999)—Sibley Dr. This 40-acre tract, the largest azalea garden in the world, features more than 4,000 native and cultivated azaleas and more than 2,000 other trees and shrubs. Along the bowl's network of footpaths are a picnic pavilion, gazebo, and a footbridge over Mirror Pond.

4. Ida Cason Callaway Memorial Chapel (1962)—Set amidst the pines along the banks of rustic Lower Falls

165

Creek Lake, this beautiful English Gothic stone church was built by Cason Callaway as a memorial to his mother and to serve as a place of peace, serenity, and reflection. Notable features of the chapel are the stained-glass windows. The four windows on the west wall show the progression of the seasons in the garden, while the large window on the south wall represents the colors and features of a coastal pine forest. The sanctuary is a popular setting for weddings, baptisms, and musical concerts, and interdenominational worship services are held here each Sunday morning during the summer.

5. Pioneer Cabin (c. 1830s)—Sibley Dr. at Meadowlark Way. Built by early settlers in nearby Troup County, this rustic, handhewn log cabin was occupied until the 1930s. Relocated to the Gardens in 1960 and restored, the cabin is filled with period furniture and household items, and costumed staff are happy to share stories of the rigors of frontier life.

6. Cecil B. Day Butterfly Center (1988)—Meadowlark Way. The largest free-flight enclosed conservatory in the nation, the center is home to nearly 1,000 specimens representing more than 50 different species of tropical

Walking path at Callaway Gardens

butterflies as well as a variety of songbirds and hummingbirds.

7. Mr. Cason's Vegetable Garden (1950s)—One of Cason Callaway's favorite projects was demonstrating innovative ways to coax produce from rural Georgia's worn-out soil. His 7.5-acre garden, located on several terraces, still supplies fresh vegetables to Gardens' restaurants and has often served as a setting for episodes of the popular public television series *The Victory Garden*.

8. Beach Pavilion and Robin Lake Beach (1950s)—A focal point of summer activities (Memorial Day through Labor Day), the lake features the world's largest artificial beach. Here, the Florida State University "Flying High" Circus performs daily and the lake hosts frequent water ski shows highlighted by the annual Master's Ski Tournament. Hours of operation vary by season.

9. Gardens Information Center and Gift Shop (1960s)—U.S. 27 at the original Gardens' entrance. Here visitors may enjoy an introductory slide program, learn about ongoing activities, and purchase daily or season passes. The center is open 7 A.M.– 6 P.M., daily.

10. Gardens Restaurant and Boathouse (1960s)—Scenic Dr. Designed in a half-timbered, English Tudor style, the restaurant offers panoramic views of Mountain Creek Lake. Visitors may rent canoes at the adjacent boathouse.

11. Callaway Gardens Inn (1960s)—U.S. 27 across from the Gardens entrance. This sprawling complex, set amidst landscaped grounds, features luxury accommodations, restaurants, and a conference center. (800) 225-5292.

12. Callaway Gardens Country Store and Kitchen (1960s)—U.S. 27 south of the Gardens. Located across from GA 190 and the entrance to Franklin D. Roosevelt State Park, the store features a wide selection of crafts, and canned fruits and vegetables from the gardens. The restaurant serves breakfast and lunch, featuring fresh vegetables from Mr. Cason's garden.

NOTES

167

Columbus

LOCATION

✦ Columbus is located about 105 miles southwest of Atlanta via I-85 and I-185. Follow U.S. 27 (exit 42, Veterans Parkway) southwest from I-185 to the historic district along the Chattahoochee River. The walk begins at the Columbus Iron Works on Front Ave. *Information:* Columbus Convention and Visitors Bureau, (800) 999-1613; www. columbusga.com/ccvb.

PARKING

🚗 Unless posted, on-street parking is permitted along residential streets. The central business district has both metered and commercial parking.

BACKGROUND

📖 By the time of the arrival of the first Europeans in North America, this area was a thriving community of Creek Indian villages located along both banks of the river. The largest village in the region was Coweta Town, situated on the western side of the Chattahoochee near the present site of Phenix City, Ala. Kashita (Cusseta), a smaller settlement, was on land that is now part of Ft. Benning. These towns were regional centers of the Creek Nation, whose boundaries spread from the mountains of northeastern Georgia to the Atlantic and Gulf coasts. The first recorded visit to Coweta Town was by a Spanish priest and his small party in 1679. They were viewed with suspicion by the tribal leaders and forced to flee.

For the next century, the Spanish, English, and French empires vied with one another for the lands of the Chattahoochee Valley, creating shifting alliances with the Creek tribes. In the 1730s, the English government established the Colony of Georgia to serve as a buffer against France and Spain. In 1739, Georgia's leader, Gen. James Edward Oglethorpe, sought and received permission to visit the Creek

Columbus

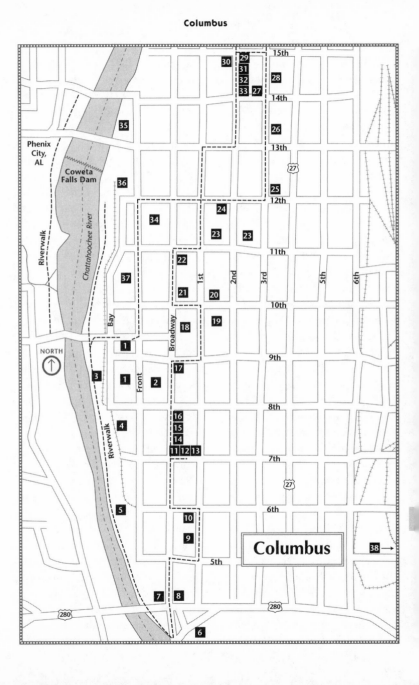

tribal leaders meeting in council at Coweta Town. Oglethorpe assured the Creeks that settlers would not encroach on their lands if they would promise loyalty to England. The Creeks agreed and stood by their British allies through skirmishes with the French and Spanish and, later, against the American Rebels during the Revolution.

Following Britain's defeat in the American Revolution, Spain wrested Florida back without challenge and, within a few years, the Spanish were again trying to align the Creeks against the new State of Georgia. To counter these efforts, Pres. George Washington signed a 1791 treaty banning settlements on Creek lands. During the War of 1812, some Creek tribes supported Britain and some served notably with the forces of the United States. Ironically, treaties growing out of U.S. victories insisted on the cession of more Creek lands, even those held by the natives who had fought with the Americans.

A decade later, Georgia Gov. George Troup, under enormous pressure to open more of the state's interior to white settlement, demanded that all remaining contested lands in Georgia and Alabama be cleared of native claims and that the Indians be removed westward. Settlers quickly moved in, and by an act of the state legislature in December 1827, a trading post was established along the Federal Road at Coweta Falls, near the head of navigation of the Chattahoochee River. Surveyor Edward Lloyd Thomas was commissioned to lay out a 1,200-acre site with streets and commons. This original survey followed a grid plan and included 614 half-acre building lots, and 45 garden lots of either 10 or 20 acres. The sale of land lots began on July 10, 1828, and at the end of 1829, a small settlement, now called Columbus to honor the famous explorer, counted more than 1,000 inhabitants.

Steamboats traveled up the Chattahoochee from Florida bringing passengers and supplies to the new settlement. Among those who came were industrialists who saw in the rushing waters of Coweta Falls the potential for great water-powered mills. Some envisioned a city, close to the cotton-producing plantations, that would someday challenge New England for supremacy in the nation's textile industry.

The Dillingham Bridge, the first to span the Chattahoochee, was completed in 1833. Constructed by engineer John Godwin and his skilled slave Horace King, it survived until 1841 when it was washed downstream in a storm (the piers of this bridge may still be seen beneath the current bridge). King proved to be a master builder, and Godwin granted him his freedom in 1846. As a free black, King built wooden bridges throughout Georgia, Alabama, and Mississippi (many still stand) and even provided lumber for the Confederate Naval Yard in Columbus during the Civil War.

Further growth in the Chattahoochee Valley region was slowed by fears of renewed hostilities with the Creeks still living along the western frontier. In early 1836, a violent uprising led by Chief Osceola took place in northern Florida, and Gen. Winfield Scott was dispatched to Columbus to supervise military operations against the Indians. Osceola was eventually captured and the rebellion crushed. By the end of the year, nearly 15,000 Creeks had been removed west to Arkansas on a journey as tragic as the more famous relocation of the neighboring Cherokees on the Trail of Tears. Interestingly, one of the commissioners sent to Columbus by Pres. Andrew Jackson to oversee the removal was Francis Scott Key, author of "The Star-Spangled Banner."

With the Indian "problem" finally resolved, the pace of development quickened. The town's first mill had been a grist mill opened in 1828 by Seaborn Jones. In 1838 the first textile mill, the Columbus Cotton Factory, opened. The E. T. Taylor Cotton Gin Manufacturing Company began operations in the mid-1840s, and Eagle Mills, manufacturers of cotton and woolen goods, followed in 1851. The Columbus Iron Works began producing cast-iron products at its large factory on Front St. in 1853, and George Woodruff established the nearby Empire Grist Mill in 1861.

With the outbreak of the Civil War in April 1861, Columbus became a major industrial center for the South. Eagle Mills made uniforms and tents for the Confederate army; the Iron Works produced cannons, ammunition, and mechanical equipment for naval gun boats; and Empire milled ground meal and baked hardtack for the troops. Also, Louis Haiman, a Prussian-born tinsmith who had settled in Columbus in the 1830s, operated the South's largest sword factory, fabricating, at its peak, more than 300 sabers and cutlasses a day.

Despite being a manufacturing center, the city was spared the wrath of Maj. Gen. William Tecumseh Sherman, whose March to the Sea moved well east of the city. Columbus finally fell to Union troops on April 16, 1865, one week after Robert E. Lee's surrender at Appomattox, in what proved to be the last eastern land battle of the Civil War. Gen. James Wilson, commander of the Union troops, ordered all the weapons plants, textile mills, and other commercial buildings destroyed. He spared only the flour mills, which were permitted to continue producing food for local citizens.

Columbus quickly rebounded from the war's devastation, and within a few years, nearly all the mills and factories were restored and new ones constructed. One of the first to

171

reopen was Eagle Mills, which had changed its name to Eagle and Phoenix Mills to signify its rebirth from the ashes of war. George Parker Swift came to Columbus in 1867 and founded Muscogee Mills, one of the world's largest producers of both cotton towels and ticking. By 1887, Woodruff's Empire Mill was the largest meal and flour mill in the South, operating 36 roller mills producing 600 barrels of flour a day. Railroads supplemented the river traffic, and by the turn of the 20th century, four lines converged in Columbus, securing its place as a regional center of commerce and industry.

In the cultural realm, Francis Joseph Springer, an immigrant from Alsace, France, opened an exquisite opera house and hotel in February 1871.

While Springer sought to satisfy people's artistic tastes, druggist John Pemberton wanted to cure their ills with patent medicines and elixirs. After operating an apothecary in Columbus from 1855 to 1869, Pemberton moved to Atlanta and continued his experiments. In 1886, he developed a tonic he called "Coca-Cola" and sold it over the counter at Atlanta's Jacob's Drug Store. Expecting little return on his concoction, Pemberton sold the rights to the formula in 1888 for $1,750! In another Columbus connection with Coca-Cola, it was Empire Mills owner

George Woodruff's grandson, Robert Woodruff, who would one day steer the small soft-drink company to international prominence.

Columbus's historic downtown and Victorian residential areas have become the hub of an urban renaissance that draws local citizens and visitors alike to shop, dine, or simply stroll along the wide avenues or the beautifully landscaped Chattahoochee Riverwalk. The significance of this area has been recognized by its designation as a National Historic Landmark District.

WALK DISTANCE AND TERRAIN

The walk through the historic industrial, residential, and business district is about 4 miles. The walk begins and ends at the Columbus Iron Works Convention and Trade Center on Front St. The route takes you south along the Riverwalk to Golden Park, before turning north and proceeding up Broadway, through the historic residential district, to downtown. After crisscrossing downtown, the path returns to Riverwalk and Front Ave. for the return to the starting point. The terrain is level with many old shade trees. There are good sidewalks along most of the route.

SIGHTS ALONG THE WAY

 1. Columbus Iron Works Convention and Trade Center (1853)—801 Front Ave. Built

to meet the growing needs for river ships and barges and to provide equipment for the surrounding cotton plantations, the Iron Works operated at this location for more than a century. The factory was burned by Federal troops in 1865 but was quickly rebuilt. In the mid-1900s, it became a major manufacturer of ice-making machines.

Entrance to Riverwalk along the Chattahoochee River at Columbus

The Iron Works closed in the late 1960s, and in 1976, the buildings were restored and adapted for use as a trade and convention center overlooking the Chattahoochee River. The restoration received a National Trust for Historic Preservation award in 1981. The complex also houses a Columbus Welcome Center. *Information:* (706) 327-4522.

2. Empire Mill Building/ Columbus Hilton (1854)—Front Ave. at 9th St. Using steam power generated from the nearby river, George Woodruff built and operated the region's largest flour mill. The mill closed in 1931, and the building was adapted for use as a hotel in the 1970s.

3. Chattahoochee Riverwalk and Columbus Plaza (begun 1992)— Along the river between 12th St. and Golden Park. Walk north to see the unique "Four Images" statue of Christopher Columbus, the brick piers of the original Dillingham Bridge—the first span across the Chattahoochee— and the observation point at Coweta Falls Dam. The falls are the head of navigation for the Chattahoochee River and mark the geologic Fall Line that separates the Piedmont Plateau from the ancient Coastal Plain. River tours aboard the replica 1885 steamboat *Chattahoochee Princess* begin at the pier just west of 9th St. (The Riverwalk continues another 10 miles to the National Infantry Museum at Ft. Benning by crossing the Dillingham Bridge and following the path on the Alabama side of the river.)

4. Coca-Cola Space Science Museum (1996)—701 Front Ave. Operated by Columbus State University, this modern museum houses a fascinating variety of exhibits, including the Challenger Center (commemorating the crew of the *Challenger*

173

space shuttle), other displays on space travel, an astronomical observatory, and the Omnisphere theater. *Hours:* 10 A.M.–4 P.M., Tues.–Fri.; 1:30–5 P.M., Sat.; and 1:30–4 P.M., Sun. (706) 649-1470.

5. Site of Confederate Naval Yard (1862-65)—Riverwalk west of 6th St. A small historical marker notes the site of the yard where ironclad rams were built and other gunboats were repaired. Detailed information about the naval yard is available at the Woodruff Museum of Civil War Naval History on U.S. 280 at Veterans Parkway. (706) 327-9798.

6. Golden Park (c. 1920s), Civic Center (1996), and Recreation Complex—Victory Drive at Broadway. Golden Park, home of the Columbus Red Stixx Class A baseball team, is one of the oldest minor league ballparks in the country. It underwent a complete renovation for use as the women's softball venue for the 1996 Olympic Games. This extensive sports and recreation complex includes the Civic Center, a multipurpose facility used for conventions, trade shows, and athletic events (it is the home of the Columbus Cottonmouths of the Central Hockey League); Memorial Football Stadium (where the Georgia-Auburn game was played until 1959); and a modern softball stadium that is home to the Georgia Pride women's professional fast-pitch softball team.

7. Goetchius–Welborn House (1839)—405 Broadway. This antebellum house, noted for its New Orleans–style wide verandah and wrought-iron ornamentation, was once owned by Gen. William Welborn, a veteran of the Creek Indian War in 1836. The home was moved from its original location to this site in 1969 and is now used as a restaurant. *NR*

8. Church Rectory Building (c. 1835)—412 Broadway. In the original city plan, a land lot was set aside for use by Catholic settlers. The Church of Sts. Philip and James was built, and this structure served as clergy residence. It was moved from its original location to this site in the 1970s and now serves as an architect's studio.

9. The "Folly" (1831, remodeled 1861)—527 1st Ave. This antebellum cottage was built by pioneer settler Alfred Iverson. Iverson served in the U.S. Congress and Senate and had two sons who were generals in the Confederate army. The house was purchased by cabinetmaker Leander May in 1861. He built the octagonal addition and remodeled the original house as a second octagon. It is believed to be the only double-octagon house in the nation. *NL*

10. Wells-Bagley House (c. 1840)—22 E. 6th St. Originally located on Front St., this early

Columbus residence was moved to this location and restored for use by the Columbus Jaycees. *NR*

11. Historic Columbus Foundation (1870)—An excellent example of the Italianate style, this house was once owned by Stirling Price Gilbert, a justice of the Georgia Supreme Court. It was restored in 1977 and now serves as foundation headquarters. The foundation's "Heritage Corner" walking tours begin here. *Information:* (706) 323-7979.

12. Pemberton House (c. 1855)— 11 W. 7th St. Once the home of Coca-Cola creator Dr. John S. Pemberton, the structure was originally located on 3rd St. It was moved to the present site in the 1970s. The adjoining kitchen/apothecary museum features a Coca-Cola exhibit.

13. Butler-Barker House (1835)— 13 W. 7th St. This Federal-style cottage is believed to be the oldest 2-story house in Columbus.

14. Woodruff Farm House (c. 1840) and Traders Cabin (c. 1800)—708 Broadway. These two structures have been relocated to this site from rural Muscogee County and restored as museums depicting life on Georgia's western frontier.

15. Pemberton Country Home (c. 1860)—712 Broadway. Dr. Pemberton lived in this house, originally about 4 miles outside of town, from 1860 until he moved to Atlanta in

1869. He continued to experiment on his formula for Coca-Cola while living here. The structure was moved to this location and restored in 1977.

16. Walker-Peters-Langdon House (c. 1828)—716 Broadway. Designed in the simple Federal style, this small cottage was built by Col. Virgil Walker. It is believed to be one of the oldest houses still standing in Columbus and was restored in 1966. Across from the house, on Broadway's grass median, is the memorial to the Confederate dead erected by the Ladies Memorial Association in 1879.

17. Isaac Joseph House (c. 1842)— 828 Broadway. Considered an excellent example of the Greek Revival Cottage style, this house was owned by Joseph and his descendants for more than a century. It is now owned by the Historic Columbus Foundation. *NR*

18. River Center (2000)— 900 block of Broadway. When completed, this $84 million complex will be one of the finest performing arts centers in the Southeast. It will serve as a venue for traveling performers and will be home to the music department of Columbus State University.

19. Consolidated Government Building (1980s)—1st Ave. at 10th St. In 1970, Columbus became one of the first municipalities in the nation to combine city and county government operations. This modern 14-story complex houses the consolidated government offices. One of the Confederacy's largest military hospitals was located on this site during the Civil War.

20. Springer Opera House (1871) —103 10th St. Among the many notables who have graced the stage of Francis Springer's lavishly decorated auditorium are Edwin Booth (brother of John Wilkes Booth), "Blind Tom" Bethune, Oscar Wilde, boxer John L. Sullivan, humorist Will Rogers, and political leaders William Jennings Bryan and Franklin D. Roosevelt. Once called "the finest house between Washington and New Orleans," the Springer narrowly escaped demolition in 1964 and was designated the state's Official Theater by Gov. Jimmy Carter in 1971. It has undergone several renovations, the most recent in 1999, and continues to host a full range of dramatic and musical productions. Tour and event information: (706) 324-5714. *NL*

21. Rankin Square (c. 1880s)— 1000 Block of Broadway at 1st Ave. Developed by Scottish immigrant James Rankin, this block of buildings is considered an excellent example of Victorian commercial architecture.

22. Bank of Columbus Building (c. 1850s)—1048 Broadway. This elegant building is notable for its distinctive white-painted, cast-iron facade, which was manufactured in Pittsburgh, Penn., and shipped to Columbus in pieces for installation.

The building now houses offices and retail shops. *NR*

23. Church Square (c. 1828)—1st and 2nd Aves. between 11th and 12th Sts. In the original city plan of 1828, surveyor Edward Lloyd Thomas set aside several lots in this area for the construction of churches. Today, four large congregations—First Presbyterian (c. 1862, 1925), Trinity Episcopal (1890), First Baptist (1859), and St. Luke Methodist (c. 1900s)—have churches here.

A nearby marker notes the site of Columbus's first hotel, the Oglethorpe House, built in 1836 and used as headquarters by Gen. Winfield Scott during the Creek Indian War. Presidents James Polk and Millard Fillmore were honored at receptions held at this hotel.

24. U.S. Post Office and Courthouse (1933)—12th St. at 2nd Ave. This Depression-era public building features the exterior ornamentation and design characteristic of the Art Deco style popular at the time. *NR*

25. Swift-Kyle House (1857)— 303 12th St. This Greek Revival mansion with its unusual U-shaped porch supported by 11 Corinthian columns was acquired by Col. George P. Swift in 1864 and is still owned by his descendants. *NR*

26. The Lion House (c. 1850)— 1316 3rd Ave. This unusual house reflects Egyptian influences in its Greek Revival architectural style. Especially notable are the six large "Tower of the Winds" columns and a flying balcony. *NR*

27. Hawks House (c. 1850)—1401 3rd Ave. Built for the Rev. William Hawks, pastor of Trinity Episcopal Church (1855–65), the house was moved to this location in 1988 from its original site at 1332 3rd Ave.

28. Bullard-Hart House (1887)—1408 3rd Ave. This grand Victorian house, built for Dr. Lewis Bullard, was the first residence in Columbus to have electricity. Notable guests in this home have included Pres. Franklin D. Roosevelt and Gens. George Patton and George C. Marshall. *NR*

29. Rankin House (c. 1870)—1440 2nd Ave. Begun prior to the Civil War, the house was not completed until 1870. It was built by James Rankin, a wealthy planter and owner of the nearby Rankin Hotel, who developed Rankin Square. The structure is especially notable for its ornamental cast iron. It is the headquarters of the Columbus Junior League. *NR*

30. Schley-Peabody-Warner House (1840)—1445 2nd Ave. This residence was built by Capt. Philip T. Schley, who was sent to Columbus in 1834 to command the soldiers stationed here. Originally located on the site of the First Presbyterian Church, it was moved to this site in 1858. The house was later sold to the Peabody family and was the boyhood home of noted financier and philanthropist

George Foster Peabody. The Peabodys sold the house to James Warner, former chief engineer for the Confederate Naval Iron Works. *NR*

31. Iliges House (1850)—1428 2nd Ave. With its Corinthian columns and balcony, this antebellum house is considered a classic example of Greek Revival architecture. *NR*

32. Robert W. Woodruff Birthplace (c. 1870s)—1414 2nd Ave. The son of Ernest Woodruff and grandson of Empire Mills founder George Woodruff, Robert Woodruff was born in this house in 1884. In 1896, Ernest was named president of the Trust Company of Georgia and the family moved to Atlanta. In 1919, Ernest purchased the Coca-Cola Company from Asa Candler and placed Robert in charge of the corporation. Over the next fifty years, Robert Woodruff made "Coke" a household word around the globe.

33. Garrett-Bulloch House (c. 1880s)—1402 2nd Ave. An excellent example of the Queen Anne style, this house was built by Joseph S. Garrett, U.S. Postmaster for Columbus.

34. The *Columbus Ledger-Enquirer* Building (1931)—17 W. 12th St. This Mediterranean-style building was constructed to house Columbus's two daily newspapers. The *Columbus Enquirer* was established by Mirabeau Buonaparte Lamar in 1828. Lamar moved to Texas in 1835 and fought for the Republic of

Texas in its war with Mexico. He succeeded Sam Houston as president of the Republic of Texas in 1838 and served until 1841. He later fought with the U.S. Army in the Mexican War and died in 1858 while serving as U.S. ambassador to Nicaragua. The *Columbus Ledger* was founded in 1886. The two newspapers combined in 1988. *Information:* (706) 324-5526.

35. Fieldcrest-Cannon Mills (1844)—Front Ave. and Broadway at 14th St. Originally named Coweta Falls Mill, this was one of the first textile mills in Columbus. After the Civil War, the damaged buildings were repaired and expanded, reopening as Muscogee Mills. Fieldcrest purchased the mill in 1963. Within the complex is the Mott House (c. 1840), which is now used for offices. *NR*

36. Eagle and Phoenix Mills (1851)—Front Ave. between 12th and 13th Sts. Another of the early mills that made Columbus the industrial center of the region. The mill was burned by Federal troops in 1865, but was quickly repaired and back in operation a year later.

37. W. C. Bradley Company (c. 1860s)—1017 Front Ave. The cotton warehouses originally on this site were burned by Union forces in 1865. Most of the buildings were restored and expanded in the late 1800s. The W. C. Bradley Company was established in 1883 and still operates the warehouses. The complex also con-

tains a conference center and an art museum. *Museum hours:* 8 A.M.– 5 P.M., Mon.–Fri. (706) 571-6041.

A nearby historical marker notes the site of the E. T. Taylor Cotton Gin Company established in 1847. In 1867, Frank Cummins acquired the company and by the turn of the 20th century, it was the world's largest manufacturer of cotton gins. The buildings are now part of the W. C. Bradley warehouse complex.

38. Gertrude Pridget "Ma" Rainey House (c. 1900s)—805 5th Ave. This house was the final home of blues and gospel performer "Ma" Rainey (1886–1939). Considered to be the "Mother of the Blues," Rainey was inducted into the Georgia Music Hall of Fame in 1993. *NR*

NOTES

CHAPTER 27

Ft. Benning Historic District

LOCATION

✦ Ft. Benning is located about nine miles south of Columbus. The fort's visitor information and orientation center may be reached by traveling south on I-185 and Custer Rd., or from Victory Dr. and Lumpkin Rd. The walk begins at the National Infantry Museum located on Baltzell St. east of Lumpkin Rd. The museum may also be reached by exiting I-185 at First Division Rd. and traveling west to Baltzell St. *Information:* (706) 545-2211; www.benning.army.mil.

PARKING

🚗 The walk begins at the National Infantry Museum on Baltzell St. There is a large parking area adjacent to the museum.

BACKGROUND

📖 The U.S. Army's Ft. Benning is one of the most important military installations in the world. Here soldiers come for advanced training in infantry tactics and airborne assault. It is an army post steeped in military tradition, yet surprisingly open and accessible to visitors. Its location on the bluffs and hills above the Chattahoochee River is a place rich in Georgia and U.S. history.

A large Creek Indian village, Kashita (Cusseta) Town, was located on the grounds of what is now Ft. Benning. In Creek culture, important villages were either "White Towns" or "Red Towns." White Towns were "peace" centers where tribal civil affairs were conducted, while Red Towns were "war" centers where warriors gathered to plan military strategies against their enemies. Interestingly, Coweta Town, which was just across the river, was a Red (war) Town, and Kashita—now the site of one of the world's largest military posts—was a White (peace) Town.

In the years following the Creek Removal by the terms of the 1825 Treaty of Indian Springs, the area of the present fort was rural farmland surrounding the small settlement of

Eelbeck, which had a grist mill, a few stores, and a post office. An old Indian trail that crossed the hills toward the river became part of the Federal Road connecting Charleston and New Orleans, and was a major pathway for westward-bound pioneers. The route of the old road passed close to the present site of the Infantry Museum and crossed the Chattahoochee River southwest of Marchant St.

Military attention focused on this area as the nation mobilized for combat in World War I. In May 1918, Col. Henry E. Eames was charged by the Army with finding a new site for a dedicated infantry training school. Columbus, Ga., civic leaders worked tirelessly to persuade the Army to consider a vast tract of farmland south of their city for the proposed fort. Their efforts were successful, and the site selected was a plantation owned by Arthur Bussey. The terrain was ideal for infantry training, and the farm's buildings would be adequate for initial camp operations. The camp officially opened on October 7, 1918, and, at the request of Columbus citizens, was named in honor of a prominent early resident, Gen. Henry Lewis Benning. With this choice, Ft. Benning became the first U.S. military post named in honor of a Confederate soldier.

In the early days, most of the soldiers stationed at Ft. Benning lived in tents or temporary facilities, and the farm buildings served multiple purposes until more permanent structures could be built. During the Great Depression, the Army was called on to tackle a number of domestic tasks, and Ft. Benning became a major induction and training facility for men preparing for work in Civilian Conservation Corps (CCC) camps around Georgia and the Southeast. The large numbers of civilians and soldiers stationed at the fort during this time contributed to the construction of many new buildings that would prove necessary a short time later when the nation mobilized for World War II. During WWII, Ft. Benning became home to the First Infantry Division, the famed "Big Red One," as well as the primary training ground for a new type of soldier, the paratrooper.

Throughout its history, Ft. Benning has served as a training ground for some of our nation's best-known military leaders. Gens. Dwight D. Eisenhower and Omar Bradley were stationed here in the mid-1920s while undergoing infantry training. Gen. George C. Marshall once served as assistant commandant of the Infantry School, and Gen. George Patton carried out tank and infantry combat preparations here during the early days of World War II. More recently, Gulf War commanders Gen. Colin Powell and Gen. Norman Schwarzkopf spent time in training at Ft. Benning.

Ft. Benning Historic District

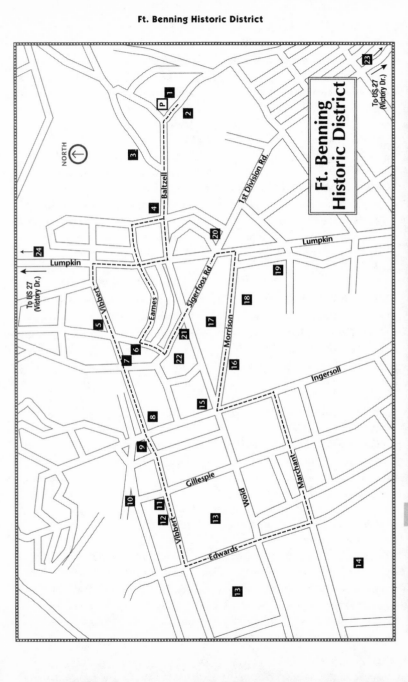

From the waning days of World War I to present-day conflicts in far-away places like Iraq, Somalia, and Kosovo, soldiers trained at Ft. Benning have served their country with honor, upholding the Infantry motto, "I am the Infantry, the Queen of Battle. Follow me!"

WALK DISTANCE AND TERRAIN

 The post sits amidst rolling hills above the Chattahoochee River, and the 3.5-mile loop through the historic district has an abundance of shade trees and sidewalks.

SIGHTS ALONG THE WAY

1. **National Infantry Museum (1923)**—Building 396, Baltzell St. This rambling complex of buildings served for more than 35 years as the Ft. Benning Hospital. In 1958, it was converted to an outpatient clinic and, in 1975, became permanent home to the National Infantry Museum. Displays trace the role of the infantry from the earliest colonial period to the present day. Artifacts include weapons, uniforms, and equipment from every war in which American soldiers have been involved. There is a large auditorium for films, a gallery of military art, and a gift shop. Tanks, artillery pieces, and other heavy equipment are displayed on the grounds. Recently, the building that served as Gen. George Patton's headquarters while he was stationed

at Ft. Benning as commander of the 29th Armored Division, has been relocated to the grounds of the museum and is undergoing restoration. Admission is free. *Hours:* 8 A.M.–4:30 P.M., Mon.–Fri.; 12:30–4:30 P.M., Sat.–Sun. (706) 545-6762.

2. **Sacrifice Field**—Baltzell St. across from the museum. This open field is dedicated to the soldiers who have made the ultimate sacrifice for their country. Monuments located on the field include the 11th Airborne Memorial (World War II), the 119th Light Infantry Memorial (Vietnam), and the SS *Leopoldville* Memorial (dedicated to soldiers who died aboard a transport ship torpedoed off the French coast on December 24, 1944).

3. **Rainbow Row (1920s)**—Rainbow Rd. Named for the Rainbow Division, which earned fame in World War I, the Mediterranean-style stucco houses along this street are painted in bright pastel colors.

4. **Patch School (1931)**—Baltzell St. at Lumpkin Rd. This was Benning's first permanent school building for use by military families. It is named for Gen. Alexander M. Patch, commander of the U.S. 7th Army in World War II.

5. **Eisenhower Marker**—Vibbert Ave. at Austin Loop. This marker identifies the residence at 206 Austin Loop occupied in 1926–27 by future General of the Army and Pres. Dwight D. Eisenhower. He was, at the time,

Tanks on display at the National Infantry Museum

serving as a major in the 24th Infantry (one of the Army's premier regiments composed primarily of African-American soldiers).

6. Riverside (1909)—Vibbert Ave. across from Austin Loop. The main house of the Bussey Farm from 1909 to 1918, this rambling house has served as the residence of the post's commanding general for many years. It is not open to the public.

7. Office of the Judge Advocate (1915)—Vibbert Ave. at Sigerfoos Rd. Built as the creamery for the Bussey farm, the building first housed the post headquarters and quartermaster's office. It serves now as the legal affairs office.

8. Doughboy Stadium (1924)—Vibbert Ave. at Ingersoll Rd. Built by infantrymen, the 8,000-seat football stadium was constructed as a memorial to comrades killed in World War I. Lining the exterior walls are symbols

representing many infantry divisions. Gen. John J. Pershing, commander of U.S. Forces in World War I, turned the first shovel of dirt in the stadium's construction.

9. Fire Station No. 1 (1939)—Vibbert Ave. at Ingersoll Rd. This building replaced an earlier station built shortly after the post opened.

10. Railroad Station (1919)—Ingersoll Rd. at the railroad tracks. From 1919 until 1946, Ft. Benning operated its own narrow-gauge railway with more than 27 miles of track and 18 locomotives. One surviving locomotive is on display at the Infantry Museum.

11. Cooks' and Bakers' School (1939)—Building 89, Vibbert Ave. It is an old saying that an army "marches on its stomach," and this building was used to train hundreds of Army cooks to serve the many thousands of soldiers in World War II. The school closed after the war, and the building was converted to financial offices.

12. Gymnasium (1928)—Building 358, Vibbert Ave. This was the first gym built for use by the soldiers stationed at the fort.

13. Cuartels (1920s)—Vibbert Ave. between Gillespie and Anderson

Sts. These three enormous U-shaped buildings were completed in the 1920s to house entire regiments of soldiers (nearly 3,000 men). The buildings were featured in the 1941 edition of *Ripley's Believe It or Not* because they were believed to have the longest continuous porches (more than 2,500 ft.) in the world.

Two of the three cuartels are seen on this walk. As you pass them on Edwards St., Olson Hall is on the left and Henry/Wilkins Hall is on the right.

14. Airborne Training Center (1942)—Edwards at Marchant Sts. Three 250-ft.-high, red-and-white metal towers dominate the open field across Marchant St. The towers were erected in the early days of World War II to provide student paratroopers with experience in parachute descents. They continue to serve the same purpose today. Beyond the towers are lower jump buildings where students practice proper landing techniques. On display behind the field is a World War II–era airborne troop transport aircraft.

15. Gowdy Baseball Field (1925)—Wold Ave. at Ingersoll St. Sgt. Harry Gowdy, for whom the field was named, was a professional baseball player who served in the 166th Infantry, 42nd Division, during World War I. Gowdy was captain in charge of athletics and physical training at Ft. Benning during World War II. The field was dedicated on March 31,

1925, and the ceremony was followed by an exhibition game between the New York Giants and the Washington Senators.

16. Officers' Club (1934)—Morrison Rd. Though the club was organized at the fort in 1919, construction on the present building did not begin until 1932. The project was supervised by Lt. Col. George C. Marshall (see #23).

17. Old Infantry School (School of the Americas) (1935)—Morrison Rd. Construction of this enormous Neoclassical-style building solidified Ft. Benning's role as the Army's primary infantry training center. The building housed the school and the post headquarters until 1964 when a new school building was completed on Burr St., south of the Airborne Training Center. In 1986, this structure reopened as the School of the Americas, a center for training military officers from Central and South American countries. The facility is controversial because of human rights concerns associated with a number of these countries. In 2001, the school's name was changed to the Western Hemisphere Institute for Security Cooperation.

18. Chinese Arch (1925)—Morrison Rd. The simple arch was a gift from the people around the Chinese city of Tientsen to the 15th Infantry Regiment in appreciation for the soldiers' protection of the city's inhabitants during the Chinese Civil War in 1924. The 15th Infantry was stationed in China from 1912 until 1938. The arch was placed permanently at Ft. Benning in 1938.

19. Doughboy Statue (1958)—In front of Building 35 on Lumpkin Rd. Dedicated on April 1, 1958, the statue is a memorial to the soldiers of World War II. It is a duplicate of the original sculpted by German artist Ernst Kunst shortly after the war as a token of reconciliation. The original still stands in Berlin. The six stones supporting the soldier are from the Remagen Bridge, the first bridge over the Rhine River captured by American troops in 1945.

20. Kashita Town Monument— In the field between Lumpkin and First Division Rds. This tablet marks the location of the Creek peace town of Kashita.

21. Field of Four Chaplains (c. 1944)—Wold Ave. at Sigerfoos Rd. This green space near the Infantry Chapel is dedicated to four chaplains who were lost at sea on February 3, 1943.

22. The Infantry Chapel (1934)— Sigerfoos Rd. The simple Georgian Colonial–style chapel is an interdenominational house of worship. The Liberty Carillon in the belfry was a gift of industrialist Harvey Firestone and was first played during the Victory Day Celebration on August 14, 1946.

23. Marshall House (1920s)— Baltzell Ave. at First Division Rd. Named in honor of five-star General of the Army, George C. Marshall, who served as assistant commandant of the Infantry School in 1932–37, this house is now used for visiting dignitaries. Marshall went on to serve as chairman of the Joint Chiefs of Staff during World War II and as Secretary of State under Pres. Harry Truman. He authored the Marshall Plan, a program to rebuild war-torn Germany and Japan that earned him the Nobel Peace Prize.

24. Main Post Cemetery (1920s)— Lumpkin and Custer Rds. In addition to the many American soldiers buried in the cemetery, 70 Italian and German POWs who died while imprisoned at Ft. Benning during World War II also rest here.

NOTES

CHAPTER 28

Providence Canyon State Conservation Park

LOCATION

✦ Providence Canyon State Conservation Park, established in 1971, is about 36 miles south of Columbus. Travel south to Lumpkin via U.S. 27, then west on GA 39C for about 8 miles to the park entrance. The walk begins at the visitor center. *Information:* (229) 838-6202.

PARKING

 There is a parking area adjacent to the visitor center and another by the picnic ground on the north side of the canyon. A daily parking fee is charged.

BACKGROUND

Long known as "Georgia's Little Grand Canyon," Prov-idence Canyon is a testament to human impact on the natural landscape. Like its more famous and much larger namesake in Arizona, the steep walls and deep chasms of Providence Canyon were carved by the forces of wind and water. However, while it took the Colorado River countless millions of years to wear away the hard stone of the Grand Canyon, Providence Canyon was created in a little more than a century.

Before settlers moved into this area of western Georgia in the early 1830s, the region was a vast forest of shortleaf and loblolly pines, oaks, hickories, and dogwoods, punctuated by the flaming colors of the now rare Plumleaf Azalea (*Azalea prunifolia*), all clinging to the thin topsoil above the sands of the ancient Coastal Plain. Native Americans hunted and traded throughout the area and grew a few crops, but agriculture really began after the land was ceded to the state of Georgia by the Creeks in the 1820s. Settlers cleared the forests and prepared the land for farming. The common method of planting at the time was to plow straight rows of deep furrows instead of the contour farming practiced today. These furrows channeled rainwater down the treeless, sloping

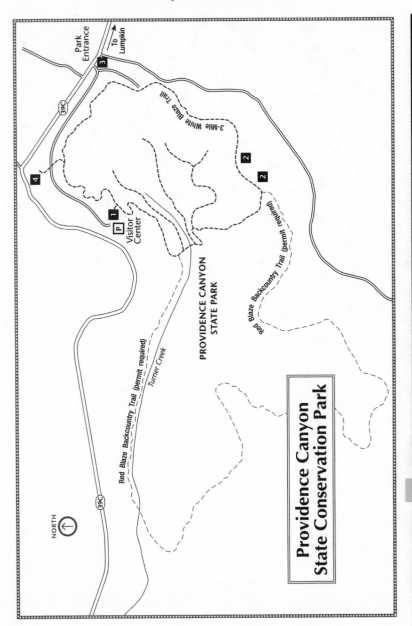

Providence Canyon
State Conservation Park

Providence Canyon

hillsides and accelerated erosion. Before long, the furrows became gullies, gullies later became ravines, and ravines eventually turned into canyons. The rapid pace of the erosion was a direct result of poor farming practices and the composition of the subsoils, which are soft sands of the Coastal Plain (which makes up nearly 60 percent of Georgia), laid down during a 20-million-year period beginning about 85 million years ago.

These soils were deposited as sediments in the ancient shallow seas that covered the lower half of the state several times during what geologists refer to as the Tertiary and Quarternary periods. As erosion continues to slowly remove soil from the walls and floors of the canyon, it is not un-usual for fossilized remains of sea creatures and marine organisms to be exposed.

Geologists have identified three distinct soil formations exposed in the walls and floor of Providence Canyon. As you descend on the trail into the canyon, you first pass through the Clayton Formation. This is a red-orange, sandy clay that was laid down during the latter part of the period. The reddish color of the soil here is a clear indication that it is rich in iron.

The next level, the Providence Sand, is the thickest layer in the canyon, at some places extending down nearly 120 feet. The buff-colored sand of this formation reveals much of the geologic evolution of the area. Visible in some places are thin sedimentary layers called "cross-beds" where the sands were deposited from fast-flowing streams. The Providence Sand is, in fact, a mixture of sand and kaolin, a white clay-like mineral used in many products including paper coatings, paint, detergents, and fertilizers. Georgia's Coastal Plain is the world's richest source of commercial kaolin.

The oldest level of the wall, dating back more than 85 million years, is the Perote Member located near the canyon floor. It is a mixture of sand, silt, and clay with a texture similar to putty.

At the bottom of the canyon, hikers may wander along streambeds to nine different canyons stretching northward like bony fingers. Hiking through the narrow canyons offers a close-up look at the brilliant colors and textures of the steep canyon walls. Along the return loop, the trail follows closely along the canyon rim providing a completely different perspective on this unique geological anomaly.

Human intervention during the last 60 years has slowed, but not stopped, erosion of the canyon. One of the first concerted attempts to arrest the deterioration occurred in the1930s when CCC workers planted kudzu to hold the soil. In recent years, the canyon floor has been planted with more stable and less aggressively growing pine trees. Nonetheless, Providence Canyon continues to change and evolve, making each visit a different visual experience.

TRAIL DISTANCE AND TERRAIN

The Canyon Trail is a white-blazed, 3-mile loop that descends from the visitor center on switchbacks to the floor of the canyon, then climbs again to follow the north rim along its return to the starting point. At the bottom of the canyon, the red-blazed, backcountry trail veers west and south on a 7-mile loop, reconnecting with the canyon trail near the eastern rim. There are six overnight campsites, and permits are required for hiking and camping on this trail.

Hikers venturing up the canyons should have waterproof boots or shoes, as much of the travel is through soft sand and along shallow, silt-laden streams. At most times, the water is only a few inches deep, but may become impassable after heavy rains. A round-trip up any canyon will add about a one-half to three-quarters of a mile to the trail distance.

189

SIGHTS ALONG THE WAY

1. Visitor Center (1970s)— This low building just west of the canyon rim offers displays on canyon geology and history. Staff are available to provide information, answer questions, and accept registrations for backcountry travel. *Hours:* 8 A.M.–5 P.M., daily.

2. Abandoned Automobiles (1950s)—On the eastern rim. As the adjacent signs explain, these wrecks were left in place when the park was established because they had become habitats for a wide variety of plant and animal life.

3. Site of the Rev. David Walker Lowe House (c. 1825)—On the park entrance road by the picnic area. Pioneer settler David W. Lowe was a circuit-riding Methodist minister who settled in this area shortly after the land was ceded by the Creek Indians. He donated land on which the original Providence Methodist Church and school were built. This site is now within the canyon. Lowe died in 1843 and is buried in a nearby family cemetery.

4. Providence United Methodist Church (1859)—On the park road, north of the picnic area. The original church was constructed south of the park road in 1833, but the rapid erosion of the soil forced its abandonment in the late 1850s. The present structure was completed just before the Civil War and is still occasionally used for services. Many pioneer families are buried in the adjacent cemetery.

Historic Westville

LOCATION

Historic Westville is on Martin Luther King Jr. Dr., 1 mile south of the Lumpkin town square. Lumpkin is 35 miles south of Columbus via U.S. 27, and 60 miles west of I-75 on U.S. 280/GA 30 at Cordele (exit 101).

PARKING

There is a large, unpaved parking area adjacent to the village's entrance gates.

BACKGROUND

Nestled deep in the rolling pine hills of southwestern Georgia, there is a community seemingly untouched by the passage of time, with dirt streets and no electricity, and where the newest building was completed before the Civil War. In the living-history village of Westville the town's motto proclaims, "It is always 1850."

The dream to create a place where visitors could experience the pace of life in the pre–Civil War South was the vision of Col. John Word West, historian and longtime president of North Georgia College in Dahlonega. West, a native of rural Georgia, spent much of his academic career studying the era and building an extensive collection of period artifacts. At the time of his death in 1961, his will stipulated that his private collection be used to re-create an authentic, functioning village of antebellum Georgia.

A few years later historian Dr. Joseph Mahan approached the Stewart County Historical Commission with a proposal to found such a living-history museum near the small town of Lumpkin. Mahan planned to locate and acquire authentic antebellum structures, relocate them to a central site where they would be restored, furnished, and opened to the public. To honor Col. West's memory, the village would be called "Westville."

Westville Historic Handicrafts, Inc., was established to raise funds

191

and begin the search for suitable structures. The Singer family, prominent residents of Lumpkin since 1838, donated 58 acres of property just south of town to the project. Planners were determined that this site would not just be an assortment of buildings but would be a working town, filled with the necessary businesses and services—blacksmiths, coopers, apothecaries, a school, and a court house—that would have been important to the prosperity of an actual antebellum community. It would also be a town that was always growing; as additional structures were found, they would be added to Westville's mythical community.

In January 1968, the first building was relocated to the site, and, as the planners had hoped, once word of the project spread, more contributions of funds, furniture, tools, and buildings came pouring in from across Georgia. A formal town-founding ceremony was held on August 31, 1968, and on April 2, 1970, Westville welcomed its first visitors.

Westville continues to grow, and the town now includes more than 30 buildings reflecting the styles and social strata of the times. Staff and volunteers don period clothing and work in the village, demonstrating the crafts and trades that made up daily life in a small Georgia town in the years before the Civil War. As you meander through town, let the aroma of fresh-baked biscuits, the heat from the blacksmith's furnace, the squeak of the wheels on a mule-drawn wagon, and the clanging of the schoolhouse bell draw you back to another time.

Historic Westville has received numerous historical preservation awards and is open 10 A.M.–5 P.M., Tues.–Sat.; and 1–5 P.M., Sun. *Information:* (800) 733-1850.

WALK DISTANCE AND TERRAIN

Westville is located on a gently sloping hillside and creek bottom. The dirt streets are level with occasional board sidewalks. There is an abundance of shade trees throughout the village, and there are numerous places to sit and relax and watch time go by—as they may have done 150 years ago. A meandering walk through the village is a distance of about 1.5 miles.

SIGHTS ALONG THE WAY

1. Randle-Morton Store (c. 1850)—Outside the village gates. Relocated from Webster County, the old general store now houses the Westville ticket office and a shop selling gifts and crafts, many made by Westville artisans.

2. Singer Gates (1960s)—Irwin and Troup Sts. The formal entrance to the village, these gates are reproductions of those that surround the old State Capitol grounds in Milledgeville.

192

Historic Westville

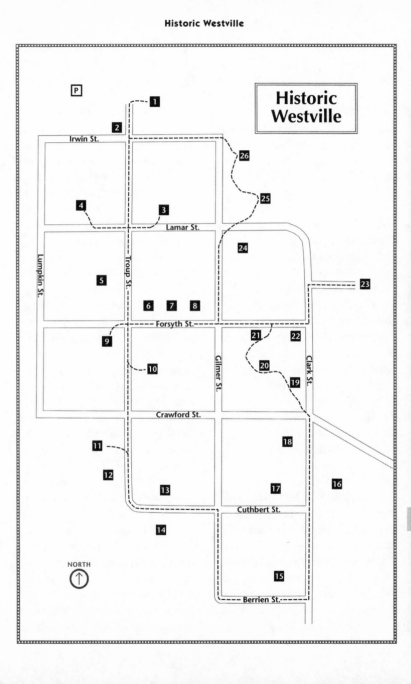

3. Stewart County Academy
(c. 1832)—Troup and Lamar Sts. Built to house a private academy, this structure was later converted for use as a Masonic lodge. The 2-story building is furnished with desks and benches donated from a school in Eufaula, Ala.

4. Grimes-Feagin House (1842)—Lamar and Lumpkin Sts. Built by John Grimes for his son-in-law, Henry Feagin, this 1-story, Greek Revival–style house is typical of middle-class homes of the period.

5. McDonald House (1843)—Troup St. between Lamar and Forsyth. The largest house in Westville, this elegant Greek Revival house began as a modest, 2-room cabin built near Cuthbert, Ga., by Scottish immigrant Edward McDonald. As both his wealth and the size of his family grew (Edward and his wife, Elizabeth, had seven children), McDonald completed the transformation of the cabin into this large mansion in 1859.

6. Cabinet Shop (c. 1836)—Forsyth and Troup Sts. Built by John Singer III for use as a tailoring and leather goods shop, the building was moved here from the Lumpkin town square and is furnished as a period cabinetmaker's business.

7. Shoemaker's Shop (c. 1838)—Forsyth St. Built in nearby Lumpkin by German-born immigrant Johann George Singer when his shoemaking business outgrew his house and shop next door. The second story of the shop served as lodgings for Singer's apprentices in the cobbling trade.

8. Singer House (1838)—Forsyth St. Originally built on the Lumpkin square by Johann Singer for both his residence and cobbler's shop, the house is notable for its two entrances—one for family and another for customers. The large 12-over-12–pane windows offered both light for living quarters and display space for Singer's wares. By the end of his first year in Lumpkin, Singer's business required more space, so he built the shop next door. This building was put to good use as Singer and his wife, Louisa, filled it with 11 children. Singer's son, George, apprenticed to the cobbler's trade, while another son, John, became a leather tanner and tailor (see #6).

9. Doctor's Office (c. 1845)—Troup and Forsyth Sts. Built by Dr. William L. Paullin, a physician in nearby Fort Gaines. the office is filled with period instruments, medicine bottles, and textbooks.

10. Chattahoochee County Courthouse (1854)—Troup St. This large, 2-story frame structure was the original courthouse built when Chattahoochee County was established in 1854. It was in active use until 1975. The building was relocated to Westville from its original site in Cusseta and dedicated by presidential candidate Jimmy Carter during the Westville

McDonald House, Westville

Bicentennial Celebration on July 4, 1976. Pres. Carter's great-grandfather and grandfather served as Chattahoochee County tax collector and clerk, respectively, and had offices in this building. With its original courtroom furnishings and woodwork, the building is the center for educational programs at Westville.

11. Climax Presbyterian Church (c. 1850)—Troup and Crawford Sts. This simple frame structure was built in nearby Lumpkin and served the congregation of Curry Presbyterian Church for more than 120 years. The congregation merged with Bainbridge Presbyterian Church in 1970 and donated this old church building to Westville at that time.

12. Rawson House (c. 1850)— Troup and Cuthbert Sts. Built by William Rawson, the house now serves as the manse for the adjacent Presbyterian church. It houses Westville administrative offices and is not open to the public.

13. Bryan-Worthington House (c. 1831)—Troup and Cuthbert Sts. Furnished to represent the house of the owner of the cotton-ginning business across Cuthbert St., the house was originally constructed in rural Stewart County by cotton planter Loverd Bryan. A notable feature of the 2-story, Plantation Plain–style house is the Federal-style portico.

14. Bagley Gin House (c. 1840s)— Cuthbert St. The building houses the

195

equipment necessary for successful cotton harvesting and marketing. The cotton gin (engine) removed seeds and husks from the raw cotton, and the screw press compressed the fibers into 600-lb. bales ready for transport to the market in nearby Columbus. The cotton gin building was constructed near Cusseta by plantation owner William Bagley.

15. Pioneer Log Cabins (c. 1820s) —Berrien and Clarke Sts. These rough-hewn wooden structures represent the primitive houses built by the region's earliest white settlers. Typically, these cabins served as temporary shelter while the family built a more permanent house.

16. Patterson-Marett Farmhouse and Outbuildings (c. 1850)—Clarke St. The living areas of this simple log structure with its clapboard addition are separated by a breezeway often called a "possum-trot" or "dog-run." The house is oriented to capture summer breezes and hold warmth in winter. The surrounding outbuildings and equipment include a pantry, mule barn, cane mill, syrup kettle, and whiskey still. The complex represents the rugged, self-sufficient life of a rural farmer of a century-and-a-half ago.

17. Wells House (c. 1825)—Clarke and Cuthbert Sts. The oldest house in the village, it was built by a Yuchi Indian family near Buena Vista. Following the Indian removal in the 1830s, it was acquired by the Wells family who occupied it for more than a century.

18. Kiser House (c. 1850s)— Berrien St. between Clark and Gilmer. Relocated from Marietta, this cottage with its wide front porch has been restored as the village's restaurant, serving authentic Southern cooking.

19. Blacksmith Shop (c. 1850)— Crawford and Gilmer Sts. A small town could not survive without a blacksmith. Here, the smith would manufacture and repair farm tools and household items of all kinds.

20. Carriage Shelter (c. 1850)— Gilmer St. The shed protects the wagons and carriages used at Westville. Included in the collection of horse- or mule-drawn vehicles are a fine black carriage once owned by Gov. George Towns and a packet that once hauled the mail between Gainesville and Dahlonega.

21. Adams Store (c. 1850)—Gilmer and Forsyth Sts. Built as a stagecoach stop near Lumpkin, the building served as a travelers' rest, general store, and local gathering place.

22. Lawson House (c. 1835)— Forsyth and Clarke Sts. Originally erected as a simple log cabin in rural Stewart County by Davenport and Margaret Lawson, the rough wood has been covered with clapboard. The house is notable for the fine quality of its workmanship.

23. Yellow Creek Tabernacle (1840)—Clarke St. This shed-roofed, open-sided building was constructed for religious camp meetings and was originally located at the Yellow Creek Campground in Hall County. Camp meetings were popular annual events in the antebellum South that usually took place in late summer and lasted a week or more. Families would travel from many miles away, set up camps around the tabernacle, and spend their days and evenings hearing preachers, listening to religious music, and singing hymns.

24. Moye-White House (c. 1840) —Gilmer and Lamar Sts. Considered the finest Greek Revival–style house in Westville, the structure was relocated to the village from its original site near Cuthbert, where it was the main house for a 3,000-acre plantation. In the 1880s, the rear portion of the house was moved and used by the owners as rental property. In 1970 the Moye family donated the front half of the house to Westville, and they donated the rear half a decade later. The two halves are now connected by a breezeway.

25. Potter's Mill and Shop (c. 1850s)—Gilmer and Lamar Sts. Another essential tradesman in 19th-century rural communities, the potter made jugs, pitchers, churns, tableware, bricks, and other important items for everyday life. This complex of buildings, assembled from sites around rural Stewart County, includes a pottery pug mill for mixing

clay and a wood-burning kiln for firing the completed pieces.

26. West House (c. 1850)—Gilmer and Irwin Sts. Included in Col. West's extensive collection was this simple frame house that once belonged to his grandparents.

NOTES

197

CHAPTER 30

Kolomoki Mounds State Historic Park

LOCATION

Kolomoki Mounds State Historic Park is located about 85 miles south of Columbus via U.S. 27. To reach the park from I-75, exit at Tifton (exit 62) and travel west on U.S. 82/GA 520 to Albany. Turn south on GA 91, then west on GA 62 to Blakely. The park is about 6 miles north of Blakely on U.S. 27. *Information:* (229) 723-5296.

PARKING

Parking is available at the museum and at a small lot near the nature trail. A daily parking fee is charged.

BACKGROUND

The earliest evidence of mound building in the Southeastern United States dates to the rise of the Mississippian Culture around 700 C.E. This culture descended from the Hopewell Culture, which spread from the Ohio Valley, and was also strongly influenced by the Aztec people of Mexico. By 900 C.E., the Mississippian Culture had spread throughout the Lower Mississippi Valley and beyond.

The first permanent settlers arrived in the area of Kolomoki around 750 C.E., traveling inland along the Chattahoochee River and its tributaries. They gradually adopted a blend of two local Woodland subcultures— the Swift Creek of the southern Appalachians and the Florida Gulf coast–based Weeden Island. Archaeologists were able to draw this conclusion after examining pottery styles and types of other early artifacts found at the Kolomoki site.

Small settlements flourished in this area of the Chattahoochee Valley, and by 1100, they had come under strong influence of the Mississippian peoples. For the next two centuries, the social structure and organization of

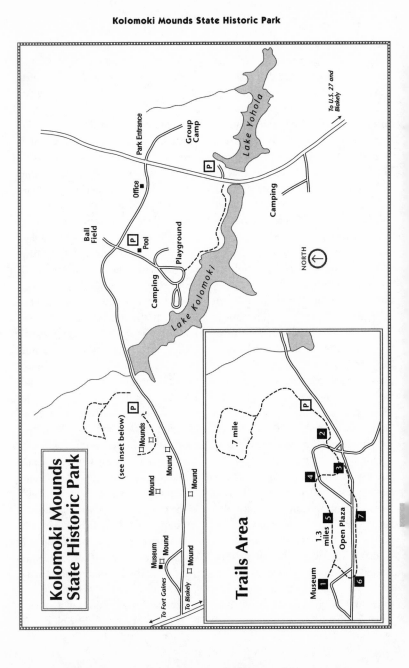

the people of Kolomoki changed dramatically. The population of the central village, never more than a few hundred inhabitants, swelled to more than 2,000 people, with an equal number living in smaller satellite farming settlements. These people were part of a regional variation of the Mississippian Culture that came to be known as the "Southern Cult."

This larger population, combined with the more elaborate religious life of the Mississippians, led to the construction of the ceremonial mounds at Kolomoki. The massive temple mound, the smaller ceremonial mounds, and the burial mounds here represent the work of a tightly knit society heavily influenced by strong religious beliefs and powerful ceremonialism. The religious and political structures were intertwined, with enormous power vested in influential clans who controlled nearly every aspect of village life.

The tremendous labor resources required to construct the temple mound and the increasingly intricate pottery and tools suggest a reliance on advanced hunting and agricultural techniques permitting relatively few people to supply the sustenance, housing, and support for all those involved in the construction work.

The burial mounds also provide clues to the religious life and social organization of the people of Kolomoki. The two large burial mounds at the site were each built as a monument to hold the remains and earthly possessions of a single individual, probably a priest-chief. The nature of the burials suggests that the people believed in some form of an afterlife. Also found in the mounds were other human remains, possibly those of servants, slaves, or spouses whose lives were sacrificed so that they might continue to accompany or serve their master after death.

Mound building did not spread further south from Kolomoki. By 1300, the village and culture had shifted to the Lamar Culture, then prevalent at Ocmulgee, and were already in decline. When the first Europeans arrived, probably Spanish explorers in the 1500s, the region's natives knew little about the mysterious mounds or the ancient people who had built them.

The first archaeological work at Kolomoki was carried out by Dr. Charles A. Woodruff in 1847. This was followed by more extensive research conducted as part of the American Ethnological Survey in the late 1800s. The most current knowledge about the mounds of Kolomoki and the area's inhabitants was the result of careful excavations of the site during the 1940s and 1950s by a team of researchers from the University of Georgia's Department of Anthropology.

The area around the Kolomoki Mounds was given to the state of

Atop one of the Kolomoki mounds

Georgia by the citizens of Early County in 1933. Scientists and historians continue to sift through the artifacts at Kolomoki, now designated a National Landmark, and other sites, interpreting the lives of these early inhabitants. In addition to the preservation of the mounds, the 1,293-acre park features a campground, picnic areas, and a wide variety of recreational facilities, including two fishing lakes, two swimming pools, and a miniature golf course.

WALK DISTANCE AND TERRAIN

From the parking area east of the temple mound, a walk from across the ancient plaza, including a climb to the top of the temple mound, is about 1.3 miles. A hike on the nearby nature trail will bring the total walk distance to about 2 miles. The plaza area is mostly level and open, while the nature trail traces a loop through a mature Southern hardwood forest. Brochures with descriptions of natural features along the trail are available at the museum.

SIGHTS ALONG THE WAY

1. Kolomoki Visitor Center/Museum—Exhibits depict our interpretation of life at Kolomoki during the era of the mound builders. Enclosed within the museum is a scientifically excavated burial mound (Mound E) just as the archaeologists left it when they completed their work in the 1950s. *Hours:* 9 A.M.–5 P.M., Tues.–Sat.; 2–5 P.M., Sun. (912) 723-5296. (After visiting the museum, you may walk or drive to the starting point of the walk, near Sight 2.)

2. Mound A, Temple Mound (c. 1100s)—Believed to be the oldest mound of its type in Georgia, this 325 ft. x 200 ft. mound is about 56 feet high. The flat top appears to be on two levels, suggesting that a ceremonial structure may have stood on the highest point. Archaeologists estimate that more than 2 million basket-loads, each holding one cubic foot of

201

earth, were required to construct the mound. Historians believe that this mound was the religious center of Kolomoki and the surrounding villages, and was the site for rituals and ceremonies. The temple mound is located at the eastern end of a large plaza that contains several smaller mounds. The plaza may have been used for gatherings and ceremonies and was likely surrounded by the thatched-wood dwellings of the village's 2,000 inhabitants.

3. Mound B (c. 1100s)—This unusual, small mound is roughly 50 feet in diameter and about 5 feet high. It contains evidence of a series of wooden posts that may have supported a pavilion or served some other unknown purpose. Pottery shards unearthed during excavations of the mounds date its construction to the Kolomoki period.

4. Mound C (c. 1100s)—Another small Kolomoki-period mound of uncertain purpose, it has roughly the same dimensions as Mound B. After excavation revealed no artifacts, some archaeologists speculated it may have simply been a pile of earth accumulated from cleaning and leveling the adjacent plaza.

5. Mound D, Burial Mound (c. 1200s)—At 20 feet in height and 100 feet in diameter, this is one of the largest and most elaborate burial mounds in the southeastern U.S. Excavations in the 1950s revealed a

treasure of artifacts including pottery, decorative beads, log supports, and both complete and partial human remains. Archaeologists have suggested that this may have been the burial mound for a ceremonial leader of the Late Kolomoki period who was interred with female companions, slaves, and "trophy" skulls of enemies. Some of the remains are intact while others appear to have been cremated. This is the most recent of all of the mounds at the site.

6. Mound F (c. 1100s)—This oval-shaped, 6-ft.-high mound contains pottery shards from the earlier Weeden Island period (c. 900–1000s C.E.), but archaeologists date construction in the later Kolomoki period. The purpose of the mound is unknown.

7. Mound H (c. 1000s)—Similar in proportion to Mound F, this mound also contains a few pottery shards that may have been dumped on the site during the mound's construction. While archaeologists are uncertain as to the purposes of Mounds F and H, they have speculated—given their proximity to Burial Mounds D and E —that they may have been constructed for funeral ceremonies.

CHAPTER 31

Albany and Chehaw Park

LOCATION

✴ Albany is about 90 miles southeast of Columbus. Travel south on U.S. 280 to GA 520. At Dawson, continue south on GA 520/U.S. 82 to Roosevelt Ave. (GA 234). Turn left and travel about 2 miles to the Thronateeska Heritage Center. *Information:* Albany Convention and Visitors Bureau, (800) 475-8700.

To reach Chehaw Park from downtown Albany, travel north about 2 miles on Jefferson St. (GA 91), crossing Liberty Expressway (U.S. 19), then turn right on Philema Rd. (continuation of GA 19). Chehaw Park will be directly ahead on the left. *Information:* (229) 430-5275.

Albany may also be reached from I-75 by exiting on GA 300 (exit 99),

south of Cordele, and traveling southwest for about 40 miles to U.S. 82. Turn right and go about 3 miles, crossing the Flint River, to Washington St. Turn right and travel about half a mile to Roosevelt Ave. and the entrance to Thronateeska Heritage Center.

PARKING

🚗 In downtown Albany, curbside parking is available at Thronateeska Heritage Center and along other city streets. At Chehaw Park, there is ample parking in the picnic area adjacent to the nature trails.

BACKGROUND

📖 Albany

Kick the dirt around Albany and you find rich, loamy, sandy soil, the remnants of the sediments laid down by an ancient, shallow sea that once covered what geologists identify as Georgia's ancient Coastal Plain. Over many millennia, the Earth's water levels have risen and fallen. In its retreat, the water left behind rolling sand dunes, some of which are still visible east of the city, nearly 50 million years removed from, and 200 miles west of, the present Atlantic Coast.

203

More than 10,000 years ago semi-nomadic groups survived by hunting wild game and fishing in the abundant rivers and streams of the area. By the time of the arrival of the first European explorers in the 1500s, people of the Yuchi Indian Tribe (part of the Creek Nation) lived near the present site of Albany. They called their village "Thronateeska," which meant "the place where flint is picked up."

In the early years of the 19th century, as settlers moved deeper into Georgia's interior, the Creek Indians were forced to cede more of their ancestral lands to the state and relocate farther to the west. Despite the fertility of the soil, the Indians held on to their lands in southwestern Georgia longer than in other sections of the state. This was probably due, in large part, to the heat, humidity, and remoteness of the region—an area viewed by many settlers as filled with marshes, impenetrable forests, and incessant malarial mosquitoes.

Despite the rigors of the climate, settlers did begin moving into the region in the early 1800s and, in 1819, engineer D. W. Porter surveyed a tract known as "Land Lot 324." In a lottery held in 1821, Gov. John Clark granted rights to this parcel of land to Orren Wiggins. It was one of the four original land lots for the future city of Albany.

The first county in the region was Baker County, chartered in 1825 and named for Revolutionary War hero Col. John Baker. The county, nestled on the Indian frontier, was the site of a major engagement, the Battle of Chickasawhachee Creek, during the Creek Indian War in 1836. At war's end, the Creeks were forced to cede all their remaining lands in Georgia and move to new homes west of the Mississippi River.

A short time after the Indian removal, land lots for a new settlement were purchased by Alexander Shotwell, a New Jersey Quaker, who commissioned a surveyor to lay out the site for an as-yet-unnamed town. That same year, Col. Nelson Tift, a Connecticut-born businessman from Augusta and later Hawkinsville, traveled by barge up the Flint River from Apalachicola, Fla., to the site of the rough, new settlement. Tift saw immediately that the village had potential and, without hesitation, he built a log home and store on the banks of the river and put down roots. A visionary, Tift believed that the community could, someday, become the commercial and industrial center for the entire region. Considering his Northeastern roots, he suggested that the town be named "Albany" for the city in New York that was itself a regional trade center on the Hudson River. In 1841, a charter was granted to the new City of Albany by the Georgia legislature.

In 1845, Tift began publishing the *Albany Patriot*, a newspaper that he circulated widely. He used the paper

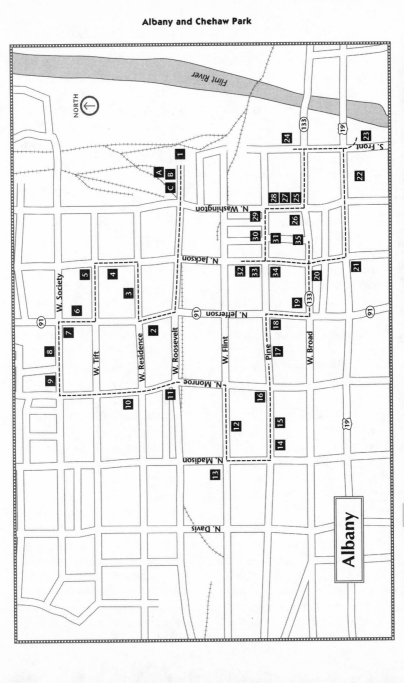

Albany

to promote the new town and debunk the widely believed stories that the southwestern Georgia climate was unhealthy. Eventually, the rich soil brought wealthy planters who developed large cotton plantations worked by thousands of slaves. For most of the planters, the climate was not an issue. They retreated to homes in northern Georgia during the summers, leaving their laborers to battle the heat, humidity, and insects.

In 1853, Dougherty County (named for Judge Charles Dougherty of Athens, Ga.) was carved out of Baker County and Albany was selected as the county seat. The city was rapidly developing into the major cotton transportation and trade center that Tift had envisioned. The Flint River waterfront bustled with traffic and the adjacent commercial district thrived with a mix of mercantile businesses and professional offices.

Ever the entrepreneur, Tift operated the first ferry across the Flint River and, in 1857 contracted with a black freedman, Horace King of Columbus, to build the first bridge across the river. Tift built the Bridge House on the western bank of the river with a central archway that led to his toll bridge. The ground floor contained Tift's office and the toll-collector's station, while the second floor housed a gaily decorated ballroom that hosted theatrical performances, masked balls, and other social events. Among the actors who performed at the Bridge House in the late 1850s was Laura Keane, who would later be on the stage at Ford's Theater in Washington, D.C., when Pres. Abraham Lincoln was assassinated.

With the outbreak of the Civil War in 1861, many of Albany's and surrounding Dougherty County's young men enlisted in the Confederate army and marched off to battlefields from Virginia to Tennessee. Back home, local plantations and farms provided cotton and food supplies to the government. Tift's Bridge House was converted into a packing plant where thousands of cattle and hogs were slaughtered, pickled, and placed in barrels to feed sailors in the Confederate Navy. Interestingly, Tift sold his goods to the Confederate government at cost, unlike many business owners, both North and South, who sought to earn enormous profits from the conflict.

After the Confederacy's defeat in 1865, Albany like so many communities across the South, found its slave-based, agricultural economy in ruins. Thousands of freed slaves still lived on the old plantations where they worked for their former owners as tenant farmers, laborers, or sharecroppers. Others flocked to Albany in search of jobs. On the surface, there appeared to be a degree of harmony between the races, but strict segregation laws enacted throughout the South in the late 19th century planted seeds of

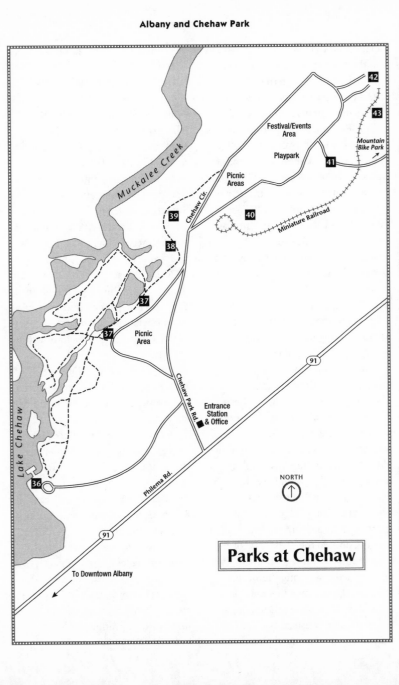

Muckalee Creek

Festival/Events
Area

Playpark

42

43

Mountain
Bike Park

41

Picnic
Areas

Chehaw Cir.

39

40

Miniature Railroad

38

37

37

Picnic
Area

91

Chehaw Park Rd.

Entrance
Station
■ & Office

Lake Chehaw

36

NORTH

Philema Rd.

91

Parks at Chehaw

To Downtown Albany

racial unrest that would thrust Albany into the national spotlight years later.

Much of southwestern Georgia rests atop rich deposits of limestone—fossilized remnants of the ancient seabed. Encased in the porous stone is a vast reservoir of fresh water, believed to be one of the largest underground aquifers in North America. This water gave a significant boost to the area's agricultural economy in 1881, when John P. Fort drilled Georgia's first artesian well just outside Albany. The well provided local citizens with fresh, pure water and offered area farmers an opportunity to tap this vast reservoir to irrigate their fields.

At about the same time, Albany began draining the surrounding marshes and floodplains that were breeding grounds for disease-bearing mosquitoes. By the 1890s, the city, like Thomasville to the south, had become a winter resort for wealthy Northern families seeking respite from the harsh weather back home. Many bought up old cotton plantations, assembling vast tracts of land that would eventually be developed as quail hunting reserves. This sport, with the development of sporting shotguns and the breeding of hunting dogs in the early years of the 20th century, became an immensely popular activity among the wealthy. While it may no longer be the sole domain of the super rich, the quail plantations of southwestern Georgia still draw many thousands of hunters each year during hunting season (October–March).

Another draw for tourists was Radium Springs, located just across the Flint River from downtown Albany. The largest natural spring in Georgia, the water bubbles up from the limestone at nearly 70,000 gallons a minute and maintains a constant year-round temperature of 68°F. Touted as both a tourist attraction and a health resort, the springs each year attracted thousands of people who came to "take the waters." In 1926, stone walls were built to encase the pools, and the elegant Radium Springs Hotel was erected to provide vacationers with luxurious accommodations. The hotel thrived for many years before falling into decline and closing in the early 1960s. The building and grounds were restored and reopened for a period of time but are currently closed.

A decade before the Great Depression gripped the nation, Albany and the surrounding farmlands were devastated by the boll weevil infestations that destroyed cotton crops across the South. Georgia farmers and the businesses that supported them found themselves in a deep, unrelenting economic recession that the rest of the country would soon share. These hard times would last until the late 1930s when the country began to gear up industrial production for World War II.

After the war, the local economy, bolstered by new agricultural crops like peanuts and pecans (Albany is now the self-proclaimed "Pecan Capital of the World"), Albany rebounded, attracting new industries and businesses to the area. At the height of the Cold War in the 1950s, the U.S. Marine Corps established a facility outside the city to coordinate the shipment of supplies and equipment to Marine units around the world. The Marine Corps Logistics Base is the county's largest employer and a key component of the local economy. Other businesses have also grown and thrived. Among these are Bob's Candies, a small company that started with the sale of pecan and peanut confections and is now the world's largest manufacturer of candy canes. Also, Miller Brewing Company, attracted by the abundance of fresh water, built a large production facility just north of the city in the 1970s.

While Albany returned to prosperity in the 1950s, the benefits to its citizens were uneven as many black citizens still struggled against discrimination. In 1961, local civil rights leaders met at Shiloh Baptist Church to form the Albany Movement, an to actively protest continued segregation and promote voter registration among local black citizens. After an Albany protest march during which nearly 500 people were arrested, the movement's leaders invited the Rev.

Martin Luther King Jr. to come to Albany. Originally planning only to preach at Mt. Zion Baptist Church, King decided to stay in Albany and join the protests. During a march in downtown Albany, King and several other Civil Rights Movement leaders were arrested and jailed for a short time. King's participation brought national media attention to the city, and eventually, brought about sweeping changes in local segregation laws. The restored Mt. Zion Church houses the Albany Civil Rights Museum profiling the powerful story of the Albany Movement and its impact on the achievement of civil rights across the nation.

Through the 1970s and 80s, Albany solidified its position as the business and cultural center of southwestern Georgia. Among the many facilities and programs fostered and developed during this time were the highly regarded Albany Museum of Art, the Albany Symphony, Theatre Albany, and the Thronateeska Heritage Center.

By the early 1990s, Albany was in the preliminary stages of a major revitalization of the downtown business district when disaster struck. On a sultry summer day in July 1994, Tropical Storm Alberto stalled over southwestern Georgia, filling the sky with dark clouds and rain. What was at first an annoyance became a catastrophe as the rain continued unabated for several days, dropping record amounts of rainfall across the region. Before long, the Flint River and its tributaries overflowed their banks and deluged the adjacent flood-plain, where many of Albany's poorest citizens lived. In a flood that a local writer described as being of "biblical magnitude," the river eventually crested at 43 feet. More than 23 square miles of Dougherty County were under water, including down-town Albany and nearby Oakview Cemetery, where long-buried caskets began to resurface and float away. Bridges across the Flint were shut down, the campus of Albany State University was inundated, and over 23,000 people were driven from their homes.

During and after the flood, called by Georgia Gov. Zell Miller, "the worst natural disaster in Georgia history," citizens of all races truly came to-gether for the first time to battle a common enemy—the rising water. In many ways, the "Great Flood of 1994" did more to foster harmony and unity within the community than any other single event in the city's history. A monument erected on the corner of Front and Oglethorpe Sts. commemo-rates the contributions of the thou-sands of volunteers who joined the efforts to save the city.

Chehaw Park

Visitors in search of a bit of the region's natural beauty, should drive a few miles north of downtown to Chehaw Park. This 800-acre public park, originally developed in the 1930s by workers from the Civilian Conservation Corps as a new state park, was later turned over to the city as a local recreation area. Today the parks at Chehaw include an acclaimed Wild Animal Park that is the state's only American Zoological Association accredited zoo in Georgia outside Atlanta, a miniature railroad called the Wiregrass Express, a campground, a BMX bicycle track and mountain biking trails, playgrounds, picnic areas, and a network of hiking trails along the shores of Chehaw Lake and Muckalee Creek.

WALK DISTANCE AND TERRAIN

The terrain is mostly level or gently rolling. The city enjoys an abundance of shading pines and live oak trees throughout the downtown walk, which traces a 3.5-mile loop through the commercial district and several century-old neighborhoods.

The nature trails at Chehaw Park provide a walk of about 2 miles, a dis-tance that may be doubled if you take a round-trip stroll along the shaded park loop road to visit the Wild An-imal Park. The nature trails are laid out in loops off of a main path and are blazed with different colors of paint. Park maps, including a layout of the trails, are available at the entrance station.

SIGHTS ALONG THE WAY

 Downtown Albany

1. Thronateeska Heritage Center (1910)—100 Roosevelt Ave. Built as Albany's railroad passenger depot, this long, single-story, red-brick structure features elements of the Prairie style popularized by noted architect Frank Lloyd Wright. (NR) At the time of its construction, the depot and surrounding businesses bustled with passengers arriving or departing on more than 30 trains a day. Passenger rail service to Albany ceased many years ago, and the depot closed in 1971. A few years later, the complex was acquired by the Thronateeska Heritage Foundation, a nonprofit organization dedicated to preserving the history of Albany and southwestern Georgia. Among the facilities here are the Discovery Depot History Museum, the Wetherbee Planetarium, and the Children's Discovery Center. The complex includes several historic buildings, some moved to this location from other parts of the city. Among them are:

A. Tift Warehouse (c. 1859)—Albany's first railway depot, this building was converted for use as a storage building for Tift Grocery.

B. Wetherbee Planetarium (c. 1900s)—The planetarium is located in the former Railway Express Agency office. For times of planetarium shows: (912) 432-6955.

C. Hilsman Kitchen (c. 1850s)—Once an outbuilding of a 19th-century home, it now serves as an office.

D. The Jarrard House (c. 1850s), believed to be the oldest existing house in Albany, has been relocated to the complex from its original site on Broad Ave. and is awaiting restoration.

Heritage Center hours: 10 A.M.–4 P.M., Mon.–Fri.; 12–4 P.M., Sat.

2. Patterson House (1871)—415 Jefferson St. Built by local foundry owner Thomas Patterson, this residence features ornate metalwork on the porch that was produced in his factory. The house now serves as attorneys' offices.

3. St. Theresa's Roman Catholic Church (c. 1861)—313 Residence Ave. Construction of this simple, brick Gothic-style church was begun with slave labor in 1859, and the exterior was finished in 1860. According to local lore, interior plaster work had just begun in January 1861 when word came that Georgia had seceded from the Union. Plasterer Thomas Churchill immediately put down his trowel and enlisted in the Confederate army, and the church remained unfinished until after the war ended. During the war the building was used as a hospital. St. Theresa's is the oldest Catholic Church in continuous use in Georgia. NR

4. J. W. Gillespie House (1896)—509 Jackson St. One of the city's most elegant Victorian homes, this 3-story house features two porches,

211

a square tower, and ornate woodwork. The house was built by A. W. Muse as a wedding gift to his daughter, Mary Muse Gillespie.

5. Charles Tift House (c. 1885)— 603 Jackson St. Charles Tift, brother of Albany's founder Nelson Tift, built this large home after moving to the city from Florida. According to local lore, when the Tift family moved out many years ago, the original surveyor's chains used to lay out the town, were found in the attic. The house is currently undergoing restoration.

6. Woolfolk House (c. 1880s)— 604 Jefferson St. The longtime home of Nelson Tift's daughter Clara and her husband, T. N. Woolfolk, the residence later served as a music school.

7. Dr. William L. Davis House (1892)—611 Jefferson St. Built by Col. Ed White, a former Confederate officer and early mayor of Albany, this large, white brick house was later purchased by Dr. Davis, one of the founding physicians of nearby Phoebe Putney Hospital.

8. Parker-Malone House (c. 1880s)—407 Society Ave. Built by Knott Parker, this was later the home of Dougherty County judge Hudson Malone. The gables and ornate woodwork are notable architectural features.

9. Spence House (c. 1890s)— 425 Society Ave. Built by the Arthur family, this large, white frame Victorian house was purchased by Judge W. N. Spence in 1919.

10. Mamie Brosnan School (1915)—601 Monroe St. This large, red-brick schoolhouse was named for a popular teacher of the day. The facility now houses the Oak Tree

Wild Animal Park in Parks at Chehaw

educational program for disadvantaged children.

11. Vason Jones House (c. 1850s)—405 Monroe St. This New Orleans–influenced Greek Revival house was acquired in 1947 and completely restored by renowned, Albany-born architect Edward Vason Jones, designer of the American Wing of the Metropolitan Museum of Art in New York, the Diplomatic Reception Room at the U.S. State Department, and various projects at the White House.

12. Capt. William Smith House (1860)—516 Flint Ave. The first brick house erected in Albany, this handsome 2-story home with columned portico and Italianate detailing was built from bricks hauled by wagon from Macon. The house had several advanced features for its day including an indoor water system supplied by attic reservoirs. Smith was a local civic leader, Confederate officer and legislator, and later a Georgia state senator. The house is now owned by the Albany Junior League. *NR*

13. Albany Academy Building (1919)—601 Flint Ave. Albany's first public school, Albany Academy, opened on this site in 1886. That structure burned in 1888 and was rebuilt. The present masonry and sandstone brick building was constructed as a replacement and now houses school system administrative offices.

14. Keaton House (c. 1860)—526 Pine Ave. This large frame house, notable for its second-story columned portico, is now an antiques shop.

15. Theatre Albany (1857)—514 Pine Ave. Built by Martha Ryals as a gift to her son, Newton Brinson, the large Neoclassical-style mansion was acquired by Capt. John Davis in 1860. Davis entertained former Confederate Pres. Jefferson Davis in the home in 1888, and a chair occupied by the executive is now on display. For many years, the house served as a Masonic lodge until it was given to the Albany Little Theatre Company for use as a performing arts center. Renamed "Theatre Albany" in the 1990s, the company continues to put on productions in an enlarged auditorium skillfully attached to the back of the house. *Information:* (912) 439-7193. *NR*

16. Pray House (1905)—501 Pine Ave. This large, Victorian Gothic–style home was built by John Pray, cofounder of the Citizens National Bank in Albany.

17. Cochran-Morrison House (c. 1860)—422 Pine Ave. Considered a superb example of the transition between the Federal and Victorian eras of architecture, this carefully preserved 1-story cottage displays elements of the Greek Revival and Italianate styles. The ornately carved woodwork of the full-length front porch is notable.

18. First Baptist Church (c. 1890s)—400 Pine Ave. One of the oldest religious congregations in Albany, the

213

church was organized in 1839 and began meeting on this site in 1844. The present Gothic Revival–style church is notable for its stained glass.

19. Old Federal Building and Post Office (1912)—345 W. Broad Ave. Designed in the Renaissance Revival style, this sandstone brick building features polished oak interior woodwork. Postmistress Nellie Brimberry, the first woman to hold that post in a major U.S. city, served here for many years. A new courthouse building is scheduled to open in 2001 at Broad Ave. and Washington St. This structure will continue to serve as a community center. *NR*

20. Farkas House (1889)—328 W. Broad Ave. This large, French Second Empire–style house, with its distinctive mansard roof and elegant ironwork, was built by local businessman Samuel Farkas. *NR*

21. Ritz Cultural Center (c. 1930)—225 Jackson St. Originally built as a movie house, the theater was restored and reopened in 1991 as a multipurpose cultural center for Albany-area youth. The facility includes an auditorium, exhibit area, gallery, and classrooms. *Gallery hours:* 9 A.M.–6 P.M., Mon.–Fri. (912) 889-1473.

22. James H. Gray Civic Center (1988)—100 W. Oglethorpe Blvd. This modern facility, the largest of its kind in southwestern Georgia, features a 10,000-seat performing arts center and a large exhibition space for conventions and trade shows. *Information:* (912) 430-5200.

23. Veterans Park and Amphitheater (1988)—200 Front St. Carved into a wooded hillside above the Flint River, this green space commemorates area residents who saw military service during the nation's wars. The 1,200-seat outdoor amphitheater is a popular venue for festivals, plays, and concerts.

24. Bridge House (1853)—112 N. Front St. This whitewashed brick building was constructed by Nelson Tift to serve as his office and the entrance to his toll bridge across the Flint River. The theater on the second floor was the social center of early Albany. Note the now-sealed brick arch that was once the entrance to the bridge. During the Civil War, this building served as a meat-packing plant for the Confederate navy. *NR*

25. Exchange Building (c. 1900s)—100 S. Washington St. At the time of its construction, this 6-story tower was one of the largest office buildings in southwestern Georgia. *NR*

26. C. B. King Federal Courthouse (2000)—Washington St. at Broad Ave. A significant part of the revitalization of Albany's downtown district, this new stone and glass complex will replace the 1912 courthouse a few blocks west on Broad Ave. It is named for an early leader of the Albany Civil Rights Movement.

27. Mayer-Cline-Brown Building (1886)—112–116 Washington St.

Built of multitextured red brick and stone, this 3-story office building may be considered Albany's first "skyscraper." The mixed pattern of arches is a notable architectural feature.

28. The *Albany Herald* Building (c. 1900s)—128–130 Washington St. Built as a department store, this Renaissance Revival–style building, with its distinctive arched windows, has served as home to Albany's daily newspaper for many years.

29. Gordon Hotel Building (1925) —205–209 Pine Ave. Only two blocks from the railway depot, this 6-story structure was one of Albany's two major hotels for many years. In 1978, the building was converted for use as offices for local government. Note the painted, terra-cotta designs along the exterior roofline.

30. Dougherty County Courthouse and Judicial Center (1966)— 225 Pine Ave. This large, sandstone brick building houses county government offices and courtrooms.

31. Government Center (1992)— 222 Pine Ave. Directly across from the courthouse, this modern glass-and-brick tower houses additional city and county offices. The construction of this building in the early 1990s marked the beginning of downtown Albany's renewal movement.

32. Old Carnegie Library (1906)— 215 N. Jackson St. One of the many public libraries around the nation erected through the philanthropy of industrialist Andrew Carnegie, this attractive Neoclassical building served as Albany's main library for more than 70 years. It has been restored as offices for the Albany Area Arts Council. The building is open to the public. *Hours:* 9 A.M.–5 P.M., Mon.–Fri. (912) 439-2787. *NR*

33. Municipal Auditorium (1916, restored 1990)—200 N. Jackson St. The cultural heart of Albany for more than three-quarters of a century, this large, red-brick building also served as a shelter for hundreds of families whose homes were destroyed in a devastating 1940 tornado, and as a popular USO venue for World War II soldiers training nearby. The restored 965-seat theater is home to the Albany Symphony and Chorale and is a regular venue for productions by Theatre Albany and the Albany Ballet. *Information:* (912) 430-5200. *NR*

34. Dougherty County Library (1985)—300 Pine Ave. Occupying a restored automobile dealership building, this large facility replaced the old Carnegie Library located a block north on Jackson St.

35. Albany Chamber of Commerce and Welcome Center (1915)—225 W. Broad Ave. The directors of the Citizens First National Bank envisioned a 7-story "skyscraper" as their signature headquarters, but cost estimates were prohibitively high and they settled on this elegant, 2-story Greek Revival building designed by

215

renowned Atlanta architect A. Ten Eyck Brown. In 1940, it became Albany's first air-conditioned building. In 1990, the building was acquired by the Albany Chamber of Commerce and carefully restored. The interior is notable for its vaulted ceiling and beautiful murals. *Hours:* 8:30 A.M.–5 P.M., Mon.–Fri. (800) 475-8700.

Chehaw Park

The nature trail begins a short distance past the park entrance station behind the playground and picnic area on the right. *Hours:* 9 A.M.–dusk, daily. (229) 430-5275.

36. Boat Dock—Adjacent to a picnic area, this dock is a place for fishing or launching small boats on Lake Chehaw.

37. Site of CCC Structures (c. 1930s)—A solitary chimney and a low stone wall and steps are evidence of the work performed here by workers from the Civilian Conservation Corps during the Depression.

38. Staff Office Building (c. 1930s)—This small, cabinlike structure was built for the original state park.

39. Creekside Education Center (2000)—With porches and balconies overlooking the nature trails and the waters of Muckalee Creek, this large facility serves as a state-of-the-art outdoor education center for both youth and adult programs.

40. BMX Bicycle Track—With its hills and banked curves, this compact track is a popular venue for local bicycle competitions.

41. RV Area and Campground—In the shade of loblolly pines and live oaks, this facility offers full hook-up spaces for trailers, motor-homes, and tent campers.

42. Wild Animal Park—Set in a shaded location along the creek banks and floodplain, Chehaw's Wild Animal Park was laid out by well-known naturalist and Albany native Jim Fowler (star of *Mutual of Omaha's Wild Kingdom*) and features habitats for such wildlife as bald eagles, African elephants, monkeys, cheetahs, and American black bears. Other facilities in the park include a reptile and small-animal house, a gift shop, snack bar, and picnic area. *Hours:* 9 A.M.–6 P.M., daily.

43. Wiregrass Express Train—This miniature train travels a loop from the zoo area through other parts of the park. Tickets available at the Zoo station. Seasonal.

NOTES

Thomasville

historical and architectural treasure set in a forest of pines and live oaks. The city's broad avenues, flower-filled parks, and elegant antebellum and Victorian homes make it an ideal place to explore on foot.

For the first half-century after the city's founding in 1831 as the seat of Thomas County (named for Gen. Jett Thomas, a hero of the War of 1812), Thomasville was an agricultural center surrounded by the fertile fields of vast cotton plantations worked by thousands of slaves. Before the coming of the railroads to the city in the late 1850s, the harvested cotton was hauled by wagon from the isolated community to Tallahassee, Fla., and on to ports on the Gulf of Mexico.

LOCATION

Thomasville is about 150 miles southeast of Columbus via U.S. 280, GA 55, and U.S. 82 to Albany, then south from Albany on U.S. 19. Thomasville may also be reached by traveling west from I-75 at Valdosta via U.S. 84/GA 38 (exit 16). *Information:* Thomasville Tourism Authority, (800) 704-2350; www.thomasville.com.

PARKING

There are commercial lots and metered curbside parking in the downtown area.

BACKGROUND

 Tucked deep in southwest Georgia, Thomasville is an

From the outset, Thomasville was marked by fine homes, many designed by English architect and master builder John Wind, who came to the area in the 1840s to design and build the plantation of early settler Jefferson Jackson Marsh. Wind remained in Thomasville for more than a decade designing plantation homes, townhouses, and the elegant Thomas County Courthouse, all notable for their classical styling. Because Thomasville was spared destruction during the Civil War, many of these structures still stand.

217

The region's plantation economy was almost solely dependent on slave labor, so the area's young men rushed to join the Confederate army after Georgia seceded from the Union in early 1861, enthusiastic to protect their way of life from outside interference. They quickly formed military companies with such colorful names as the Dixie Boys and the Thomas Dragoons. Of the 1,600 men from Thomasville and surrounding Thomas County who marched off to war, nearly a third never returned.

While Thomasville was spared from combat during the Civil War (Union troops did not occupy the city until May 8, 1865), local citizens got a close-up look at the war's horrors when 5,000 prisoners from Andersonville were temporarily relocated to the city in early December 1864 to prevent their liberation by Gen. William T. Sherman's invading Union army.

With the war's end and the emancipation of the slaves, the region's plantation agricultural system was destroyed, leaving both owners and former slaves in a desperate situation. Many former slaves remained on the land working for wages or as tenant farmers and sharecroppers. With patience and perseverance, they struggled to forge a new place for themselves in Southern society.

One former Thomasville-area slave became a true pioneer and hero. Henry O. Flipper became the first black to attend the U.S. Military Academy at West Point. Despite severe racial abuse from fellow cadets, Flipper graduated in 1877 and served as a cavalry officer on the Western frontier (one of the famed "Buffalo Soldiers," as the Indians called the black troops). In 1880, Flipper was charged by a white officer with embezzlement, court-martialed, and dishonorably discharged from the army. The charges later proved to be racially motivated and untrue, but Flipper died in 1940 with this tarnish on his record. In 1978, Flipper's body was relocated from Atlanta to Thomasville and buried at Magnolia Cemetery with full military honors. Two decades later, Pres. Bill Clinton gave Flipper a posthumous pardon. To commemorate Lt. Flipper, students at West Point give the Flipper Award each year to the cadet who has displayed the most courage and perseverance in the face of adversity.

While cotton still contributed to the revitalization of the area's postwar economy, Thomasville found another, even more lucrative, path to prosperity—tourism. Shortly after the war, local physician Dr. T. S. Hopkins began promoting the city as a health resort. Citing the therapeutic benefits of the area's mild climate and fresh air, he published a pamphlet called "Thomasville as a Winter Home for Invalids," which was distributed throughout the North. By the

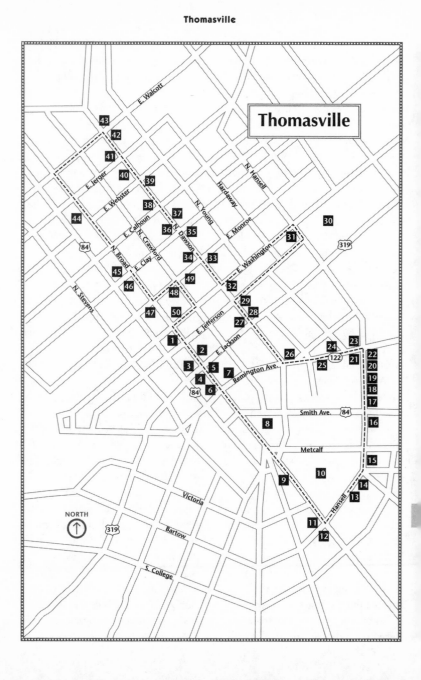

Thomasville

mid-1870s, Thomasville was entertaining several hundred tourists each winter, including many Union veterans who recalled the pleasant climate from the March Through Georgia with Gen. Sherman in 1864. A decade later, winter visitors more than doubled the resident population (from 5,500 to more than 12,000), and the city's renowned "Hotel Era" began. Within a few years, ten large hotels and more than two dozen boarding houses offered visitors comfortable, sometimes luxurious, accommodations and fine dining. Possibly the most elegant was the Queen Anne–style Piney Woods Hotel, whose name belied its luxurious amenities that included an Otis elevator, suites with private baths, a bowling alley, billiards, and tennis courts.

While many winter visitors were content to stay in hotels, some of the wealthiest built grand Victorian "cottages" along city lanes or purchased antebellum plantations, turning them into opulent estates. By the end of the 19th century, Thomasville was the winter playground of some of America's wealthiest businessmen, industrialists, celebrities, and politicians. The prosperity rubbed off on local businessmen who grew wealthy satisfying the needs of their Northern guests, and many built homes that equaled those of the visitors in their elegance. While the Northerners were always treated cordially, memories of

the Civil War were still fresh. Along Hansell St., Northerners built their homes on the west side of the street and locals built on the east side. Many in town still refer to Hansell St. as Thomasville's "Mason-Dixon Line."

Tourism peaked in the early 1900s, then virtually disappeared with the development of resort communities further south in Florida. By the time of the First World War, Thomasville had returned to the ways of a sleepy Southern town. Many wealthy owners of plantations around Thomasville, however, stayed and developed their holdings into hunting preserves with vast wooded tracts that were ideal grounds for raising game birds such as ducks and quail. Sports enthusiasts from around the world continue to come to Thomasville for sport shooting.

The region's climate offers a long growing season, and the city is awash in color nearly all year—much of it coming from the many varieties of roses that thrive in the mild climate and rich soil. In the early 1900s, county home demonstration agent Lilla Forest won a $25 prize in a competition and decided to use the money to develop a flower show in Thomasville. Forest, along with Mrs. W. M. Harris, founder of the Thomasville Garden Club, and Sam Hjort, co-founder of Thomasville Nurseries, was instrumental in staging the first Thomasville Rose Festival in 1922.

The event, held each April, has grown larger and more popular each year. Never resting on their laurels, researchers continue to experiment with new varieties of flowers at the Rose Test Gardens near downtown. Today Thomasville proudly claims the title "Rose Capital of the World."

WALK DISTANCE AND TERRAIN

The walk route from the Thomas County Courthouse forms a 4-mile loop. The terrain is mostly level with sidewalks along many streets and an abundance of shade trees.

SIGHTS ALONG THE WAY

1. Thomas County Courthouse (c. 1858)—N. Broad St. Set on the highest point in southwestern Georgia (330 feet above sea level), this stately 3-story Greek Revival building, designed by John Wind, is topped with an ornate clock tower. *NR*

2. Izzo's Pharmacy (c. 1890)—122 N. Broad St. A trio of arched windows and a patterned belt course are the outstanding architectural details of this late 19th-century pharmacy. Locals still flock to the soda fountain for sodas and milkshakes.

3. Neel's Department Store (c. 1883)—101 N. Broad St. The store incorporates portions of the Mitchell House Hotel, the only one of the fine hotel buildings that still exists. The

best view of the original part of the building is from the rear parking area.

4. Thomas Drug Store (c. 1869)—108 S. Broad St. Located in one of the oldest commercial buildings in Thomasville, Thomas Drug has been in operation since 1881. Prescriptions from this pharmacy have been filled for such notables as Presidents William McKinley and Dwight Eisenhower and the English Duke of Windsor. The building was badly damaged in a 1982 fire but has been restored.

5. The Gift Shop (c. 1885)—103 S. Broad St. Believed to be the work of architect T. J. P. Rommerdall, architect of the eccentric Lapham-Patterson House (see #39), this building reflects some of the same mix of unusual design features and styles. Especially striking is the bay window over the store entrance.

6. Jerger-Johnson Jewelers (c. 1884)—130 S. Broad St. Established in 1857, Jergers is the oldest continuously operating business in Thomasville. The attractive, brick Victorian building has long been a Broad St. landmark. Especially noteworthy are the beautiful cherrywood display cabinets, which are original.

7. WPAX Radio Station (1930)—117 Remington Ave. WPAX is the third-oldest station in Georgia and the twentieth oldest in the nation. Founder Hoyt Wimpy also built and sold radios so that locals would listen

221

to his station. One of Wimpy's early sound trucks was used by Franklin D. Roosevelt for a speech in Warm Springs during the 1932 presidential campaign.

8. Site of Piney Woods Hotel (c. 1885)—Dawson and Broad Sts., north of Paradise Park. The most luxurious accommodations in town during Thomasville's "Hotel Era," the Piney Woods stretched more than 400 feet across the front and featured long porches and decorative towers. The hotel burned in 1906.

9. Neel House (1907)—502 S. Broad St. This stately Neoclassical-style house was built by Elijah Leon Neel, founder of Neel's Department Store. As teenagers, Elijah Neel and his brother, John, left Thomasville to serve in the Confederate army. They both survived to return and build their fortunes. This was, for many years, the family home of Marguerite Neel Williams, a founder of the Georgia Trust for Historic Preservation and a driving force in the preservation movement both in Georgia and in the nation. The house has been adapted for use as a restaurant.

10. Paradise Park (1889)—Bordered by S. Broad, S. Hansell, and Metcalf Sts. This 26-acre wooded park, crisscrossed by trails, was purchased by the city from Dr. Alex Smith for $500 an acre. It was a popular gathering place for guests who stayed in the luxury hotels nearby. The park was so popular with Northern visitors that locals referred to it as "Yankee Paradise." John Philip Sousa's band once performed in the park's Strawbridge Bandstand.

11. Bailey-Willett House (1900)—110 W. Hansell St. Built for the Bailey family of Boston, Mass., this was the first house constructed on this block. Especially notable are the Palladian-style windows flanking the front entrance portico.

12. Strawbridge House (1899)—704 S. Broad St. Built for Justus Strawbridge, a Philadelphia, Pa., clothier who wintered in Thomasville for many years. The Strawbridge family were active in local affairs and donated the bandstand in Paradise Park.

13. Forbes Cottage (1891)—717 E. Hansell St. Designed in the Queen Anne style, this shingled structure is reminiscent of an English country cottage.

14. Charles Hebard House (1899)—711 E. Hansell St. Called "Park Front" when it was built, because it faced Paradise Park, this imposing, 19,000-sq.-ft. Neoclassical-style house was built for Hebard, a lumber company owner from the upper Midwest. After wintering in Thomasville for a few years, Hebard purchased vast tracts of the Okefenokee Swamp and harvested many of its rich stands of cypress trees. A notable interior feature of the home is a large second-story ballroom.

15. Charles S. Hebard House (1899)—701 E. Hansell St. Built by Hebard for his son, the house was designed to resemble the barges that carried lumber across the Great Lakes. Consequently, it was nicknamed "Steamboat." A distinctive feature of the house is the 2-story rounded front porch. The large dormers are modern additions.

16. State Farmer's Market—502 Smith Ave. This second-largest (after Atlanta) fresh produce market in the Southeast offers a rich variety of regional fruits and vegetables in season. The Market Diner, featuring fresh produce prepared country style, is a local favorite. *Market hours:* 8 A.M.–5 P.M., Mon.–Sat. (912) 225-4072.

17. All Saints Episcopal Church (1881)—443 S. Hansell St. Originally constructed to serve the local Roman Catholic congregation, this quaint Queen Anne and Colonial Revival– style sanctuary is the oldest existing church in Thomasville. Slated for demolition in the 1970s, the building was instead moved to this site and preserved by Thomasville Landmarks. When it was still a Catholic church, Jacqueline Kennedy attended services here while recovering at a nearby planta-

All Saints Episcopal Church

tion from the assassination of Pres. Kennedy in 1963.

18. Balfour House (1900)—435 S. Hansell St. This eclectic Neoclassical residence features a pedimented bay on one side and a rounded, 2-story porch on the other. The original owner, R. C. Balfour, was the proprietor of a Thomasville saloon and a crate-manufacturing company.

19. Augustin Hansell House (c. 1853)—429 S. Hansell St. One of the oldest existing homes in Thomasville, the house was designed by John Wind for Judge Augustin Hansell. Hansell served as a delegate to Georgia's Secession Convention in

223

Milledgeville in 1861 *and* as a delegate to the convention that voted to rejoin the Union after the Civil War. *NR*

20. James Watt House (1893)— 421 S. Hansell St. Originally topped with an ornate tower, this Victorian home was built by Watt, the owner of hardware stores in Thomasville and several surrounding communities. Some historians believe Watt's may have been the first hardware chain in Georgia and possibly the nation.

21. David Harrell House (c. 1853) —420 S. Hansell St. The original structure was a small cottage that faced Remington Ave. When a portion of the property was sold, the house was expanded and the front entrance moved to its present location facing Hansell St.

22. Bruce-Driver House (1885)— 403 S. Hansell St. A frame Victorian house with large front porch, the structure was the residence of Dr. Bruce, a local physician who tragically drowned trying to ford a rain-swollen stream in his buggy after visiting a patient during an outbreak of typhoid fever.

23. Paxton House (1884)— 445 Remington Ave. This Victorian Gothic house with a central tower was built for Col. J. W. Paxton, a winter resident from West Virginia. The house is now a bed-and-breakfast inn.

24. Burbank Cottage (c. 1875)— 437 Remington Ave. Built for Evelyn Burbank, a winter resident from Wisconsin, this quaint Victorian cottage is

one of the most photographed buildings in town.

25. John Dyson House (c. 1854)— 406 Remington Ave. Built as a honeymoon cottage, the house was once flanked by giant magnolias planted by Dyson and his bride. The twin trees fell together in a 1985 storm.

26. Ransom Reid House (c. 1857) —331 Remington Ave. Built with slave labor, the house was renovated in the Classical Revival style at the turn of the 20th century.

27. First Presbyterian Church (1889)—Dawson and Jackson Sts. Pres. Dwight Eisenhower attended this rough-hewn brick and stone, Romanesque Revival sanctuary when he visited Thomasville on golf and hunting trips.

28. Hawkins House (1891)— 108 N. Dawson St. This house and the Ball house next door are almost identical in design. The builder of this house liked the style of the adjacent house and asked permission from the owner to copy it.

29. Ball House (1889)—116 N. Dawson St. This house became one of the first in Thomasville to be connected to the city water system when its owner requested permission to tap into the pipes behind his home that supplied water to the nearby Piney Woods Hotel.

30. Thomasville Cultural Center (1915)—600 E. Washington St. The former East Side Public School building was saved from demolition and adapted for use as the community's cultural and performing arts center. It houses a 500-seat auditorium, library, gallery space, studios, and classrooms. *Hours:* 9 A.M.–5 P.M., Mon.–Fri.; 1–5 P.M., Sat.–Sun. (912) 226-0588.

31. Joanne Woodward House (1925)—528 E. Washington St. This comfortable Craftsman-style house was the childhood home of the Academy Award–winning actress. Woodward made her acting debut in a play at nearby East Side School.

32. Royal Miller House (1903)—216 N. Dawson St. This Classical Revival–style house was patterned after Greenwood Plantation, a Thomas County mansion that many believe was the inspiration for "Twelve Oaks" in Margaret Mitchell's novel *Gone with the Wind.*

33. Ephraim Ponder House (c. 1856)—324 N. Dawson St. A large Classical Revival antebellum home, the building was constructed to serve as the dormitory for Young's Female College, a school for the wealthy daughters of local plantation owners. It was later converted to a private residence and purchased by Ephraim Ponder, who owned the Flipper family of slaves, one of whom, Henry, was the first black graduate from West Point. *NR*

34. Seixas House (c. 1835)—403 N. Dawson St. A simple, raised cottage, this is the oldest 1-story house in Thomasville. A few years ago, the house was threatened with demolition. It was relocated and restored by Thomasville Landmarks and is now used for office space.

35. Brown-Cooper House (1885)—420 N. Dawson St. Built from a prefabricated kit assembled on the site, this house was placed on the extreme right side of the property. The owners planned to expand the house but never did, so locals have long referred to it as the "Half House."

36. B. P. Walker House (1884)—503 N. Dawson St. Once an ornate Victorian, this house was remodeled with simpler lines several years ago.

37. Hardaway House (c. 1856)—522 N. Dawson St. Designed by John Wind, this Classical Revival house was built for Thomasville's first mayor. The structure is now owned by the Colonial Dames and is used as a special events facility.

38. Ainsworth House (1882)—603 N. Dawson St. Ainsworth owned the largest livery stable in Thomasville. The city's first telephone system connected the stable with the Mitchell House Hotel so that carriages could be summoned to pick up arriving hotel guests at the railway station.

39. Lapham-Patterson House (1885)—626 N. Dawson St. Winter visitor Charles W. Lapham, a shoe manufacturer from Chicago, Ill., built this rambling Queen Anne–style

225

house for the then-enormous sum of $45,000. Very modern for its time, the house featured gas lights, hot and cold running water, indoor plumbing, and numerous closets. Lapham survived the Great Chicago Fire of 1871 and remained deathly afraid of being trapped by fire. To allay his fears, he had the house built with 45 exterior doors. By the 1960s, the house had fallen into disrepair. It was acquired by the city, with the help of Thomasville Landmarks, in 1970 and later deeded to the state, restored, and opened to visitors as a state historic site. *Hours:* 9 A.M.–5 P.M., Tues.–Sat.; 2–5:30 P.M., Sun. (912) 226-0405. *NL*

40. Thomas County Historical Society and Museum (1923)—725 N. Dawson St. Exhibits, artifacts, and restored buildings tell the story of Thomasville and its surrounding area. The main building, constructed in 1923, replaced an original 1893 structure that burned. A single-lane bowling alley survived the fire and is believed to be the oldest in Georgia. *Hours:* 10 A.M.–12 P.M., Mon.–Sat.; 2–5 P.M., Sun. (229) 226-7664.

41. Stevens-Butler House (c. 1857)—803 N. Dawson St. This Classical-style house was used for many years as a winter rental cottage for Northern visitors.

42. Hanna-McKinley House (1883)—830 N. Dawson St. An elegant Victorian Renaissance Revival–style house, it was the winter residence for

many years of Ohio industrialist Mark Hanna. Hanna was influential in national politics and at a gathering in this house in 1896, William McKinley was offered the Republican nomination for the presidency. McKinley promised to make a return visit to Thomasville if he was elected and was again a guest of Hanna's in 1899. During the visit, locals referred to the Hanna residence as the "White House of the Nation."

43. Eaton House (c. 1856)—912 N. Dawson St. This Classical Revival–style house with its large central portico was originally a much smaller, slave-built cottage.

44. Old City Cemeteries (c. 1850s–present)—N. Broad at Webster Sts. The northernmost burial ground is Magnolia Cemetery, one of the city's oldest burial grounds for blacks. A state historical marker notes the location of the grave of Lt. Henry Flipper. Just south of Magnolia Cemetery is the Old Thomasville Cemetery, the city's earliest public burial ground; the earliest interments date to the 1840s.

45. Amason House (1910)—503 N. Broad St. This large, Classical Revival–style house was constructed with distinctive local materials.

46. First United Methodist Church (1885)—425 N. Broad St. The original, wooden church on this site was used as a hospital during the Civil War. The present, Victorian Gothic sanctuary is the third church on the site. Pres. William McKinley attended services here during his visit to Thomasville.

47. Hayes House (c. 1858)— 329 N. Broad St. Originally, this was a Georgian-style cottage built by Tom Jones, owner of Greenwood Plantation, as a wedding gift to his daughter. In the 1870s, the house was purchased, expanded, and remodeled in the Second Empire style by the Hayes family.

48. The Big Oak (c. 1680)— Monroe and Crawford Sts. At more than 300 years of age, this massive tree is believed to be one of the oldest and largest live oaks in Georgia. It has a trunk that is more than 8 feet around and a limb span greater than 160 feet. Many limbs are supported by steel cables so that the tree will not topple in high wind.

49. William Miller House (1888)— 216 Monroe St. Miller worked tirelessly to beautify Thomasville by planting trees along city streets. Locals affectionately called him the "Johnny Appleseed of Thomasville."

50. Hardy Bryan House (c. 1833) —312 N. Broad St. Built by Bryan, a pioneer settler to Thomasville, this Classical Revival–style structure is the oldest 2-story house in the city. It is now headquarters for Thomasville Landmarks, Inc., the local historic preservation organization. *Hours:* 2–4 P.M., Fri.; and by appointment. (229) 226-6016. NR

CHATTAHOOCHEE VALLEY ANNUAL EVENTS

March
- Spring Celebration
  (Callaway Gardens)
- Dulcimer Festival (Westville)
- Easter Egg Hunt
  (March or April, Kolomoki
  Mounds State Historic Park)
- River Days (Chehaw Park)

April
- Spring Celebration
  (Callaway Gardens)
- Azalea Festival (Pine Mountain)
- FDR Commemorative Celebration
  (Warm Springs)
- Riverfest Weekend (Columbus)
- Wildflower Hikes (Providence
  Canyon State Conservation Park)
- National Indian Festival
  (Chehaw Park)
- Spring Festival (Westville)
- Rose Festival (Thomasville)

May
- Masters Water Ski Championship
  (Callaway Gardens)
- Great Southern "Ham-It-Up"
  Parade (Columbus)
- May Day (Westville)

July
- Independence Day Celebration
  (Westville)
- Surf and Sand Spectacular
  (Callaway Gardens)
- Independence Day Celebration
  (Columbus)
- Independence Day Festival
  (Thomasville)
- Fiddlers Contest (Westville)

August
- Kudzu Takeover Day (Providence
  Canyon State Conservation Park)

September
- Sky High Hot Air Balloon
  Festival (Callaway Gardens)

October
- Harvest Festival (Pine Mountain)
- Columbus Day Celebration
  (Columbus)
- Fall Wildflower Hikes (Providence
  Canyon State Conservation Park)
- PGA Buick Challenge Golf
  Tournament (Callaway Gardens)
- Fair of 1850 (Westville)
- Kolomoki Festival (Kolomoki
  Mounds State Historic Park)
- Boo at the Zoo (Chehaw Park)
- Halloween Celebration (Westville)

November

- Southwest Georgia Fair (Albany)
- Steeplechase (Callaway Gardens)
- Plantation Wildlife Arts Festival
  (Thomasville)
- Candlelight Tour (Warm Springs)

December

- Yuletide Season Celebration
  (Westville)
- Christmas Festival of Lights
  (Pine Mountain)
- Fantasy in Lights
  (Callaway Gardens)
- Christmas Lights at Kolomoki
  (Kolomoki Mounds State
  Historic Park)
- Festival of Lights (Chehaw Park)
- Holiday Tour of Homes (Albany)
- Celebration of Lights (Albany)
- Victorian Christmas (Thomasville)

Monument to Bibb County's Confederate dead, downtown Macon

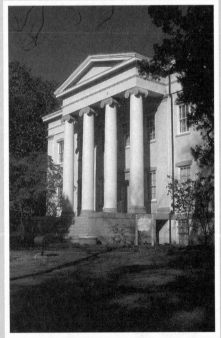

Old Governor's Mansion, Milledgeville

HEART OF
GEORGIA

Georgia's heartland is a broad and varied region stretching from
the Piedmont Plateau to the ancient Coastal Plain. While Macon,
located at nearly the geographic center of the state, is the largest city
in the region, the area is filled with sites of distinctive natural beauty
and small towns rich in Southern charm and history.

Geologically, the Piedmont Plateau was formed by erosive forces
on the Appalachian Mountains over hundreds of millions of years.
The wide plateau stretches from just north of Atlanta to the fall
line, then west to east from Columbus, through Macon, and on to
Augusta. At the fall line, the terrain drops off noticeably to the
Coastal Plain. Rivers that flow from north to south cut more deeply
into the sandy soils of the Coastal Plain and have created waterfalls
along the line. These drops in elevation are especially notable on the
Chattahoochee, Ocmulgee, and Savannah Rivers. The softer soils also
contribute to the rivers' broadening and deepening south of the fall
line, a characteristic which makes these waterways navigable by
barges and boats below the line, but not above it. Early settlers found
the waterfalls to be excellent sources for generating power to run
mills and factories.

Even before the arrival of the European settlers, the region was an
important cultural center. Evidence unearthed during excavations at
Ocmulgee National Monument outside Macon showed that this site
along the banks of the Ocmulgee River was occupied for more than
10,000 years. The monument's major features are the large ceremonial mounds constructed by Mississippian-period Indians around
1000 C.E. At its peak, Ocmulgee may have been one of the largest and
most culturally important communities in the Southeast.

Another site of great national importance, but for a very different reason, is Andersonville National Historic Site. Here in early 1864, the Confederate government established a primitive prison camp for Union soldiers being relocated from Virginia and for those captured during fighting in northern Georgia. Originally intended to house about 12,000 men, the camp was forced to hold more than 30,000, a condition that led to widespread outbreaks of disease, starvation, high mortality, and practically unbearable conditions. Today, the former prison site is preserved as a reminder of the terrible human cost of war. On the grounds are the Andersonville National Cemetery and the new National Prisoner of War Museum, a facility chronicling the stories of American prisoners of war (POWs) in all the nation's conflicts from the Revolution to the Persian Gulf War.

The Johnston-Hay House, Macon

Not far from Andersonville is the historic city of Americus. While the city is a treasure of Victorian architecture, its focus is not just on its past. A restored downtown building serves as international headquarters for Habitat for Humanity, the charitable organization committed to building homes for needy people around the world. It is not uncommon to see Habitat's best-known volunteers and residents of the nearby community of Plains, Pres. Jimmy Carter and Rosalynn Carter, coming to town to shop or attend meetings.

There are several other fascinating destinations in the heartland. East of Macon is the city of Milledgeville, one of only two cities in the nation founded to serve as capitals (the other is Washington, D.C.). Established in 1807, the city served as Georgia's capital until the government moved to Atlanta in 1868. Still located here are the unusual Gothic-style capitol building, now part of Georgia Military College, and the Old Executive Mansion, completed in 1838 and considered one of the state's finest examples of Greek Revival architecture.

Further south is the small city of Fitzgerald. Born during the era of reconciliation following the Civil War, the town was founded as a colony for aging Union soldiers anxious to escape the harsh winters of the North and Midwest. Located at the southern boundary of the heartland, Valdosta is an important regional business and educational center. Its Victorian downtown has been preserved and the Spanish Mission–style campus of Valdosta State University draws students from throughout the state.

Beautiful turn-of-the-20th-century homes lining South Main Street in downtown Fitzgerald

This region is nearly bisected by Interstate 75 and many of the destinations are just a short drive from the highway, offering an enjoyable side-trip for those who wish to explore the scenic and historic Heart of Georgia.

CHAPTER 33

Macon

LOCATION

✦ Macon is adjacent to the intersection of I-75 and I-16 about 85 miles south of Atlanta. Exit on Martin Luther King Jr. Blvd. (exit 2 off I-16) and travel south to Cherry St. The walk begins at the Welcome Center in the old railroad station at Cherry and 5th Sts. *Information:* Macon–Bibb County Convention and Visitors Bureau, (800) 768-3401; www.maconga.org.

234

PARKING

🚗 Street parking and commercial lots are available throughout the downtown area.

BACKGROUND

Situated on the Ocmulgeee River midway between the mountains and the sea, Macon may be both geographically and symbolically the heart of Georgia. Although evidence exists that Hernando de Soto and his explorers visited this area in the 1540s (possibly even conducting the first recorded baptism in North America along the banks of the Ocmulgee), there was no permanent non-native settlement here until 1806.

That year a crude fort was constructed on the southern boundaries of the Creek Nation. Commanding the soldiers stationed there was Capt. Benjamin Hawkins, an Indian agent originally appointed by Pres. George Washington. The soldiers named their small garrison "Ft. Hawkins" in his honor. Over the next decade and a half, troops from the fort took part in the War of 1812 and in various conflicts with native tribes. By the early 1820s, additional treaties with the Creeks opened more land in Georgia's interior for settlement, and pioneers homesteaded the fertile Ocmulgee River valley. In 1822, Bibb County was created, and surveyor James Webb was retained to lay out a town site across

Macon

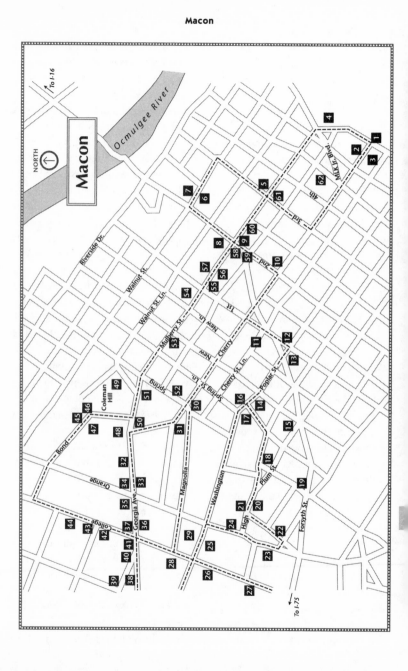

the river from Ft. Hawkins. Citing ancient Babylon as his inspiration, Webb's town plan included wide boulevards, parks, and gardens. Today, broad thoroughfares such as Mulberry and Cherry Streets and green spaces like Coleman Hill and Washington Park are reminders of Webb's vision for the "Queen Inland City of the South."

Within a few years flatboat traffic on the river and the expansion of the fledgling railway system through Macon into the Deep South made the town a center of commerce, from which agricultural products from farms and plantations could be shipped to markets throughout the region. The decade before the Civil War was a time of prosperity for Macon, and homes such as the Hay House, the Woodruff House, and several others reflected the wealth accumulated by some of the city's business leaders.

During the war, Macon continued to supply both agricultural products and manufactured goods to the Confederacy, with textile mills providing clothing and local factories turning out rifles and sabers. Many of these goods were shipped to the arsenals in Atlanta for later distribution to Confederate armies in the field.

The invasion of Georgia in 1864 by Union armies commanded by Maj. Gen. William T . Sherman led to fierce fighting through the summer and the destruction of Atlanta in the fall. Macon's defenders, a mix of regulars and militia, waited for an anticipated attack that never came. Instead, Sherman divided his army. The main body followed an easterly route toward the state capital at Milledgeville while a second, smaller wing protected the western flank.

That smaller force reached the outskirts of Macon in late November 1864 and fired a few artillery shells into the city from the bluffs north of the Ocmulgee River. One shell smashed through the walls of Judge Asa Holt's home earning the structure lasting recognition as "The Cannonball House." Federal troops never captured the city, apparently content to occupy the attention of the Rebels and allow Sherman's main force to march south virtually unopposed. Shortly before the fall of Milledgeville in November 1864, Gov. Joseph Brown relocated the government to Macon, and the city served as the temporary state capital until war's end.

Due in part to the city's stout defense as well as Sherman's strategy on the March to the Sea, Macon was spared wholesale destruction, and many antebellum homes and buildings remain. In addition, the city boasts important regional museums, fine institutions of higher education, and various outdoor festivals.

WALK DISTANCE AND TERRAIN

The 3.8-mile route traces a loop through the historic downtown district and nearby residential area. The area southeast of First Street is fairly level with a gradual, at times steep, ascent of Coleman Hill along Georgia Ave. and Magnolia St. There are good sidewalks throughout most of the route and an abundance of shade trees in the residential areas.

SIGHTS ALONG THE WAY

 1. Macon Welcome Center (1916)—200 Cherry St. This Roman Classical–style building long served as Macon's railway station. Today it houses Georgia Power Co. offices as well as the Macon–Bibb County Convention and Visitors Bureau. *Hours:* 9 A.M.–5:30 P.M., Mon.–Sat. (800) 768-3401.

2. Georgia Sports Hall of Fame (1999)—301 Cherry St. This museum celebrates the accomplishments of many of Georgia's finest amateur and professional athletes including Hank Aaron, Herschel Walker, Bill Elliott, and dozens more. The 43,000 sq. ft. of exhibit space features photographs, memorabilia, and interactive exhibits. Films are shown in a 205-seat theater designed in the style of an "old-time" ballpark. *Hours:* 9 A.M.–4:30 P.M., Mon.–Sat.; 1–4:30 P.M., Sun. (478) 752-1585.

3. Harriett Tubman African-American Museum (1981)—Cherry at 5th St. (planned relocation from 340 Walnut St.) Named to honor Tubman, a former slave and founder of the Underground Railroad that aided slaves in their escape to freedom before the Civil War, the museum is dedicated to preserving Macon's and America's African-American history through art and historical exhibits. Especially notable is the 63-ft.-long wall mural *From Africa to America* by Macon artist Wilfred Stroud. *Hours:* 10 A.M.–5 P.M., Mon.–Fri.; 2–5 P.M., Sat. (478) 743-9740.

4. Georgia Music Hall of Fame (1996)—200 Martin Luther King Jr. Blvd. Georgians have contributed much to America's rich musical traditions. Artists performing in such varied areas as Gospel, Blues, Soul, Country, Classical, and Rock-and-Roll are highlighted in this 43,000 sq. ft. museum, which features such renowned performers as "Ma" Rainey, Jessye Norman, Brenda Lee, Billy Joe Royal, Lena Horne, and Robert Shaw. A highlight is a Georgia village called "Tune Town," where there is always a music festival going on. *Hours:* 9 A.M.–5 P.M., Mon.–Sat.; 1–5 P.M., Sun. (888) 427-6257; www. gamusichall.com.

5. William A. Bootle Federal Building (1908)—475 Mulberry St. This impressive granite building is in the Beaux Arts style. It was recently dedicated to Judge William Bootle, who was appointed to the bench by Pres. Dwight Eisenhower in 1954 and served as Federal District Court judge during the turbulent Civil Rights era

237

of the 1960s. Bootle retired in 1981. *NR*

6. Christ Episcopal Church (1852)—Walnut St. between Second and Third Sts. This Gothic-style building is the oldest church still standing in Macon. The poet Sidney Lanier (see #21) was married here in 1867. *NR*

7. Baber House (1831)—577 Walnut St. Built for Dr. Ambrose Baber, the home was occupied during the Civil War by Maj. Gen. Howell Cobb, commander of the state militia during the Union invasion of 1864. The building now houses attorneys' offices. *NR*

8. Bibb County Courthouse (1926)—Second and Mulberry Sts. The building, with its large domed clock tower, occupies the site of the former courthouse constructed in 1870. *NR*

9. Washington Block (1854)—Second and Mulberry Sts. These buildings are an excellent example of Macon's antebellum commercial architecture.

10. Willingham Building (1860s)—Second and Cherry Sts. In an upstairs office, Sidney Lanier studied law with his father, Robert, and his uncle, Clifford Anderson (see #22).

11. Municipal Auditorium (1925)—First and Cherry Sts. This structure is designed in the Greek Temple style. Particularly notable is the massive colonnade supported by Doric columns and the large copper dome. In the Great Hall hangs a mural of Macon history painted by Don Carlos Dubois and Wilbur Kurtz. *NR*

12. Volunteer Armory (1884)—First and Poplar Sts. Note the busts of Stonewall Jackson and Robert E. Lee above the doorway of this brick Victorian building.

13. City Hall (1836)—700 Poplar St. Originally built for a bank, this building served briefly as the state capitol when Milledgeville was threatened by the invading Union army in late 1864. The Confederate Congress met here while in flight from Richmond, Va., in 1865.

14. St. Joseph's Catholic Church (1903)—830 Poplar St. This congregation was established in 1840. The Romanesque brick church features a beautiful stained-glass rose window. St. Joseph's was designed by Br. Cornelius Otten, architect of Sacred Heart Cultural Center in Augusta. *NR*

15. First Baptist Church (1887)—behind St. Joseph's at 595 New St. This African-American church grew from the slave congregation that worshiped at the First Baptist Church on High St. The land was provided for the church in 1845.

16. Green-Poe House (1840)—843 Poplar St. Built by Dr. Mercer Green, surgeon in charge of Macon hospitals during the Civil War, the home is an excellent example of the Federal style. *NR*

Downtown Macon

17. First Baptist Church (1887)—511 High St. Macon's earliest Baptist congregation was organized in 1826. The present Victorian Gothic church was completed in 1887.

18. Ruth Haitly Mosely Memorial Women's Center (c. 1880)—626 Spring St. Named in honor of one of Macon's most prominent African-American women, the center provides a variety of community and family services.

19. Steward Chapel A.M.E. Church (1889)—887 Forsyth St. This congregation was established by emancipated slaves in 1865. Dr. Martin Luther King Jr. preached here in 1957.

20. Monroe-Dunlap-Snow House (1857)—920 Plum St. This attractively restored antebellum cottage is noted for it gingerbread trim. *NR*

21. Lanier Cottage (c. 1830s)—935 High St. Writer and musician Sidney Lanier, now best known for such poems as "Song of the Chattahoochee," was born in this simple, Gothic-style frame cottage in 1842. Today it is headquarters of the Middle Georgia Historical Society and is open to the public. The park across the street from the house contains a live oak reminiscent of those described in one of Lanier's most famous poems, "The Marshes of Glynn." *Hours:* 9 A.M.–1 P.M. and 2–4 P.M., Mon.–Fri.; 9:30 A.M.–12:30 P.M., Sat. (478) 743-3851. *NR*

22. Judge Clifford Anderson House (1859)—642 Orange St. This large clapboard house with its notable square central tower was built for Anderson, a Confederate congressman, judge, and later Georgia attorney general. *NR*

23. The Navarro Apartments (c. 1900s)—Orange St. west of High St. Situated on the ridge at the top of High Street, this large, 3-story apartment building combines elements of Federal and Dutch Colonial architectural styles.

24. John H. Lamar House (c. 1830s)—544 Orange St. This large, frame house, designed in the Greek Revival style, was the home of Sidney Lanier's fiancée, Mary Day.

239

25. Washington Memorial Library (1920)—1180 Washington Ave. The library is widely known for its archives and genealogical records. *Hours:* 9 A.M.–9 P.M., Mon.–Thur.; 9 A.M.–6 P.M., Fri. and Sat.; 1:30–5:30 P.M., Sun. (478) 744-0800.

26. Hill-O'Neal Cottage (c. 1880s)—College St. near Hardeman Ave. A prominent feature of this Victorian home is the iron railing, which came from the balcony of the old Union Depot. *NR*

27. North-Tinsley House (1854)—Forsyth and College Sts. This antebellum cottage was built in the Mississippi Delta style by Henry North. The second story was added at the turn of the 20th century.

28. Federal Building (1930s)—College St. between Georgia and Hardeman Aves. This building occupies the original site of Wesleyan College, the first college in the world chartered to grant degrees to women, and was designed to resemble the original college. *NR*

29. Washington Park—Magnolia and College Sts. at Washington Ave. The focal point of this small hillside park is a spring that once served as Macon's main water supply.

240

30. Temple Beth-Israel (1902)—892 Cherry St. This well-proportioned masonry structure is notable for its large central dome and beautiful stained-glass windows. The congregation was organized in 1859.

31. Edward Dorr Tracy House (c. 1830s)—974–80 Cherry St. at Magnolia Ln. Once located on the site of the Hay House (see #51), this house was originally composed of two sides with a dogtrot. It was divided into two homes when moved, but the structures were later rejoined.

32. Isaac-Scott-Johnston House (1846, remodeled 1893)—1073 Georgia Ave. This residence is an excellent example of Greek Revival architecture.

33. Schofield House (1831)—1074 Georgia Ave. Built by A. D. Schofield, this cottage is one of Macon's oldest surviving structures.

34. Burke House (1901)—1085 Georgia Ave. This distinctive Queen Anne–Victorian house with its large, adjoining carriage house was built by T. C. Burke. *NR*

35. Holt-Peeler-Snow House (1840)—1129 Georgia Ave. This attractive Greek Revival mansion is notable for its horseshoe-style steps and wrought-iron trim. *NR*

36. Hatcher-Groover-Schwartz House (1880)—1144 Georgia Ave. This mansion, in French Second Empire style, features an intricate wrought-iron porch and patterned shingle roof. *NR*

37. Raines-Miller-Carmichael House (1840s)—1183 Georgia Ave. Built in the shape of a Greek cross, the home dominates a small hillside. Note the curved portico. Inside, a free-standing, spiral stairway leads to the rooftop cupola. *NR*

38. Walter T. Johnson House (1911)—1238 Jefferson Terr. Situated on a small triangular lot, this Neel Reid–designed house has been described as "English Medieval" in style.

39. Nisbet-Budsey-Domingos House (1843)—1261 Jefferson Terr. This excellent example of Greek Revival style has a Doric-columned portico. Note the inverted laurel wreath along the entablature. *NR*

40. Randolph-Whittle-Davis House (1837)—1231 Jefferson Terr. This unusual antebellum structure features a mixture of round and square columns. *NR*

41. Schinholzer House (1890, remodeled 1911)—397 College St. A once-rambling Victorian, this home was masterfully remodeled in the French Neoclassical style by architect Neel Reid.

42. 1842 Inn (1842)—353 College St. This restored Greek Revival–style house is now a bed-and-breakfast inn with elegant Victorian furnishings. 800-336-1842.

43. Massee Apartments (c. 1910s)—347 College St. An imposing, 8-story building set amidst single family homes, the structure's Georgian design is attributed to noted architect Neel Reid.

44. 1860 House (1860)—315 College St. Originally built as a plain 2-story frame house, it was remodeled in the Greek Revival style in 1901. A popular restaurant for several years, it has recently undergone adaptive restoration as an office building. *NR*

45. Zettler-Nisbet-Robertson House (1880s)—1019 Bond St. This beautiful Queen Anne Victorian overlooks Coleman Hill. *NR*

46. 1013 Bond Street (1880s)— This rambling, 3-story Queen Anne house perched atop Coleman Hill has a panoramic view of downtown Macon. *NR*

47. Cowles-Bond-Woodruff House (1836)—988 Bond St. Designed and built by architect Elam Alexander for wealthy Macon banker Jerry Cowles, this house is an excellent example of the Greek Revival style. In 1877, the house was sold to Col. Joseph Bond, one of the South's richest plantation owners. A grand ball was held here to honor Winnie Davis, daughter of Confederate Pres. Jefferson Davis. The home is now owned by Mercer University and is used for special functions. *NR*

48. Walter F. George School of Law of Mercer University (1950s)— Bond St. and Georgia Ave. Named for U.S. Sen. Walter F. George, the building is designed to resemble Independence Hall in Philadelphia. From the Marshall Johnston home previously on this site, Jefferson Davis reviewed a parade of Confederate veterans in 1887.

241

49. Coleman Hill Park (1830s)—Georgia Ave. and Spring St. The green slopes of this hillside park feature a monument honoring longtime Georgia Congressman Carl Vinson and memorials to Macon citizens killed in both World Wars.

50. Harris-Pliny House (1902)—990 Georgia Ave. This home sits atop a spring that once provided water to the nearby Hay House.

51. The Johnston-Hay House (c. 1855)—934 Georgia Ave. This magnificent Italian Renaissance Revival home, built by wealthy Macon businessman William Butler Johnston, is considered an architectural masterpiece. It was owned for many years by the P. L. Hay family. Especially notable are the 500-pound, hand-carved front doors, the stained-glass windows, and ornate trim. The home is administered by the Georgia Trust for Historic Preservation and is open to the public. *Hours:* 10 A.M.–5 P.M., Mon.–Sat.; 1–5 P.M. Sun. (478) 742-7155. *NL*

52. Middle Georgia Art Association (c. 1880)—372 Spring St. This Victorian-era building houses a non-profit gallery of work by local artists.

53. Cannonball House (1853)—856 Mulberry St. Built by Judge Asa Holt, the house was struck by a Federal cannonball during an artillery bombardment in July 1864. The hole made by the ball is still in the wall, while the ball remains in the living room where it rolled to a stop. The attractive Greek Revival structure is now home to the Sidney Lanier Chapter of the United Daughters of the Confederacy and houses a museum. *Hours:* 10 A.M.–4 P.M., Mon.–Sat. (478) 745-5982. *NR*

54. Mulberry Street Methodist Church (1928, remodeled 1967)—713 Mulberry St. Organized in 1826, the congregation originally built on this site in 1828. The Georgia Conference was organized here in 1831, and the church is considered the mother church of Georgia Methodism.

55. First Presbyterian Church (1858)—690 Mulberry St. The congregation was organized in 1826 and hosted formation of the Georgia Synod in 1844. The Rev. Francis Goulding, author of *The Young Marooners*, preached here during the Civil War, and Sidney Lanier was a member. *NR*

56. Old Macon Library (1889)—652 Mulberry St. Notable for the high-vaulted ceiling in the reading room, the building is now home to the Macon Heritage Foundation. *NR*

57. Grand Opera House (1906)—651 Mulberry St. Built on the site of the 1884 Academy of Music, the building has one of the largest stages in the south. The theater has been restored and now serves as the Mercer University Performing Arts Center. Tour information: (478) 749-6580. *NR*

58. Hardeman Building (1850)— 303 Cotton Ave. This antebellum commercial building, with its second- and third-story bay windows, once housed a concert hall. The pharmacy on the ground floor has been in business for more than a century. *NR*

59. Confederate Monument (1879)—Second and Mulberry Sts. Created of Italian marble with a base of Georgia granite, this monument is a memorial to Bibb Countians who died fighting for the Confederacy.

60. Brown Stone Front (1859)— 564 Mulberry St. This narrow 3-story brick structure was built by Dr. George Emerson as an office and residence. The ornate trim, round-head windows, and balcony are in the style of an Italian villa.

61. William Wadley Monument (1886)—Median of Third and Mulberry Sts. The monument was erected in memory of a founder and president of the Georgia Railroad.

62. Douglass Theater (c. 1920s)— 361 Martin Luther King Jr. Blvd. Built as a vaudeville and movie house for Macon's African-American community, the Douglass was a popular venue for many great artists including Macon-born Otis Redding. The theater was restored in 1996. *Information:* (478) 742-2000.

NOTES

243

CHAPTER 34

Ocmulgee National Monument

LOCATION

✤ The national monument is located on the northern banks of the Ocmulgee River a short distance from downtown Macon. It may be reached by taking Emery Highway (GA 22) east from I-16 (exit 1-B) and following the signs. The park is open 9 A.M.–5 P.M., daily, with extended summer hours. *Information:* (478) 752-8257; www.nps.gov/ocmu.

244

PARKING

🚗 There is a large parking area at the visitor center and smaller lots adjacent to the park's significant sites. A 2-mile road connects the center with the parking area at the Great Temple Mound.

BACKGROUND

📖 The mysterious mounds at Ocmulgee National Monument, as well as companion sites at Etowah and Kolomoki, speak to us of a remarkable era in social development and cultural evolution.

Although archaeological evidence shows that nomadic Ice Age hunters traveled through this region during the last ice age about 10,000 years ago (the first Ice Age "Clovis" spearhead found in the southern U.S. was found on the Macon Plateau), the story of Ocmulgee truly begins with the establishment of the Hopewellian and, later, the Mississippian Cultures in the Middle Mississippi Valley around 700–800 C.E. Unlike earlier loose bands of nomadic hunter-gatherers, the Mississippians were an agricultural people who built permanent settlements in fertile river valleys and supplemented hunting and fishing with skillful cultivation of beans, squash, pumpkins, tobacco, and other crops. Their agricultural contributions may have been more significant, but their most tangible links to us are the unusual mounds they constructed.

It isn't known exactly when the site at Ocmulgee was settled, but archaeological evidence shows that the village

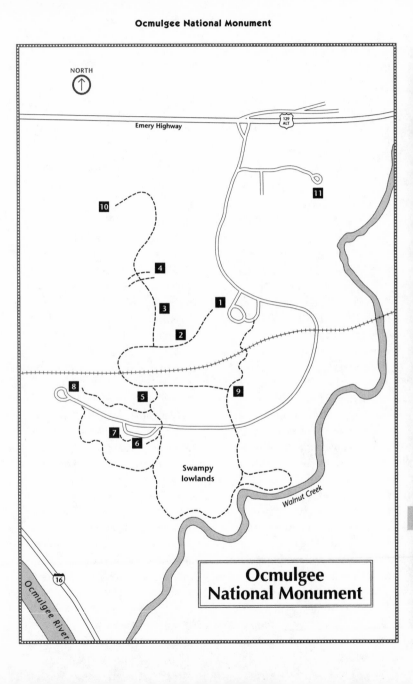

was bustling with activity by 1000 C.E. Excavations at the site indicate that one of the mounds was used as a burial site, probably for religious or political leaders, while the other mounds likely served as locations for religious or secular ceremonies. Also, careful digging revealed that the mounds were built gradually over a period of years, possibly representative of some cycle of cultural change.

Another significant structure from the height of the Mississippian Culture at Ocmulgee, the Earth Lodge, has also been excavated and carefully restored. Here, the present-day visitor enters what may have been a council house where village leaders gathered to govern or conduct religious ceremonies more than a millennium ago.

By 1150 C.E., the large village at Ocmulgee was in decline and eventually abandoned. Over the next two centuries, the Lamar Culture (named for the family on whose land the village sites were excavated), evolved in the area. The Lamar people established several small villages nearby and reoccupied the old Ocmulgee village site. These people, known as the Southeastern Ceremonial Complex, or "Southern Cult," blended the cultures of the earlier Woodland period and the Mississippian, developing religious ceremonies and artworks filled with flamboyant motifs and specialized objects. These were likely the natives who greeted the first European

explorers, Hernando de Soto and his soldiers, on their expedition north from Florida in 1540.

Ultimately, contact with the Europeans proved catastrophic for the indigenous people. Disease, political entanglements, and pressure for lands destroyed their way of life. The natives, now known as the Creeks, found themselves trapped between the Spanish in the south and the encroaching English on the east. In the late 1500s, the Spanish, from their settlement in St. Augustine, sent priests accompanied by soldiers into Georgia's interior intent on converting the Indians to Christianity— either by choice or by force. The English established the city of Charles Town (Charleston, S.C.) in 1670 and set up a trading post at Ocmulgee in 1690.

Conflict spread between the native tribes and the competing European invaders. Twenty-five years later, in 1715, the Creeks attacked British settlers in middle Georgia in protest against the taking of Indians to work as slaves on Caribbean sugar plantations. The conflict, known as the Yamassee War, ended with the British burning Ocmulgee Town and driving other Creeks from the area.

With the establishment of the Royal Colony of Georgia in 1733, colony founder Gen. James Oglethorpe established friendly relations between the Creeks and the English colonists. Oglethorpe proved so successful in earning the allegiance of the Creeks that most served as allies to the British during the American Revolution.

Just prior to the Revolution, pioneer naturalist William Bartram passed through the old Ocmulgee village site during his journey through the South to collect botanical specimens. In his diary he wrote, "On the east bank of the [Ocmulgee] river lie the famous Ocmulgee fields, where are yet conspicuous very wonderful remains of the power and grandeur of the ancients in this part of America."

After the Revolution, the new State of Georgia exerted increasing pressure for expanding settlement into the Creek Nation, especially along the fertile river bottomlands. The Creeks yielded slowly to these demands, continuing to claim sovereignty over their ancestral homelands, and Pres. George Washington initiated a policy of purchasing lands from the Indians. Several Creek chiefs, recognizing that opposition to American expansion was fruitless, urged that the tribe negotiate for the sale of their lands, with an exchange for lands elsewhere, before it would be taken from them by force.

Col. Benjamin Hawkins, a Revolutionary War veteran, was appointed by Washington as Federal agent for all of the Indian tribes south of the Ohio River. In the Treaties of Ft. Wilkinson (1802) and Washington (1805), he negotiated with the Creeks for nearly all of their lands in Georgia. In the 1805 treaty, the Creeks excluded a 3- by 5-mile strip of land known as the Ocmulgee Old Fields Reserve, just north of the river. On this parcel of land, in 1805, the Creeks permitted the government to construct an extension of the Federal Road (eventually connecting Washington with New Orleans) along the route of the Old Lower Creek Trading Path (GA 49 follows this route) and, in 1806, to construct a blockhouse fort, to be called Ft. Hawkins. At the time, this pioneer outpost was along the southwestern border of the United States. Within a few years, the frontier settlement that grew around the fort became the bustling city of Macon.

Over the years, the ancient mounds at Ocmulgee were neglected and forgotten. Prior to the Civil War, much of the old village land was purchased by Samuel Dunlap for his plantation, and he built his main house between the mounds and the Federal Road. More than a half-century later, land from one of the mounds was removed for use in grading Macon's Main St. This event galvanized a small group of local citizens to call for preservation of the ancient mounds. The group asked the Smithsonian Institution in Washington to examine the site to determine its historical significance. In 1934, the Smithsonian, in what became the largest archaeological excavation in

247

Restored Earth Lodge

the United States, unearthed numerous objects and artifacts reflecting the rich history of the area.

In 1936, legislation created the Ocmulgee National Monument. Approximately 700 acres have been preserved, and some of the ancient structures (including the 1,000-year-old Earth Lodge) have been restored. Ocmulgee National Monument stands as a tangible link to the ancient peoples who have inhabited this fertile river valley.

WALK DISTANCE AND TERRAIN

248 The round-trip from the visitor center along the Opelofa Trail is about 2.5 miles. A side trip to the McDougal Mound will add about 1.7 miles to the walk. Much of the terrain is rolling, forested land with large open spaces around the mounds and the Earth Lodge. Steps make ascent of the larger mounds easier. The south-

ern portion of the trail and the spur Loop Trail wind through river bottomland and marsh areas.

SIGHTS ALONG THE WAY

 1. Visitor Center (1930s)—Designed and built by Civilian Conservation Corps workers in the 1930s, the building's unusual design—Art Deco/Temple Mound—is eye-catching. The center contains extensive exhibits on life at Ocmulgee over the past 10,000 years. A theater screens a regular schedule of films about Ocmulgee National Monument, while the gift shop offers handcrafts and books on Native American and regional history. *Hours:* 9 A.M.–5 P.M., daily; extended hours in summer.

2. The Earth Lodge—Reconstructed by the CCC workers in the 1930s, the lodge depicts the ceremonial building that archaeological evidence indicates was on this site about 1000 C.E. The clay floor encircled by a low bench with molded seats, the firepit, and the central platform in the shape of a raptorial bird with forked eyes, are original.

3. Cornfield Mound—This small mound once stood about 8 ft. high and probably served as a platform for a ceremonial building. Archaeologists discovered evidence that the mound was built over previously tilled farm fields.

4. Prehistoric Trenches—These shallow trenches may have served a defensive purpose or simply as "borrow pits" from which the soil was taken to construct nearby mounds.

5. Trading Post Site—About 1690, English traders from Charleston, S.C., built a wooden structure here. Merchants exchanged firearms, cloth, and other goods for furs and deerskins. Disease and conflict led to abandonment of the post and the village around 1715.

6. Great Temple Mound—The largest Mississippian mound on the Macon Plateau, this mound was probably once topped with a building used for religious ceremonies. Archaeological evidence indicates that the mound was constructed in seven stages, likely over several years. During each stage, the mound was topped by wooden buildings probably used for religious ceremonies.

7. Lesser Temple Mound—Like its larger neighbor, this mound was used for ceremonial purposes and had a building atop its summit. Portions of the mound were destroyed during construction of the railroad in the 1840s.

8. Funeral Mound—Archaeological excavations have unearthed more than 100 human burials, thought to be of village leaders, in this mound, which was also built in seven stages. Like the Lesser Temple Mound, parts of this mound were destroyed by railway construction.

9. Southeast Mound—The significance of this small mound, like several others on the property, is not known.

10. McDougal Mound—Little is known about the purpose of this small mound at the far-northern edge of the village site.

11. Dunlap House (c. 1840s)—Once the main house of the Samuel Dunlap plantation, this house served as Federal cavalry headquarters during a 1864 raid on Macon. It is currently the residence of the park superintendent and is not open to the public. The woods behind the house still contain evidence of Civil War artillery fortifications.

NOTES

249

CHAPTER 35

Milledgeville

LOCATION

✢ Milledgeville is located on U.S. 441 about 39 miles south of I-20 (exit 114). It may also be reached from I-16 by exiting on U.S. 129/GA 22 near Macon (exit 1A). Go north on U.S. 129/GA 22 to GA 49 and follow this road east for about 25 miles to Milledgeville. The walk begins at the Tourism and Trade Building on W. Hancock St. *Information:* Milledgeville-Baldwin County Convention and Visitors Bureau, (800) 653-1804; www.milledgevillecvb.com.

PARKING

🚗 On-street parking is plentiful, and there are several surface lots near the Tourism and Trade Building.

BACKGROUND

📖 By the close of the 18th century, an increasing number of people were pushing farther into the interior of Georgia in search of land for farming and settlement. To avoid conflicts with the Creek Nation, Pres. George Washington in 1790 and, later, Pres. Thomas Jefferson in 1802, dispatched Federal officials to negotiate treaties with the Indian inhabitants for land cessions to the state.

Following the 1790 treaty, a wooden stockade called Ft. Fidius was constructed on the banks of the Oconee River to protect the frontier. By the mid-1790s, it was home to the largest garrison of soldiers south of the Ohio River. In 1797, the original fortification was replaced by the larger Ft. Wilkinson where, in 1802, chiefs from 32 villages met with government officials and reluctantly agreed to further land concessions.

With the land openings leading to both an increase and a shift in the location of the population, Georgia recognized the need to move its capital from the town of Louisville to a more central location. In 1803, the legislature established a commission to select an appropriate site near the head of navigation of the Oconee

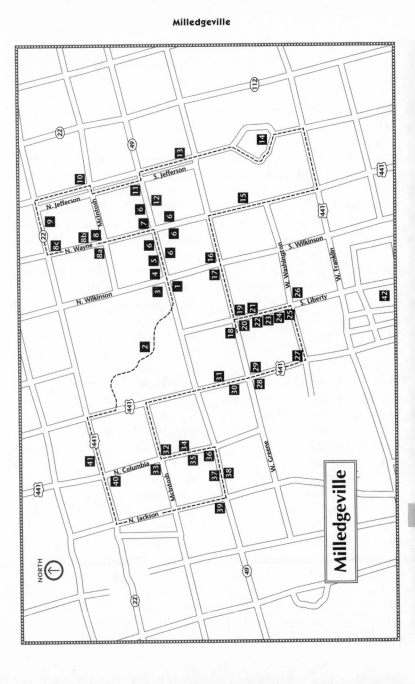

Milledgeville

River, and in 1804, work began to carve a new capital city out of the wilderness.

Three 16-acre squares were planned, one for the State House, one for the Governor's Mansion, and one for a penitentiary or other suitable purpose. A fourth square, for a cemetery, was added a short time later. Two main streets, both 120 ft. wide, were laid out and 4-acre land lots in the community were created and sold by lottery. By popular choice, the new town was named in honor of the current governor, John Milledge. Milledgeville and Washington, D.C., are the only two cities in the nation created and developed specifically to serve as capitals.

On October 8, 1807, 15 wagons containing the state's records and treasury left Louisville with a military escort and headed for the new seat of government. Shortly before the move, Milledge vacated the governorship to fill a vacancy in the state's delegation to the U.S. Senate, and Jared Irwin was elected to fill out the unexpired term. So Irwin became the first chief executive to preside in Milledgeville.

252

For a number of years after the move, the legislature met in an unfinished State House while workers sought to complete and, later, expand the building to meet the government's growing needs. Irwin's first executive mansion was a simple log home that was replaced a short time later by two successive modest frame houses. Eleven governors would occupy these simple homes until, in 1838, Gov. George Gilmer moved into the magnificent Greek Revival Governor's Mansion.

During its tenure as state capital, Milledgeville was the focal point for significant events both glorious and tragic. Here, in 1825, the entire town welcomed the Marquis de Lafayette on his grand tour in celebration of the 50th anniversary of the American Revolution; while, in 1831, the legislature, bending to enormous pressure from settlers greedy for gold, revoked the sovereignty of the Cherokee Nation, in violation of Federal treaties, setting in motion the Indian nation's removal west on the infamous Trail of Tears.

Shortly after the election of Abraham Lincoln to the presidency in November 1860, several Southern states, led by South Carolina, seceded from the Union. In January 1861, the nation's attention focused on Milledgeville, where Georgia's secession convention was being held. Many believed that, as the largest and most populous state in the Deep South, Georgia's decision would determine the fate of the newly formed Confederacy. After lengthy and heated debate, the Ordinance of Secession was passed on January 19. Georgia had cast her lot with the Rebel cause and would pay dearly.

Over the course of the war, Georgia sent more young men to battle than any other Southern state, and, during Sherman's famous March to the Sea over the course of nearly 8 months—from May to December 1864—Federal troops carved a 60-mile-wide path of destruction through the heart of the state.

The state government departed Milledgeville for Macon as the Union army approached, and the town was left to be defended by an assortment of militia and students from Georgia Military Academy who had fled south from Marietta. This meager force offered little resistance to the advance elements of the Union army that entered Milledgeville on November 22, 1864. The next day, the main body of the Federal force marched down Main Street with flags unfurled, and Sherman established his headquarters at the vacant executive mansion.

During their brief stay, Federal troops held mock sessions of the legislature to repeal the Ordinance of Secession. Surprisingly, they did not burn the capital, and left most of downtown undisturbed.

Following the war, the government returned to Milledgeville, but only briefly. In 1868, at the urging of Military Governor George Meade (the Union hero of the Battle of Gettysburg) and others, the civil government was relocated to Atlanta. When the change was made, local author Nellie Womack Hines wrote, "Milledgeville was born a capital city in the fading light of an Indian War dance; it died as a capital city in the fading light of a burning bridge as Sherman passed on."

Although Milledgeville faded from the limelight, it remained a regional economic hub and a center of higher education. The city also gained distinction as the home of noted writer Flannery O'Connor (1925–64), author of several award-winning books, including *Wise Blood* and *The Violent Bear It Away*. The Flannery O'Connor Room in Georgia College and State University's Ina D. Russell Library contains copies of her works and artifacts from her life.

For the casual tourist or the serious student of Georgian history, Milledgeville, with its grand homes and historic buildings, remains a treasured link to the past.

WALK DISTANCE AND TERRAIN

Winding along tree-shaded streets, the gently rolling trail follows an approximately 3-mile-long loop through the city. Well-maintained sidewalks are plentiful along the route.

SIGHTS ALONG THE WAY

 1. Tourism and Trade Building (1900s)—200 W. Hancock St. This turn-of-the-century building houses the local tourism

253

office. Maps and guides are available. A guided trolley tour, offered on Tuesday and Fridays at 10:00 A.M. begins here. *Hours:* 9 A.M.–5 P.M., Mon.–Fri.; 10 A.M.–2 P.M., Sat. (800) 653-1804.

2. Georgia College and State University (GCSU) (1889)—W. Hancock St. Founded as the Georgia Normal and Industrial College for Women, the name changed to Georgia College for Women in 1922. The school became coed in 1968. The attractively landscaped campus has several significant buildings including magnificent, Neoclassical-style Parks, Atkinson, and Terrell Halls, three massive red-brick structures with columned porticos and ornate balconies. Atkinson, built in 1896, is the oldest building on the campus and is listed on the National Register of Historic Places. *Ina D. Russell Library hours:* 8 A.M.–5 P.M., Mon.–Fri.; 1–5 P.M., Sat.; and 2–5 P.M., Sun. (478) 453-4047.

3. Old Baldwin County Courthouse (1883)—W. Hancock St. at Wilkinson St. This large brick Neoclassical building, topped with a Second Empire–style clock tower, is the fourth courthouse on this site. After completion of the new courthouse across the street, the building was conveyed to GCSU. NR

4. New Baldwin County Courthouse (1997)—W. Hancock St. at Wilkinson St. This imposing 4-story brick and masonry building with

central clock tower, designed in the Georgian style, now houses county offices and courtroom facilities. On display in the lobby on Wilkinson St. are early photographs of Milledgeville and a replica of the Liberty Bell. *Hours:* 8 A.M.–5 P.M., Mon.–Fri.

5. Campus Theater (1930s)—137 W. Hancock St. This Depression-era movie house still retains its original marquee and facade. It closed in the early 1980s, but there are plans for its reopening as a cinema and restaurant.

6. Commercial District (c. 1880s–1910s)—Hancock and Wayne Sts. The heart of Milledgeville's downtown is a treasure of Victorian-era commercial buildings. Many have been preserved or adaptively restored for retail and dining establishments.

7. Masonic Hall (1832)—Hancock and Wayne Sts. This Federal-style building with Italianate details was designed by John Marlor (see #8) and made from locally produced, handmade bricks. The fine wrought-iron work, which features the Masonic emblem, is notable, as is the 87-ft. unsupported, circular interior stairway. NR

8. John Marlor House and Arts Center (1830)—201 N. Wayne St. Designed in the Milledgeville Federal style with Greek Revival influences by Marlor, an English-born architect and master builder, the house was a wedding present for his second wife. It is now part of the Milledgeville–Baldwin County Allied Arts Center and houses the Elizabeth Marlor Bethune Art Gallery. (478) 452-3950. Other properties that are part of the Marlor Arts Center include:

A. Allan's Market Building (1911)—This 2-story brick building is used for additional gallery and studio space.

B. Marlor Cottage (c. 1820)—Marlor's residence while the main house was under construction now houses a pottery studio and living quarters for an artist-in-residence.

Stetson-Sanford House

C. Griffin-Baugh Cottage (c. 1810)—This small New England saltbox-style cottage is one of the oldest structures in Milledgeville. It was relocated to the center from its original site south of downtown.

9. Delaney-Joseph-Hobbs House (1825)—151 Montgomery St. John Marlor designed this white clapboard, Greek Revival–style house, one of Milledgeville's oldest existing residences.

10. Breedlove-Scott-Tate House (1838, remodeled 1887)—201 N. Jefferson St. Originally designed in the Georgian style, the home underwent extensive changes, including addition of the Mansard roof, in the 1880s. Note the front door, which is made from 28 different kinds of wood and features the Masonic symbol.

11. Sacred Heart Roman Catholic Church (1874)—Hancock and Jefferson Sts. This small Gothic-style church was designed to complement the nearby state capitol building. It occupies the site of the elegant Lafayette Hotel completed in 1824, at which Lafayette was a guest during his grand tour of the U.S. in 1825.

12. Milledgeville City Hall (1907)—Hancock St. between Wayne and Jefferson Sts. Designed in the Beaux Arts style, the red-brick building is notable for its large, ornate portico supported by four Corinthian columns.

13. Confederate Memorial (1912)—Jefferson St. Median. This large granite sculpture commemorates local men who fought for the Confederacy.

14. Old State Capitol (1807)— 201 E. Greene St. Constructed by army engineers Jett Thomas and John Scott, the building is one of the oldest Gothic-style public structures in the nation. This was the seat of Georgia's government from 1803 to 1868. The north and south gates were built in the late 1860s from the rubble of the nearby Confederate arsenal. The capitol building and grounds now house Georgia Military College, chartered in 1879. The building has undergone a recent restoration to return it to its original 1807 appearance, and a Museum of Milledgeville and Baldwin County History is planned for the building's main lobby. A marker by the north entrance gate commemorates the visit to Milledgeville of French aristocrat and writer Alexis de Tocqueville during his 1831–32 tour of America. *NR*

15. St. Stephens Episcopal Church (1841)— 220 S. Wayne St. Described as Carpenter Gothic, the church originally had a flat roof that was destroyed by fire when the nearby arsenal was blown up during the Civil War. The beautiful chancel window was a gift from the members of Christ Episcopal Church in Savannah.

16. McComb-Holloman-Waddell House (1879)— 138 S. Wilkinson St. An unusual feature of this asymmetrical, brick Victorian house is its ornate, rooftop steeple. The house now serves as attorneys' offices.

17. Stovall-Conn-Gardner House (1825)— 141 S. Wilkinson St. Designed by John Marlor, the house was built in the Federal style with later Greek Revival additions. The house has 13 columns, reputed to represent the original 13 colonies.

18. Gordon-Cline-O'Connor House (1820)— 311 W. Greene St. This 2-story clapboard house represents another example of the Milledgeville Federal style. It briefly served as the governor's residence while the nearby executive mansion was under construction. It was the longtime home of Flannery O'Connor's mother, Regina Cline O'Connor.

19. Bell-Martin House (1898)— 200 S. Liberty St. Constructed as a simple, 2-story clapboard house, it was later remodeled in the Neoclassical style.

20. Paine-Jones House (1820)— 201 S. Liberty St. Built by early Milledgeville resident Dr. Joshua Paine, the plain 2-story clapboard house was similar in design to houses in Paine's native Connecticut. The house has undergone several renovations and additions.

21. Myrick-Jenkins-Switch House (1890)— 220 S. Liberty St. This asymmetrical Victorian house is notable for its ornately carved exterior trim.

22. Pound-Flemister-Alton House (1893)— 221 S. Liberty St. Built by J. B. Pound, this large, frame Victorian house with two squared turrets features a wraparound porch with rounded corners and ornate woodwork. Early owners named it "Buena Vista."

23. Alling-Bethune-Combs House (1895)—231 S. Liberty St. This handsome Victorian was designed by architect E. T. Alling for his own residence. It later served as parsonage for the First Baptist Church.

24. Bearden-Montgomery House (1898)—241 S. Liberty St. An attractive, asymmetrical 2-story Victorian with wraparound porch, this house was also designed by Alling.

25. Orme-Sallee House (1822)—251 S. Liberty St. An excellent example of the Milledgeville Federal style, this residence is attributed to architect Daniel Pratt and is listed in the Historic American Buildings Survey.

26. Williams-Ferguson-Lewis House (1818)—240 W. Washington St. Known locally as "The Homestead," this is the oldest Milledgeville house built in the transitional Georgian-Federal style. Adjacent to the house is the original brick kitchen building. The boxwood and wisteria surrounding the house were planted by the first owner.

27. Blount-Parks-Mara-Williams House (c. 1818)—220 S. Clarke St. This superb example of the Milledgeville Federal style was originally located at the northeast corner of Clarke and Greene Sts. It was moved in 1901 and again in 1991.

28. Newell-Watts House (1825)—201 S. Clarke St. Built in the Georgian style, the house was later renovated and the Greek Revival portico added.

29. Sanford-Powell-Binion-Mara House (c. 1825)—330 W. Greene St. Originally built in the Federal style for Gen. W. A. Sanford, the house started with four columns with more added as the porch was extended around the structure. The house was remodeled in the Neoclassical style by Dr. T. O. Powell in 1890. It is now "Mara's Tara," a bed-and-breakfast inn. (478) 453-2732. *NR*

30. Museum and Archives of Georgia Education (1900)—131 S. Clarke St. The building is ornate Greek Revival Renaissance style with Corinthian columns and Palladian windows. The museum is operated by the Georgia College School of Education and is open 1–4 P.M., Mon.–Fri., and by appointment. (478) 445-4391.

31. Old Governor's Mansion (1838)—120 S. Clarke St. Exquisite example of Greek Revival style, the design is attributed to architect Charles Clusky. It served as the executive mansion in 1838–68. The mansion is open to the public. Guided tours: hourly, 10 A.M.–4 P.M., Tues.–Sat.; 2–4 P.M., Sun. (478) 453-4545. *NL*

32. Compton-Fowler-McKnight House (c. 1815)—McIntosh at N. Columbia St. This clapboard structure, designed in the style of a New England cottage, is one of the city's oldest

257

buildings. The porch was a Victorian-era addition.

33. Roberts-Jones-Johnson/ Thompson House (1890)—200 N. Columbia St. Designed by E. T. Alling, this large frame house displays elements of the Victorian and Greek Revival styles. It is now the Antebellum Inn, a bed-and-breakfast lodging. (478) 454-5400.

34. Howard-Jarratt-Garrard House (c. 1823)—131 N. Columbia St. Locally known as "The Cedars," the home is another excellent example of the Milledgeville Federal style. The design is attributed to Daniel Pratt.

35. Trippe-Bell-Speer House (1821) —140 N. Columbia St. This 1-story, Greek Revival–style clapboard house has remained virtually unchanged since before the Civil War. A notable feature is the row of floor-length windows along the front of the house.

36. DuBignon-Brown-Massee-Moore House (c. 1850)—N. Columbia St. at Hancock St. Intricate woodwork frames the porch of this well-preserved antebellum cottage.

37. Cathy Alumni Center (1921) —517 W. Hancock St. Built as a private residence, this attractive English Tudor–style house now serves as headquarters for the GCSU Alumni Association.

38. Gobert-Baston-Snyder House (c. 1850)—520 W. Hancock St. Designed by E. T. Alling, this single-story clapboard cottage, with a period-style,

modern addition, is now The Guest House bed-and-breakfast inn. (478) 452-3098.

39. Stetson-Sanford House (c. 1825)—Jackson and W. Hancock Sts. This house was designed by John Marlor and was originally located on Wilkinson St. near the courthouse. Notable features include the Palladian double portico and fanlights with ornamental trimwork. In the early 1950s, the house was converted into a tea room. In 1966 it was acquired by the Old Capital Historical Society and moved to its present location. A tour of the home is included in the Trolley Tour, and the house is also open by appointment. (478) 452-4687.

40. Beeson-Andrews House (1898)—210 N. Columbia St. The design of this attractive 2-story Victorian is believed to be based on the Admiral Raphael Semmes House in Mobile, Ala. The original owner was J. L. Beeson, first president of Georgia College.

41. Harris-Vinson-Snead House (c. 1825)—421 W. Montgomery St. A recently restored Federal-style home with Victorian enhancements, the house was for many years the residence of Carl Vinson, a U.S. congressman for more than 50 years.

42. Memory Hill Cemetery (c. 1803)—Liberty and Franklin Sts. Milledgeville's oldest burial ground is the resting place of Georgia governors, legislators, Confederate soldiers, and slaves.

CHAPTER 36

Piedmont National Wildlife Refuge

LOCATION

The refuge is about 25 miles north of Macon via I-75. In Forsyth, follow Juliette Road (exit 186) for 18 miles, passing the small community of Juliette and crossing the Ocmulgee River. After crossing the river, the refuge headquarters will be about 5 miles ahead on the left. The refuge is open 8 A.M.–5 P.M., daily. *Information:* (478) 986-5441.

PARKING

There is a parking lot adjacent to the headquarters/visitor center and a smaller lot at the end of the road above Lake Allison.

BACKGROUND

"This land has changed more in the last 200 years than in the previous 10,000 years...." This statement from an exhibit in the refuge visitor center is a serious commentary on human impact in the area.

The first human beings entered the hardwood forests of the Piedmont (the word literally means "foot of the mountains") more than 10,000 years ago. These nomadic Paleo-Indians trod lightly on the land, building no permanent settlements and subsisting on edible plants and what fish and game they could kill. Little evidence remains of their passage.

The Archaic Indians of 5,000 years ago built semipermanent villages and practiced primitive agriculture. They, too, left only scattered artifacts such as spear and arrow points, pottery shards, and other small items to mark their tenure on the land. Their descendants, the Mississippians, the great mound builders, lived in large towns of several thousand inhabitants and practiced more advanced agriculture. While they hunted and traveled through the rugged Piedmont forests, they, too, left much of it unchanged.

259

The arrival of the first European settlers to Georgia in the mid–18th century was the watershed event in the history of the once-vast wilderness of Georgia's interior. By the early 1800s, pioneer farmers, taking advantage of treaties with the Creek Indian descendants of the mound builders, moved into the fertile hills and river valleys of the Piedmont Plateau and began carving farms and plantations from the wild country. So rapid was the influx of settlers anxious to build a life on the frontier, that by 1820, Jones County (where the refuge is located) was the most populous in Georgia.

The land was ideal for cotton, and enormous tracts were cleared for large-scale planting and harvesting made possible by thousands of slaves. By the time of the Civil War, most of the ancient forests were gone, and, at harvest time each year, the rolling hills, covered in white cotton bolls, resembled a winter snow scene. By the 1870s, the last remnants of the virgin forest had fallen to the lumberman's ax.

Such intensive farming and timbering led to severe erosion and loss of the topsoil on more than 90 percent of the land. Nearly impenetrable hardwood forests had been transformed into treeless hills and widening gullies. This destruction of the landscape, followed in the 1920s by boll weevil infestations and then the Great Depression, wiped out farmers,

who gave up and left the land in record numbers.

The century-long devastation also destroyed important wildlife habitat. By the 1930s, there was little forage left to sustain even a population of squirrels, much less white-tailed deer or migrating birds on their seasonal journeys.

The Federal Government acquired much of the abandoned land and, in 1939, established the 35,000-acre Piedmont National Wildlife Refuge, operated by the U.S. Fish and Wildlife Service. As a tangible demonstration in land reclamation, the property was retired from agriculture. Ponds and lakes were built, and the forest, with its important wildlife habitats, slowly began to renew itself. The despoiled countryside has now been replaced by a healthy intermediate forest of loblolly pines along drier slopes and ridges and hardwoods in creek valleys and coves. Unhindered, the forest will slowly evolve to its ancient status of a climax hardwood forest, just as the first occupants found it more than a hundred centuries ago.

As trees and plants have returned in profusion, the refuge has again become a haven for wildlife, filled with more than 200 species of birds and a wide variety of mammals, reptiles, and amphibians. Scientists estimate that the populations may now even exceed the numbers that were here when the pioneer settlers arrived in

Piedmont National Wildlife Refuge

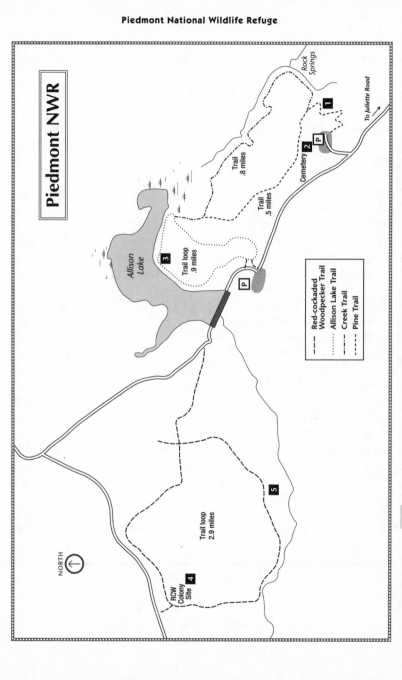

Piedmont NWR

Allison Lake

Rock Springs

To Juliette Road

Cemetery

Trail .8 miles

Trail .5 miles

Trail loop .9 miles

Trail loop 2.9 miles

RCW Colony Site

NORTH

--- Red-cockaded Woodpecker Trail
······ Allison Lake Trail
-·-·- Creek Trail
- - - Pine Trail

the early 1800s. Two wildlife species, once plentiful in the region, have received special attention. First, wild turkeys were returned to the refuge lands in 1944, when nine nesting pairs were transplanted from South Carolina's Cape Romaine National Wildlife Refuge. Second, the endangered red-cockaded woodpecker, a native of the South's old-growth pine forests, most of which were wiped out during the period of intensive agriculture and logging, have reestablished a foothold. Today, several family groups inhabit nesting sites in the refuge.

Visitors are welcome to enjoy exhibits in the visitor center, hike refuge trails, tour by automobile along the 6-mile Little Rock Wildlife Dr., and observe wildlife from a photography blind overlooking Lake Allison. Today, the Piedmont National Wildlife Refuge is a functioning, healthy ecosystem—a true success story in environmental restoration and protection.

WALK DISTANCE AND TERRAIN

Three connecting loops combine to provide about 5 miles of hiking trails. The longest trail, the 2.9-mile Red-Cockaded Woodpecker Trail, ascends from the Allison Lake dam into the loblolly pine forest and through prime woodpecker habitat, before descending to follow the creek valley back to the trailhead. The .9-mile Allison Lake Trail winds along

the shores of the small lake, offering several vantage points for observing waterfowl and other wildlife. Two other trails, the .8-mile Creek Trail and the .5-mile Pine Trail, combine to explore the marshy lowlands, with their ferns and hardwoods, and the drier upland slopes beneath a canopy of evergreens. Along all of the trails there are benches where hikers may pause to rest or quietly observe the surroundings.

The terrain is heavily wooded and rolling with some moderately strenuous climbs along upland slopes. All the trails are identified with either metal or wooden directional markers. The Red-Cockaded Woodpecker and Allison Lake Trails also feature descriptive markers offering details about the surrounding fauna or wildlife habitats. There is also a short, wheelchair-accessible pathway behind the visitor center that leads to a bird nesting and feeding area.

Plans are under development for the addition of a new network of trails in the Bond Swamp area of the refuge near Macon. These trails are expected to be completed in 2003–04.

Occasionally, some sections of the trails may be closed during the limited deer and wild turkey hunting seasons in the refuge.

Note: In winter, after the leaves fall, some sections of the trails may be obscured and difficult to follow. The markers are spaced about 25–50 yards apart. If you travel for more than a few minutes without seeing a marker, you may want to retrace your steps to determine if you have strayed from the trail.

SIGHTS ALONG THE WAY

 **1. Refuge Headquarters and Visitor Center (1970s)**—The building houses staff offices

Pioneer Cemetery

and exhibits tracing the natural and human history of the refuge lands. The center exhibits were completely updated in 2000. Maps and information are available at the center. *Hours:* 8 A.M.–4:30 P.M., Mon.–Fri.; 9 A.M.–5 P.M., Sat. and Sun. (478) 986-5441.

2. Old Cemetery (c. 1800s)—As the fading inscriptions indicate, this was the burial ground for members of the Gunn and Bradley families. The earliest interment was of Daniel Gunn who died in 1825.

3. Allison Lake Wildlife Observation Blind (1960s)—Perched on the shores of the small pond, this blind allows bird-watchers and photographers to observe waterfowl on the lake without being detected. The blind is an especially popular destination during the spring and fall bird migrations.

4. Red-Cockaded Woodpecker Colony Site—Several nesting pairs of

woodpeckers have made their homes in the old-growth pines along this section of the trail. The birds bore holes in the trunks of live trees and build their nests in the cavities. They then drill holes around the nest so that resin coats the surrounding wood. Ornithologists believe they do this to protect the nest from snakes and other predators. Trees with known nesting cavities are marked with a white horizontal stripe, and spring is the best season for observing the birds.

5. Pioneer Cemetery (c. 1800s)—A low, fieldstone wall surrounds two long-faded tombstones marking the burial site of early settlers to the area.

263

CHAPTER 37

Fitzgerald

LOCATION

Fitzgerald is located about 110 miles south of Macon via I-75. Exit the interstate at Ashburn (exit 78) and travel east on GA 112 and GA 107 for about 25 miles to the town center. *Information:* Fitzgerald Tourism and Visitors Association, (800) 386-4642; www.fitzgeraldga.org.

PARKING

 There is ample curbside parking throughout the central business district and on nearby residential streets.

BACKGROUND

At first glance, Fitzgerald seems little different from dozens of small towns across the South. Farmers in dusty pickups sidle up to the feed store; mechanics tinker at the corner auto shop; merchants greet customers they have served for generations; and retirees relax beneath stately shade trees on the courthouse lawn.

A stroll across that lawn yields an important clue to Fitzgerald's unique place in Georgia's, and perhaps, America's history. A clue revealed not from what is there, but from what is missing. Survey the scene and you will find no marble soldier from the Confederacy's "Lost Cause," facing northward in a defiant pose. In Fitzgerald, this is no oversight. Instead, it is part of the marvelous story of Georgia's "Colony City."

The story began in 1893–94 when the nation was in the grips of a deep recession. Summer droughts, followed by brutal winters, ravaged the Midwest, leaving many farm families on the brink of starvation. When calls for help spread across the nation, Georgians were among the first to respond, sending trainloads of grain, supplies, and clothing to the sufferers.

This generosity, from a state still recovering from the devastating effects of defeat in the Civil War, caught

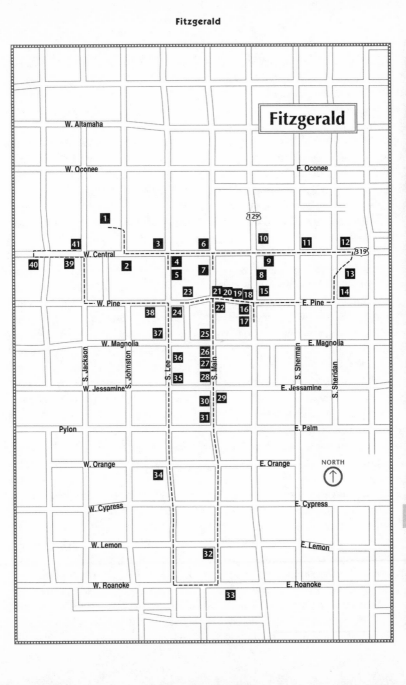

the attention of Philander H. Fitzgerald, a Union Army veteran, Indiana pension attorney, and editor and publisher of the *American Tribune* newspaper.

In his legal work with the Grand Army of the Republic—the national association of Union veterans of the war—Fitzgerald saw firsthand how many of the aging soldiers and their families were suffering from the effects of the economic hard times and the harsh northern climate. Several years before, he had proposed the idea of establishing a community where the old veterans could work and live in more comfortable surroundings. Watching waves of immigrants arrive in America and continue on to the western frontier, Fitzgerald initially considered locations in the West and Southwest for his planned colony. He ultimately rejected several possible sites due, in large part, to their remoteness. With the humanitarian gesture of the Georgians fresh on his mind, he considered for the first time the possibility of establishing his colony in the Deep South.

In a letter to Georgia's governor, William J. Northen, Fitzgerald outlined his idea and inquired about possible sites. Northen responded enthusiastically, and in the summer of 1894, Fitzgerald and several of his associates rode by train to Atlanta, where they were met by the governor, and after exploring several locations, they finally chose a tract of dense pine forest in southern Georgia about 100 miles south of Macon.

To finance the purchase of about 50,000 acres of this land, Fitzgerald formed the American Tribune Soldier's Colony Company. Through the sale of stock in the company, the money was raised and the land acquired. Shares in the company were of two kinds: investment stock and allotment stock. Both types sold for $10 per share, and no family could purchase more than ten shares. Allotment stock could be redeemed for a lot or tract of land in the colony at the company's cost. If the family moved to the colony and built on their land, the money would be refunded. A 1,000-acre square in the center of the property was set aside for a planned city. This tract was surveyed and divided into 4 wards, each containing 4 blocks with 16 squares in each block, yielding 256 squares of equal size. One block in each ward was set aside for a school, and 3 for parks. In the heart of the city, 36 blocks were subdivided into business lots, and the remainder were available for residential development. Bisecting the city were two grand thoroughfares: Central Avenue was laid out east to west, and Main Street, north to south.

At the time the land was acquired by the company, the only people living in the area were a handful of residents of the backwoods village of

Swan, located on the northern edge of the property. By the summer of 1895, even before a survey of the land was finished, people began coming by the hundreds, then the thousands—by rail, wagon, or on foot—to start a new life in the colony to be carved from the trackless woods. At first they made their homes in a vast tent city while streets were laid out, timber was cut and milled, and the first permanent buildings erected.

While the property was initially intended as a home for Union veterans, the colony's charter stated that ownership was "open to all good people." Soon, native Southerners, many of them Confederate veterans, purchased shares and joined the colony. Past animosities were set aside as everyone pitched in to build a city. Many of the town's settlers were craftsmen and artisans, and they worked both quickly and skillfully to create a complete city in an extraordinarily short time. By the time Fitzgerald was incorporated on Dec. 2, 1896, many of the early wooden structures were already giving way to permanent buildings constructed of brick and stone. The continued immigration of settlers and the pace of construction was such that the growing town soon boasted 13 saw mills, a brickyard, and an ironworks. Within a few years, the city also had two factories producing distinctive masonry blocks for residential and commercial construction. These

blocks, commonly called "granitoid," were notable because they were smooth on three sides and rough on the fourth—giving the impression of hewn stone. Not surprisingly, Fitzgerald has a large number of buildings constructed of this unusual material.

As the city was surveyed, colonists chose to use the newly laid out streets as symbols of reconciliation by naming them for Union and Confederate generals. Confederates Lee, Johnston, Jackson, Bragg, and Longstreet parallel Main Street to the west, while Federals Grant, Sherman, Sheridan, Thomas, and Logan parallel it to the east. Another example of the sense of reconciliation of past enemies that filled the town was the establishment of Blue and Gray Park, not by the Colony Company, but by the Blue and Gray Association, a group composed of veterans from both sides.

Probably the grandest display of peace and harmony among former adversaries occurred in 1897 during the festival celebrating the first anniversary of the town's incorporation. According to plans, the festival's many events were to culminate with two parades accompanied by a band playing martial music. The first parade would feature Confederate veterans; they would be followed by marching Union veterans. But the old soldiers had another idea. As the band started, the men of both sides joined together and marched as one behind the Stars and Stripes. When Fitzgerald saw this from his seat in the reviewing stand, he turned to Gov. Northen and proclaimed, "We are watching our nation reunite before our eyes."

WALK DISTANCE AND TERRAIN

Located along the upper edge of Georgia's ancient coastal plain, Fitzgerald is situated on level, rolling terrain. Most residential streets have good sidewalks and an arching canopy of shading pines, hardwoods, and live oak trees. The distance of the loop through the downtown business district and close-in neighborhoods is about 2.5 miles.

SIGHTS ALONG THE WAY

 1. Blue and Gray Museum (1902)—116 Johnston St. Located in the municipal building, which is housed in the Spanish Mission–style Atlanta and Birmingham Railroad depot, the museum offers a rich collection of photographs and artifacts tracing the history of the colony and its people. Plans are under development to relocate the museum to a site on Pine Street (see #24) in 2001. *Hours:* 10 A.M.–4 P.M., Mon.–Fri.; weekends by appointment. (478) 426-5069.

2. Site of Lee-Grant Hotel (1897)—W. Central Ave. at S. Lee St. A grocery store and shopping center now occupy the site of the elegant hotel, which was torn down in the early 1970s. Of all the early structures built in Fitzgerald, none was grander than the 4-story, wood frame, 150-room hotel (the largest wooden building in Georgia when completed). Colonists initially planned to call the hotel the "Grant-Lee," but in deference to their new Southern friends and neighbors, changed the name to the "Lee-Grant."

3. Central United Methodist Church (1920)—W. Central Ave. at N. Lee St. This large Georgian-style church was erected by a local Methodist Episcopal congregation. In 1939, when the Southern and Northern branches of the denomination consolidated, the congregation reorganized as a Methodist church.

4. Old Federal Building (c. 1930s)—W. Central Ave. and S. Lee St. Built in the Georgian style, this single-story brick building once housed local Federal agency offices and the post office.

5. Old Carnegie Library (1915)—116 S. Lee St. Built with funds donated by industrialist Andrew Carnegie, the building served as the local library until a new facility was completed in 1984. The building is owned by the city, and its planned renovation will be part of the Historic Pine Street Development project.

6. Mother Enterprise Monument—Median of S. Main St. at Central Ave. This small monument commemorates the work of Nettie C. Hall (1841–1908), editor of the

Enterprise, one of the city's first newspapers. The very literate population of Fitzgerald once supported seven daily newspapers.

7. The Grand Theatre (c. 1920s, rebuilt 1936)—115 S. Main St. The present structure replaced the original theater badly damaged in a fire in 1935. The Grand operated as a movie theater until it closed in 1977. It was purchased by the city a year later and was eventually restored and converted to an 847-seat state-of-the art performing arts center. Today, with its distinctive Art Deco facade and marquee, the theater is again the cultural heart of the city, featuring a variety of dramatic and musical productions each year. Plans currently in development include installation of the latest in conferencing equipment for meetings, and the restoration of a roof garden for special events. The facility is managed by the Fitzgerald–Ben Hill County Arts Council whose offices are located next door. *Information:* (478) 426-5033.

8. Home Savings Bank (1908)—114 S. Grant St. This unusual Romanesque Revival–style building with distinctive marble facade was built for a local bank. The original bank closed in 1928, and the building has served numerous functions since that time.

9. Kruger-Davis Building (c. 1898)—S. Grant St. at E. Central Ave. Built to house a hardware store, this large, 2-story painted brick building is notable for its distinctive brickwork and ornate cornices. It has served numerous purposes through the years including use as an athletic club, dry goods store, Dr. Pepper bottling plant, and furniture store.

10. *Herald-Leader* Building (1897)—202 E. Central Ave. One of the oldest and most distinctive buildings in Fitzgerald, this 2-story structure originally housed a grocery store on the first floor and rooms of the Windsor Hotel on the second floor. It was later converted for use as a hardware store. It was acquired by the *Fitzgerald Herald-Leader* in 1991 and extensively renovated. Noted for its ornate metal cornices, brackets, and finials (manufactured by the Fitzgerald Ironworks), the building won an award for its restorers from the Georgia Trust for Historic Preservation.

11. Fire Station (c. 1902)—302 E. Central Ave. Originally built to house City Hall, the building once included a 3-story clock tower (plans are under consideration to restore the tower). The building was expanded in 1938. The city owns several pieces of antique firefighting equipment, and there are plans to use a portion of the building for a small museum.

12. Standard Supply Company (c. 1897)—406 E. Central Ave. Built in the Spanish Mission style, this long, 1-story, painted brick building is the oldest, continuously operating family-owned business in Fitzgerald.

269

13. Ben Hill County Courthouse (1909)—E. Central Ave. at S. Sheridan St. Notable for its large Corinthian columns, this Greek Revival sandstone-brick building was recently restored and modernized. *NR*

14. Ben Hill County Jail (c. 1909)—402 E. Pine St. The city's first jail is significant as Fitzgerald's only Gothic Revival–style structure. The building was restored and modernized in 2000.

15. Corbutt-Donovan Building (1897)—128 S. Grant St. This large, 5-story building featuring elegant iron cornice work, was completed only two years after the city's founding. It originally provided space for professional offices on the upper floors and retail businesses at street level. The building was renovated in the 1980s and now houses several county agencies.

16. First National Bank Building (1902)—102 W. Pine St. Originally constructed for use as a bank, this building has also housed the Blue and Gray Museum and, most recently, an insurance company. The structure is notable for its brickwork and the marble steps leading to an ornate entrance facade with arched transom.

17. Martin Insurance Building (1901)—207 S. Grant St. Built of the distinctive granitoid blocks manufactured in Fitzgerald, this building has served a variety of uses through the years.

18. Colony Art Gallery (c. 1910s)—126 E. Pine St. This former retail building now houses a gallery featuring works of local and regional artists. Hours vary. *Information:* (478) 426-5035.

19. Holzendorff Building (1905)—Mid-block of E. Pine St. between Grant and Main Sts. The unusual roughened exterior and three-sided bay window on the second floor are distinctive features of this building built by Dr. Holzendorff, a local dentist. The first floor has housed Dock's Jewelry Store for many years.

20. Haile Drug Store (c. 1900)—114 E. Pine St. This building originally housed the apothecary of Dr. Haile, one of Fitzgerald's first druggists.

21. Third National Bank (c. 1900)—102 E. Pine St. Originally constructed to house a bank and the local Elk's Club, the building was later converted for use as a hotel. It now houses retail businesses on the first floor.

22. Jay, Sherrell, and Smith Law Offices (1920)—101 E. Pine St. Built to house a bank, this brick structure with distinctive Ionic columns has served as attorneys' offices for many years.

23. Holzendorff Apartments (1915)—105 W. Pine St. Also built by Dr. Holzendorff (see # 19), this building is distinctive for its second-story recessed porch. *NR*

24. Swan Laundry Building (1920s)—Pine and S. Lee Sts. This former laundry and dry-cleaning business is the site for the planned relocation of the Blue and Gray Museum.

25. W. R. C. Building (c. 1898)—215 S. Main St. One of the early structures erected in town, the building was constructed by the Union veterans and their sons to serve as headquarters for the Grand Army of the Republic's Women's Relief Corps, which provided services and support for veterans and their families. Note the distinctive carved "WRC" beneath the roof gable.

26. Paulk Funeral Home (1925)—301 S. Main St. This elegant Greek Revival–style structure, featuring four large Doric columns, was built originally as a residence. It was later adapted for use as a funeral home and the adjacent chapel was constructed in the 1960s.

27. Ware-Mashburn House (1906)—315 S. Main St. Designed in the Georgian style, this brick residence is noted for its stained-glass windows and porch supported by Doric columns. The building was converted for use as attorneys' offices in 1986. *NR*

28. Bowen-Sheppard House (1900)—327 S. Main St. Constructed by the same family that erected the adjacent Ware-Mashburn House, this residence also features elements of the Georgian style.

29. Jessamine Place (1910)—402 S. Main St. Originally constructed by the Littlefield family, this brightly painted, Georgian-style frame house features a 2-story porch beneath a central portico.

30. Broadhurst-Paulk House (1920)—409 S. Main St. One of the newer residences on Main St., this is an elegant, Neoclassical-style mansion with a large shed porch supported by Ionic columns.

31. Maffett-Ritter House (c. 1900)—507 S. Main St. Distinctive features of this Georgian-style house are the diamond-paned casement windows and the unusual hipped dormer. The house was originally constructed on an adjacent lot and moved on logs to its current location in 1905.

32. McLendon-Walker House (1912)—801 S. Main St. This large frame house is typical of many of Fitzgerald's early residences. It is notable for the large, 2-story bay front and hipped roof.

33. Farmer House (1915)—100 W. Roanoke Dr. An elegant, Georgian-style mansion with a semicircular porch, this former residence has served as headquarters for the Fitzgerald Elks Club for many years.

34. Russell-Harris House (1905)—605 S. Lee St. A rambling,

Dorminy-Massee House

Queen Anne–style structure with a central turret and full-length front porch, the house was built for the family of a Dr. Russell. It was later subdivided into apartments, and, most recently, has been restored for use as a personal care home.

35. Faith Baptist Church (1906)— 326 S. Lee St. Built by the congregation of Central Christian Church, the sanctuary was acquired by the Baptist congregation in the late 1980s. The building is constructed of the distinctive granitoid blocks manufactured in Fitzgerald. Notable are the rich stained-glass windows.

36. Fitzgerald Hebrew Congregation (1906)— 302 S. Lee St. Originally built by the Methodist Episcopal congregation (see #3), the sanctuary was acquired by members of Fitzgerald's Jewish community in 1939 and remodeled as a Hebrew synagogue. Today, the synagogue serves Jewish families from around southern Georgia.

37. Philip Jay House (1905)— 225 S. Lee St. Constructed of granitoid blocks, this Greek Revival–style house is notable for having only three Doric columns, instead of the usual four, to support the central portico. According to local stories, the house was erected by a thrifty Scottish family who believed that the portico could be supported by three columns, rendering the fourth an unnecessary expense. The ivy surrounding the house is said to have originated with cuttings from the garden of Scottish poet Robert Burns.

38. Episcopal Church (1905)— 212 W. Pine St. Designed in the Gothic style, this small church is notable for its rock-faced bell tower and extensive use of stained glass.

39. Glover-Smith House (1900)— 412 W. Central Ave. This rambling Queen Anne–style house with large wraparound porch and Victorian turret, is constructed largely of granitoid blocks.

40. Dorminy-Massee House (1915)—516 W. Central Ave. An elegant Greek Revival mansion, the house was built by banker, businessman, and lumber company owner Capt. Jack Dorminy. The Dorminy family had lived in the area since antebellum times and were among the first to welcome and join the colony. Considered one of the grandest homes in town, it is now a bed-and-breakfast inn operated by Dorminy's great-grandson and his family. (478) 423-3123.

41. Fitzgerald "T" House (c. 1900) —401 Jackson St. This carefully preserved residence is an excellent example of a "T" house (with the front porch extending from the main part of the house to form a rough "T"). The style, with its steeply pitched roof

designed to handle heavy snowfall, was common throughout the Midwest in the 1880s–90s, and brought south with the colonists.

NOTES

CHAPTER 38

Little Ocmulgee State Park

LOCATION

✴ Little Ocmulgee State Park is located about 80 miles southeast of Macon via I-16 and U.S. 441 (exit 51). It is about 2 miles north of the town of McRae, the seat of Telfair County. *Information:* (229) 868-7474.

PARKING

🚗 A large parking area ajoins the trailhead. There is a daily parking fee, and annual state park passes are available.

274

BACKGROUND

📖 In the early 1800s, immigrants moving inland came to the lands of central Georgia only recently ceded by the Creek Indians, and many settled in the pine woods of what became Telfair County. The economy, dependent on agriculture and timber, thrived until the early years of the 20th century when prolonged drought and the infamous cotton infestations by the boll weevil brought hard times to much of rural Georgia. Failed crops and worn-out lands left residents with an unsure future.

In the depths of the Great Depression, the citizens of the area sought assistance from one of Pres. Franklin D. Roosevelt's most popular New Deal agencies, the Civilian Conservation Corps (CCC). CCC camps offered employment opportunities for healthy young men and local adults with necessary work experience.

With the help of Gov. Eugene Talmadge, a McRae native, a CCC camp was established in 1933 to carry out forest recovery and soil conservation work in an area called Shamrock Springs. Located just east of the Little Ocmulgee River, Shamrock Springs had once been a popular spa and local citizens believed that with the help of CCC workers, the scenic area could be an attraction once again. In early 1935, local citizens raised the funds to purchase more than 1,000 acres around

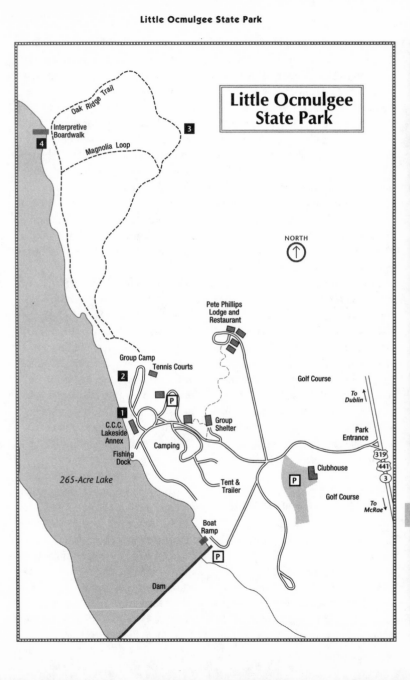

Little Ocmulgee
State Park

NORTH

the springs for the creation of a new park. Later that same year, a second camp, composed of unemployed World War I veterans, began work on the newly created recreation area.

For nearly five years, workers built roads, carved trails, constructed rustic log buildings, and planted nearly 100,000 trees. The centerpiece of the park was the 265-acre lake created by the fabrication of a 1,500-ft. concrete dam, much of it mixed and poured by hand. In 1940, with the approach of World War II, the camp closed and the land was turned over to the state.

Little Ocmulgee, with its variety of amenities, is one of the most popular units in Georgia's state park system. Visitors flock to the park to enjoy 18 holes of golf on the Wallace Adams Memorial Golf Course, dine in the restaurant, stay overnight at the 30-room Pete Philips Lodge or the shaded campground, play tennis on two lighted courts, or to hike, boat on the lake, swim in the pool, or simply relax as their grandparents did years ago.

TRAIL DISTANCE AND TERRAIN

276

The park's Oak Ridge Trail carves a 3-mile loop through the sandy, tree-shaded hills of the upper coastal plain. The Magnolia Trail is a shorter loop (1.7 miles) created by a connecting path between the eastern and western sides of the Oak Ridge Trail. There is only a moderate elevation change along the trails, which travel through pines, magnolias, and live oaks heavily draped in Spanish moss.

The park is prime habitat for the endangered gopher tortoise. The telltale signs of the animal's burrow (which can reach 30–40 ft. in length beneath the ground) may be seen along the route. The tortoise and another rare and endangered animal, the nonvenomous indigo snake, often share a burrow. Both are very reclusive and unlikely to be seen by hikers.

SIGHTS ALONG THE WAY

1. Lakeside Pavilion (1930s)—South side of the parking area adjacent to the lake. This large, rustic wooden building was constructed by CCC workers from heavy cypress logs culled from the plains flooded to create the lake. The fieldstone used for the foundations and chimneys of this and the other CCC-era buildings was brought from Fort Mountain in northwestern Georgia because there is no stone suitable for this purpose in southern Georgia. Behind the pavilion is a fishing dock and playground. (Note: There are alligators in the lake and nearby swamp, so swimming is not permitted and pets should be kept on a leash.)

2. Outdoor Amphitheater (1997)—Located west of the trailhead. This open-air stage each September

Little Ocmulgee State Park

hosts the drama, *The Lightered Knot,* tracing the tumultuous history of the timber barons of the Dodge family and the land wars fought in this part of the state in the late 1800s.

3. Oak Ridge—This area along the northern edge of the loop is unusual for its open sand dunes and trees that may be centuries old but whose growth has been stunted by the nutrient-poor soil, clear reminders that in ancient geological times, this land was on the bottom of a shallow ocean.

4. Lake and Marsh Overlook— This short boardwalk leads to a platform overlooking the northern edge of the lake and surrounding marsh, an ideal place to watch for waterfowl and migratory birds.

NOTES

277

CHAPTER 39

Andersonville National Historic Site

LOCATION

✦ Andersonville is located about 58 miles southwest of Macon. Travel south on I-75 to GA 26 (exit 127). Follow this highway west to Montezuma, then travel south on GA 49 to the park entrance. The grounds and National Cemetery are open daily 8 A.M.–5 P.M. The walk begins behind the National Prisoner of War Museum. *Information:* (229) 924-0343; www.nps.gov/ande.

PARKING

🚗 There is a large parking area adjacent to the museum. There are smaller lots near the Star Ft., near Providence Spring, and at the National Cemetery.

BACKGROUND

📖 Two years deep into the Civil War, the pine hills of southwestern Georgia remained far from the horrors of the battlefield. Yet, when Confederate soldiers and slave laborers arrived near the small community of Andersonville in January 1864 to begin construction of a prisoner-of-war (POW) camp, the incalculable human cost of the war would soon be evident to all.

Since the war's outbreak in April 1861, most soldiers captured by either side had been paroled (sent home with a promise not to take up arms again) or exchanged for a like number of prisoners from the opposing army. Consequently, most POW camps were small and soldiers stayed only a short time. This situation irrevocably changed in the early spring of 1864 when the new Union commander, Lt. Gen. Ulysses Grant, ended the exchange system. He argued that most exchanged Rebels quickly returned to combat, so it would be better to hold prisoners because the South had few men to replace them. He firmly believed this strategy would decimate the Confederate armies and shorten the war. As a result of Grant's order, POW camp populations, on both

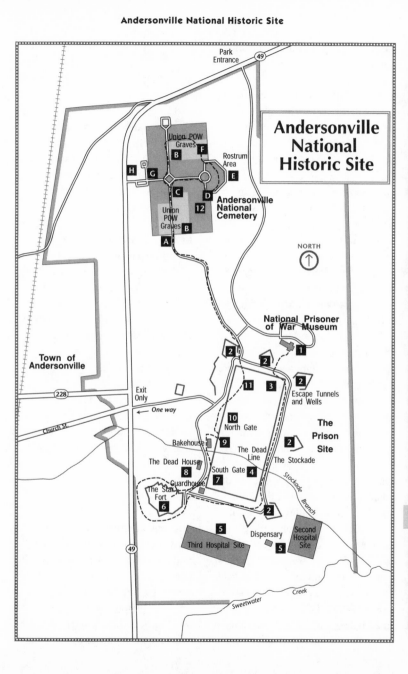

Andersonville National Historic Site

sides, exploded, and in most camps, conditions were poor and prisoners suffered horribly.

In the fall of 1863, two significant events occurred that hastened the need for a POW camp in southwestern Georgia. First was the Battle of Chickamauga in northwestern Georgia, where several thousand Union soldiers were captured and held at temporary camps close to the battlefield and outside Atlanta. Second was Gen. Robert E. Lee's defeat at Gettysburg and retreat to Virginia. When Union armies began massing in northern Virginia, the Confederate government decided to move many of the Union prisoners held near Richmond to locations farther from the battle fronts. Because southwestern Georgia was considered the "breadbasket" of the Confederacy, a prison site there would be secure and have readily available food for both the prisoners and the soldiers guarding them.

In January 1864, slaves began felling pine trees along the banks of a small stream just east of the Andersonville railway station. By the end of the month, a rectangular, 15-ft.-high wooden stockade enclosed an open space of about 16.5 acres. The prison, called Camp Sumter by the Confederates, was intended to house 10,000 prisoners and the first began arriving in early February 1864. Until June, about 400 additional prisoners ar-

rived each day, swelling the prison population to nearly twice its intended capacity. Many more would soon come.

In May 1864, Maj. Gen. William T. Sherman launched his invasion of Georgia with Atlanta as his objective. The fighting yielded thousands more Union captives for the bleak stockade at Andersonville. To accommodate these new arrivals, Andersonville's stockade was expanded in June 1864 to 26.5 acres. By the end of that month, the prison incarcerated almost 26,000 soldiers, with more arriving each day. The prison population peaked at 32,000 in August 1864. Then, with impending threats of attack from Sherman's cavalry, many prisoners were transferred to other camps in eastern Georgia and in South Carolina.

While Sherman's troops marched through Georgia, there was one aborted attempt by Federal cavalry to free the prisoners at Andersonville. In July 1864, as the main body of the Union army surrounded Atlanta, Gen. George Stoneman and a cavalry brigade rode southwest to destroy rail lines and attempt an attack on Andersonville. Outside Macon, Stoneman and 600 troopers were captured. The general was held in Macon, but his men finally made it to Andersonville—as prisoners.

While conditions at nearly all Civil War–era POW camps were terrible by modern standards, the conditions at Andersonville made this small camp a true hell-on-earth. Overcrowding, lack of shelter from the brutal summer sun, contaminated water and almost nonexistent sanitation, a deteriorating Confederate economy, and the failing transportation system, all conspired to make interment at Andersonville a death sentence for more than 12,000 prisoners, most succumbing to disease and malnutrition.

Not all the privations suffered by the prisoners came at the hand of their captors. Within the stockade itself, gangs of thugs preyed on their fellow prisoners. They even resorted to beatings and murder to take what few possessions a man had. These gangs, called "Raiders" by other prisoners, numbered in the hundreds and, for several months, their brutal behavior went unchallenged. Finally, in July 1864 a band of soldiers calling themselves the "Regulators" stood up to the predators and succeeded in rounding up six of their leaders. With the approval of prison commander Maj. Henry Wirz, these men were put on trial before a jury of other prisoners. They were found guilty and hanged. Their bodies were buried in dishonor, their graves set apart from those of other prisoners.

Lack of access to clean water was one of the most serious problems within the stockade. A shallow creek, dubbed "Stockade Branch" by the prisoners, was a muddy, slow-moving stream that meandered on an easterly course through marshy "sinks." While the official camp latrines were positioned on the downstream side of the creek, the water was little more than a fetid cesspool harboring disease. Despite the risks, men routinely drank from and bathed in the stream, and many came down with severe, waterborne illnesses.

On August 15, 1864, at the height of summer's most ferocious temperatures, a heavy thunderstorm struck the camp. Amidst heavy rains, fresh water began gushing from a hillside just south of the stockade's North Gate. John Maile of the 8th Michigan Infantry witnessed the event and wrote in his journal, "A spring of purest crystal water shot up into the air. Looking across the dead line, we beheld with wondering eyes and grateful hearts the fountain spring."

Unfortunately, the spring flowed from the hill inside the dead line, a wooden barrier 19 ft. inside the stockade wall. Prisoners crossing the line were shot. At first, men tied strings to tin cups and tossed them toward the spring to get water. Eventually, Maj. Wirz permitted construction of a trough to channel the water to a safe place within the stockade. As if it were the answer to a thousand prayers from parched throats, the prisoners dubbed the water "Providence Spring."

281

At first at Andersonville, there were only a handful of deaths each day, but as conditions worsened, the number rose to nearly 100 per day. Detachments of soldiers, many of them Negro troops who were being held prisoner at the camp, worked full-time digging shallow, trenchlike graves. The loved ones of many of those who died might never have known their fate if it were not for the efforts of one prisoner, Dorence Atwater, who fell ill and was sent to the camp hospital. The prison surgeon, Dr. White, noted Atwater's excellent handwriting and arranged for him to remain at the hospital as a records clerk. In this capacity, he was responsible for maintaining the register of deaths in the camp. Each record listed the soldier's name, his company and regiment, cause of death, and a chronological number corresponding to a numbered wooden stake marking each grave. Realizing the value of this list to relatives and friends of the deceased, Atwater secretly made a duplicate record. When he was exchanged in February 1865, he carried his list, containing the names of 12,165 men, hidden in the lining of his coat.

In April 1865, Atwater offered the record to the government if they would publish it. Receiving no promise of immediate publication, Atwater sought out Clara Barton, the famous Civil War nurse, who was herself attempting to locate missing and dead Union soldiers. In July 1865, Atwater and Barton traveled together to Andersonville accompanied by a group of army clerks and laborers under the command of Capt. James Moore. Their task was to replace the crude stakes on each grave with lettered, wooden markers containing the information on Atwater's list. When the task was completed, all but 460 graves were identified. The burial ground at Andersonville was designated a National Cemetery on July 26, 1865, and, in a solemn ceremony on August 17, Clara Barton raised the American flag over the hallowed ground.

In 1890, the prison site was purchased by the Georgia Chapter of the Grand Army of the Republic (an association of Union veterans) and then sold to the association's Women's Relief Corps (WRC) for $1.00. The corps undertook a nationwide fund-raising campaign to preserve the site as a permanent memorial to the men who had suffered and died there. Pecan trees were planted on the grounds and the fruit harvested and sold as a means of raising money. Eventually, more than a dozen states erected monuments at the prison site or cemetery to honor their native sons who had been held captive at Andersonville (prisoners at the camp came from 26 different states, including Union loyalists from Virginia, North Carolina, Tennessee, Alabama, and Louisiana).

In 1901, the WRC erected a marble pavilion over Providence Spring to permanently preserve the flow of life-saving water. Nine years later, the corps donated the prison site to the people of the United States as a perpetual memorial. The site was administered by the War Department and later the Department of the Army until it was made a National Historic Site and transferred to the National Park Service in 1971.

The Congressional legislation that formalized the establishment of the National Historic Site stipulated that Andersonville would be set aside to honor the memory of all American prisoners from every war in which they fought. In the beginning, little attention was paid to this larger mission, but in the 1990s, representatives from ex-POW associations, veterans groups, and the Park Service staff planned and raised funds for the National Prisoner of War Museum. It was dedicated on April 9, 1998, 56 years to the day after beleaguered U.S. soldiers on the island of Bataan in the Philippines surrendered to the Japanese. Today, visitors come to Andersonville from around the nation to remember the sacrifices of all American POWs—from the Revolution to the Persian Gulf War. It seems fitting that this important museum be located at Andersonville, for it makes true the wish inscribed on the Pennsylvania Memorial on the grounds of the cemetery:

". . . and while the stars their vigil keep, across the silence of the sky,

The Nation's love for those who sleep at Andersonville shall not die."

WALK DISTANCE AND TERRAIN

A loop hike from the museum along the stockade road and through the cemetery is about 3.7 miles. The ground around the prison site is open.

SIGHTS ALONG THE WAY

 1. National Prisoner of War Museum/Visitor Center (1998)—This brick-and-masonry building is designed to give the appearance of a prison as visitors must pass through gates in front of low towers before entering the lobby and exhibit areas. Inside, large clerestory windows bathe the building in light—a stark contrast to the darkness of most prison cells. Exhibits starkly profile, in sight and sound, the experiences of the nearly 800,000 Americans who have been prisoners of war. Artifacts on display include journals kept by captured soldiers, homemade clothing, hand-stitched flags, and numerous other items men and women used to survive their captivity. Behind the museum is the Commemorative Courtyard with its powerful bas-relief sculpture of massed prisoners behind a free-standing statue of a captive with his arms finally unshackled. According to sculptor Donna Dobberfuhl, the message she sought to convey in the work is "the price of freedom fully paid."

The visitor center also houses a small theater and a gift shop. *Hours:* 8:30 A.M.–5 P.M., daily. (478) 924-0343.

2. Confederate Earthworks (1864)—Located at the four corners of the stockade, these fortifications held artillery that pointed into the prison to prevent disturbances and outward to repel possible attacks.

3. Reconstructed Stockade—This recently built corner section of the prison depicts the layout of the pine-log walls, the guard's "crow's nest," prisoners' crude shelters called "she-bangs," and the placement of the dead line.

4. Stockade Branch—Located at the lowest point between two hills, this slow-moving, shallow creek was the only source of drinking water for the entire prison population until August 1864.

5. Hospital Sites (1864)—Pine woods and open fields were once the location of two large hospitals where doctors feebly attempted to treat prisoners' illnesses with only the most meager medical supplies and equipment. Many soldiers who fell ill refused to go to the hospital, preferring to die among their friends.

6. Star Fort (1864)—This was the largest fortification at the prison. Maj. Wirz's headquarters was located here.

7. Site of South Gate (1864)—Fieldstone pillars mark one of the two gates of entry into the stockade.

8. Site of the Dead House (1864)—The bodies of soldiers who died in the prison were brought to a log shelter here prior to being transported to the cemetery for burial.

Some of the more than 16,000 Civil War POW graves at Andersonville

9. Providence Spring (1864, building 1901)—Fresh water from this underground spring surfaced on August 15, 1864. The ornate marble spring house was erected by the Women's Relief Corps of the Grand Army of the Republic.

10. North Gate Reconstruction—Archaeological excavations identified the location of this main gate, through which new prisoners entered the stockade after their arrival at the Andersonville railway station a half-mile away. Recalling his own arrival, Pvt. John McElroy, 16th Illinois Cavalry, wrote in his journal:

"... five hundred weary men moved along slowly through double lines of guards. Two massive wooden gates, with heavy iron hinges and bolts swung open as we stood there and passed through into the space beyond. We were in Andersonville."

11. Escape Tunnels (1864)—Evidence of escape tunnels remains at several locations among the trees and monuments at the northern end of the stockade.

12. Andersonville National Cemetery (1864)—Set aside in February 1864 as a burial ground for prisoners who died in captivity, the cemetery eventually contained the remains of 12,636 prisoners. After the Civil War, the ground was designated a National Cemetery, and the remains of nearly 800 other Union soldiers—many from field hospitals, battlefield graves, and other prisons—were reinterred here. Andersonville continues to be an active cemetery open to military veterans. The cemetery is divided into 17 sections, arranged alphabetically A–R (there is no section O). Notable sites within the cemetery include:

A. The Georgia Monument (1976)—Commissioned by then-Gov. Jimmy Carter, this powerful sculpture captures the essence of the captive's experience, depicting three weary prisoners supporting each other. Inscribed in the base is a scriptural passage, "Turn you to the stronghold, Ye prisoners of hope" (Zechariah 9:12).

B. Union POW Graves (1864–65)—Located in sections E, F, H, J, and K, these closely spaced graves mark the mass interments of the prisoners who died at Andersonville. The wooden markers placed here by Barton and Atwater were replaced by stone markers in the 1870s.

C. Raiders Graves (1864)—These six graves of prison gang leaders were placed just outside section J as a mark of shame.

D. Memorial to Prisoners at Stalag 17 B—This large monument commemorates American fliers held prisoner by the Germans during World War II at a camp in Austria. Stalag 17 was featured in a popular movie filmed in the 1950s.

E. Rostrum (1941)—This marble structure is used for funerals and special ceremonies.

285

F. Andersonville's Dove (18??)—
Perched on the section H headstone
of L. S. Tuttle of Maine (#12196) is a
carved stone dove. No one knows
when the dove was placed on the
marker, who did it, or why.

G. Park Headquarters (1878)—
This 2-story house was constructed as
the cemetery caretaker's residence.
Hours: 7:30 A.M.–4 P.M., Mon.–Fri.

*H. National Cemetery Office and
Information Center*—Staff provide
assistance to visitors or relatives
searching for the grave of a loved one
or ancestor.

NOTES

CHAPTER 40

Americus

LOCATION

Americus is about 75 miles southwest of Macon via I-75. Exit on GA 27 (exit 112) and travel west for about 30 miles to downtown Americus. The walk begins in front of the Windsor Hotel on W. Lamar St. (U.S. 280). *Information:* Americus–Sumter County Tourism Council, (888) 278-6837; www.Americustourism.com.

PARKING

Streetside parking is available in downtown Americus and along nearby residential streets.

BACKGROUND

 Following the Treaty of Indian Springs in 1825 and the Treaty of Washington in 1831, all of the Indians living in western Georgia were forced to give up their ancestral lands and relocate to the western territories. Even before the removal was finalized, settlers had moved into the western part of the state and established counties and towns.

Sumter County, named for Col. Thomas Sumter of South Carolina, a hero of the French and Indian War and the Revolution, was created in 1831, and a year later, the new county seat of Americus was laid out. According to a popular story, a drawing was to be held to name the town when a man stepped from the crowd and suggested the village be called "Americus" to honor the Italian navigator and mapmaker Amerigo Vespucci. The townspeople liked the name so much that they canceled the drawing and immediately adopted it.

The surrounding land proved ideal for growing cotton, and soon Americus was the center of Georgia's "Cotton Kingdom," an area of vast plantations worked by thousands of African slaves. The town prospered as a regional center for the cotton trade, and many planters built elegant town homes, a few of which still stand.

287

During the Civil War, three large Confederate hospitals were located in Americus. Some of the patients were guards stationed at Camp Sumter, the large prisoner-of-war camp located near Andersonville a few miles northeast of Americus. Nearly a third of the prisoners died from disease and malnutrition, and hundreds of Rebel soldiers guarding them succumbed to the same illnesses.

In the latter years of the 19th century, many communities in southern Georgia boomed as winter retreats for wealthy Northerners. Americus set out to compete for this lucrative business, and several wealthy investors raised the funds to construct an elegant hotel in the center of the city. Unlike many hotels of the period, which were built of wood and consequently fire hazards, the new Windsor Hotel was constructed of locally made brick. In 1884 much of downtown Americus had been razed by a devastating fire that destroyed many of the antebellum buildings. Most were replaced by the late-19th- and early-20th-century commercial structures that remain today, giving Americus the atmosphere of a Victorian city.

While Americus began in the midst of the tragedy of slavery, this area has become best known as the home of leaders dedicated to peace and racial equality and as the headquarters for a humanitarian organization that builds houses around the world.

Former Pres. Jimmy Carter grew up near the tiny community of Plains, 9 miles west of Americus, and traveled frequently to Americus to shop with his family, to attend educational programs, and to take in movies at the Rylander Theater. According to one story, Carter lost his place as senior class valedictorian at Plains High School as punishment for skipping school one day to go to a matinee at the Rylander. The future First Lady, Rosalynn Carter, also grew up in Plains and attended college at Georgia Southwestern College (now University) located in Americus.

In the early days of World War II, Christian missionaries Clarence and Florence Jordan and Mabel and Martin England came to rural Sumter County to establish Koinonia Farms, a Christian commune intended as "a demonstration plot for the kingdom of God." Dedicated to peace and racial harmony, Koinonia was a radical and, at times, highly unpopular departure from the social norms of racial segregation.

In the late 1960s, Koinonia Partners began a housing ministry by building modest homes on their 1,500 acres of land. These homes were built by volunteers and sold to selected families who paid 20-year, no-interest mortgages. Two partners who had been involved in this program, Millard and Linda Fuller, left the farm in 1976 to develop their own housing

288

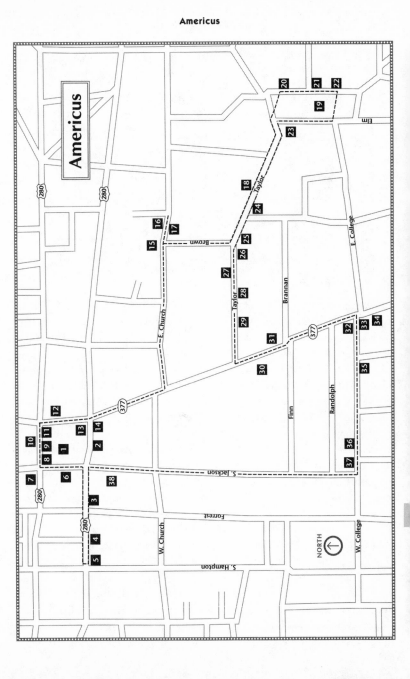

Americus

The second-floor grand balcony of the Windsor Hotel

ministry. Their program, Habitat for Humanity, has gone on to construct thousands of houses for needy families in more than 44 countries. Habitat's international headquarters is located in a restored building in downtown Americus, and Pres. and Mrs. Carter are two of their most famous volunteers.

Today, Americus is a widely recognized architectural treasure, filled with superb 19th- and early-20th-century commercial buildings and houses that are easily enjoyed on foot.

WALK DISTANCE AND TERRAIN

The 3-mile loop from the Windsor Hotel winds through the restored commercial district and along nearby residential streets. There are good sidewalks and shade trees along most of the route.

SIGHTS ALONG THE WAY

1. Windsor Hotel (1892)— 125 W. Lamar St. The castle-like Windsor Hotel with its turrets, towers, dormers, and grand balcony, occupies the heart of Americus's commercial district. Designed by Atlanta architect Gottfried Norrmann, the red-brick Victorian structure was built to accommodate business travelers and to attract a share of the Northern winter-resort trade.

While the Windsor did not keep Northern tourists from continuing on to Florida, it hosted a number of famous guests including statesman and orator William Jennings Bryan, Pres. Franklin D. Roosevelt, and notorious gangster John Dillinger. Despite being the center of Americus social life for many years, the Windsor fell into decline and closed in the early 1970s.

After an award-winning renovation, it reopened in 1991 and is again the place to see and be seen in Americus. The Americus–Sumter County Tourism Council's visitor center is adjacent to the hotel lobby. Hotel: (478) 924-1555; Welcome Center: (888)278-6837.

2. Allison Building (1907)— 124 W. Lamar St. This well-preserved, 3-story sandstone building is notable for its large arched windows.

3. Empire State Bank Building (c. 1910)—Forrest Ave. and W. Lamar St. The entrance to this imposing former bank building is flanked by massive columns, reflecting the importance of the local bank in small town life.

4. Rylander Theater (1921)— 308–20 W. Lamar St. This elegant 630-seat theater served as both a vaudeville and cinema house when it first opened. It was a popular gathering place until it closed in 1951. Shuttered for almost 50 years, the Rylander was recently restored and is now one of the premiere performing arts centers in Georgia. It is also the home of two powerful dramas: *Grace Will Lead Me Home*, a POW story, and *The Jimmy Carter Story*. Event information: (478) 931-0011.

5. Habitat for Humanity International Headquarters (1920s)—322 W. Lamar St. The home of this renowned organization, dedicated to providing housing for needy families, was once an automobile dealership. It was creatively restored in 1996, and the atrium-like lobby is crafted to resemble the surroundings of a small home. Building hours are 8 A.M.–5 P.M., Mon.–Fri., and guided tours are available. These tours include the building and the nearby international village that contains reproductions of the different types of houses built by Habitat volunteers across the globe. (800) 422-4828.

6. Barlow Block (c. 1890s)— Jackson St. across from the Windsor Hotel. This block of ornate buildings reflects the architectural style common in late-19th-century commercial buildings. During the Civil War, a large Confederate hospital occupied this site.

7. Thomas Block (1890s)—W. Forsyth and Jackson Sts. Another of the late-19th-century commercial buildings flanking the Windsor Hotel block.

8. 1889 Building (1889)—124 W. Forsyth St. A former retail shop sitting in the shadow of the Windsor Hotel, the building now houses a restaurant.

9. Thornton-Wheatley Building (1892)—122 W. Forsyth St. This red-brick Victorian building, with its granite and terra-cotta exterior features and rounded corner with a circular window, is believed to have been designed to complement the Windsor Hotel and to serve as the model for other downtown buildings of the period. The building was once called

"Pythian Castle" when it served as the meeting place for the Knights of Pythia fraternal order.

10. Byne Block (1887)—105 W. Forsyth St. This was one of the first commercial blocks rebuilt following the 1884 fire.

11. Citizens Bank Building (c. 1900)—120 N. Lee St. This 4-story structure opened as the Planters' Bank, owned and operated by Lee Council. Council was so rich that he once purchased the Windsor Hotel as a Christmas gift for his wife. The building is now a restaurant.

12. Old Fire Station (1890)—107 N. Lee St. Designed by Windsor Hotel–architect Gottfried Norrmann, this red-brick double-bay station once housed horsedrawn fire wagons. It has been restored as lawyers' offices.

13. Americus City Hall and Municipal Building (1910)—101 W. Lamar St. Built as the Federal Building, this Italian Renaissance–style structure was acquired by the city in 1969. Today it houses offices of city government as well as nonprofit community service and cultural organizations.

14. 102–6 Lamar Building (1890)—Rounding out the tour of the commercial district is this 2-story, blue-painted brick building noted for its ornate, arched windows.

15. Lee Council House (1902)—318 E. Church St. Considered the "most beautiful house in Americus," this brick and terra-cotta Victorian-style structure features several stained-glass windows attributed to Louis C. Tiffany. The house was built by local businessman Lee Council, owner of the Planters' Bank. Today, the house serves as headquarters for the Sumter Historic Preservation Council and is available for use as a special-event facility. The house is occasionally opened to the public for tours. (478) 924-1163.

16. 406 E. Church St. (1890)—In Neo-Jacobean style, this house features shingle siding and a wide, circular verandah.

17. 405 E. Church St. (1890)—This Italian Renaissance-style house features a campanile tower.

18. 234 Taylor St. (1850)—Originally located in Oglethorpe, Ga., this antebellum cottage was moved to Americus to serve as a planter's town house.

19. Rees Park (c. 1880s)—One of the first public parks in Americus, Rees Park quickly became the center of an affluent residential district of the same name. The north side of the park features the Confederate Memorial while the south side contains the "Spirit of the American Doughboy" statue sculpted by Americus artist E. M. Visquesney and unveiled on Armistice Day, Nov. 11, 1921. The statue was originally located at the intersection of Lamar and Lee Sts., and local veterans A. B. Turpin and Walter Rylander served as models. Nearly 140 life-sized copies of this statue have been placed as World War I monuments in 35 other states.

20. Rees Park Inn (c. 1848)— 504 Rees Park St. This elegant antebellum house, with its Italianate-style front portico and verandah, has been beautifully restored as a bed-and-breakfast inn. (478) 931-0122.

21. 602 Rees Park St. (1890)— This eclectic Victorian house has several notable features including a 2-tier portico and corner porch.

22. 606 Rees Park St. (1905)— Another elegant Victorian-style home overlooking the park, this structure is notable for its tower, columns, and ornate baluster.

23. Rees Park School (1910)—409 Rees Park St. Built as Americus High School, this Greek Revival–style building now houses a theater troupe, the Sumter Players.

24. 217 Taylor St. (1859)— An excellent example of Greek Revival architecture, this antebellum house is distinguished by its Greek entablature and Doric columns.

25. 201 Taylor St. (1907)— This early-20th-century house was designed in a style reminiscent of the nearby antebellum Greek Revival structures.

26. D.A.R. Chapter House (1893)—155 Taylor St. This Neoclassical–style house now serves as headquarters of the local chapter of the Daughters of the American Revolution.

27. 144 Taylor St. (c. 1850)—This small antebellum cottage features sidelights, transom, and pediments typical of the Greek Revival style.

28. Charles F. Crisp House (1893)—139 Taylor St. This finely crafted frame house was built by Crisp, a British native and former Confederate officer. Crisp served as Federal judge and later as a U.S. congressman. He was Speaker of the House of Representatives during the 1880s and was elected to the U.S. Senate in 1896, but died before he could serve. His son, Charles R. Crisp, was appointed to fill his seat and later won election to Congress in his own right.

29. Walter B. Hollis House (c. 1850)—133 Taylor St. Hollis built this house shortly before the Civil War, and it was occupied by his daughter "Miss Florence" Hollis until her death in the 1960s at the age of 106. Miss Hollis told stories of carrying food in horsedrawn wagons to the Union prisoners at Camp Sumter (Andersonville).

30. 401 S. Lee St. (c. 1840)—One of the oldest houses in Americus, this Greek Revival–style cottage now serves as a medical office.

31. Calvary Episcopal Church (1919)—408 S. Lee St. This simple brick church in Carpenter Gothic style is the work of Ralph Adams Cram, one of the nation's most renowned architects of church and academic buildings. Accustomed to much larger commissions (Cram designed buildings for Princeton and Rice Universities, and he served as dean of the architecture school of Massachusetts Institute of Technology), Cram accepted this project following a direct appeal from the church's pastor.

32. Hancock Funeral Home (1892)—427 S. Lee St. Built as a private residence, this Victorian-style structure is noted for its corner tower and dormers.

33. 1906 Pathway Inn (1906)—501 S. Lee St. An elegant, Victorian house featuring a 2-story central portico with rounded balcony, this is now a bed-and-breakfast inn. (800) 889-1466.

34. Cobb House (c. 1823)—505 S. Lee St. This structure is one of nearly 100 antebellum houses moved from Oglethorpe, Ga., following a devastating smallpox epidemic there. The house was purchased by Col. Charles Malone in 1855 and moved to this site by oxcart. It was acquired in 1883 by Capt. John Cobb, son of Confederate general Howell Cobb. His descendants lived in the house until 1963. It was purchased in 1975 by the late Dr. Henry King Stanford, retired president of the University of Miami and one-time interim president of the University of Georgia.

35. 202 W. College St. (c. 1860)—This small cottage has excellent examples of the Gothic style, most notably the trefoil and delicate bargeboard.

36. 309 W. College St. (c. 1850)—This house is a finely crafted antebellum Greek Revival cottage.

37. 317 W. College St. (c. 1840)—This antebellum cottage is a simple and well-proportioned residence.

38. Presbyterian Church (1884)—125 S. Jackson St. This frame church is designed in the Carpenter Gothic style.

NOTES

Valdosta and Valdosta State University

LOCATION

Valdosta is 152 miles south of Macon via I-75 (exit 16) and U.S. 221 and 84 and GA 38. Follow U.S. 84/GA 38 (Hill Ave.) east to downtown. The walk begins at the north side of the Lowndes County Courthouse. *Information:* Valdosta–Lowndes County Convention and Visitors Bureau, (800) 569-8687. Valdosta State University, (229) 333-5980; www.valdosta.edu.

PARKING

Metered, on-street parking and commercial lots are available in the downtown area. Visitor parking is available at the Valdosta State University Center on N. Patterson St., just north of the campus on Georgia Ave.

BACKGROUND

 At the time of the first European contact, this area was the home of the Lower Creeks, an advanced culture that lived in permanent villages, hunted game, fished, and cultivated crops of beans, corn, and squash. Despite persistent legends that Hernando de Soto passed through this area, the earliest recorded contact with European settlers occurred in the late 1600s when Spanish priests from Florida traveled north into Georgia's interior to convert the "savages" to Christianity.

Their missionary trail, locally known as the "Saint Augustine Road," was soon followed by traders who established a lucrative commerce with the natives, seeking every opportunity to take advantage of them. By the late 1700s, the Creeks had sold many thousands of acres of their lands as payment for debts incurred in acquiring manufactured goods from traders and merchants.

Following the American Revolution, the government of the new state of Georgia faced unrelenting pressure to acquire more Creek lands and to

295

remove the Indians from Georgia. After three decades of conflict and various short-lived treaties, the Federal government succeeded in removing the Creeks from Georgia and Alabama and turned the land over to the states. The fertile lands drew thousands who came to establish small farms, to build mills for grinding corn or harvesting lumber, and to carry goods to ports along the Flint and Chattahoochee Rivers.

Cotton thrived in the sandy soil and, in the decades prior to the Civil War, wealthy landowners assembled vast plantations, importing thousands of slaves to work the fields. In many southern Georgia counties, including Lowndes, slaves often greatly outnumbered the white population.

The key markets for the cotton were in New England and in Europe, but the plantation owners found the primitive roads and limited river access increasingly ill-suited to getting their products to coastal ports for shipping. A railroad was the answer, and by the late 1850s, work was under way on the construction of the Atlantic and Gulf Railroad line connecting Thomasville, Albany, and other towns in southern Georgia with ports on both the Atlantic and Gulf coasts.

Railroad surveyors determined that the terrain around the county seat of Troupville was unsuitable for railway construction and built the line about four miles east of the town. The citizens of Troupville established a new county seat adjacent to the rail line in 1860. They called this settlement "Valdosta," a name drawn from Gov. George Troup's estate, "Val d'Osta," which is thought to have been derived from "Val de Aosta," an especially scenic area in the Italian Alps.

With the election of Abraham Lincoln in November 1860, Georgia followed several other Southern states into secession from the Union in early 1861. When the war ended, the fields were overgrown and the slavery-based agricultural economy in ruins. But, the fertile soil remained, and through tenant farming and sharecropping with former slaves, cotton farmers were soon thriving again.

In the years after the war, a young Valdostan named John Holliday developed a modest dental practice in town until he contracted tuberculosis. In 1872, he left for the drier climates of the West where he ultimately traded his dental tools for a six-gun, gaining immortality as the famous gambler and gunfighter "Doc" Holliday. At the same time that Holliday was practicing dentistry, a young composer named James L. Pierpont was teaching music in Valdosta. He would later gain fame as the author of "Jingle Bells," one of the nation's favorite Christmas songs.

By the 1890s, Valdosta was a major center for producing and shipping

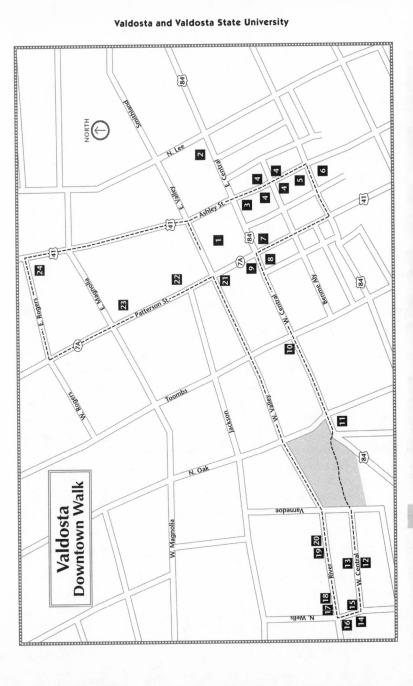

highly prized Sea Island cotton. The trade made many local citizens so wealthy that a 1910 survey recognized Valdosta as the richest city (per capita) in the United States. Many elegant Victorian homes were erected near the heart of the city, while the stately Lowndes County Courthouse, completed in 1905, was surrounded by a bustling business district. In 1910, the world's second Coca-Cola Bottling Co. (the first was in Chattanooga, Tenn.) opened in Valdosta.

In 1899, Valdosta constructed an electric trolley system that carried passengers from downtown to the grounds of the Georgia State Fair in Pine Park (near the present site of Valdosta State University). After the fair, the system expanded to serve downtown businesses and the residential areas to the west and north of the city, making Valdosta the smallest town in the nation to have its own public transportation system. The trolleys operated until 1924.

Shortly after the turn of the 20th century, Valdosta became a regional center for higher education. In 1906, the South Georgia State Normal College was established in Valdosta for the education of women. In 1922, the name was changed to the Georgia State College for Women (GSCW), and the Spanish Mission–style buildings on its campus in the northern suburbs became a Valdosta landmark. Six years later, Emory University opened a junior college for men a short distance from GSCW. The two schools thrived until 1950, when GSCW became coed and changed its name to Valdosta State College. With males now able to attend that school, Emory-Valdosta's enrollment declined and the school closed its doors in 1953. Its classroom and administration buildings were given to the University System of Georgia and are now part of the campus of Valdosta State University (the college was granted university status in 1993).

During the prosperous years of the first quarter of the century, Valdostans undertook a remarkable effort to beautify their city. With the strong encouragement of R. J. Drexel, superintendent of Valdosta's parks department, citizens began planting azalea shrubs by the tens of thousands. Public parks and private yards exploded with color each spring, and Valdosta became widely renowned as the "Azalea City." A large public park near the Valdosta State campus is named in honor of Drexel, and the "Azalea Trail" is a popular driving tour of some of the city's most colorful neighborhoods. Maps are available at the Welcome Center at I-75 and GA 133 (exit 18).

Like much of the South, Valdosta and Lowndes County suffered terribly during the late 1920s as an agricultural recession brought on by drought conditions and boll-weevil infestations of

298

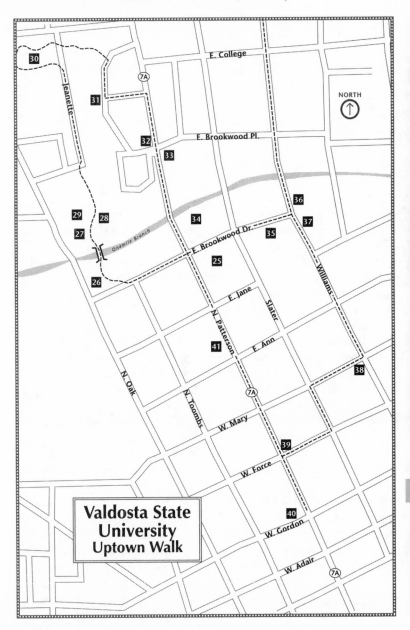

cotton crops devastated the local economy. The hard times were compounded when the nation plunged into the depths of the Great Depression in 1929. The failure of cotton forced local farmers to turn to corn, tobacco, and pine products as replacements. Through the years these crops—and the revived cotton industry—have been staples of the local agricultural economy.

For many people in southern Georgia and around the country, Valdosta may be best known for high school football. Beginning in 1942 when young Wright Bazemore took over as head coach of the local team, Valdosta High School embarked on an annual journey to become the top football team in the state, if not the nation. During Bazemore's nearly 30-year tenure (1942–71), followed by 20 years under coach Nick Hyder (1974–95), the Valdosta High School Wildcats won 22 state football championships and 6 national high school championships. Under coach Mike O'Brien, the Wildcats won a 23rd state championship in 1998.

WALK DISTANCE AND TERRAIN

There are two distinct walks. The first traces a 2.5-mile loop through the historic downtown area and nearby Fairview Residential District. Both are notable for their rich mix of Victorian and early 20th-century structures. The second walk follows a meandering 3-mile route through the campus of Valdosta State University and past elegant, older homes along N. Patterson St. and surrounding side streets. You may choose to connect the two routes by walking about a half-mile up Patterson St. The Valdosta State University Admissions Office offers campus walking tours at 10:30 A.M. and 2 P.M., Mon.–Fri., and at 11 A.M. on Sat. *Information:* (478) 618-1878.

Valdosta is situated on the Coastal Plain, and the land is predominantly flat with some gentle hills. The residential areas are shaded by live oaks and other stately old trees. There are sidewalks throughout much of the walk route.

SIGHTS ALONG THE WAY

Downtown Walk

1. **Lowndes County Courthouse (1914)**—Patterson St. between E. Valley St. and Central Ave. The imposing Neoclassical structure, designed by Frank P. Milburn, is the third courthouse on this site since the original was built in 1860. It is notable for its central tower and corner domes, and has been the anchor of downtown Valdosta's business and government community for nearly a century. *NR*

2. **Federal Building/City Hall (1910)**—216 E. Central Ave. Complementing the nearby courthouse, this 3-story, Italian Renaissance–style building originally served as the

Federal courthouse and post office. It was sold to the city in 1968 and was damaged in a 1987 fire. It received an award from the Georgia Trust for Historic Preservation for its 1989 restoration. Open 9 A.M.–5 P.M., Mon.–Fri.

3. Dosta Theatre (1941)—122 N. Ashley St. This Art Moderne–style structure served as a local movie house for many years before closing in 1977. After an award-winning restoration, the auditorium reopened in 1993 and now houses the Valdosta Theatre Guild. Information on upcoming productions: (478) 247-8243.

4. Commercial Buildings (c. 1900) —100 block of N. Ashley St. Both sides of the street are lined with well-preserved and adaptively used turn-of-the-20th-century commercial buildings notable for their distinctive Victorian style and ornamentation. The second floor of the building at 112 N. Ashley once held the offices of the *Valdosta Daily Times.*

5. European House Hotel (c. 1884) —100 N. Ashley St. This Victorian-era brick building with central pediment was constructed by the Sloat Brothers as a retail shop for their popular Vegetable Bitters. W. P. Renfroe operated a small hotel on the second floor. Today it houses professional offices.

6. Daniel Ashley Hotel (1926)— 109 E. Hill Ave. For many years, the Daniel Ashley was Valdosta's premier hostelry. After years of decline, the 7-story building was rehabilitated and now serves as a retirement residence.

7. McKey Building (1906)— 135 N. Patterson St. This 4-story building in the Italian Renaissance style was constructed by T. S. McKey from profits earned in Florida's orange groves. The building is noted for its rounded top-floor windows and

Ceremonial entrance gate, Valdosta State University

301

entablature. It now houses a mix of offices and retail businesses.

8. C. C. Varnedoe Building (c. 1880)—134 N. Patterson St. Varnedoe's has been providing retail goods and clothing to Valdostans since 1871. After a 1979 fire, the store purchased this 2-story Victorian building, with central turret, that had been built as a buggy and harness shop. It had been operated as a ladies' clothing shop for more than 60 years.

9. Peeples Building (c. 1885)—200 N. Patterson St. This Victorian commercial structure was built by Judge R. A. Peeples to house Valdosta's first insurance agency. Since the 1940s, it has been operated as King's Grill, one of the city's landmark eateries.

10. First Baptist Church (1899)—200 W. Central Ave. A blend of Queen Anne and Romanesque styles marks this church designed by architect Stephen Fulghum. The church's interior is noted for its rich use of wood and stained glass. The church bell came from the congregation's original 1850 sanctuary.

11. Lowndes County Historical Society and Museum (1913)—305 W. Central Ave. Designed by local architect Lloyd Greer, this building served for many years as the public library—a gift from philanthropist Andrew Carnegie. In 1968, the library moved into a new facility. This building became

home to the Historical Society in 1976. The museum houses an extensive collection of artifacts and photographs chronicling the history of the county and the city of Valdosta. *Hours:* 10 A.M.–5 P.M., Mon.–Fri.; 10 A.M.–2 P.M., Sat. (478) 247-4780. *NR*

12. Dasher House (1901)—413 Central Pl. This restored cottage in the heart of the Fairview Historic District is an excellent example of the Queen Anne style. It is one of the "Five Sisters' Houses" in the neighborhood built by J. A. Dasher for his daughters.

13. Varnedoe-Scott-Man House (c. 1890)—404 Central Pl. Originally built by James Oglethorpe Varnedoe as a small cottage, the house was moved by Luther Scott to this location in 1906. Scott remodeled and expanded the house into a large Victorian-style home.

14. Wisenbaker-Roberts House (c. 1840)—206 Wells St. The oldest structure in Valdosta, this house was built by pioneer settler William Wisenbaker. The simple "Plantation Plain" cottage was purchased by J. T. Roberts in 1900 and greatly remodeled with the addition of the wings and gingerbread ornamentation.

15. Monroe-Sutton House (1896)—303 Wells St. Considered the finest example of Queen Anne style architecture in Valdosta, this house was designed by Stephen Fulghum for

W. F. Monroe, a local druggist and patent-medicine salesman. It later served as a boarding house and was eventually abandoned before being restored in 1979.

16. Winn-Wilson-Hamm House (1917)—208 Wells St. A rare example of the Prairie style popularized by Frank Lloyd Wright, this house was designed for Abial Winn by Lloyd Greer.

17. Pardee-Cranford-Cribbs House (1903)—418 River St. This residence is a superbly restored Folk Victorian house.

18. Myddelton-Green House (1895)—416 River St. This squarish, vernacular Victorian house was built for R. T. Myddelton.

19. Sam's Place (c. 1850)—410 River St. This simple cottage, believed to have been built in Troupville, was purchased by Sam Myddelton and moved to this site in 1852. Known throughout the county as "Sam's Place," the house features hand-hewn beams and heart-pine flooring.

20. Hunt House (1906)—402 River St. This fine example of Queen Anne style has remained in the Hunt family since it was built.

21. First United Methodist Church (1909)—220 N. Patterson St. An excellent example of the Romanesque Revival style, this church is noted for its rich interior woodwork and stained-glass rose window.

22. Converse-Dalton-Ferrell House (1902)—305 N. Patterson St. This carefully restored Neoclassical house now serves as headquarters for the Valdosta Junior League. It is occasionally opened to the public for special community functions. *NR*

23. First Presbyterian Church (1909)—313 N. Patterson St. Designed as a Romanesque variation of a Greek temple, the church is noted for its large portico supported by Corinthian columns. *NR*

24. Barber-Pittman House (1915)—416 N. Ashley St. Designed in the Neoclassical style by Lloyd Greer, this house was built for E. R. Barber, owner of the Valdosta Coca-Cola Bottling Company. The house was bequeathed to the people of Valdosta by Barber's daughter, Ola Barber Pittman, and restored in 1979. Today it houses the Valdosta Chamber of Commerce. *Hours:* 9 A.M.–5 P.M., Mon.–Fri. (478) 247-8100. *NR*

Valdosta State University/Uptown Walk

25. Valdosta State University (VSU) Plaza And Information Center (1995)—Brookwood Dr. at N. Patterson St. This large modern building houses recreational facilities, offices, classrooms, dining facilities, meeting rooms, and the campus information center. *Hours:* 8 A.M.–8 P.M., Mon.–Fri.;

10 A.M.–2 P.M., Sat.; 2–4 P.M., Sun. (478) 333-5980.

26. VSU Fine Arts Center (1969)—Brookwood Dr. at N. Oak St. The Fine Arts Center houses the music, art, and commercial art departments. The art gallery and Georgia Sawyer Theater offer a full schedule of exhibitions and musical and dramatic performances.

27. Georgia State Women's College Chimney (c. 1910s)—Between the Fine Arts Building and Odum Library. Once part of the original campus power plant, this tall red-brick chimney still has "GWSC" in stenciled white paint along its shaft.

28. Odum Library (1972)—East of the old gymnasium. The main campus library houses nearly a half-million volumes. Included in its holdings are the Archives of Contemporary South Georgia History and the Southern History Collection.

29. University Union (1966, expanded 1976)—North of the old gymnasium. The main student gathering place on campus, the Union houses the bookstore, post office, snack bar, student association offices, and the studio of radio station WVVS.

30. Jewel Whitehead Camellia Trail (1944)—VSU campus between Georgia Hall and Georgia Ave. This winding path lined with winter-blooming camellia plants, grew from 150 plants given as an unusual 1944 Christmas gift to the college by Mr.

and Mrs. A. B. Whitehead. Mrs. Whitehead designed the trail and continued to add plants for many years. By the time of her death in 1972, the trail was 1,700 feet long and contained more than 500 camellia plants. The construction of campus buildings in the 1970s required shortening the trail to 1,310 feet. The concrete pathway was added In 1984.

31. West Hall (1917)—1500 N. Patterson St. Named for U.S. Sen. William West, this large Spanish Mission–style building was the second building completed on the campus and is still one of the largest. With its fountain and palm tree-lined walkway to N. Patterson St., it is a campus landmark.

32. Valdosta State College Trolley Station (1917)—1500 N. Patterson St., just south of West Hall. This small, stucco, open-sided structure was built for the electric trolley line that ran from downtown to the college and uptown residential areas from 1899 until 1924. This station is the only tangible reminder of the trolley car system.

33. Women's Club Building (1925)—1409 N. Patterson St. This red-brick structure, with a central pedimented porch, was designed by Lloyd Greer. The building was constructed to house local women's clubs, a function it still serves today. *NR*

34. Drexel Park (1916)—N. Patterson St. and Brookwood Dr. Several local families donated land for what was known for many years as Brookwood Park. In 1925, Robert Drexel began work as Valdosta's parks superintendent and spent many years beautifying these public spaces with varieties of colorful camellias and azaleas. To commemorate his work, this park was renamed for him in 1979.

35. Bazemore-Hyder Stadium/ Cleveland Field (1923)—Brookwood Dr. at Williams St. The stadium is home to the Valdosta High School Wildcats and the Valdosta State University Blazers, who play NCAA Division II football. The field is named for Dr. A. G. Cleveland, longtime superintendent of Valdosta schools, while the stadium is named for the high school's two legendary coaches.

36. Miller-Burns-Underwood House (1938)—1407 Williams St. This International-style house, designed by Lloyd Greer, is the only one of its type in Valdosta. It was commissioned by local builder and concrete contractor Leo Miller.

37. American Legion Building (1931)—1301 Williams St. Valdosta's American Legion Post No. 13 was established in 1919. This building has served as post headquarters since 1931.

38. Decorator Show House (1925)—1016 Williams St. This whimsical, Spanish Eclectic–style house was constructed by the Georgia Realty Company for the Valdosta House

Beautiful show in 1925. A notable feature is the wing-shaped stairway along the front of the house.

39. Rose House (1899)—1007 N. Patterson St. Originally a 1-story house, the second floor and ornate portico with Ionic columns were added in 1910. The house reflects the elegant style that once marked N. Patterson Street as Valdosta's premier residential address.

40. The Crescent (1898)—900 N. Patterson St. Possibly the most lavish home in Valdosta, this grand Neoclassical mansion with its curving front portico was built for Sen. West. The massive portico is supported by 13 Doric columns, representing the original American colonies. Shortly after World War II, the structure was in a state of decline and slated for demolition. It was saved by the Garden Club of Valdosta and is now the club's headquarters and garden center. It is open to the public for tours Mon.–Fri., 2–5 P.M. *Information:* (478) 244-4537. *NR*

41. Lowndes–Valdosta Cultural Arts Center (1980s)—1204 N. Patterson St. This converted commercial building houses the offices of several arts guilds and associations. *Information:* (478) 247-2787.

HEART OF GEORGIA ANNUAL EVENTS

March
- Cherry Blossom Festival (Macon)
- Lantern Light Tours
  (Ocmulgee National Monument)
- Rattlesnake Roundup (Fitzgerald)

April
- Earth Day
  (Ocmulgee National Monument)
- March for the Parks
  (Ocmulgee National Monument)
- Arts and Crafts Festival
  (Little Ocmulgee State Park)
- Swine Fest (Americus)
- Spring Flower Show (Valdosta)

May
- Spring Antiques and Crafts Fair
  (Andersonville)
- Memorial Day Ceremonies
  (Andersonville National Cemetery)
- Remerton "Mayfest" Celebration
  (Valdosta)

June
- Midsummer Celebration (Macon)
- "Ocmulgee University" Heritage
  Preservation Workshops
  (Ocmulgee National Monument)
- Ebony in Arts Festival (Fitzgerald)

July
- Fireworks Extravaganza
  (Americus)
- Independence Day Celebration
  (Valdosta)

September
- Southern Jubilee (Macon)
- Fest of Ville (Milledgeville)
- *The Lightered Knot*
  Outdoor Drama
  (Little Ocmulgee State Park)
- Peanut Festival (Plains)
- Sumter Civic Fair (Americus)
- Remerton Cotton Patch Festival
  (Valdosta)

October
- Arrowhead Arts and Crafts
  Festival (Macon)
- Brown's Crossing Fair
  (Milledgeville)
- Yank-Reb Festival (Fitzgerald)
- Civil War Days
  (Andersonville Village)

November
- American Indian Heritage Month
  (Ocmulgee National Monument)
- Veterans' Day Ceremonies
  (Andersonville National Cemetery)
- Lowndes County—
  South Georgia Fair (Valdosta)
- Camellia Show (Valdosta)
- White Columns and Holly
  Christmas (Macon)

306

December

- ◆ Twelve Days of Christmas
  (Milledgeville)
- ◆ Christmas in the Country
  (Milledgeville)
- ◆ Downtown Christmas Open House
  (Valdosta)
- ◆ Christmas Arts and Crafts Show
  (Valdosta)
- ◆ Wild Adventures Animal Park
  Festival of Lights (Valdosta)

Tupper-Barnett House,
Washington

The Old Medical College
of Georgia in Augusta

CLASSIC
GEORGIA

Classic Georgia is a region of rolling Piedmont hills, broad and fertile fields, and meandering waterways. In the decades following initial settlement of the new colony of Georgia in 1733, pioneers moved into this area and pushed back the frontier as they cleared the land and built farms and towns.

The first city of the region, and the second largest in the state, is Augusta. Founded in 1736 as a fort on the banks of the Savannah River, Augusta slowly evolved into a major inland port and industrial center, a role strengthened by construction of the 9-mile-long Augusta Canal in the 1840s. While the canal is no longer a vital transportation route, it has been preserved as an engineering landmark and a popular recreational resource for boaters, hikers, and bicyclists.

A decade before the Revolution, homesteaders settled on the edge of the wilderness about 40 miles northwest of Augusta, building a small block-house garrison called Ft. Heard. During the Revolution, these fiercely independent farmers embraced the patriot cause and waged bloody guerilla warfare against the British stationed in Augusta. On February 14, 1779, a British force marched out from the city intent on destroying the rebels. Instead, the king's forces were ambushed and soundly defeated at the Battle of Kettle Creek a few miles from Ft. Heard. The following year, the settlers living around the fort changed its name to Ft. Washington to honor the Continental Army's commanding general. As a result, the small community became the first in the nation to be named for the country's future first president.

Confident from victory in the Revolution, Georgia's leaders and citizens sought more lands for settlement from the native Creek and

Cherokee Indians. In a series of treaties, the natives ceded more of their ancestral lands to the state, and by the early years of the 19th century, new communities were thriving. Among them were Athens, founded in 1806 to serve as the home of the new University of Georgia, and Madison, established in 1807 and named for Pres. James Madison. Both cities prospered as mercantile and trade centers during the antebellum years, and many classically styled houses and commercial buildings built by wealthy business owners and planters still stand as evidence of life in the "Old South."

Whether it is the excitement of college football in Athens, a stroll through the State Botanical Garden, or a visit to a restored antebellum home, there is much to see and do in Classic Georgia.

Middle Oconee River at
Georgia's State Botanical
Garden near Athens

CHAPTER 42

Augusta

LOCATION

✦ Augusta is located adjacent to I-20, just west of the Savannah River. To reach downtown, exit on Washington Rd. (GA 28, exit 199) and travel south about 2 miles (along the way you will pass the entrance of the famous Augusta National Golf Club). Washington Rd. becomes Greene St. on the edge of downtown. Turn left on 8th Ave. and follow it to the Cotton Exchange Building on Reynolds St. The walk begins at the Cotton Exchange. *Information:* Augusta–Richmond County Convention and Visitors Bureau, (800) 726-0243; www.augustaga.org.

PARKING

🚗 There is limited, metered street parking around the Cotton Exchange

Building, and commercial lots are available throughout the downtown area.

BACKGROUND

📖 Only three years after the Colony of Georgia's founding in 1733, Gen. James Oglethorpe established a fort and trading post 150 miles up the Savannah River on the colony's boundary with the Creek Nation. Ft. Augusta, named for the daughter of England's King George II, began as a crude wooden stockade on the bluffs above the river. Within a few years, it was the heart of a thriving trading community located between the English and the Creeks, Chickasaws, Cherokees, and other tribes who brought furs from Georgia's interior and the upland Carolinas.

By the time of the French and Indian War in 1755, Augusta was the colony's second largest community and was situated on the edge of an unfriendly frontier, as the Cherokees were allied with the French. Only isolated fighting occurred in the area but this would not be the case 20 years later during the American Revolution.

Early in that war, Augusta was bitterly divided as feuds between Whigs (patriots) and Tories (British loyalists)

311

erupted in the community. When the British occupied Savannah they rapidly moved on to capture Augusta as well, holding it against repeated attacks until a Colonial force under command of Col. "Light Horse" Harry Lee (father of Gen. Robert E Lee) liberated the town in 1781. By war's end, Augusta lay in ruins, its trade-based economy in shambles. The introduction of tobacco farming into the area after the Revolution proved the community's salvation and, for many years, Augusta was the state's leading market for the crop.

In 1783, Gov. John Martin used the newly acquired powers of the "sovereign State of Georgia" to call a council meeting in Augusta of the Indian nations to establish boundaries between their lands and the state. Within a few years, the increasing pressures of western migration forced the Creeks to cede all their lands east of the Oconee River. A precedent was now established, and within 50 years all the natives would be forced to give up their lands in Georgia.

By the early 1800s, steamboats replaced flat-bottom barges on the Savannah River, and in the 1830s, a railway line connected Augusta with Charleston, S.C. As more Indian lands opened for settlement, pioneers moved northwestward and the rails followed. By the mid-1840s, a line connected Augusta to the new community of Atlanta, and was inching

toward Ross's Landing (later Chattanooga) in Tennessee.

Cotton became a major regional product, and Augusta quickly developed as a center for both the tobacco and cotton trade. Initially, the raw cotton was carried downriver to Savannah for transport to northern mills; but by the late 1840s, local textile mills began to manufacture their own finished goods, signalling the beginnings of a pre–Civil War industrial boom. The Augusta Canal was also built around this time to provide safe passage for cotton barges and to divert water from the river to the mills and spur more industrial growth.

During the Civil War, Augusta's industries focused their resources on war production. Constructed along the canal in 1862, the Confederate Powder Works was, at the time, the largest munitions factory in the world. Today, a massive brick chimney is all that remains of this once-sprawling complex.

Although the invading Union armies bypassed Augusta in their March to the Sea, the city suffered considerable hardship and deprivation during the conflict. An eyewitness to these struggles was the young son of the Rev. Joseph Wilson, pastor of the First Presbyterian Church. The boy, Woodrow, would have a successful career as a lawyer and educator before his election to the presidency of the United States in 1912. Many

Augusta

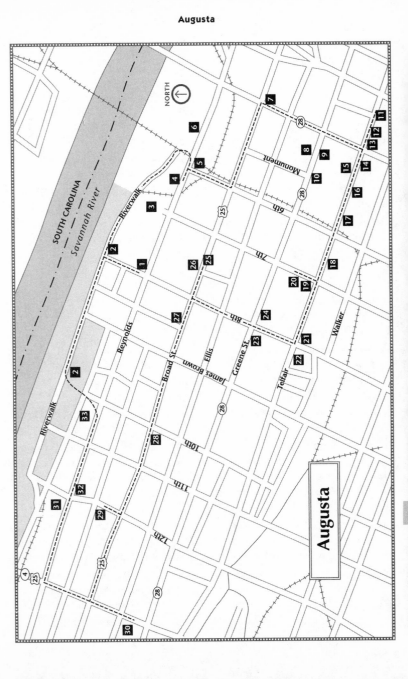

historians believe that Wilson's reluctance to involve America in the First World War and his fervent efforts to secure lasting peace through establishment of the League of Nations were grounded in his memories of the devastation in his native South after the Civil War.

Augusta's mills and factories returned rapidly to peacetime production and, by the 1880s, the city's economy was again prospering. Many of the fine homes in the city's Victorian "Old Town" neighborhood date from this boom time. In Old Town's heyday, locals called it "Pinch Gut" for the fashionable, tight-corseted waistlines of dresses worn by the ladies of the day. The city also became a popular winter resort for wealthy Northern industrialists, and grand hotels like the Bon Air and the Partridge Inn were built to accommodate them. In 1910, pioneer aviators Orville and Wilbur Wright opened a flying school in Augusta, and for a brief period in 1911, the entire fleet of the U.S. Army Air Force, all six planes, was stationed here. The mild climate also brought major league baseball teams to Augusta for Spring Training. Ty Cobb and the Detroit Tigers worked out here for many years as did the National League's New York Giants.

Golf also grew in popularity, and in 1931, golfing legend Bobby Jones, along with several associates, acquired "Fruitlands," an antebellum plantation that was then a defunct nursery. On the rolling grounds, they set about creating one of the finest golf courses in the world. Today, the Augusta National Golf Club, with its tournament known simply as "The Masters," is a mecca for professional golfers from around the world.

On two occasions near the turn of the 20th century (1888 and 1912) Augusta suffered devastating floods that inundated the downtown business district. Then, on March 22, 1916, a fire began in a building at 8th and Broad Sts. and spread over 40 blocks, destroying nearly 700 structures. Despite these catastrophes, the business district was rebuilt and prospered until the 1960s when, as in many other communities, suburbanization drained business away from downtown merchants.

In recent years, active efforts to revitalize the area have taken place. The growing popularity of such places as Old Town, with its inns, shops, and Victorian atmosphere; Riverwalk, with its promenade; the Broad St. shopping district fronting the second widest street in the country (only Canal St. in New Orleans is wider); and the former Enterprise Mill, adaptively restored as luxury apartments, are all examples of the community's commitment to remaining a vibrant city filled with the hustle and bustle that has made

Augusta a colorful part of Georgia history for more than 250 years.

WALK DISTANCE AND TERRAIN

The loop along the river front, through Old Town, and along Broad St. covers about 3 miles. The sidewalks are sheltered with shade trees and the terrain, for the most part, is level.

SIGHTS ALONG THE WAY

1. Cotton Exchange Building (1886)—8th and Reynolds Sts. Once the hub of economic activity for one of the world's largest

Sacred Heart Cultural Center

cotton markets, the building now houses the Augusta Welcome Center, Cotton Exchange Museum, and the Augusta–Richmond County Convention and Visitors Bureau. *Hours:* 9 A.M.–5 P.M., Mon.–Sat.; 1–5 P.M., Sun. (800) 726-0243. *NR*

2. Riverwalk—East of Reynolds St. along the Savannah River. Main entrance at 8th and Reynolds. This shaded riverside esplanade winds along the banks of the Savannah River from 6th to 10th Sts. Locals call it Augusta's "front porch," the perfect place for a leisurely stroll, a picnic, or a concert at the Jessye Norman Amphitheater (named for the world-renowned opera star and Augusta native). There are children's playscapes in Oglethorpe Park near the southern end of the walk and statues of famous golfers behind the Georgia Golf Hall of Fame at the northern end.

3. Fort Discovery/National Science Center (1997)—1 7th St. This $24-million, hands-on science center invites the curious of all ages to explore nearly 300 interactive exhibits. The center, a joint project of the U.S. Army and the Georgia Department of Education, houses both permanent and traveling exhibits. Audiovisual programs are presented in the Paul S. Simon Discovery Theater. *Hours:* 10 A.M.–6 P.M., Mon.–Sat.; 12–6 P.M., Sun. (800) 325-5445; www.nscdiscovery.org.

4. St. Paul's Episcopal Church/Site of Fort Augusta (1919)—605 Reynolds St. The first wooden church was built on this site in 1750. It was replaced in 1820 by a brick structure that was destroyed in the 1916 fire. The present church, designed to resemble the 1820 structure, was completed in 1919. Of particular note, the original baptismal font, brought from England in 1751, is located inside the church foyer. The churchyard contains the remains of William Few, a signer of the U.S. Constitution, while a crypt beneath the church is the burial site of Leonidas Polk, the Episcopal bishop and Confederate general who was killed in fighting near Atlanta in 1864. A Celtic cross behind the church marks the site of Ft. Augusta. *NR*

5. Augusta–Richmond County Museum (1996)—560 Reynolds St. The museum utilizes a variety of creatively designed exhibits to trace Augusta's colorful history. Highlights of the collection include a 19th-century steam locomotive and a replica of a "Petersburg" boat, a craft used for many years to float cotton from upland plantations down the Savannah River to Augusta. *Hours:* 10 A.M.–5 P.M., Tues.–Sat.; 2–5 P.M., Sun. (706) 722-8454.

6. Antiques Depot (c. 1866)—Reynolds and 5th Sts. These 19th-century cotton warehouses have been adaptively preserved and now house a mix of antiques dealers.

7. Haunted Pillar (c. 1820s)—Broad and 5th Sts. This lonely pillar is all that remains of the thriving Lower Market which once stood in the middle of Broad St. According to local legend, in the mid-1870s, a traveling evangelist, upset that local authorities would not permit him to preach in the market, cursed the city and prophesied that the market would be destroyed. In 1878, a tornado struck Augusta and leveled the market—leaving only this pillar standing. In 1879, a new market was built, and a local businessman purchased the pillar and moved it to its present location.

8. Phinizy House (c. 1835)—519 Greene St. This house is architecturally significant with features from both the Federal and Greek Revival styles. Especially notable are the curving, horseshoe steps and ornate wrought-iron railings.

9. Cullum House (1900)—510 Greene St. This well-preserved house is an excellent example of the very ornate and occasionally exaggerated Neoclassical Revival style that was popular in Augusta's (and the nation's) upscale neighborhoods at the end of the 19th century.

10. Signers Monument (1848)—Greene and Gwinnett Sts. The 50-ft. obelisk was erected in honor of George Walton, Lyman Hall, and Button Gwinnett, Georgia's signers of the Declaration of Independence. Walton and Hall are interred beneath the monument.

11. Old Government House (1801)—432 Telfair St. Built to house the first city government, the building is constructed of brick overlaid with stucco to resemble cut stone. The building was used for many years as a private residence. In the 1970s it was acquired by the City of Augusta and renovated for use as a special events facility and conference center. *NR*

12. Amanda Dickson House (1851)—452 Telfair St. Born in 1849, Amanda Dickson was the daughter of wealthy Hancock County planter David Dickson and his slave Julia. Upon her father's death in 1885, Amanda inherited the bulk of his estate (estimated to exceed $500,000), and she spent years defending against numerous claims against the estate from parties who did not believe that she, as an illegitimate, mixed-race child, could inherit the property. Dickson's case went all the way to the Georgia Supreme Court, where her rights were upheld. She purchased this house and moved to Augusta in 1886.

13. Brahe House (1850)—456 Telfair St. Built by Frederick Adolf Brahe, a German-born silversmith, this house was the first in Augusta to be wired for electricity. The home is now owned by the Augusta–Richmond County Museum and is open by appointment. *Information:* (706) 722-8454. *NR*

14. Gertrude Herbert Memorial Art Institute (1818)—506 Telfair St. Built by one-time Augusta mayor and later U.S. Sen. Nicholas Ware, this remarkable house, which cost the then-unheard-of sum of $40,000 to build, was once called "Ware's Folly." Architectural details of particular interest include the horseshoe entrance steps and Palladian fanlights and sidelights on three levels. The institute contains exhibit space and offers art classes. *Hours:* 10 A.M.–5 P.M., Tues.–Fri.; 10 A.M.–2 P.M., Sat. Information: (706) 722-5495. *NR*

15. Augusta–Richmond County Planning Commission Building (1872)—525 Telfair St. Designed by

317

Charleston, S.C., architect D. H. Abraham, this building was originally constructed to serve as the synagogue for the Congregation Children of Israel.

16. Old Richmond Academy (c. 1801)—540 Telfair St. The Academy of Richmond County, a secondary school for boys, was established in 1783 and occupied this impressive Gothic-style building from 1801 until 1929, when it moved to a new campus. For many years the building housed a library and, until 1996, the Augusta–Richmond County Museum. It is undergoing renovations. *NR*

17. Old Medical College of Georgia (1835)—598 Telfair St. Designed by noted Georgia architect Charles Clusky, this imposing Greek Revival building with massive Doric columns was the state's first medical school and one of the nation's oldest. Not surprisingly, the building was used as a hospital during the Civil War. The school was located here until 1912, when it moved to a new campus in the suburbs. The building has been fully renovated and now serves as a community special events facility. *Information:* (706) 721-7238. *NR*

18. First Presbyterian Church (1810)—642 Telfair St. The congregation was organized in 1804, and the cornerstone for this church was laid in 1809. The architect was Robert Mills, designer of the Washington Monument and the U.S. Treasury Building,

who won a national design competition for this commission in 1807. The Rev. Joseph Wilson served as pastor here from 1858 to 1870. His son, Woodrow, went on to become the 28th President of the United States. *NR*

19. Woodrow Wilson Boyhood Home (1822)—419 7th St. This brick home served as the Presbyterian Church manse when the Wilsons occupied it. It was from a window in this house that young Woodrow Wilson watched as Confederate Pres. Jefferson Davis was escorted through the city under armed guard after his May 1865 capture by Federal troops outside Irwinville, Ga. Restored by Historic Augusta, Inc., this house and the Lamar House next door are open to the public. Hours vary. *Information:* (706) 724-0436. *NR*

20. Joseph Lamar House (1850)—415 7th St. next to the Wilson House. This red-brick house was the family home of Woodrow Wilson's boyhood friend Joseph R. Lamar. Lamar became a prominent attorney and judge and was appointed by Pres. William Howard Taft to serve on the U.S. Supreme Court. *NR*

21. Holy Trinity Roman Catholic Church (c. 1856)—720 Telfair St. Home to one of Georgia's oldest Roman Catholic congregations, established in the 1790s, this is the oldest existing Catholic church building in the state. It served as a hospital during the Civil War. Its rare Jardine organ was installed in 1868 and is still played today. *NR*

22. Old Federal Courthouse (1916)—Telfair and 8th Sts. Built to house the Post Office, the building has been renovated to serve as the Federal Court for the Southern District of Georgia.

23. Site of the First Baptist Church of Augusta (1902)—802 Greene St. On this site, in 1845, the First Baptist Church hosted a meeting to found the Southern Baptist Convention. This building replaced the original church in 1902, and the congregation moved to a new sanctuary in 1975. The building is now home to the congregation of Grace Way Baptist Church.

24. St. John United Methodist Church (1844)—734 Greene St. Organized in 1798, the Methodist congregation built a small wooden church here in 1801. In 1844 the old building was sold to Springfield Baptist Church, a congregation of freeblacks (see #32), and moved to its present location on 12th St. to make way for construction of the new church. This elegant Romanesque Revival structure has been expanded several times through the years. *NR*

25. Confederate Monument (1878)—700 block of Broad St. Nearly 10,000 people attended the unveiling of this monument in October 1878. To honor the common soldier, an enlisted man stands atop the column while four Confederate generals—Robert E. Lee, Stonewall Jackson, T. R. R. Cobb, and W. H. T. Walker—flank its base.

26. Imperial Theater (1917)—745 Broad St. Built to replace an earlier theater lost in the 1916 fire, the Imperial served a variety of uses from vaudeville stage to downtown movie house. It has been renovated and continues to host both live performances and films. *Information:* (706) 722-8293.

27. Modjeska Theater (1916)—811–17 Broad St. Like the Imperial, this theater replaced the original Modjeska destroyed in the downtown fire. Designed in the Moorish Revival style by G. Lloyd Preacher, it operated as a theater stage and movie house until 1977. The theater was named for 19th-century opera star Helene Modjeska.

28. Claussen Building (c. 1870s)—1002 Broad St. Paine College, established in 1882 by two congregations of freed slaves, offered its first academic classes in this building in 1884. The college quickly outgrew the facility and moved to the site of its present campus. The building was purchased by H. H. Claussen, a baker from Charleston, in 1888.

29. Old Fire Department Headquarters (1911)—1253 Broad St. Believed to be one of the earliest

319

buildings designed by architect G. Lloyd Preacher, this red-brick building housed the fire department's offices until 1968. The outbuildings behind the main structure were used as stables for the horses that pulled the fire wagons.

30. Sacred Heart Cultural Center (1901)—1301 Greene St. This beautiful twin-spired brick and masonry church, designed in the Romanesque Revival style, served for more than 70 years as home to the Roman Catholic parish of Sacred Heart. In the early 1970s, many parishioners had moved to the suburbs and the congregation chose to build a new church west of the city. Recognizing the beauty of this structure, a private partnership purchased and preserved the building, which now serves as community cultural center with art galleries, meeting spaces, and a gift shop. The former sanctuary now hosts wedding receptions, art shows, musical performances, dances, and other cultural events. Tours are offered by appointment. *Information:* (706) 826-4700. *NR*

31. Georgia Golf Hall of Fame (scheduled opening Spring 2001)—Reynolds St. between 13th and 11th Sts. Currently under construction, this $32-million complex will utilize interactive exhibits and treasured artifacts to trace the rich history of golf in Georgia. Hall of Fame inductees are a mix of Georgia-born golfers and champions of the fabled

Masters and other professional tournaments. The building will be surrounded by lush gardens modeled after the famous Butchart Gardens in British Columbia. (706) 724-4433.

32. Springfield Baptist Church (1801)—114 12th St. This congregation, founded in 1787, is believed to be the oldest independent African-American church on its original site in the U.S. The current red-brick building was completed in 1897, but the most notable structure is the white clapboard building behind it that was constructed by the congregation of St. John's Methodist Church in 1801 and sold to Springfield in 1844 to replace the congregation's original small wooden building. Morehouse College, now located in Atlanta, was founded here in 1867. *NR*

33. Morris Museum of Art (1997)—1 10th St. Opened in 1992 and located in this space since 1997, the museum houses a superb collection of nearly two centuries of Southern art. It is the only museum in the nation dedicated to collecting and displaying the works of Southern artists. Galleries are designed to give the viewer the feeling that they are enjoying the paintings and sculpture in a private home. Included in the permanent collection are works by Augusta-born artists Jasper Johns and Robert Rauschenberg. *Hours:* 10 A.M.– 5:30 P.M., Tues.–Sat.; 12:30–5:30 P.M., Sun. Information: (706) 724-7501.

CHAPTER 43

Augusta Canal

LOCATION

The canal forms a linear park extending from Evans Rd. to Locks Rd. and south to the Riverwalk in the heart of downtown Augusta. To reach the northern trailhead, follow GA 28 (Washington Rd.) northward from I-20 (exit 199). In about a mile, the road forks and GA 28 becomes Furys Ferry Rd. Continue on Furys Ferry for about 2 miles and turn right on Evans to Locks Rd. Follow Locks to its end at Savannah Rapids Park. The southern terminus of the canal is located at 13th St. on the edge of downtown, a few blocks from Broad St. and the Riverwalk. *Information:* Augusta Canal Authority, (888) 659-8926; www.augustacanal.com.

PARKING:

Parking is available at several locations along the canal route. There are parking lots at the canal dam and head locks, off Riverwatch Pkwy. at the old pumping station, on Goodrich St. east of Riverwatch Pkwy., at Lake Olmstead, around Chaffee Park, at the old canal basin, and at the Riverwalk.

BACKGROUND

In the early 1800s, the invention of the cotton gin vastly increased production of this crop throughout inland Georgia. The bustling river-port city of Augusta, 150 miles upriver from the seaport of Savannah, was the destination for much of this cotton. However, treacherous shoals on the Savannah River (along the Fall Line where the Piedmont Plateau drops to the Coastal Plain) made transportation by barge a risky venture. In 1844, Augusta businessman Col. Henry H. Cumming first proposed the idea for construction of a canal to bypass the dangerous rapids and provide safe passage to the city for the cotton and other plantation goods.

Cumming and other visionaries saw a canal not just as a safer route to the sea, but as the first step in a bold move to turn Augusta into a major Southern industrial center. Up to that point, much of Georgia's cotton was being exported to large mills in the North and even across the Atlantic to Great Britain for spinning into cloth and finished goods. These entrepreneurs rightly reasoned that a canal could provide the necessary water power to drive textile mills along its banks and that Augusta could become a final destination for the raw cotton and the manufacturer of finished goods to be shipped to the entire nation.

A short time after the meeting, Cumming hired engineers to lay out a proposed canal route from Bull Sluice rapids to Beaver Dam Creek. With the favorable results of the survey, Cumming and several other investors established the Augusta Canal Company and began raising the money necessary to begin construction. Contracts were signed and construction crews, composed mostly of slaves, free-blacks, and Irish laborers, worked to build a dam across the Savannah River and carve a canal along the river's western bank. The first phase of construction was completed and water flowed for the first time through a 7-mile-long, 40-ft.-wide, 5-ft.-deep channel on November 23, 1846. Two years later, the canal was extended to its present length of 9 miles, and, in 1849, ownership of the canal was transferred to the city of Augusta.

The next year, with the banks raised to deepen the channel to 7 feet, more than 25,000 bales of cotton were shipped to the city via the waterway.

Now that cotton could be shipped to Augusta without risking the treacherous shoals above the city, newly designed barges, called "Petersburg" boats (named for the town where they were constructed, which is now beneath the waters of Lake Thurmond), were built for use on the river and canal. These long, shallow-draft vessels were particularly suited for carrying heavy loads in the canal and were widely used for nearly a half-century.

The canal helped to turn Augusta into one of the key inland ports in the South and spurred early industrial development along the waterway. After the outbreak of hostilities between the North and South in 1861, the Confederate government constructed a massive munitions factory on the banks of the canal as well as other industries that supplied materials throughout the war.

In 1872, with renewed growth of Georgia's agricultural economy, especially cotton production, the Augusta Cotton Exchange was established to track cotton markets and prices worldwide. That same year, the city acquired the abandoned munitions factory and demolished the buildings to make way for the construction of a large textile mill. The old factory's

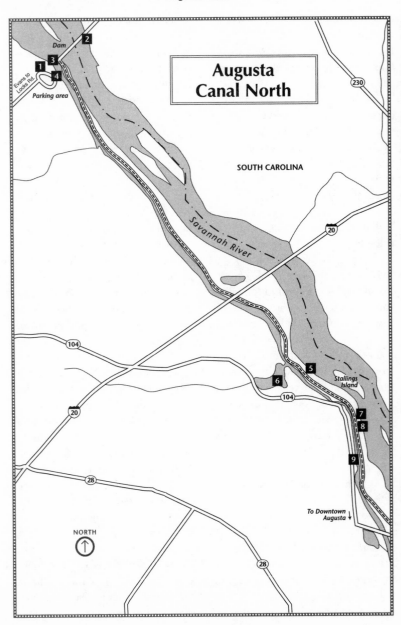

Augusta
Canal North

SOUTH CAROLINA

Savannah River

Dam

Evans to Locks Rd

Parking area

Stallings Island

To Downtown Augusta

NORTH

octagonal chimney was retained as a monument to the South's "lost cause." It is the only permanent structure built by the Confederate government still in existence.

In keeping with Henry Cumming's original vision, the canal was soon lined with bustling mills, including the Enterprise (1877), the Sibley (1881), and the King (1882) textile mills and the Granite (1848) and Crescent (1874) grain mills. The City of Augusta's water pumping station, built on the canal in 1899, still provides the city's drinking water.

Within a few years, Augusta bustled as the second-largest inland cotton market in the world (only the port of New Orleans was larger). This prosperity was reflected in the construction of the ornate Cotton Exchange Building completed in 1886 (now the Augusta Welcome Center on 8th St.). In addition to carrying barge traffic, the water flowing through the canal also provided hydroelectric power to run businesses and factories, illuminate the city, and charge local streetcars.

As with other inland canal systems in the U.S., the canal was eventually made obsolete by the expansion of railway lines and construction of paved roads that made overland delivery of agricultural goods to markets quicker and less expensive. The 13th St. Dock Basin was closed in 1912, and barge traffic ceased soon after.

When the old textile mills began closing in the 1960s and 70s (Sibley Mill and King Mill are still in operation), the Augusta Canal became a largely forgotten relic of a bygone age.

In the 1980s and 90s, there was a renewal of interest in restoring and preserving the canal as a recreational and historical resource, and the Augusta Canal Authority was established in 1989. In 1996, Congress designated the canal as one of only 16 National Heritage Areas in the nation. That same year, the state Department of Community Affairs selected it as Georgia's first "Regionally Important Resource," a designation earned through the cooperation of the several communities along the canal that joined together to support and plan its future.

Today, while work continues on canal restoration, hikers and bikers enjoy the towpath trail, tourists take an excursion on an electrically powered replica of a Petersburg boat, canoeists and kayakers paddle the slow-moving waters, schoolchildren get hands-on lessons on ecology, history buffs explore, and urban pioneers set up housekeeping in old mills and row houses turned into modern homes and apartments.

TRAIL DISTANCE AND TERRAIN

The area through which the canal passes is part of the Savannah River flood plain. The 9-mile

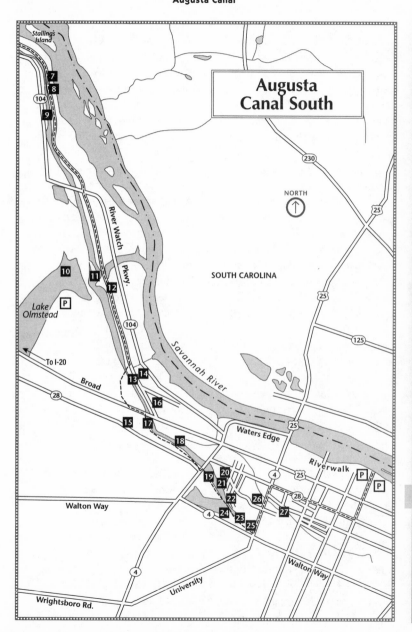

Augusta
Canal South

NORTH

SOUTH CAROLINA

Stalling's
Island

River Watch Pkwy.

Lake
Olmstead

To I-20

Broad

Savannah River

Waters Edge

Riverwalk

Walton Way

Walton Way

University

Wrightsboro Rd.

route (one-way) is mostly flat, with some gentle elevations along the towpath. The canal is divided into three sections. The *Upper Reach* includes the head gates, dam, and inlet where the water flows from the Savannah River into the canal. This area is the least developed, with views of the natural river front and Stallings Island, one of the nation's richest Paleo-Indian archeological sites

Beyond Warren Lake, the *Mid-Reach* marks the beginning of the industrial section of the canal with views of the Augusta Pumping Station and Sibley Mill. Located along this stretch is recently refurbished Chaffee Park.

The *Urban Reach* is the heavily industrialized portion of the canal. The Confederate Powder Works was located in this area, and visitors can see structures of the Sibley, King, and Enterprise Mills. Across the canal, an inlet leads to Lake Olmstead, centerpiece of the city's largest public park. At the site of the old Canal Basin on 13th St., signs mark the walking/biking route along downtown streets to the Riverwalk.

Parking areas located at several intervals along the canal make it easy to arrange shuttles for hikers and bikers.

SIGHTS ALONG THE WAY

 1. Savannah Rapids Pavilion (1994)—Evans to Locks Rds. This modern shelter recalls the early days of the canal when Augustans would travel by carriage for all-day picnics and "lock parties."

2. Bull Sluice Rapids and Dam (c. 1852, extended 1875)—Avoiding these and other treacherous rapids provided the impetus for building the canal. The rapids mark the change in Georgia's geological landscape where the Piedmont Plateau drops to the Coastal Plain, an area know throughout the state as the fall line. The dam, extending across the river to South Carolina, creates a pool above the rapids and diverts water into the canal gates.

3. Head Gates and Locks (1845 and 1875)—These gates and locks at the canal opening controlled the flow of water into the basin. The original gate and lock used a wooden dropgate that limited the size of boats that could enter the canal. In 1875, the original gate was replaced with a swing-gate that permitted larger craft to use the waterway. The present concrete abutment and retaining wall were constructed by the Works Progress Administration (WPA) in the 1930s.

4. Lockkeepers Cottage (c. 1870s)—The lockkeeper was responsible for controlling the opening and closing of the locks for canal traffic. This cottage served as home for the keeper and his family. A nearby springhouse captured water from the river for the family's use.

5. The Clearing—Today, this open area serves as a gathering place for bikers and hikers and as a launchpoint for canoeists and kayakers. Archaeological excavations here and at nearby Stallings Island (in the river a short distance southeast) suggest that people have been meeting and living in this area for nearly 10,000 years.

Augusta Canal's old locks on the Savannah River

6. Warren Lake— This lake is located on property once owned by Judge Benjamin Warren. It was during an 1844 reception in Warren's home, attended by Henry Cumming, that Whig presidential candidate Henry Clay may have first suggested the idea for the construction of a canal.

7. WPA Spillway (1930s)—The stone revetment along the river side of the canal was constructed by WPA workers as an emergency overflow in the event of flooding.

8. Water Pumping Station (1899, several expansions during the years) —The turbines inside this complex pump water from the canal into the city's reservoir and treatment plant for use as drinking water.

9. Electric Pumping Station (1919)—Equipment in this building provided water for Augusta's hydroelectric power.

10. Lake Olmstead—Constructed as a reservoir during the canal's expansion in the 1870s, Lake Olmstead was a local tourist attraction complete with zoo, amusement park, and a private lake club. The lake was named for Charles Olmstead, an engineer who worked on the Erie Canal and was superintendent on the Augusta Canal expansion project. It remains a popular recreation area and includes Lake Olmstead Stadium, home of minor league baseball's Augusta Greenjackets.

11. Aqueduct (1840s–70s)—In the design of the original canal, a wooden aqueduct atop stone piers carried canal water over Rae's Creek, while draw-gates controlled the flow of water through the creek. The original wooden aqueduct was replaced in 1850 by a larger masonry structure, faced with Stone Mountain granite. During the 1872–75 canal expansion, Olmstead raised the canal bank and closed off the gates to allow Rae's Creek to flow into the canal. A 1936 flood broke through the 1875 dam and destroyed portions of the canal bank and spillway. WPA workers repaired the damage and realigned the bank to its present configuration. Today, a dirt path crosses the old aqueduct.

12. Levee (1913–18)—From this point to Savannah Bluff Lock and Dam, 7 miles downriver from Augusta, the raised levee was constructed to protect the city from flooding. There are only six breaches and each may be quickly closed in the event of flooding. One of these breaches is located at the 8th St. entrance to the Riverwalk in downtown Augusta.

13. Confederate Powder Works Chimney (1862)—Goodrich St. in front of Sibley Mill. The 168-ft. chimney is all that remains of the 26 buildings of the munitions factory that lined both sides of the canal. During its three years in operation, the powder works produced nearly three million pounds of gunpowder, much of it using saltpeter brought from Europe through the U.S. Naval blockade. Other war factories along the canal produced items ranging from baked goods to uniforms and hospital supplies.

When the city purchased the abandoned powder works from the Federal government in 1872, local citizens urged that at least the chimney be preserved as a "monument to the dead heroes who sleep on the unnumbered battlefields of the South."

14. Sibley Mill (1881)—Goodrich St. at the canal. The ornate brickwork

and artistic embellishments of this large cotton mill reflect the architectural styles of the late Victorian period when it was built. It is similar in style to the Confederate Powder Works complex that previously stood here. The mill continues in service, producing cotton denim fabric.

15. Sibley Mill Row Houses (c. 1880s)—Pearl Ave. and Eve St. These small cottages were constructed to house mill workers and their families.

16. King Mill (1882)—Goodrich St. west of Broad St. Named for John Pendleton King, one of the city leaders instrumental in construction of the original canal, this mill once had nearly 2,000 water-powered looms. The mill continues to produce cotton products.

17. Ezekiel Harris House (c. 1797)—1840 Broad St. This raised cottage, featuring architecture usually found in coastal areas, was constructed by Harris, a tobacco merchant. The house is open to the public. *Hours:* 9 A.M.–4 P.M., Tues.–Fri.; 10 A.M.–3 P.M., Sat.; and 1–4 P.M., Sun. (706) 733-6768. *NR*

18. Augusta Railway Power Station Gate (c. 1900s)—Canal west of 15th St. This gate controlled the flow of water from the first to the third levels of the canal that generated hydroelectric power for the city's streetcar system.

19. Butt Memorial Bridge (1914) —15th St. at the canal. Dedicated by Pres. William Howard Taft, the bridge was named in memory of Augusta native Archibald Butt, military aide to both Theodore Roosevelt and Taft. Butt died in the sinking of the *Titanic* in 1912.

20. Enterprise Mill (1877)— Greene St. east of 15th St. This former textile mill recently underwent an award-winning renovation and conversion to a loft apartment complex.

21. Granite Mill (c. 1848)—Adjacent to Enterprise Mill. Built as a flour mill, this is the only structure still in existence that was built on the original 1845 canal.

22. Sutherland Mill (c. 1880s)— On the canal east of Calhoun Expy. Originally the Dartmouth Spinning Mill, the looms were once powered by a 13-ft. waterfall from the first to the second level of the canal.

23. Meadow Garden (c. 1794)— 1320 Nelson St. This Sand Hills–style cottage was the home of George Walton, a Georgia signer of the Declaration of Independence. It is now a museum. *Hours:* 10 A.M.–4 P.M., Tues.–Sat.; 1–4 P.M., Sun. (706) 724-4174. *NR*

24. Site of Canal Basin (1850s)— 13th St. at the canal. From the 1850s until it was closed in 1912, docks on this pond were used for unloading supplies from barges for transport either to local factories or to the Savannah River wharf for continued transport to the seaport in Savannah. In 1912, the basin was closed and the docks removed, bringing an end to barge traffic on the canal.

25. 13th St. Gatehouse (1910)— 13th St. at Walton Way. The gates located here continue to regulate the flow of water between the canal's first and second levels. The ornate design of the house and gate structure is typical of the "City Beautiful" style popular at the time.

26. Davidson Fine Arts Magnet School (c. 1880)—West of 12th St. between Walton Way and Telfair St. This school incorporates existing buildings from the 1876–80 Globe Mill. This was the first Augusta mill to have electric lights. Nearby, the school's Visual Arts Building occupies the former Georgia Iron Works Pattern Shop, located on the site of a factory that made pistols for the Confederacy.

27. 12th St. Gates (1852)— 12th and Telfair Sts. These gates control the flow of water through the canal's third level east of this point.

Note: Sights along the remainder of the route to the Riverwalk are found in the previous chapter, "Augusta."

329

CHAPTER 44

Washington

LOCATION

Washington is about 52 miles northwest of Augusta via I-20. Travel west about 30 miles to U.S. 78 (exit 172), then north for 22 miles to the town square. The walk begins in front of the Wilkes County Courthouse. *Information:* Washington–Wilkes County Chamber of Commerce, (706) 678-2013; www.washingtonga.org.

330

PARKING

 There is ample street parking by the Wilkes County Courthouse on East and West Square.

BACKGROUND

During the American Revolution, Georgia was bitterly divided as the King's soldiers, supported by loyal citizens, sought to retain control of the colony and brutally suppress the rebellion. On February 14, 1779, a pivotal battle was fought near the confluence of the Broad and Savannah Rivers in the hills above a slow-moving stream called Kettle Creek. There, a ragged band of Patriots, led by John Dooley, Andrew Pickens, and Elijah Clarke, defeated a large British force that had marched out from Augusta to secure the backcountry. The battle was described by Pickens as "the severest check and chastisement the Tories ever received in South Carolina or Georgia." Victory in the Battle of Kettle Creek proved a turning point. Although two more years of bloodshed remained, the British were never again able to control Georgia's interior.

In 1780, the new state of Georgia, still in the midst of war, laid out plans for a new town to be the seat of Wilkes County (named for John Wilkes, a pro-American member of Parliament). So proud of their claim for independence were the local citizens that they chose to honor the commander of the Continental army by naming their community for him. Thus, it became the first city in the

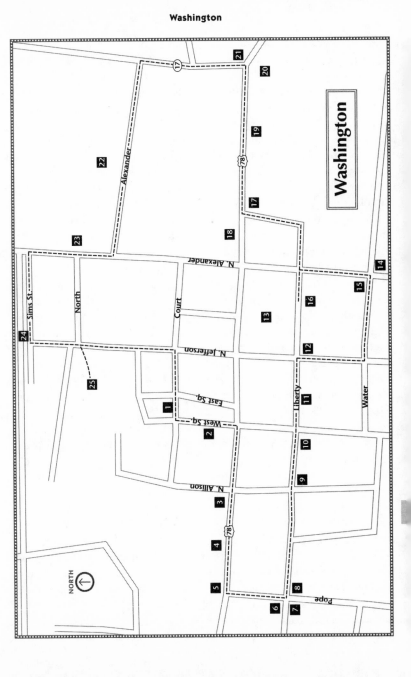

Washington

nation to be named for General, and future president, George Washington.

In July 1781, Patriot troops mustered in Washington for the assault on British-held Augusta. Augusta's recapture, followed by the fall of Savannah, highlighted a triumphant summer that culminated in Gen. Washington's stunning victory over Lord Cornwallis at Yorktown, Va.

Following the Revolution, the small town of Washington grew to prominence as the center of an expanding agricultural region built on cotton and slavery. During the first half of the 19th century, wealthy planters built many fine town homes in Washington. Here they socialized, politicked, raised families, and transacted business. This aristocratic style of life ended forever on January 19, 1861, with the arrival of a messenger from the capitol in Milledgeville carrying news of Georgia's secession from the Union.

Although Washington escaped the fighting, it still had its share of Civil War excitement and lingering mystery. In early May, 1865, Jefferson Davis, his cabinet, and military escort arrived in Washington on their flight southward from Richmond. Included in their baggage were, as the story is told, millions of dollars in gold, practically all that remained of the Rebel treasury. The funds were secured in the vault of a local bank, while Davis held his final cabinet meeting on

May 4. Shortly afterward, Davis and his party left Washington. A week later, they were captured by Union cavalry outside Irwinville, Ga.

Only a small quantity of gold was found with Davis. When Federal troops had arrived in Washington on May 5, a mere $100,000 in bullion was found in the bank vault. For more than a century, historians and treasure hunters alike have speculated that the "lost gold of the Confederacy" remains hidden somewhere in or near Washington; yet no clue has ever revealed its location.

Today, Washington is a village delightfully suspended in time. Many of its finest homes and buildings have been carefully preserved and restored for visitors to enjoy.

WALK DISTANCE AND TERRAIN

The walk is a 3-mile loop along downtown streets and quiet residential lanes. There are good sidewalks along most of the route. The terrain is gently rolling with a moderate climb to a hill overlooking downtown.

SIGHTS ALONG THE WAY

 1. Wilkes County Courthouse (1903)—Court St. An unusual Romanesque Gothic structure, the courthouse is built on the site of the bank building where Jefferson Davis held his final cabinet meeting. *NR*

2. Fitzpatrick Hotel (1898)— W. Square at Toombs Ave. This massive red-brick structure, with its turret, bay windows, and cast-iron entrance columns, was once one of the grandest hotels between Augusta and Atlanta. Vacant for more than 25 years, it is now being restored as a bed-and-breakfast inn.

3. Tupper-Barnett House (1853)—101 W. Toombs Ave. This magnificent Greek Revival house encircled by 18 Doric columns was built by Dr. Henry Tupper, pastor of the Baptist Church nearby. Tupper was a member of a wealthy family and never accepted any salary from his congregation. Tupper's granddaughter married Gen. George C. Marshall, chief of staff during World War II and secretary of state under Pres. Harry Truman. *NR*

4. First Baptist Church (1884)— W. Toombs Ave. Established in 1827, the congregation's first pastor was the Rev. Jesse Mercer for whom Mercer University was named. Henry Tupper served as pastor here for 20 years.

5. New Haywood (1887)— W. Toombs Ave. at Pope St. Designed by Atlanta architect E. G. Lind for T. M. Green, the house, with its expansive porch and 3-story cupola-topped turret, is a superb example of Queen Anne–style architecture.

6. Hynes-St. Gaudens-Standard-Barnett House (c. 1800s)—Pope and W. Liberty Sts.

This early 19th-century home was erected on land set aside in the original town charter for use as the militia's drilling ground.

7. Lane-Cheney-Lindsay House (1820)—Pope and W. Liberty Sts. This frame structure was originally located at a site near the square.

8. Poplar Corner (1810)—210 W. Liberty St. One of the town's most historic homes, the original house, built in 1810 by Oliver Hillhouse Prince, was a simple Federal-style structure. In 1820, Alexander Pope purchased and enlarged it, adding two rooms that had been part of the original county courthouse. It was later remodeled in the Greek Revival style popular with wealthy landowners and businessmen. The house has been occupied by members of the Pope family for four generations. *NR*

9. Walker House (1793)—W. Liberty and Allison Sts. One of the town's oldest homes, it is now the Liberty Bed and Breakfast Inn.

10. First Methodist Church (1900)—100 W. Liberty St. Established in 1819, this congregation traces its roots to one of Georgia's earliest Methodist churches, built just north of Washington in 1787.

11. City Hall Annex and Chamber of Commerce (1912)—104 E. Liberty St. The former Zirbes-Ledbetter house now serves as government offices and welcome center. *Hours:* 9 A.M.–5 P.M., Mon.–Fri. (706) 678-2013.

333

12. Mary Willis Library (1889)— E. Liberty and S. Jefferson Sts. Built by Dr. Francis T. Willis in memory of his daughter, this beautiful red-brick Victorian-style structure was the first free library in Georgia. Inside there is a portrait of Mary created in Tiffany stained glass. *NR*

13. Allied Bank Building (1980s)—Between E. Liberty St. and E. Toombs Ave. Although new, this building was designed to resemble the Georgia Bank building originally located on the square where Confederate Pres. Jefferson Davis held his last cabinet meeting in May 1865.

14. Holly Court (c. 1840s)—301 S. Alexander Ave. The present house is actually the marriage of two earlier structures, an 1817 residence built on this site and a farmhouse relocated from rural Wilkes County by Dr. Fielding Ficklen in the 1840s. Jefferson Davis's wife, Varina, and their children were guests of Dr. Ficklen in May 1865 as they awaited the president's arrival from Richmond. *NR*

15. Carroll-Colley House (1810)—Water St. at Alexander Ave. This Federal-style structure was built in the country and later moved into town.

16. Aiken-Griggs House (c. 1786)—208 E. Liberty St. This home was once owned by Duncan Campbell, a state legislator and author of the treaty that removed the Cherokees from Georgia on the infamous Trail of Tears. His son John A. Campbell, who was born in the house, served as a U.S. Supreme Court justice and later as assistant secretary of war for the Confederacy. *NR*

17. Washington Presbyterian Church (1825)—206 E. Toombs Ave. The congregation was established in 1790 and the present building, erected in 1825, is Washington's oldest church. Its original pastor, the Rev. John Springer, was the first Presbyterian minister ordained in Georgia. Young Woodrow Wilson attended services here when his father, the Rev. Joseph Wilson, came from his church in Augusta to preach.

18. Hillhouse-Toombs House (c. 1814)—E. Toombs and Alexander Aves. This was once the home of Sarah Hillhouse, Georgia's first woman newspaper editor and publisher. In 1869, it was acquired and enlarged by Gabriel Toombs, brother of Robert Toombs.

19. Robert Toombs House State Historic Site (c. 1797)—216 E. Toombs Ave. This structure was purchased and remodeled by Toombs in 1837. A noted lawyer and politician, Toombs served in the U.S. Senate from 1853 to 1861, resigning when Georgia seceded and accepting appointment as Confederate secretary of state. After frequent disagreements with Pres. Davis, he left the post and entered military service as a brigadier general under Gen. Robert E. Lee's command.

Holly Court

20. Washington Historical Museum

(1836)—308 E. Toombs Ave. Located on land once owned by Micajah Williamson, the town's original surveyor, the present structure was built in 1836 by Albert Semmes, cousin of the swashbuckling Raphael Semmes, Confederate sea-raider and captain of the CSS *Alabama*. Many of the museum's furnishings belonged to Dr. Francis Willis and were donated by his grandson Edward Willis. The upper floors contain display cases reflecting the area's Indian heritage, the Civil War period, and other facets of local history. *Hours:* 10 A.M.–5 P.M., Tues.–Sat.; 2–5 P.M., Sun. (706) 678-2105.

When Federal troops came to arrest Toombs in 1865, he narrowly escaped from the back of the house while his wife stalled the soldiers at the front door. He fled to France, returning to Washington only after the 1867 death of his daughter. Stubbornly refusing to sign the oath of loyalty to the United States, Toombs preferred to spend the remainder of his life an "unreconstructed Rebel." *Hours:* 9 A.M.–5 P.M., Tues.–Sat; 2–5:30 P.M., Sun. (706) 678-2226. *NR*

21. Dugas House (c. 1790)—E. Toombs Ave. at Poplar Dr. Set back in the trees, this elegant Greek Revival house was originally a simple frame structure built by Louis Dugas, a refugee from Santo Domingo. It was remodeled in the current style in the 1830s. For many years, Mrs. Dugas operated a school for girls in the home. Their son, Dr. Louis Dugas, born here in 1806, was a founder of the Medical Association of Georgia and the Medical College of Georgia in Augusta.

22. Gilbert-Alexander House (1808)—Alexander Dr. at Alexander Ave. Set well back from the street, this was the first brick house built in Georgia's interior. It was the home of Confederate general E. P. Alexander, commander of artillery for Gen. Robert E. Lee's Army of Northern Virginia.

23. Gaines House (1827)—Alexander Ave. at North St. Built to serve as the Female Seminary, it was converted to a private home when the school for girls closed in 1895.

24. The Cedars (1800)—Sims St. at Jefferson Ave. This house sits on land once owned by George Walton, a Georgia signer of the Declaration of Independence. The builder was Frenchman Anthony Poulain, who came to the colonies to fight in the Revolution. His son, Dr. T. N. Poulain, served as the Marquis de Lafayette's physician during Lafayette's 1825 tour of Georgia. The house was remodeled in the Victorian Italianate style in the 1880s.

336

25. Fort Washington Park—Jefferson Ave., behind the courthouse. This pleasantly shaded green-space, with a nature trail and picnic tables, is located on the site of the original frontier stockade built in the 1770s. In a corner of the park is the "Nelson Stone," an inscribed granite boulder that once marked the boundary of land granted to John Nelson by King George III in 1775. It was moved to the park from its original site in rural Wilkes County.

NOTES

CHAPTER 45

Athens and the University of Georgia Campus

LOCATION

✦ Downtown Athens is located about 100 miles northwest of Augusta via I-20 and U.S. 78 (exit 172). Travel north on U.S. 78 through Washington and Lexington to Athens. In downtown Athens, U.S. 78 becomes Broad St. Athens is also about 70 miles northeast of Atlanta via I-85 and GA 316 (exit 106: University Pkwy.). The walk begins at College Square on Broad St. *Information:* Athens Convention and Visitors Bureau, (800) 653-0603; www.visitathensga. com. University of Georgia, Visitors Center, (706) 542-0602; www.uga.edu.

PARKING

🚗 There is metered street parking along several downtown streets, and commercial parking lots offer daily rates. There are also visitor parking lots on the university campus: on North Campus on Thomas St., adjacent to the Tate Student Center and Bookstore off Lumpkin St., next to the Center for Continuing Education on Lumpkin, and near the Georgia Museum of Art and Performing Arts Center on E. Campus Dr.

BACKGROUND

📖 Athens and the University of Georgia offer a marvelous mix: brash young college students and active senior citizens, raucous rock music and marching bands, roaring football Saturdays and quiet Sunday afternoons. To many people, Athens and the university are inseparable— the perfect blend of "town and gown."

While proud Georgians boast that the University of Georgia, chartered by the legislature in 1785, is the oldest state college in the United States, the school truly existed only in name until 1801, when a search committee finally chose a permanent site for construction of the campus. The land, situated on a wooded bluff above the confluence of the North and Middle Oconee Rivers near an old Indian settlement called "Cedar Shoals," was still

337

wilderness, only recently ceded by treaty from the Cherokee Indians. The school's founders, among them Abraham Baldwin and Gov. John Milledge, believed the school's location was ideal—far from the corrupting influences of city life.

As work began on the college's buildings, a small village began to grow on a hill just north of the campus. Though it was rough in appearance, early settlers dubbed it "Athens," envisioning the community's future role as a seat of classical education. Land for the town was purchased from the university by Gov. Milledge, lots were created, streets laid out and, by the time the first classes were held in a crude log cabin, a small town had been established.

The school's first permanent building, Old College, was completed in 1806. It was called Franklin College and served as both dormitory and classroom. In 1832, Alexander Stephens (future U.S. congressman, Confederate vice-president, and Georgia governor) and Crawford Long (physician and discoverer of ether anesthesia) were roommates there. Construction of other structures followed, including literary halls, a chapel, and faculty residences. Today, the shaded grounds of the old North Campus contain eight historic 19th-century buildings.

Like most college towns, as the school grew so did Athens. It attracted scholars, lawyers, and businessmen who built fine Federal-style and, later, Greek Revival homes along winding, shaded lanes. By the time of the Civil War, enrollment at the college remained small (around 100 students), but Athens was a thriving city of 4,000 and the seat of Clarke County.

In addition to businesses established to support the college, Athens was also home to a foundry and textile mills (Georgia's first cotton mill was established here in 1829). During the Civil War, the Athens Foundry cast a unique double-barreled cannon, designed to fire two cannon balls connected by a chain and "mow down Yankees like a scythe cuts wheat." However, when the gun was tested, the two barrels would not reliably discharge simultaneously and the cannon was never used in combat. Although it was a failure, the cannon has long been an object of curiosity, occupying a prominent place on the lawn of Athens' City Hall.

Following Sherman's capture of Atlanta, the Union Army moved southeastward toward Milledgeville and bypassed Athens. As a result, many of the town's exquisite antebellum homes and buildings were spared destruction.

With Georgia's economy in ruins, financial difficulties plagued the university during the years of Reconstruction. The school's survival was greatly aided by grants awarded through the terms of the Morrill Act,

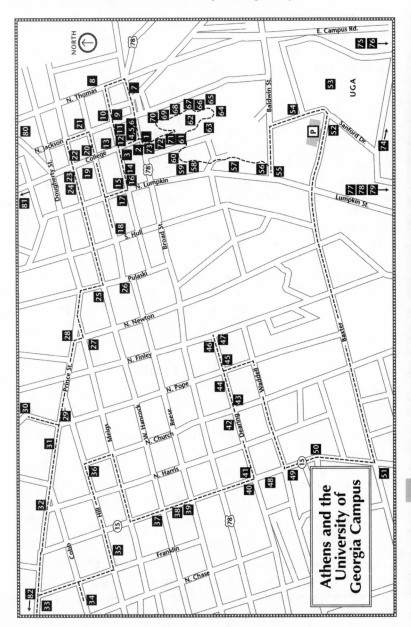

Athens and the
University of
Georgia Campus

a Federal law enacted in 1862 to provide for the establishment and maintenance of public, land-grant colleges across the nation.

The postwar years also saw the introduction of social fraternities at the university. (Sororities followed with the change to coeducation in 1918.) As time passed, many of the fine old houses near the campus, particularly along Milledge Ave., were transformed from private homes to chapter houses. Despite the wear and tear college students inflict, the change served to preserve many historic structures that might otherwise have been lost.

While few could imagine the impact at the time, college life at Georgia changed forever when, in 1892, Professor Charles F. Herty introduced to a handful of students the new game of football. A team was formed and began playing in a field behind the college. The sport caught on with a passion (a near-riot erupted following the 1893 contest with rival Georgia Tech) that continues unabated to the present day.

The early years of the 20th century were a time of rapid growth for both the university and the town. As the university has continued to grow in enrollment and academic standing, Athens has prospered, enjoying the many cultural and intellectual benefits associated with an academic community. Poetry readings, chamber music recitals, cutting-edge rock-and-roll

(Athens is the birthplace of R.E.M. and the B-52s), world-class art exhibitions and theatrical performances, NCAA championship gymnastics or tennis—whatever your interests, there is an extraordinary variety of activities that make Athens a lively place to visit and explore.

Today, the university's enrollment approaches 30,000, and the once-small college town is a bustling metropolitan area of more than 150,000 (a population that nearly doubles on football Saturdays). From the white-columned antebellum mansions lining Athens' tree-shaded streets to the ultra-modern buildings that dot the university campus, the city and school, both carved from the rugged frontier, share a colorful history and a promising future.

WALK DISTANCE AND TERRAIN

This winding route around the heart of downtown and through historic residential areas traces a 4.5-mile loop. The downtown area is hilly with Athens City Hall occupying the highest point. There is a steep descent along Baxter St. to the university campus and a moderate climb through the old North Campus back to the starting point.

SIGHTS ALONG THE WAY

1. The University Arch (1858)—Broad St. at College Ave. This three-columned, wrought-iron arch, patterned after the Great Seal of the State of Georgia, has long served as the ceremonial entrance to the campus.

2. College Square Building (1845)—Broad St. at College Ave. Originally known as the Newton House, it was once considered Athens' finest hotel. The building was remodeled in the Colonial Revival style during the 1920s and, today, houses a variety of shops, restaurants, and offices.

3. Myers Building (1892)—171 College Ave. Designed in the Victorian Romanesque style, the building is highlighted by an ornamental tower.

4. University Bank Building (1885)—279 E. Broad St. Built by the University Bank of Athens on the site of one of the town's first pharmacies, the building now houses retail shops and restaurants.

5. Parrott Building (1885)—283 E. Broad St. Designed in the Victorian Romanesque style, it served for many years as the Athens Savings Bank. The building now houses street-level shops and restaurants. *NR*

6. National Bank Building (1866)—295 E. Broad St. This Gothically inspired commercial building with its crenelated parapets and arched windows was built as the bank's headquarters.

7. Franklin House (1845)—464–80 E. Broad St. Originally built as a hotel, with street-level retail space,

this building contains fine Greek Revival details. It was renovated in the 1970s and now serves as commercial offices. *NR*

8. Classic Center (1996)—300 N. Thomas St. Athens' civic center is a venue for a wide variety of cultural events, trade shows, and conventions. *Information:* (706) 357-4444.

9. Michael Brothers Building (1922)—320 E. Clayton St. Designed by noted architect Neel Reid, this retail store is built in the Second Renaissance Revival style.

10. Heery Building (1890)—361 E. Clayton St. Designed in the Victorian Romanesque style, the small commercial structure is noted for the beautiful Gothic arches over the second-floor windows.

11. Victorian Building (1885)—264 E. Clayton St. This commercial structure is designed in the Victorian Romanesque style.

12. Moss-Heery Building (1880)—216 E. Clayton St. Originally built to house a print shop, this Victorian-era building is noted for its unusual pressed-tin facade, the last of its type in Athens.

13. Georgia National Bank Building (1909)—202 College Ave. Constructed by the Southern Mutual Insurance Company, this 7-story building was Athens' first "skyscraper."

14. Moss-Scott Building (1910)—164 E. Clayton St. Designed in the Beaux Arts Classical style, this building

Athens City Hall and double-barreled cannon

has served many functions, from pool hall and soda fountain to furniture store.

15. Haygood Building (1885)—151 E. Clayton St. This 3-story brick structure contains architectural features of the Victorian Romanesque style. Especially notable are the stone window moldings.

342

16. Citizens & Southern National Bank Building (1915)—110 E. Clayton St. Athens' tallest building, it was originally built as a hotel. During the 1960s it was remodeled in the Colonial Revival style.

17. Georgia Theatre (1889)—215 N. Lumpkin St. This building has served a variety of purposes including use as a YMCA, hotel, and vaudeville theater. In 1935, it was remodeled in the Art Deco style and converted to a movie theater.

18. Morton Building (1910)—199 W. Washington St. This building houses the 550-seat Morton Theatre, one of the first vaudeville theaters built, owned, and operated by African-Americans. Closed for many years, the theater was restored and reopened as a performing arts center in 1994. *Information:* (706) 613-3770. *NR*

19. Athens City Hall (1904)—College Ave. at Washington St. Sitting atop the city's highest hill, this Beaux Arts Classical building, designed by Augusta, Ga., architect L. F. Goodrich, is a local landmark. The building houses offices for the consolidated government of Athens and Clarke County. The unique double-barreled cannon is located at the northeast corner of the building.

20. Georgian Hotel (1909)—247 E. Washington St. Designed by Atlanta architect A. Ten Eyck Brown in the Georgian Revival style, this was Athens' first modern luxury hotel. It is now used for offices and apartments.

21. Clarke County Courthouse (1914)—Washington and Jackson Sts. Also designed by Brown, the courthouse is in the Beaux Arts Classical style.

22. First American Bank and Trust Building (1906)—300 College

Ave. Originally built to house the post office and Federal court, the building was designed in the Second Renaissance Revival style by James Knox Taylor, architect for the U.S. Treasury Department building in Washington, D.C. The structure's 1978 conversion to a bank was Athens' first historic-building, commercial adaptive, reuse project.

23. Tinsley-Stern House (1830)— 193 E. Hancock Ave. The second oldest residence in Athens, this home was built in the Federal style by pioneer citizen Dr. James Tinsley. It is currently used for offices.

24. First Presbyterian Church (1855)—185 E. Hancock Ave. Designed in the style of a Greek Revival Temple, the church still contains its original pews. The beautiful marble pulpit is an especially notable feature. The original church bell is displayed on the lawn by the main entrance.

25. First Baptist Church (1920)— Hancock Ave. and Pulaski St. Also in the Greek Revival Temple style, this imposing building houses one of Athens' oldest religious congregations, established in 1830.

26. Ross Crane House (1842)— 247 Pulaski St. Many of the fine antebellum homes in Athens and around Georgia were the work of architect Ross Crane. He built this well-appointed Greek Revival house for his personal residence. The house was purchased by the Sigma Alpha

Epsilon Fraternity for use as a chapter house in 1929. *NR*

27. James Camak House (c. 1830) —279 Meigs St. Built in the Federal style, this was the residence of James Camak, who originally came to Athens in 1817 to teach mathematics at the university. By the 1830s, Camak had turned to business for his livelihood. In 1834 a meeting was held in this house to organize the Georgia Railroad, the state's first. Camak was selected as its first president. *NR*

28. Joseph H. Lumpkin House (c. 1837)—248 Prince Ave. Originally built as a small frame house, the structure was greatly enlarged by Lumpkin, who purchased it in the early 1840s. A noted attorney, Lumpkin was one of the first three men elected by the legislature to serve on the State Supreme Court, becoming chief justice in 1863. The house is an excellent example of Greek Revival architecture. *NR*

29. Fire Hall No. 2 (1901)— 489 Prince Ave. This unusual triangular brick building was constructed to house a single horse-drawn fire wagon. It was an active fire station until 1979 and has now been adapted for use as headquarters for the Athens-Clarke Heritage Foundation. The building is occasionally open for tours. (706) 353-1801.

30. Howell Cobb House (1835)— 698 Pope St. Another prominent Georgian who called Athens home,

343

Cobb served as Georgia governor, secretary of the treasury under Pres. James Buchanan, president of the Georgia Secession Convention in 1861, and as a general in the Confederate army, commanding "Cobb's Legion" in the army of Northern Virginia. This attractive Greek Revival home was the first of two residences in Athens owned by Cobb.

31. University of Georgia President's Home (1857)—570 Prince Ave. This imposing Greek Revival house has 14 Corinthian columns extending around three sides of the structure and Doric columns across the back. It was built by Col. John T. Grant, an 1833 graduate of the university and a successful civil engineer and railroad contractor. After the war, Grant moved to Atlanta, and the home was purchased by noted lawyer and Confederate legislator Benjamin H. Hill. Hill later served for many years as a U.S. senator from Georgia and was instrumental in persuading Pres. Rutherford Hayes to end the Reconstruction period throughout the South in 1877. The house had a succession of owners until 1949, when it was purchased by the University of Georgia and renovated for use as the official residence of its president. It is occasionally opened to the public for special events. (706) 542-0602) *NR*

32. Taylor-Grady House (1840)— 634 Prince Ave. This beautiful Greek Revival home, with its unusual

twisted-wire railing between Doric columns, was built by wealthy businessman and planter Robert Taylor. In 1863 the house was purchased by Maj. William Grady while on furlough from the Confederate army. Grady was fatally wounded at the Battle of Petersburg, and his widow and five children did not occupy the house until after the war. Their oldest child, Henry, attended the university, graduating in 1868. A professional journalist, he became editor of the *Atlanta Constitution* and a nationally renowned spokesperson for the post–Civil War "New South." Today, the house is owned by the Junior League of Athens and serves as a special events facility. It is open for tours 10 A.M.–1 P.M. and 2:30–5 P.M., Mon.–Fri. (706) 549-8688. *NL*

33. E. K. Lumpkin House (1858)— 973 Prince Ave. Begun by Gen. Robert Taylor, whose father built the nearby Taylor-Grady House, this residence was unfinished when the younger Taylor died in the Civil War. The house was completed by the general's son, Richard. Following several subsequent owners, the house was purchased by Judge E. K. Lumpkin, grandson of Joseph Lumpkin (see #28). It was in this house, in 1891, that Lumpkin's wife, Mary, organized the Ladies Garden Club of Athens, the first garden club in the U.S. The house is now owned by Young Harris Memorial Methodist Church.

34. Moss Side (1838)—479 Cobb St. This simple, frame Greek Revival house was built by Hiram Hayes and sold to Joseph Maxwell in 1846.The house was purchased by John Moss and his son Rufus in 1863. At the time, the younger Moss was in charge of the Confederate Commissary in Atlanta. Rufus Moss returned to Athens after the war and had a highly successful career in textiles and railroading. His youngest child, William, born in the house in 1876, went on to a renowned career in medical research and is best known for developing the world's first system of blood typing. In 1931 William returned to Georgia to serve as dean of the Medical College of Georgia in Augusta.

35. DeRenne-Berry House (1843)—573 Hill St. One of Athens' most unique antebellum homes, this Greek Revival–style house features a massive columned portico of heart pine.

36. Cobb-Bucknell House (1850)—425 Hill St. Howell Cobb's second residence in Athens (see #30), this Greek Revival house was built shortly before Cobb was elected governor in 1851.

37. Phinizy-Hunnicutt House (1855)—325 N. Milledge Ave. Built by prominent businessman John Phinizy, the house was one of the first in the city designed in the Italianate style. It was purchased by Dr. John Hunnicutt in 1873 and remained in the family until 1986. The house is especially notable for its intricate wrought-iron work.

38. Lucy Cobb Institute (1858)—200 N. Milledge Ave. These buildings, notable for their exquisite wrought-iron scroll work, housed a school for young ladies established by T. R. R. Cobb, younger brother of Howell. The school was named in memory of one his daughters who had died of scarlet fever. T. R. R. Cobb was a prominent lawyer and a founder of the university's law school. He was killed in December 1862 at the Battle of Fredericksburg after taking command in November of his brother's "Cobb's Legion."

The institute operated as a girls' preparatory school until 1931, when the property was acquired by the university. The main building was converted for use as a women's dormitory. The institute's classroom building and the adjacent chapel underwent extensive renovations in the late 1980s and now house the university's Carl Vinson Institute of Government, named for the Milledgeville native who was a powerful member of the U.S. Congress for more than 50 years. *NR*

39. Seney-Stovall Chapel (1885)—Milledge Ave. and Reese St. This chapel was built with funds donated to the Lucy Cobb Institute by New York businessman George Seney, who also contributed money to build Seney Hall at Oxford College of

345

Emory University. The unusual double-octagon structure, designed by Athens architect W. W. Thomas, is an Athens landmark. *NR*

40. Hamilton-Hodgson House (1861)—150 S. Milledge Ave. This antebellum house with features of the Italianate style was built by Athens physician and planter Dr. James Hamilton. It was purchased by Edward Hodgson in 1902 and sold to the Alpha Delta Pi Sorority in 1939. The house's ornamental ironwork was manufactured in England and arrived in Athens on the last train from Philadelphia before the outbreak of the Civil War.

41. Sylvanus Morris House (c. 1860s)—458 Dearing St. Morris was the dean of Lumpkin Law School for many years. The house has been remodeled several times, and it is believed that the original structure was brought to the site from the Macon area.

42. Rucker-Teague House (1790)—328 Dearing St. Originally built in Oglethorpe County, the house was moved to Athens by Richard Wilson in the late 1850s. The side addition and porch were added at that time.

43. Yancey House (c. 1850)—243 Dearing St.—This architecturally interesting house features characteristics of the Italian Villa and Gothic Revival styles.

44. Young Y. G. Harris House (c. 1830s)—220 Dearing St. Designed and built by Athens architect Ross Crane, the house was purchased by Young Harris in 1843. The Victorian porch was a later addition, and the house was moved to this location from its original site on Pope St. in the early 1900s.

45. Meeker-Pope-Barrow House (1857)—197 Dearing St. Called "Boxwood" by it current owners, this attractive home with Italianate features was built as a summer residence for the cotton planter Christopher Meeker. It was purchased by Dr. John Pope in 1873 and acquired by James Barrow in 1936. The formal boxwood garden is one of only two antebellum gardens still in existence in Athens.

46. Cobb-Ward House (c. 1828)—126 Dearing St. The original house was built by John A. Cobb as a wedding gift for his sister at the time of her marriage to William Jackson, son of Gov. James Jackson. In 1832 the home was purchased by university professor Malthus Ward, curator of the school's botanical garden, which covered an adjoining hillside.

47. The Tree That Owns Itself (1875)—Dearing and Finley Sts. William Jackson was so fond of a magnificent oak tree growing on this site that he purchased the tree and the land around it in 1875. In his will, Jackson bequeathed title to the tree to the tree itself. The tree on the site today has grown from a sapling cultivated from the original tree and was planted in 1946 by the Junior Ladies Garden Club of Athens.

48. Hamilton-Phinizy-Segrest House (1858)—250 S. Milledge Ave. This antebellum home is notable for its unusual double-tiered portico and intricate wrought-iron railings. The house was built by Thomas Hamilton, who died before it was completed. His widow completed construction and lived here for 18 years. In 1964, the house was purchased by the Phi Mu Sorority, which added the two side wings and curving stairway.

49. Albion P. Dearing House (1856)—338 S. Milledge Ave. Considered one of the finest examples of pure Greek Revival architecture in the nation, this house was built by Dearing, whose father, William, had amassed a fortune in manufacturing, railroads, and real estate. Albion died in 1885, but his widow, Eugenia Hamilton Dearing, lived in the house until her death in 1912. The house remained in the family until it was purchased by the Kappa Alpha Theta Sorority in 1938. *NR*

50. Wilkins House (1860)—387 S. Milledge Ave. Built by Alfred Dearing, son of Albion, the home was later owned by university professor Leon Charbonnier. In 1909, it was purchased by John Wilkins, who added the Classical Revival colonnade. *NR*

51. Thomas-Carithers House (1895)—530 S. Milledge Ave. This marvelous example of Beaux Arts

style with its abundance of classical features was built by William W. Thomas, a local businessman and first chairman of the Clarke County Commission. Thomas was also an architect and designed the unusual Seney-Stoval Chapel (see #39). The house was purchased by state senator James Carithers in 1913 and remained in his family until it was sold to the Alpha Gamma Delta Sorority in 1939. Through the years, the home has become popularly known as the "Wedding Cake" house. *NR*

52. Tate Student Center (1983)— Baxter and Lumpkin Sts. A low red-brick structure, the Tate Center is a busy student gathering place with dining facilities, TV and reading rooms, 500-seat movie theater, post office, game rooms, and offices. The campus bookstore (1968) is adjacent to the center.

53. Sanford Stadium (1929, numerous expansions)—Sanford Dr. across from the student center. As the popularity of college football grew, the university constructed a 33,000-seat stadium in a natural valley between the northern and southern sides of the campus. The first game played at the stadium, on Oct. 12, 1929, matched Georgia against a mighty Yale team. Georgia defeated the Ivy League power 17-0. Many great teams and players have competed on this field. The stadium also hosted the Gold Medal soccer

347

match during the 1996 Olympic Games. After many expansions, the stadium now seats in excess of 90,000 fans who come to watch their Bull-dogs play "between the hedges."

54. Memorial Hall (1925)— Sanford Dr., just north of the stadium. This building, housing a variety of student services, registrar's office, and faculty dining facilities, was built to commemorate the ultimate sacrifice paid by the 47 Georgia students and alumni who died in World War I.

55. Fine Arts Building (1941)— Baldwin and Lumpkin Sts. Housing a 750-seat theater, studios, rehearsal fa-cilities, and classrooms, this building served as the university's main per-forming arts facility until completion of the new arts center on E. Campus Dr. This building remains the home of the Drama Department and the UGA Theater Company. Its Cellar Theater hosts smaller experimental and classical theater performances. *Information:* (706) 542-2838.

56. Joseph E. Brown Hall (1932) — Baldwin at Lumpkin Sts. Originally constructed as a dormitory, Brown Hall now contains classrooms and offices.

57. Old Garden Club Headquar-ters and Founders Memorial Garden (1857, 1939)—Lumpkin St., north of Brown Hall. The grounds and gardens commemorate the founding of the Athens Garden Club, the nation's first garden club, in 1891. The gardens were designed for the Garden Club of

Georgia in 1939 by Hubert Owens, professor of landscape architecture. They surround an 1857 faculty house that served for many years as a small museum and headquarters for the Garden Club of Georgia, which recently relocated its headquarters to the State Botanical Garden of Georgia, a short distance south of the campus. *NR*

58. Candler Hall (1902)— Lumpkin St., north of Gilbert Hall. Named for Georgia governor Allen Candler, this Neoclassical-style building is notable for its twin, columned porticos and symmetrical design. It was originally constructed to serve as a dormitory and later housed university offices.

59. Meigs Hall (1905)—Lumpkin St., adjacent to Candler Hall. This 2-story, red-brick building with rounded windows and a small, col-umned entrance portico, was origi-nally called LeConte Hall. It was renamed in honor of Josiah Meigs, the university's second president. For many years, the building housed sev-eral foreign language departments.

60. Moore College (1874)—Herty Dr., just east of Meigs Hall. Athens physician Richard Moore, a member of the university's board of trustees, persuaded the city of Athens to appro-priate the funds needed to construct this classroom building, the only per-manent structure built on the campus in the period between the Civil War and the turn of the 20th century. The French Second Empire–style building, notable for its sloping mansard roof, was designed by Leon Charbonnier, a professor of engineering and mathematics at the university.

61. New College (1823)—East of Herty Dr. Originally completed in 1823 and rebuilt after an 1830 fire, the structure housed classrooms, dormitory rooms, and the library. Over the years, New College has fulfilled many purposes, including service as a snack bar, bookstore, and home to the university's school of pharmacy. It now houses administrative offices.

62. Old College (1806)—Southeast of New College. The university's first permanent building, Old College is modeled after Connecticut Hall at Yale University. When built, Old College served mainly as a dormitory. Two notable Georgians—Alexander Stephens (U.S. Congressman, Confederate vice-president, and Georgia governor) and Crawford Long (physician and discoverer of ether anesthesia)—were roommates in a second-floor room in 1832. The building was abandoned and nearly demolished in the early 1900s but was saved and restored through donations from alumni and others. The building's interior was completely remodeled to house flight-training cadets during World War II. Today, Old College contains administrative offices. Just south of the building is the English-style President's Club Garden. *NR*

63. Hirsch Hall (1932)—Southwest of Old College. When the University of Georgia's Law School was founded in 1859 by local attorneys Joseph Lumpkin and T. R. R. Cobb, students were taught in their private law offices. Through the early years of the 20th century, as enrollment grew, the school moved into rented space on Broad St. across from the campus. Finally, in 1932, after a successful fundraising campaign, this permanent home for the university's law school was completed. Several modern additions have been made to the building and the nearby law library.

64. Little Library (1953)—Southwest of the law school. This grand, columned building houses the university's main library. Funds for its construction came from a 1944 gift from Ilah Dunlap Little. The building has been expanded several times to accommodate the university's growing collections, including the Hargett Rare Book and Manuscript Collection that includes the original handwritten Confederate Constitution of 1861. The public is welcome to view the library's collections and utilize its resources for study. *Information*: (706) 542-7501; www.libs.uga.edu.

65. Peabody Hall (1913)—Northeast of the library. George Foster Peabody, a wealthy New England merchant, made provisions in his will for much of his wealth to go toward improving public education,

349

especially in the South, which was still in ruins from the Civil War. Shortly after the turn of the 20th century, the university received a $40,000 gift from the Peabody estate, using it to complete this building, which for many years housed the university's school of education. The school moved into larger quarters many years ago and the building now houses other academic departments.

66. Waddell Hall (1821)—North of Peabody Hall. This whitewashed Federal-style building is the second oldest on campus. It was originally known as Philosophical Hall and housed scientific books and equipment (at the time, science was often referred to as "natural philosophy"). Through the years, the building has housed classrooms, a boarding house, and in the 1870s, the university's school of agriculture. More recently, it housed the Dean Rusk Center for International and Comparative Law until the opening of the new Rusk Center in the mid-1990s. It now serves as the administrative annex for the offices of the university's president.

67. Lustrat House (1847)—North of Waddell Hall. One of two surviving antebellum faculty houses (the other is in the Founders Garden, #57), it is named for Joseph Lustrat, a professor of romance languages who lived here with his family until 1927. After his death, Mrs. Lustrat rented rooms in the home to students. Today, the

350

house serves as the office of the university president.

68. North Campus Office Building (1905)—North of the Lustrat House. Originally constructed to serve as the university library, the Neoclassical–style building was a gift from George Foster Peabody (not the same Peabody whose estate provided funds for nearby Peabody Hall), a native of Columbus, Ga., who moved to New York after the Civil War and earned a fortune in banking. Like his contemporary Andrew Carnegie, Peabody supported many academic institutions around the nation. He may be best known as the benefactor of the Peabody Awards, one of the highest honors bestowed on journalists. The library outgrew this building, moving into new facilities in 1953. The building housed the Georgia Museum of Art until it, too, outgrew the space. Today, the building is under renovation for administrative offices.

69. Terrell Hall (1904)—North of North Campus Office Building. This building is constructed on the foundations of the science building that burned down in 1903. For many years, this Renaissance Revival–style building housed the school of pharmacy. Today Terrell Hall houses the admissions office.

70. Phi Kappa Hall (1836)—North of Terrell Hall. This red-brick, classically styled, 2-story structure with a columned portico was constructed to house the Phi Kappa Literary Society, a student club organized in 1820 to compete with the nearby Demosthenian Society. When Federal troops occupied Athens at the end of the Civil War, the building was used as a stable. The Phi Kappa Society is long gone, but the building still serves the university as offices and gathering place.

71. Chapel (1832)—North of New College. The finest building on campus at the time of its construction, this Greek Revival Temple–style building reflects the era when religious instruction and mandatory attendance at worship services were part of everyday student life—even at a public university. For many years, university commencement ceremonies were held here. Today, the chapel is most often used for musical recitals and weddings. The interior of the building contains a beautiful painting of the interior of St. Peter's Basilica in Rome, Italy, a gift to the university from industrialist Daniel Pratt in 1867. Behind the building is the chapel bell that once tolled for class changes and worship services; now it is used to celebrate athletic victories and other special occasions.

72. Demosthenian Hall (1824)—North of the Chapel. The Demosthenian Literary Society was founded in 1803, and this chapter house was constructed in 1824. It is one of the finest remaining buildings from the early campus, featuring elements of

the Federal style and notable for its symmetry and the grand Palladian window over the entrance. The Demosthenian Society still exists and uses the building for meetings.

73. Holmes-Hunter Building (1905)—North of Demosthenian Hall. The building, as currently configured, dates to 1905, but is actually the merging of two antebellum buildings, Ivy Hall (1831) and a wooden library building, completed in the 1870s on the site of the Presbyterian church (c. 1820s). At the turn of the 20th century, Charles Strahan, a professor of engineering, combined the two old buildings into a single structure by constructing the elegant Corinthian portico and rooms to fill the space. Today, the building houses university offices. In 2001, this building long known as the "Academic Building" was renamed to honor Hamilton Holmes and Charlene Hunter, two African-American students who peacefully integrated the university in 1961.

74. Lumpkin House on "Ag Hill" (1844)—Cedar St. at Brooks Dr., south of Sanford Stadium. Before the Civil War, the land south of the university campus was rolling farmland owned by Wilson Lumpkin, brother of Joseph Lumpkin. Wilson was the Georgia governor responsible for the tragic removal of the Cherokees on the Trail of Tears. In 1907, Wilson's descendants gave the land and the family home atop the hill to the university for campus expansion. One condition of the gift was that if the family home, known as the "Rock House," were ever torn down, the land would revert to the Lumpkin family. The 2-story, stone farmhouse, surrounded today by classroom and dormitory buildings, has served a variety of purposes including use as a residence hall, classroom building, and headquarters for the school of agriculture's Cooperative Extension Service. It now houses university offices.

75. Georgia Museum of Art and Performing Arts Center (1996)—E. Campus Rd. at Carlton St. The museum houses more than 7,000 works in this state-of-the-art, 52,000-sq.-ft. facility with more than 9,000 sq. ft. of gallery space. There are also classrooms, studios, an auditorium, gift shop, and café. *Hours:* 10 A.M.–5 P.M., Tues., Thurs., Fri., Sat.; 10 A.M.–9 P.M., Wed.; and 1–5 P.M., Sun. (706) 542-4662; www.uga.edu/gamuseum. On River Rd., just north of the museum, is the new UGA Performing Arts Center, considered one of the premier theaters in the state. The center features two performance halls: 1,100-seat Hugh Hodgson Hall and 360-seat Ramsey Hall. *Information:* (888) 289-8497; www.uga.edu/pac.

76. University Visitors Center—College Station Rd. just west of GA 10 (Athens Loop Rd.). Housed in the Four Towers Building, the center offers maps and information about campus facilities and events. Student-led campus tours are offered daily (reservations required). *Hours:* 8 A.M.–5 P.M., Mon.–Fri.; 9 A.M.–5 P.M., Sat.; 1–5 P.M., Sun. (706) 542-0842; www.uga.edu/uga/visitor_info.

77. Butts-Mehre Heritage Hall (1987)—Lumpkin and Pinecrest Sts. The University of Georgia's rich athletic history is chronicled in exhibits contained in this hall named in honor of legendary football coaches Harry Mehre (1928–37) and Wallace Butts (1939–60). Displays include athletic equipment from the turn of the 20th century to the modern day, the Heisman Trophies earned by football players Frank Sinkwich (1942) and Herschel Walker (1980), and national championship trophies won by the football, baseball, tennis, and women's gymnastics teams. The hall also contains offices of the UGA Athletic Association, coaches' offices, locker rooms, and athletic ticket offices. *Hours:* 8 A.M.–5 P.M., Mon.–Fri.; 2–5 P.M., Sat.–Sun. 706-542- 9036; www.sports.uga.edu.

78. Dan McGill Tennis Complex (1977, 1984)—Brooks Dr. south of Butts- Mehre Heritage Hall. Considered one of the finest collegiate tennis facilities in the nation, the complex has hosted the NCAA men's and women's national championship tournaments many times. An outdoor stadium seats 4,500, and the indoor stadium seats 1,200. Adjacent to the courts is the Intercollegiate Tennis Association Hall of Fame, which is open during events at the complex. *Information:* (706) 542-8064.

79. Stegman Coliseum (1964, renovations 1995)—Carlton St. at Brooks Dr. This 11,000-seat arena is home to the men's and women's basketball teams and the women's gymnastics team. The coliseum also served as a gymnastics and volleyball venue during the 1996 Olympic Games and has hosted the NCAA gymnastics national championships.

80. Church-Waddell-Brumby House (1820)—280 E. Dougherty St. Designed in the Federal style, this house was begun by Professor Alonzo Church, mathematics teacher and, later, university president (1829–59). Before the house was completed, Church sold it to Dr. Moses Waddell, who was then president of the school and who lived here until 1829. It was sold to the Brumby family, and in 1971, following nearly 140 years of ownership by them, the house was acquired by the Athens–Clarke County Heritage Foundation and restored for use as the Athens Welcome Center. *Hours:* 10 A.M.–5 P.M., Mon.–Sat.; and 2–5 P.M., Sun. (706) 353-1820. *NR*

81. Lyndon House Arts Center (1856)—293 Hoyt St. Built of locally made red-clay bricks, this simple home was built by Dr. Edward Ware and later sold to Athens druggist Dr. Edward Lyndon. Today, the house is owned by the Athens Recreation and Parks Department and is used as an arts center featuring the works of local artists and artisans. *Information:* (706) 613-3623.

82. U.S. Navy Supply Corps School and Museum (1954)—Oglethorpe and Prince Aves. Before the Civil War, the university proposed relocating freshman and sophomore students to this location, then known as "Rock College." Student opposition and the war intervened and the plan was dropped. After the war, the original buildings were used for preparing Confederate veterans to take college-level courses. In the late 1800s, the buildings were used for the State Normal School (a college for women). In 1933, the campus, known as the Coordinate College, began housing freshman and sophomore women attending the university. This continued for nearly 20 years, until dormitory space was provided for women on the main campus.

In 1954 the U.S. Navy Supply Corps purchased the property for use as a school. Several original buildings were demolished and new ones constructed. The oldest remaining structure is Winnie Davis Hall (1902) and the Carnegie Library (1910) (*NR*), which now houses a museum featuring ship model displays, memorabilia, and uniforms. *Hours:* 9 A.M.–5:15 P.M., Mon.–Fri. (706) 354-7349.

CHAPTER 46

State Botanical Garden of Georgia

LOCATION

The State Botanical Garden is 3 miles south of downtown Athens on S. Milledge Ave. It may be reached from Augusta by traveling northwest via I-20 and U.S. 78 (exit 172), through Washington and Lexington to Athens. Travel west on GA 10 (Athens Bypass), then south on Milledge Ave. to the garden's entrance. The botanical garden is about 75 miles northeast of Atlanta via I-85 and GA 316 (exit 106: University Pkwy.). From GA 316, travel east on GA 10 (Athens Bypass) to Milledge Ave. and turn right. The garden's entrance is on the right about a mile south of the turn. The garden is open daily from 8 A.M. to dusk.

354

Information: (706) 542-1244; www.uga.edu/botgarden.

PARKING

There are large parking areas adjacent to the Garden Club of Georgia headquarters and by the visitor center/conservatory complex. There is a small parking area by Day Chapel.

BACKGROUND

Nearly two centuries ago tiny Franklin College, located in rolling Piedmont woodlands only recently ceded from the Creek Indians, set aside a portion of its campus as a garden for the preservation and study of native plants and trees. As the small school grew to become the sprawling campus of the University of Georgia, this plot of land was lost to development and long forgotten.

However, in 1968, the university returned, figuratively, to its roots by setting aside nearly 300 acres of old farmland and forest along the Middle Oconee River as a perpetually preserved and strictly maintained botanical oasis. The University of Georgia Botanical Garden was created so scholars and scientists could study the environment and ecology of the

The State Botanical Garden of Georgia at the University of Georgia

Piedmont and conduct botanical research on land where human impact was carefully controlled. From the beginning, the garden's primary mission has been to collect, preserve, and display a rich and diverse collection of native Georgia plants, along with presenting special displays of plants introduced to the state from elsewhere, for the dual purposes of scholarly research and public enjoyment.

At the time of the opening of the Conservatory in 1985, the garden's name was changed to the State Botanical Garden of Georgia as a reflection of its broadened purpose. For three decades, the garden has benefited from the support of Friends of the Garden in close association with the Athens-based Garden Club of Georgia and its local affiliates. Generous philanthropic contributions have helped the garden to prosper. Surrounding the visitor center are a number of specialty gardens created from gifts, and a serenely beautiful addition is Day Chapel, completed in 1994. Today, the garden's exhibit areas, laboratories, research facilities, classrooms, and library host conferences and workshops for professional scholars as well as amateur gardeners from across the state and the nation. Whether visitors come for an educational event or just to wander among the flowers and trees, they share a common interest in, and love for, Georgia's rich and enduring natural beauty.

356

WALK DISTANCE AND TERRAIN

In addition to pleasant strolls through the specialty gardens, the grounds are crisscrossed by a network of nature trails offering nearly 6 miles of wooded paths to explore. The popular 3.1-mile White Trail begins at the edge of the shade garden and quickly descends to the river bank. It turns northward and follows the waterway for nearly a mile before climbing away to the upland ridges. It descends again to a creek bottom where it crosses a small stream several times before ascending on the return, past several specialty gardens, to the visitor center.

The 1.5-mile Orange/Purple Trail begins behind the Conservatory and near the International Garden. It descends southeastward, passing through an oak/hickory forest before bearing left at the river (the trail to the right connects with the White Trail). From that point, it climbs into a heath bluff forest, an area noted for rugged rock outcrops along the river's edge and an abundance of mountain laurel, before gradually winding through ravines and small ridges. The path leads past an evolving section of succession forest before ascending to the large parking area adjacent to the Garden Club of Georgia headquarters. A small guide book, available at the garden's gift shop, provides detailed information on the plant communities found along this trail.

Callaway Conservatory

The two trails may be combined for a moderately strenuous 5-mile loop that carries you through the heart of the Piedmont woodland with its wide variety of plant and animal life. Throughout the nature trail network, many trees and plants are labeled for easier identification.

SIGHTS ALONG THE WAY

 1. The Visitor Center and Conservatory (1985)—This strikingly modern glass structure, designed by the firm of Norris, Hall, and Marsh, features a large, open atrium as the focal point for the permanent display of tropical and semitropical plants. It also houses a reception area, gift shop, classrooms, theater, conference areas, and the Garden Room Café. The center is open 9 A.M.– 4:30 P.M., Mon.–Sat.; and 11:30 A.M.– 4:30 P.M., Sun. The café is open for lunch every day except Monday.

2. The Callaway Building (1975)—The first permanent structure constructed at the gardens, the building houses administrative offices, research facilities, library, conference rooms, classrooms, and a 105-seat auditorium. The building is open 8 A.M.–5 P.M. weekdays and by appointment at other times.

3. International Garden (1996)—A landscaped plaza adjacent to the visitor center contains 11 botanical and horticultural collections that reflect the origin of selected plants and their spread throughout the world. The arrangement of the collections reflects the different eras of Western culture's search for plants. For example, the Middle Ages are represented in the Herb and Physic Gardens, the Age of Exploration in gardens of different regions from the Mediterranean to the Orient, and the Age of Conservation in such displays as American Indian Plants, a Bog Garden, and Threatened and Endangered Plants.

4. Specialty Gardens. The following specialty gardens are located near the visitor center:

357

A. Shade Garden—Seven sections honor the districts of the Garden Club of Georgia. A notable feature of the Shade Garden is the John Kehoe sculpture, *La Grazia Dello Stelo* (The Graceful Stem), at the center of Mathis Plaza.

B. Native Flora Garden—This garden is home to many species common to the Piedmont woodlands, including fiddlehead fern, trillium, bloodroot, and lady slipper.

C. Rose Garden—The Elizabeth Bradley Turner Rose Garden was one of the first developed. Prominent among the many colorful species here is the Cherokee Rose, Georgia's Official State Flower.

D. Annual-Perennial Garden— A brilliant palette of color in summer, this garden is alive with bees and birds when the many species of flowers are in bloom. The All-America Selections Display Garden is located here, as is the Children's Garden where classes are held throughout the year.

E. Rhododendron Garden— Especially associated with colorful mountain ridges and summits, the rhododendron blossoms turn this garden, a gift from the Athens Garden Club, into a sea of white, pink, and red in the late spring.

F. Dahlia Garden—Established in 1987 as a memorial to Elizabeth Faust, the garden is a blaze of yellow and orange from early summer until fall's first frost.

G. Trial Garden—Here researchers plant a variety of trees and shrubs to evaluate their adaptability to the southeastern soil and climate as either landscape plants or food crops. Plants are kept here up to seven years before they are considered for transplantation or removal.

H. Groundcover Garden—From vinca and ivy to junipers and liriope, this area is used to evaluate the suitability of different groundcover plants to the southeast.

I. Native Azalea Garden—Native azalea species are abundant in the southeast, and this colorful collection of flame azaleas, pinxterbloom azaleas, and the rare plumleaf azalea, is dedicated to author Fred C. Galle.

5. Day Chapel (1994)—The exquisite, small Cecil B. Day Chapel, designed by Smith Dalia Architects, appears to spring from the surrounding forest. The stone foundation-blocks were preserved from the original paving used along Atlanta's Decatur St. shortly after the Civil War and were a gift to the chapel project, while the cypress and pine exterior seems to blend with the trees. If the chapel is open, step inside to view the magnificent sanctuary doors, carved from dogwood and cherry panels. The chapel is used for special events, recitals, and weddings. It is open to the public on Thursdays, 12–2 P.M.

CHAPTER 47

Madison

LOCATION

✦ The historic community of Madison is located about 100 miles west of Augusta via I-20 and U.S. 129/441 (exit 114). The central business district is about 2 miles north of the interstate. To reach Madison from Atlanta, travel about 60 miles east of the city via I-20 to U.S. 129/441, then follow the directions above. The walk begins on the town square. *Information:* Madison– Morgan County Convention and Visitors Bureau, (800) 709-7406.

PARKING

🚗 Curbside parking is available throughout the downtown business district and along several side streets.

BACKGROUND

Considered one of the best-preserved antebellum communities in Georgia, Madison retains much of the pastoral beauty that prompted traveler George White to write in his journal in 1845 that it was "the most cultured and aristocratic town on the stage coach route from Charleston to New Orleans." Almost 20 years later, a writer for *Harpers Weekly* traveling with Maj. Gen. William T. Sherman's invading Union Army, described Madison as "the most picturesque town in Georgia."

The seat of Morgan County, Madison sits on lands ceded to the state by the Creek Nation in 1802. Indian "problems" slowed emigration until 1809, when plans for a permanent community were drawn up. Within a short time, settlers came to the area from Virginia, the Carolinas, and southern Georgia and, with a sense of national pride, named their new town for the country's president, James Madison.

The site had been chosen for its proximity to the fresh water of "Round Bowl" Springs (located near Calvary Baptist Church on Academy St.), and the town was laid out in a series of squares. Inns and taverns were built,

359

and soon Madison was a regular stop on the stage route from the coast to the interior. For most of its early history, the community was the economic and cultural center for the surrounding cotton plantations, and many planters built fine town homes in the town. Here they could oversee their business affairs, entertain, and educate their children in one of the several private, church-sponsored, male and female academies. For sons who chose to further their education, the new state university was nearby in Athens.

The 1840s signaled the coming of the railroad, and Morgan County cotton was shipped by rail to Augusta and loaded on barges for the river trip to the port at Savannah. From there it was carried to mills in New England and abroad.

The concentration of wealth in Madison produced lavish homes lining the tree-shaded streets, from the Federal-style houses popular in the 1820s–30s to the stately Greek Revival mansions more typical of the 1840s–50s. During the Civil War, Madison lay directly in the path of Sherman's March to the Sea. Although many of the town's commercial and governmental buildings were looted and burned, much of the residential area was spared.

A popular myth maintains that Gen. Sherman once courted a young lady from Madison and that he spared the town in deference to her memory.

It is more likely that prominent Madisonian Joshua Hill, an antisecessionist and former U.S. congressman, implored Sherman to save the town. While in Congress, Hill had befriended Sen. John Sherman, the general's older brother. This relationship may have truly spared Madison. In 1868, Hill returned to Congress as a U.S. senator.

The war had other, long-term devastating effects for this area as it did throughout the region. The slave-based economy was dismantled, and many of the men who fought never returned. To compound the town's misery, in 1869 a fire swept through the heart of town, destroying many of the buildings that had survived the war.

New agricultural techniques helped reestablish cotton farming, and by the turn of the century, Madison was again thriving. New, Victorian-style homes were built, and grand hotels constructed for businessmen and vacationers. The prosperity lasted until the 1920s, when the cotton boll weevil ruined much of the region's agricultural economy. To many across the South, the blight ultimately proved to be a blessing as it forced farmers to diversify to other crops and products beside cotton. For many Morgan County families, the years before World War II saw a major shift to dairy farming, which significantly helped to restore the local economy.

Proud of their colorful history as "The Town Sherman Refused to

Madison

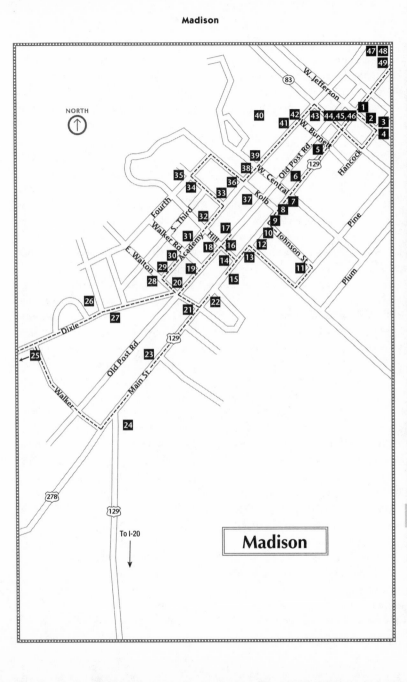

Burn," Madisonians have supported preservation and restoration of many local homes and buildings. Only a few hundred visitors came to the town's first annual tour of homes in 1951, but thousands now come each year to enjoy the architecture and cultural events and savor the charm of small-town life in the Old South.

WALK DISTANCE AND TERRAIN

The 3.3-mile loop from the Welcome Center follows rolling, tree-shaded streets. There are sidewalks along Main St. (U.S. 129/441) and on some of the side streets.

SIGHTS ALONG THE WAY

 1. Madison–Morgan County Chamber of Commerce and Welcome Center (c. 1887)—115 E. Jefferson St. Originally constructed to serve as Madison's City Hall and volunteer fire station, this 2-story brick building was acquired by the chamber of commerce in 1989 and restored as chamber offices and visitor center. The original fire bell has even been returned to the rooftop cupola. *Hours:* 8:30 A.M.–5 P.M., Mon.–Fri.; 10 A.M.–5 P.M., Sat.; 1–4 P.M., Sun. (800) 709-7406.

2. Offices of the *Madisonian* (1872)—131 E. Jefferson St. Designed in the Federal style, this building has served a variety of purposes. The *Madisonian* weekly newspaper, founded in 1840, has occupied the building since 1967. Pause to enjoy

"Editors' Walk," a small garden adjacent to the building.

3. Morgan County Courthouse (1905)—Hancock and E. Jefferson Sts. Once featured in *Life* magazine, this building is an excellent example of Beaux Arts Classical architecture. The building's grand portico and tower are unusually situated diagonally across from the town square. *Hours:* 9 A.M.–5 P.M., Mon.–Fri.

4. Rogers House and Rose Cottage (c. 1810)—179 E. Jefferson St. This Plantation Plain–style home was built by Reuben Rogers, one of the earliest settlers in Morgan County. The house was purchased by Thomas Norris in 1817. He lived there with his wife and 9 children for a year before he died. The family remained in the house, and the 1820 census showed that 18 people were living in the small house. The house has been restored by the City of Madison as it appeared in the 1870s. Adjacent to the house is Rose Cottage, a simple cabin once owned by Adeline Rose, a former slave who earned a living by taking in laundry. Both houses are open to the public. *Hours:* 10 A.M.–4:30 P.M., Mon.–Sat.; 1:30–4:30 P.M., Sun.

5. Richter-Dovecoat House (1840)—201 S. Main St. Built as a simple, frame cottage by Martin Richter, the building was extensively expanded and remodeled in the Victorian style in the 1880s. In recent years it was adapted for use as a bank.

6. Heritage Hall (c. 1835)—277 S. Main St. Built by local physician Dr. Elijah Jones, the home later served for many years as an inn. The house was moved to its present location in 1914 to make room for the Methodist Church. Considered a superb example of Greek Revival architecture, the house museum, decorated with authentic period furniture, is now headquarters for the Morgan County Historical Society. It is reputed to be haunted. *Hours:* 10 A.M.–4:30 P.M., daily. (706) 342-9627.

7. Madison Baptist Church (1858)—328 S. Main St. Built with bricks made by slaves on the plantation of John Walker, the church still has its original windows, pews, and slave gallery. According to local historians, Union troops stabled their horses in the basement.

8. The Magnolias House (1860)—356 S. Main St. Built by a local dentist who maintained his office in an upstairs room, the home was remodeled in the Queen Anne style in the 1880s. Renovations unearthed a trapdoor leading to a tunnel that ran toward the Presbyterian Church. Some believe the secret passage may have been part of the Underground Railroad.

9. Madison Presbyterian Church (1842)—383 S. Main St. Built in the style of an old English church, the church is noted for its beautiful stained-glass windows crafted by Louis Comfort Tiffany. The Rev. Samuel Axson, whose daughter Ellen was the first wife of Pres. Woodrow Wilson, was once pastor here.

10. Atkinson-Rhodes House (1893)—408 S. Main St. Originally a small Victorian cottage, the home has been expanded numerous times.

11. Foster-Turnbull-Truett House (1830)—390 Johnson St. Built by Nathan Foster, the house was moved to its present location in the late 1800s to make way for the grade school (now the Madison-Morgan Cultural Center).

12. Madison-Morgan Cultural Center (1895)—434 S. Main St. This red-brick, Romanesque Revival building with a central bell tower served for more than 60 years as the local schoolhouse, one of the first graded schools in the South. In 1976, the adaptively restored building reopened as a cultural center. It has received several preservation awards and is now home to the Piedmont History Museum, an art gallery and studios, and a theater. *Hours:* 10 A.M.–4:30 P.M., Tues.–Sat.; 2–5 P.M., Sun., (706) 342-4743.

13. Baldwin-Wiliford-Ruffin House (c. 1840)—472 S. Main St. This is the original, and only remaining, building of the Georgia Female College founded in 1849. The Greek Revival–style house once served as the academy president's home.

14. Porter-Wade-Fitzpatrick-Kelly House (c. 1850)—507 S. Main St. In the late 1800s, the house's second owner, Henry Fitzpatrick, reoriented the structure to face Main St. and had it extensively remodeled in the Neoclassical style.

15. Thomason-Miller House (c. 1871)—498 S. Main St. Constructed as a simple farmhouse on the site of the Georgia Female College's classroom building, the house was purchased and redesigned by Robert Thomason in 1877. The structure, noted for its superb interior woodwork, has received several preservation awards.

16. Stokes-McHenry House (c. 1820)—458 Old Post Rd. Once known as "Rose Hill," the house illustrates a transition in architecture with features from both the Federal and Greek Revival styles. The only casualty of the fighting around Madison during the Civil War died in a makeshift hospital located in the house.

17. Broughton-Sanders House (1850)—411 Old Post Rd. Situated between Old Post Rd. and Academy St., this Greek Revival house with Victorian influences was constructed by W. H. Broughton. It still features the original boxwood gardens.

18. Joshua Hill House (1830s)—485 Old Post Rd. During the Civil War, this Greek Revival–style house was the home of Joshua Hill.

19. Cornelius Vason House (1800)—549 Old Post Rd. One of

Madison's oldest buildings, the house was built by Vason to serve as an inn along the Charleston–New Orleans stage road. The gardens surrounding the house were planted by Vason.

20. LaFlora (1895)—601 Old Post Rd. This large, wood-frame Victorian house was built for A. K. Bell.

21. LeSeur-Meacham House (1830s)—637 S. Main St. This residence is a remarkably well-preserved antebellum cottage.

22. Hunter House (1883)—580 S. Main St. Considered one of the finest examples of high Victorian architecture in Georgia, the home is noted for the ornate "gingerbread" trim on its arched front porch. It is a favorite subject of photographers.

23. Holland-Tipton-Turbyville House (1848)—808 S. Main St. This house, an excellent example of a Greek Revival–style cottage, was the first built on "the hill" south of downtown Madison. A stone in the house's foundation has "1848" carved in it.

24. "Honeymoon" (1851)—928 Eatonton Rd. This large Greek Revival–style house was built by the Rev. Charles Irvin, a Baptist minister and political leader in antebellum Georgia. The origin of the house's name is unknown.

25. Bonar Hall (1832)—1000 Dixie Ave. Built by John Walker, this residence is considered one of the finest Georgian-style houses in the state. The building is flanked by a brick teahouse, orangery, and kitchen. The ornate porches were added to the house in 1880.

26. Thurleston (1800)—847 Dixie Ave. Originally built by the Walker family as a plantation house, the building was moved to this large lot in 1818. A subsequent owner, Dr. Elijah Jones (see #6), remodeled the house and added the front rooms in 1848. The building, situated at the end of a long drive, embodies the stereotypical image of an Old South plantation.

27. Stokes-Barnett House (1830)—752 Dixie Ave. This house is an excellent example of the Raised Cottage style popular at the time of its construction.

28. Trammell House (1898)—617 Dixie Ave. Known by locals as "Oak House," this large Greek Revival structure incorporates the kitchen of a house (c. 1800) that burned in 1890.

29. Godfrey House (1850s)—568 Academy St. This antebellum house was built by Dr. J. E. Godfrey and extensively remodeled by his granddaughter in 1915.

30. Carter-Newton House (1849)—530 Academy St. Built on the site of the Madison Male Academy, where future Confederate vice-president Alexander Stephens once taught, this is a well-preserved Greek Revival–style structure surrounded by luxuriant gardens.

31. Edward Walker House (1838)—484 Academy St. Built by Walker as a town house where his family could enjoy the educational and social opportunities in Madison, the Piedmont Plain–style home was identical to the main house of his plantation, Walker Rest, which still stands in rural Morgan County.

32. Holly Hall (1830s)—434 Academy St. This attractive Federal-style house with some Victorian modifications, may, local historians believe, have housed the nation's first kindergarten.

33. Episcopal Church of the Advent (1842)—338 Academy St. Built by the Methodists, the church was sold to the Episcopalians in 1960. Interior features of this simple Gothic Revival building include 200-year-old chandeliers and the original slave gallery.

34. Lakis (1840s)—382 Porter St. Built as a simple 2-room cottage, the building has undergone several expansions. Note the walkway built of old millstones.

35. Barrow House (1840)—420 Porter St. This house is an excellent example of a New Orleans–style Raised Cottage. Local records show that the house served as a hospital during the Civil War.

36. Episcopal Parsonage (c. 1842)—338 Academy St. Believed to have been built as part of the Madison Female Institute, the structure was converted to a private residence in the 1870s. It was acquired by the

Gardens at Boxwood

occupation of Madison in 1864 is the name of a Federal soldier etched in the glass by the main door facing Old Post Rd.

38. Foster-Boswell House (1818, 1840)—292 Academy St. Astonishingly, this large house began as a 2-room cabin. Major additions were made by Judge Frederick Foster in 1840. The house was remodeled in the Victorian style in the 1880s.

39. Cooke House (1819)—287 Academy St. Another of Madison's older homes, this frame house features characteristics of the Roman Classical and Greek Revival styles.

40. Madison Cemetery (1800s)—Central Ave. and Academy St. The city's oldest burial ground contains the graves of many pioneer citizens and a number of excellent examples of 19th-century funerary art.

Episcopal Church as a parsonage and extensively remodeled in 1967.

37. Boxwood (1851)—375 Academy St. This unusual home, with characteristics of both the Georgian and Italianate styles, is considered one of the finest antebellum houses in Georgia. It draws its name from the elaborate 150-year-old boxwood gardens that surround the house. An enduring reminder of the Union

41. Calvary Baptist Church (c. 1873)—324 Academy St. Originally this was the site of a Baptist church founded in 1833. After the Civil War, the property was acquired for $400 from the Freedman's Bureau by a congregation of newly freed slaves. Church members made the bricks on the grounds and constructed the present building.

42. Morgan County African-American History Museum (c. 1895) —156 Academy St. Located in a frame house built by African-American tradesman Horace Moore, the house was moved to its present location near Round Bowl Spring and opened as a museum in 1993. Exhibits trace the heritage of African Americans in the county from slavery to the present day. *Hours:* 10 A.M.–4 P.M., Tues.–Fri.; 12–4 P.M., Sat. (706) 342-9191.

43. Old Livery Stable (c. 1860s) — 174 W. Washington St. For many years this was Reid's Stables. It was later adapted for use as a hardware store.

44. Vason Building (c. 1870) — 217 S. Main St. One of the first commercial buildings erected after the devastating 1869 fire, the structure is still owned by the family and has been restored.

45. Fitzpatrick Building (c. 1870) —155 S. Main St. Now a medical office, this building served for many years as Fitzpatrick's Hardware.

46. Foster-Baldwin Building (c. 1870) —133-137 S. Main St. Built by Judge Foster, the building housed retail stores on the ground floor and lawyers' offices upstairs. It also contained a public auditorium called Foster Hall. It now houses retail shops.

47. Martin-Weaver-Baldwin House (1850) —488 N. Main St. Built by Felix Martin, the house was later owned by Judge H. W. Baldwin, secretary to Confederate vice president Alexander Stephens. It is considered one of the finest antebellum homes in Georgia.

48. Hill Top (1833) —543 N. Main St. This attractive Georgian-style house, situated on a small hill north of the square, was built by Samuel Shields.

49. Jeptha Vining Harris House (1850) —611 N. Main St. Considered a fine example of the Greek Revival Cottage style, the house is featured in the book *The Early Architecture of Georgia*.

NOTES

CLASSIC GEORGIA ANNUAL EVENTS

January
◆ Greenhouse Tours (State Botanical Garden of Georgia)

March
◆ St. Patrick's Day Celebration (Augusta)
◆ International Rowing Regatta (Augusta)
◆ Brewfest (Athens)
◆ Spring Wildflower Ramble (State Botanical Garden of Georgia)

April
◆ Masters Golf Tournament (Augusta)
◆ Canal Cruise and Cook-Out (Augusta Canal)
◆ Spring Tour of Homes (Washington, Athens)
◆ Earth Day Festival (Athens)
◆ Rainforest Adventure (State Botanical Garden of Georgia)

May
◆ The Great Savannah Rubber Duck Race (Augusta)
◆ Riverwalk Bluegrass Festival (Augusta)
◆ Bicycling Festival and Twilight Criterium (Athens)
◆ Spring Tour of Homes (Madison)

July
◆ Star Spangled Classic (Athens)
◆ Independence Day on the Lawn (Madison)
◆ Southern National Riverboat Races (Augusta)
◆ AthFest (Athens)
◆ Arts Festival (Madison)

September
◆ Arts in the Heart of Augusta

October
◆ Mule Day (Washington)
◆ North Georgia Folk Music and Harvest Festival (Athens)
◆ Olde Madison Days Harvest Festival (Madison)

November
◆ Festival of Lights (Augusta)
◆ Candlelight Holiday Open House (Washington)

December
◆ Jaycees Christmas Parade (Augusta)
◆ Christmas at Sacred Heart (Augusta)
◆ Christmas Tour of Homes (Washington, Madison)
◆ Christmas Parade (Athens)
◆ Classic Christmas Weekend (Athens)
◆ First Night Celebration (Athens)
◆ Holiday Open House (State Botanical Garden of Georgia)
◆ Christmas Parade (Madison)

A carriage ride past the Moss "cottage," a former retreat of one of the millionaires who came to Jekyll Island in the early 1900s

A working commercial fishing boat at the dock in Brunswick

*The ornate fountain
in Savannah's
Forsyth Park*

*Ruins of Dungeness,
Thomas Carnegie's
mansion, on
Cumberland Island*

HISTORIC COAST

Georgia's barrier islands, tidal rivers, and marshlands offer visitors a glimpse of extraordinary natural beauty and rich human history. Modern-day tourists flock to beachfront resorts that line the Georgia coast, retracing the paths taken by the state's earliest inhabitants nearly 12,000 years ago.

For many centuries, native people, called the Guale (pronounced wähl'-eh), lived and fished along this scenic coast. Their first contacts with Europeans were encounters with explorers like the Frenchman Jean Ribaut and Spaniard Pedro Menendez de Avilles in the 1560s. A few decades later, Spanish priests accompanied by soldiers traveled north from Florida and established missions along the Georgia coast in an effort to convert the natives to Christianity. After a century of nearly fruitless effort, combined with heightened tensions with the English in the Carolinas, the Spaniards abandoned the missions and returned to Florida.

Fearful of future conflicts with Spain, England's King George II granted a charter to Gen. James Oglethorpe to establish the Colony of Georgia along the coast south of the Carolinas. In February 1733, Oglethorpe led the first party of settlers to a site a few miles up the Savannah River from the Atlantic Ocean and claimed the land in the name of the British crown. As the colony grew and prospered over the next four decades, the small wilderness village of Savannah became a major regional trade port for timber, naval stores, tobacco, and other goods shipped from the colonies back to Britain.

By the 1770s, British fears of conflict with the Spanish were vastly outweighed by unrest among their own colonists, angry about unfair taxation and lack of fair representation in Parliament. Concerns turned to bloodshed and revolution in 1775, and Georgia found itself embroiled in internecine warfare where allegiance to the patriot and loyalist causes often bitterly divided friends and families. While Britain captured and firmly held Savannah for much of the war, Patriot supporters in the area carried out a vicious guerrilla war against the British.

After American victory in 1781, the borders of the new State of Georgia pushed unrelentingly westward. In the early 1790s, on a plantation near Savannah, Eli Whitney perfected the cotton gin (engine) and revolutionized the harvesting of this valuable crop that grew well in Georgia's climate. Within a few years, cotton became the staple crop grown on vast plantations across the state and the rest of the Deep South. Cotton brought enormous wealth to planters, but misery to the tens of thousands of African slaves forced to plant and harvest it.

Coastal plantation owners raised cotton on the uplands and rice in marshes that had been drained and dammed. Evidence of these century-and-a-half-old fields may still be seen in the Melon Bluff Natural Heritage Preserve east of Midway. Much of the highly prized Sea Island cotton grown along the coast and inland passed through Savannah, turning the city into one of the world's leading seaports.

The Southern Confederacy's defeat in the Civil War ended the slavery-based plantation economy, and coastal communities sought new ways to rebuild and restore their livelihoods. For some, tourism became the answer. Resorts developed to cater to wealthy Northern visitors such as the Pulitzers and the Rockefellers, who came to escape harsh winters amid lush, semitropical splendor. Tourism remains strong, while agriculture has continued to be important, with cotton rising and falling in profitability through the years and the development of timber and other crops. Shipping and commercial fishing, of course, have always been significant economic factors, with their attendant business activities.

Visitors are drawn to the state's seaboard for commerce and for recreation. Few go away untouched by the sheer esthetic experience of Georgia's hauntingly beautiful coast.

CHAPTER 48

Savannah

LOCATION

Savannah is located on the Savannah River about 15 miles inland from the Atlantic Ocean. The city is about 10 miles east of the intersection of I-95 and I-16. The two walks described here encompass the northern and southern portions of the Savannah National Historic District, one of the largest in the nation. Both walks begin at the Savannah visitor center on Martin Luther King Jr. Blvd. *Information:* Savannah Convention and Visitors Bureau, (800) 444-2427; www.savcvb.com.

PARKING

Many of Savannah's downtown streets are narrow, and curbside parking is difficult to find. Parking is available at the visitor center on Martin Luther King Jr. Blvd. and in commercial lots located throughout the historic district.

BACKGROUND

On the cold morning of February 12, 1733, several small boats put ashore at the foot of Yamacraw Bluff. For the weary but excited passengers, the landing marked the end of a long and difficult ocean voyage to begin a new life in the North American wilderness.

Led by Gen. James Edward Oglethorpe, 40 families, 110 passengers in all, had set out from Gravesend, England, four months earlier in the small merchant ship, HMS *Ann.* After crossing the stormy Atlantic Ocean, the party had paused briefly in Charles Town (Charleston) and Beaufort, S.C. In the latter port, they transferred to smaller boats to navigate 15 miles upriver from the ocean to the chosen site for their new settlement. Oglethorpe named the new colony "Georgia" in honor of his sovereign, King George II.

At the time of its founding, Georgia was the southernmost British colony in North America. It was chartered by Parliament and governed by a board of trustees for two clear purposes. First, it was to serve as a buffer between Britain's other colonies and their hated rivals, the Spanish, who controlled Florida to the south; second, the colonists were to cultivate the vast natural resources of the wilderness, seeking new opportunities for trade.

With the assistance of Mary Musgrove, a half-English princess of the Creek Nation, Oglethorpe negotiated for land with Tomo-chi-chi, chief of the Yamacraw Tribe of Creeks. Choosing a site well situated on a plain above the river, Oglethorpe laid out the village of "Savannah" in a distinctive grid pattern featuring large squares to be set aside as marketplaces and commons. Just beyond the town walls (Savannah was a walled city until 1790), settlers would have 5-acre lots for vegetable gardens, while 45-acre farms would be created for large-scale agricultural production.

The trustees had grand plans for the colony. They imported mulberry trees for breeding silk worms, and they had vineyards planted in the hopes of producing wine. They also planned to tap the colony's seemingly endless forests for naval stores (turpentine and timber) to export back to England.

Ironically, few of the early settlers had the skills needed to develop the industries envisioned by the trustees, or even to carry out the basic tasks of

clearing the land, laying out roads, and building houses. They were primarily shopkeepers and tradesmen, plus debtors who chose life in the primitive colony over years in prison. Joining this group were small garrisons of military troops posted at Savannah and in wooden forts constructed upriver at Augusta and along the coast at Sunbury, Darien, Frederica, and elsewhere.

The isolation, along with the constant threat of conflict with the Spanish in Florida or the French in Louisiana, made life in the colony arduous and recruitment of new settlers difficult. Nonetheless, hundreds came. Some sought civil freedom and new opportunities, while others, like the Moravians, Jews, Salzburgers, Catholics, and Anglicans, journeyed to Georgia in hopes of escaping religious persecution. Almost from the beginning, the colony was closely linked with the practice of Methodism, which eventually separated from the Church of England and became a new denomination. The Rev. John Wesley, an Anglican priest, was sent to Georgia by the trustees in 1736 to serve as a missionary, and his brother Charles, the great hymn composer, came as Gen. Oglethorpe's secretary. They remained in the colony less than two years, leaving after several disappointing personal experiences, but not before firmly establishing Methodism's roots in the new land.

Savannah

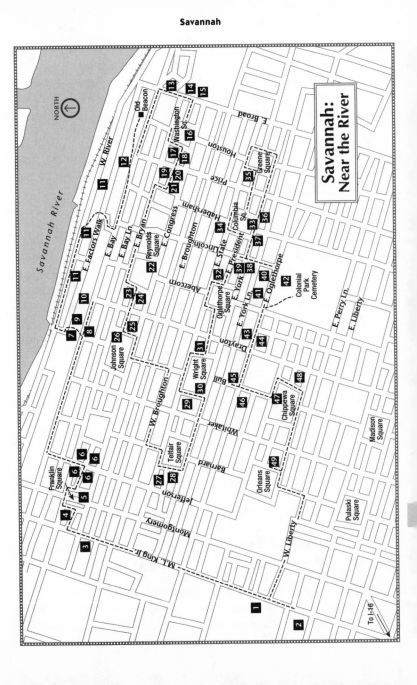

Savannah: Near the River

Oglethorpe took pride in the good relations he had fostered with Tomo-chi-chi and the Yamacraw. In 1734, the chief sailed to Britain with Oglethorpe to be presented to the king and his royal court. Tomo-chi-chi and Oglethorpe developed such a strong bond of trust and friendship that the chief, when lying on his deathbed in 1739, asked to be buried in the heart of Savannah.

Georgia's growth caused alarm among the Spanish who saw the new English colony as a direct threat to their territorial claims. In 1739, Oglethorpe launched a preemptive attack on northern Florida that ended in disaster. The Spanish retaliated with an invasion of Georgia in the summer of 1742. Spanish soldiers, marching across St. Simons Island, were ambushed and routed by Scottish Highlanders in the Battle of Bloody Marsh. The Spaniards retreated back to Florida and never again seriously threatened the colony.

While some colonial threats diminished, the settlers' need for more land led to increased conflicts with the Creek in southern and central Georgia and the Cherokee in the northern part of the colony. Tensions boiled over into war with an attempt by several tribes to destroy Savannah in 1749. A combined force of British regulars and local militia drove the warriors back deeper into the wilderness, and the colonial government laid claim to many more acres of the Indians' ancestral lands.

Although the colony's population remained small, Savannah slowly grew in importance as an export center. The primary products were not those originally planned by the trustees (silk and wine), but rice and cotton, which could be more easily grown in Georgia's climate.

As the years went by, Britain's American colonies grew more self-reliant and less willing to passively accept the dictates of a government 3,000 miles and a long sea voyage away. In the 1760s and 70s, in Savannah as well as in Charleston, Philadelphia, New York, and Boston, serious talk grew of armed rebellion against the crown.

A group of young men in Savannah, calling themselves the "Liberty Boys" and led by Noble Jones, Joseph Habersham, and Edward Telfair, began organizing resistance and corresponding with similar groups throughout the colonies, including the "Sons of Liberty" in Massachusetts. When word reached the Liberty Boys of the British attack on colonists at Lexington and Concord in April 1775, they broke into the Savannah powder magazine and smuggled 5,000 pounds of munitions to Boston, hidden in a shipment of rice.

As word of the rebellion in the North spread, irreconcilable divisions developed between patriots and

376

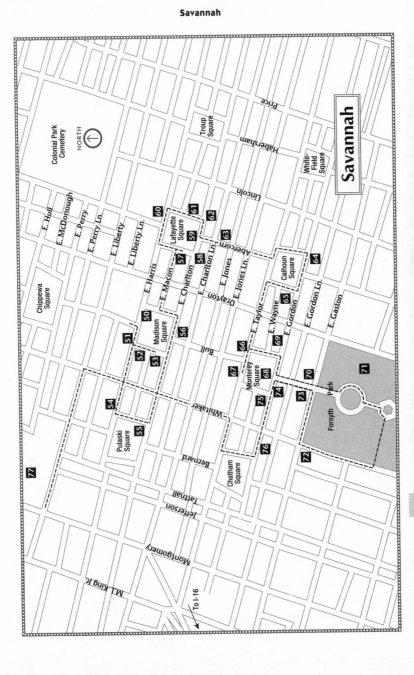

Savannah

loyalists. In July 1775, Georgia's royal governor, James Wright, unsuccessfully attempted to convene the colonial assembly, while more than 100 delegates attended a provincial congress called by the patriots at Tondee's Tavern in Savannah.

Patriot forces wrested control of colonial government from Gov. Wright and placed him under house arrest. In January 1776, with the help of loyalists, he escaped to Tybee Island and boarded a British warship bound for England. That spring, the provincial congress appointed three delegates to attend the upcoming Continental Congress in Philadelphia. The three men, Lyman Hall, George Walton, and Button Gwinnett, assured their place in American history when, on July 2, 1776, they affixed their names to the Declaration of Independence. The historic document was read to a cheering crowd assembled in Johnson Square on August 10, 1776. A new state of Georgia was declared the following February, officially separating the colony from England.

British troops stationed in South Carolina paid no heed to Georgia's newly declared independence and, in December 1778, launched an attack against Savannah. The seasoned force of nearly 2,500 British regulars overwhelmed the city's badly outnumbered and poorly trained defenders. Savannah fell and the state's government fled up the Savannah River to Augusta.

For nearly nine months, Savannah remained under firm British control. Then, in September 1779, Continental troops, with the support of French warships anchored off Tybee Island and more than 4,000 French soldiers, laid siege to the city. By the time the patriots began their bombardment of the city several days later, Savannah was well provisioned and strongly fortified. After two weeks of shelling, the combined French and American forces attacked the British lines. In a furious battle that lasted less than an hour, the patriots were hurled back with heavy casualties. Among their dead was the highly respected and dashing Polish cavalry officer, Comte Casimir Pulaski. Savannah would remain firmly in British hands until Lord Cornwallis's surrender at Yorktown and the withdrawal of English troops from the former colonies in 1781.

Following the Revolution, the seat of government remained in Augusta, but Savannah retained its importance as a trade port. This role took on a dramatic new dimension when Eli Whitney, a teacher and inventor, built the first cotton gin at Mulberry Plantation outside Savannah in 1793. Almost overnight, the machine made large-scale cotton production both practical and highly profitable.

As Savannah became a major port for the export of cotton, it also became a major gateway through which thousands of slaves passed on their way to years of unrelenting toil in Georgia's vast cotton fields. Even after the importation of slaves was outlawed in the early 1800s, Savannah and the islands along the Georgia coast became havens for smugglers bringing in more slaves. (The practice continued until the last slave ship, *The Wanderer*, was caught in 1861.)

In 1819, Pres. James Monroe visited Savannah and took a short trip on a newly developed vessel, the steamship *Savannah*, built by Robert Fulton. A short time later, Fulton's ship made its first trans-Atlantic crossing, signaling the close of the era of the great sailing ships. Celebration of this accomplishment was short-lived as the year 1820 bought dual catastrophes to Savannah. First, a massive fire consumed nearly all of the old city from Broughton to Bay Streets. This was followed, a short time later, by a deadly yellow fever epidemic that killed nearly 700 people and forced most of the 7,000 survivors to flee, leaving Savannah a virtual ghost town.

As the danger passed, residents returned to pick up the pieces of their lives and rebuild the city. Before long, Savannah was again vibrant and bustling. In 1825, the visiting Marquis de Lafayette, on a tour of the U.S. commemorating the 50th anniversary of his service in the Revolution, was feted at grand parties held in the city. An even larger celebration took place

on February 12, 1833, as thousands of citizens turned out to toast the city's Centennial.

As settlers forced the Indians west and pushed deeper into Georgia's interior, the state's first railroad, the Central of Georgia, was planned to connect Savannah with inland agricultural centers. Work began on the project in 1834, and the line reached Macon in 1843. It connected to the small rail hub of Marthasville (soon to become Atlanta) in 1846, and branched westward and northward from there. By 1860, Georgia had more than 1,200 miles of rails linking cities and towns across the state with the expanding transportation hub of Atlanta and the seaport of Savannah.

In 1855, visiting British writer William Makepeace Thackery described Savannah as "a tranquil old city, wide-streeted, tree-planted, with a few cows and carriages . . . a red river with a tranquil little fleet of merchantmen . . . no tearing northern hustle, no ceaseless hotel racket, no crowds. . . ." This picture of quiet tranquility would soon be shattered by the Civil War.

Following South Carolina's exit from the Union in December 1860, Georgia's governor, Joseph E. Brown, moved to seize Ft. Pulaski, situated on Cockspur Island near the mouth of the Savannah River. A force of volunteers from Savannah's militia units sailed

379

downriver to the fort and easily took it from the small detachment of soldiers stationed inside. This undertaking was especially risky because Georgia would not secede until January 16, 1861.

In February 1861, Federal troops set up an artillery battery at Venus Point between Savannah and Ft. Pulaski. This cut off the fort from the city, and a tense waiting game began. War became a grim reality when Confederate artillery bombarded Ft. Sumter, in Charleston harbor, on April 12, 1861.

Soon after the opening battle, Pres. Abraham Lincoln established a naval blockade of Southern ports, and Federal troops fortified artillery positions on Tybee Island, beyond the reach of Ft. Pulaski's aging cannons. In March 1862, the Union soldiers brought in new rifled cannons and began a bombardment of the brick fortress. For a month, the Rebel defenders watched helplessly as the high-velocity shells fired by the new guns tore away huge sections of the fort's masonry walls. Finally, a shell explosion near the powder magazine convinced the defenders that further resistance was futile, and they surrendered. A little more than a year after the Confederates had seized the fort, the Union flag again flew above its walls. The fall of Ft. Pulaski marked the first use of rifled cannon against a masonry fort and was compelling proof that the massive structures were now obsolete.

While they remained far from the fighting, for more than two years Savannahians lived uneasily with their port closed and Union troops nearby. In May 1864, Maj. Gen. William T. Sherman and his army of more than 100,000 men left Chattanooga with their avowed goal to destroy the railroad hub of Atlanta and capture Savannah. Sherman firmly believed that his March to the Sea would cut the Confederacy in half and bring an end to the war.

Following a summer of vicious fighting, Atlanta fell in September 1864. Milledgeville followed in November. Sherman's troops cut a 60-mile-wide path of destruction through the central part of the state as they pushed toward the coast. On December 11, 1864, Union troops were within sight of Savannah, and within a few days, Sherman had the city surrounded.

Resistance was futile, and the Confederates decided to build a plank bridge across the Savannah River to Hutchison Island, S.C., as an emergency escape route for the 9,000 soldiers defending the city. On December 20, the bridge was finished and the troops evacuated the city, burning the docks and navy yards as they departed.

The following day, Savannah mayor Richard Arnold surrendered the city to Gen. John Geary. Sherman entered the city on December 22, 1864, and, with

380

great satisfaction, wired Pres. Lincoln offering him the city of Savannah as a Christmas present.

Shortly after the city's capture, Sherman reopened the port and permitted the renewal of trade with the North. While this move certainly helped to lift spirits and soften hearts toward the conquering general, much more would be needed after the war to restore Savannah's and the South's shattered economy.

Over time, commerce increased and Savannah slowly returned to prominence as a regional trade center. A number of the buildings currently lining Factors Walk and Bay St. date from the wave of prosperity brought about by the tremendous growth in the cotton trade in the last quarter of the 19th century and first years of the 20th. Unfortunately, much construction encroached on the decaying older parts of the city and, one by one, historic structures were demolished to make way for new buildings. Savannah, like many other cities, was becoming more interested in progress and growth than in preserving links to its past.

Finally, in 1954, a small group of concerned citizens banded together to protest the planned demolition of the Old City Market for construction of a parking lot. They lost that battle, but their efforts turned into a movement to protect Savannah's structural heritage. That year the Historic Savannah

Foundation was established to "wage war" against what the group called the "demolitionists."

The foundation's first purchase, in 1955, was the Isaiah Davenport House. Historic Savannah then carried out a three-year effort to inventory more than 1,100 buildings worthy of preservation. By 1976, more than 900 of these structures had been saved, and Savannah's National Historic District, one of the nation's largest, became a mecca for visitors. In more recent years, the city's architectural treasures and colorful history, highlighted in the best-selling book and movie *Midnight in the Garden of Good and Evil*, have drawn a new generation of visitors.

Today, historic Savannah is a city known for its lively waterfront, its live oak–shaded avenues, its spacious squares, and the beautifully restored houses and buildings that hark back to earlier times. A walk through Savannah's Historic District is a journey back in time, thanks to the vision of those determined to preserve the legacy of Georgia's first city.

WALK DISTANCE AND TERRAIN

With the exception of a fairly steep ascent from the riverfront to Bay St., the terrain is level and heavily shaded by Spanish moss–draped live oaks. There are excellent sidewalks throughout the Historic District.

Due to the size of the Savannah National Historic District and the large number of sights to see, the district is divided into two walks. Walk A begins at the Savannah History Museum and visitor center and winds along a 5-mile loop through the northern, and oldest, portion of the city. Walk B begins at Madison Square and traces a 4-mile loop through Forsyth Park and the southern, mostly Victorian-era part of the historic district.

SIGHTS ALONG THE WAY

All of the listed sights are within the boundaries of the Savannah National Historic Landmark District, one of the largest in the United States.

Walk A

1. Savannah History Museum and Visitor Center (c. 1860)— 301–3 Martin Luther King Jr. Blvd. Built as a depot for the Central of Georgia Railroad, the building now houses a museum and welcome center with maps and information about the city. The Savannah History Museum traces the colorful history of Savannah and coastal Georgia. The Revolutionary War Battle of Savannah was fought near this site in 1779. *Visitor Center:* 8:30 A.M.–5 P.M., Mon.–Fri.; 9 A.M.–5 P.M., Sat.–Sun. (800) 444-2427. *Museum:* 9 A.M.– 5 P.M., daily. (912) 238-1779.

2. Historic Railroad Shops Museum and Central of Georgia

Railroad Roundhouse Complex (1850)—601 W. Harris St. Built by the Central of Georgia Railroad for storage and maintenance of the railroad's rolling stock, the large stone complex now houses Georgia's official railroad museum. Among the exhibits is America's oldest existing wheeled portable steam engine. *Hours:* 10 A.M.–4 P.M., daily. (912) 651-6823. *NL*

3. Scarborough House (1819)— 41 Martin Luther King Jr. Blvd. William Jay's second Savannah commission, this Regency-style house was built for William Scarborough, a wealthy businessman and principal investor in the steamship *Savannah*. Pres. James Monroe was entertained here during his 1819 visit to Savannah to see the revolutionary new vessel. For many years, the house served as a school for the children of former slaves and now houses the Ships of the Sea Maritime Museum. *Hours:* 10 A.M.–5 P.M., Tues.–Sun. (912) 232-1511. *NL*

4. First African Baptist Church (1861)—23 Montgomery St. The origins of this congregation date to the work of George Leile, a slave and missionary who preached at Savannah River plantations in the 1740s. The permanent congregation was organized at Brampton Plantation in 1788 and is believed to be one of the oldest continuously operating African-American churches in the nation.

Scarborough House

5. Franklin Square (c. 1740s)—Montgomery and St. Julian Sts. Named for Benjamin Franklin, the square once held the city's water reservoir. A marker placed in the square in 1983 commemorates the 250th anniversary of the founding of the colony of Georgia. Today, Franklin Square is an entertainment center surrounded by nightclubs and restaurants.

6. Site of the City Market (c. 1800s)—Jefferson and St. Julian Sts. This area of restored commercial buildings (a parking deck occupies the actual market site) is now a popular dining, shopping, and entertainment destination. The demolition of the old market in the 1950s marked the beginning of Savannah's historic preservation movement.

7. City Hall (1905)—Bay at Bull Sts. Designed in the Neoclassical style, this well-proportioned building sits astride Factors' Walk. *Hours:* 9 A.M.–5 P.M., Mon.–Fri.

8. U.S. Customs House (1852)—1–5 Bay St. Designed by noted architect John Norris, this imposing granite building was Savannah's first iron-framed structure. This was the site of Gen. Oglethorpe's first Savannah residence, erected shortly after the colony's founding. *NR*

9. Washington Guns (1791)—Bay St. in front of the Cotton Exchange. Captured from the British at the

Battle of Yorktown in 1781, these cannons were a gift to the Chatham Artillery from Pres. George Washington during his 1791 visit to Savannah. During the Civil War, the guns were buried to prevent their seizure by Union forces.

10. Cotton Exchange (1887)— Bay St. at the head of Drayton St. Built during the height of the revival of the "Cotton Kingdom" in the late 1800s, the exchange was a center for the international cotton trade. The stylish, Romanesque Revival building was designed by William G. Preston. Today, the exchange houses offices and a branch of the public library.

11. Factors' Walk and River Street (c. 1850s–90s)—Between Bay St. and the Savannah River. Built for the booming cotton trade prior to and in the years after the Civil War, these long buildings are situated at the crest of Yamacraw Bluff where Oglethorpe came ashore in 1733. The lower floors, adjacent to the wharves, once served as warehouses, while the upper floors were the offices of the cotton factors (brokers). The iron catwalks connected the buildings with Bay St. without creating obstacles to the wharves below. The cobblestone streets were laid down by slaves using ballast stones from sailing ships. Today, most of the buildings have been adapted for use as shops, restaurants, and inns.

On the river front is the statue of Florence Martus, the "waving girl" who, from 1887 to 1931, greeted the ships passing her family's home on Cockspur Island.

12. Emmett Park (c. 1800s)— North side of Bay St. Named by Irish immigrants to Savannah in memory of Irish patriot Robert Emmett (an 18th-century advocate of Ireland's independence from England), the park offers excellent views of Factors' Walk and the Savannah River. In the park are the Savannah Vietnam Memorial, the Chatham Artillery Regimental Monument, and the harbor light erected in 1858 to help warn river pilots of the dangerous wreckage of ships scuttled in the river by the British in 1779.

13. Site of Fort Wayne (c. 1770s)— Bay at E. Broad Sts. Built as part of the city's Revolutionary War defenses and known at the time as the Trustees' Garden Battery, the fortifications were later renamed to honor Revolutionary War hero Gen. "Mad" Anthony Wayne.

14. Trustees' Garden (c. 1733)— E. Broad at E. St. Julian Sts. On this site, the colony's trustees established the first experimental garden in the American Colonies. Imported and native plants were grown to evaluate their economic potential. Results from the work performed here showed that the silk industry would not likely succeed, but that the climate

384

and soil were ideal for growing cotton and peaches. The land was sold to John Reynolds in the 1750s and the buildings in the current Trustees' Garden village date from the 1800s.

15. Pirate's House (1794)—20 E. Broad St. Built as a seamen's tavern, the building has long housed a Savannah landmark restaurant. The restaurant's "Herb Room" is thought by some to be the oldest standing structure in Savannah. The Pirate's House is reputedly haunted by the ghost of a sea captain who died there.

16. Washington Square (1790)—E. St. Julian and Houston Sts. This square was laid out and named for Pres. George Washington before his 1791 visit to Savannah.

17. Charles Oddingsell House (1800)—510 E. St. Julian St. Oddingsell was a Skidaway Island planter who also owned nearby Little Wassaw Island. This Williamsburg-style house was the first constructed on the block.

18. Hampton-Lillebridge House (c. 1796)—507 E. St. Julian St. This 3-story, clapboard structure is the only 18th-century gambrel-roofed house in Georgia. The house also has the distinction of being haunted and was the site of a well-publicized, but unsuccessful, exorcism attempt by an Episcopal bishop.

19. Colonial-Era House (c. 1750)—426 E. St. Julian St. This modest cottage is typical of the structures built in early Savannah. The odd-sized windows in the front of the house are a notable feature.

20. William Pope House (1808)—419 E. St. Julian St. Built by Pope, a Hilton Head Island planter, the house was once divided into six tenement apartments before it was restored.

21. John D. Mongin House (1793)—24 Habersham St. Mongin was the owner of a Dafuskie Island (S.C.) plantation and built this for his town home. The house hosted the Marquis de Lafayette during his 1825 visit to Savannah. It later served as the rectory for Christ Episcopal Church and was used as a hospital during the city's 1876 Yellow Fever epidemic.

22. Reynolds Square (c. 1730s)—Abercorn and E. St. Julian Sts. One of the city's early squares, it is named for colonial governor John Reynolds.

23. The Pink House (1789)—23 Abercorn St. One of Savannah's finest remaining 18th-century houses, it was built for James Habersham Jr., the youngest son of James Habersham, who came to Georgia in 1738. The elder Habersham was one of the colony's wealthiest planters and served as acting colonial governor from 1771–73. The younger Habersham was a staunch patriot and Speaker of the State Assembly in 1782 and 1784.

24. Oliver Sturgis House (1813)—27 Abercorn St. One of a pair of twin structures (the other was demolished many years ago), this house was once owned by Oliver Sturgis, a major investor in the steamship *Savannah*.

25. Christ Episcopal Church (1838)—East side of Johnson Square. From the colony's beginning as an Anglican settlement, Christ Episcopal Church has been a part of Savannah's religious and cultural life. Among its pastors have been notable clergymen Henry Herbert, John Wesley, and George Whitefield. The present church building was designed by James H. Couper and is an excellent example of the Greek Revival Temple style of architecture. The church suffered damage in an 1898 fire, but was fully restored.

26. Johnson Square (1733)—Bull and E. St. Julian Sts. The earliest of Savannah's 24 original squares, it is named for Gen. Oglethorpe's friend and supporter Robert Johnson, colonial governor of South Carolina. The centerpiece of the square is the tomb of Revolutionary War hero Gen. Nathanael Greene. The cornerstone of the monument was placed by Lafayette in 1825.

From the beginning, Johnson Square has been Savannah's gathering place. Here, in August 1776, the Declaration of Independence was first read to Georgians. Pres. James Monroe (1819) and Sen. Daniel Webster (1847) were entertained here at elaborate receptions; in December 1860,

Savannahians first learned of South Carolina's secession from the Union at a public meeting in the square.

A plaque in the square, placed by the American Society of Civil Engineers, denotes Gen. Oglethorpe's original plan for the city of Savannah as a National Historic Civil Engineering Landmark.

27. Telfair Academy of Arts and Sciences (1819)—121 Barnard St. Designed by William Jay for Alexander Telfair, son of Gov. Edward Telfair, the building is on the site of the colonial governor's residence. In 1875, the Regency-style mansion was bequeathed to the Georgia Historical Society by Mary Telfair for use as a public art museum. The museum, the first of its kind in the Southeast, opened in 1885. The building has undergone several expansions through the years. *Hours:* 12– 5 P.M., Mon.; 10 A.M.–5 P.M., Tues.–Sat.; and 1–5 P.M., Sun. (912) 232-1177.

28. Trinity United Methodist Church (1848)—127 Barnard St. The oldest Methodist Church in Savannah, the interior has been modeled after London's Wesley Chapel. The Greek Revival church, with its notable Corinthian columns, was designed by architect John Hogg.

29. U.S. Post Office and Courthouse (1895)—West side of Wright Square. An excellent example of the Romanesque style, the building was designed by Jeremiah O'Rourke. *Hours:* 9 A.M.–5 P.M., Mon.–Fri.

30. Wright Square (1733)—Bull and President Sts. One of Savannah's original squares, it was first named for the colony's supporter John Percival. The name was changed in 1763 to honor James Wright, who would become Georgia's last colonial governor. The Yamacraw chief Tomo-chi-chi was buried here with great ceremony in 1739 (Gen. Oglethorpe was a pallbearer). In 1883, a monument to William H. Gordon, founder of the Central of Georgia Railroad, was erected in the center of the square.

31. Lutheran Church of the Ascension (1843–79)—Bull and President Sts. Organized in 1741 by the Rev. John Martin Bolzius of Ebenezer, a Salzburger settlement just north of Savannah, this is the city's oldest Lutheran congregation. The first church was built on this site in 1742 but burned in 1797. *NL*

32. Richardson-Owens-Thomas House (1819)—124 Abercorn St. Designed by William Jay for his brother-in-law, wealthy cotton merchant Richard Richardson, the house is considered one of the finest examples of the Regency style of architecture in the United States. Lafayette spoke to enthusiastic crowds from the side porch during his 1825 visit. The house is now open to the public as a museum. *Hours:* 10 A.M.–5 P.M., Tues.–Sat.; 2–5 P.M., Sun. (912) 233-9743. *NR*

33. Columbia Square (1799)— E. President and Habersham Sts. Laid out at the end of the 18th century, the square commemorates the poetic name for the United States. Bethesda Gate stood on this site when Savannah was a walled city (1745–90).

34. Isaiah Davenport House (1815)—324 E. State St. Constructed by master builder Isaiah Davenport as his personal residence, the house is an excellent example of Georgian style. The structure's rescue from planned demolition in 1955 drew public attention to the deterioration and possible loss of many of Savannah's most historic buildings and led to the creation of the Historic Savannah Foundation. *NR*

35. Second African Baptist Church (1925)—Houston and E. State Sts. Home to a congregation established by the Rev. Henry Cunningham, the first sanctuary on this site was completed in 1802. After that structure was destroyed by fire, the present structure was erected. The church still contains the original pulpit and pews. In December 1864, Gen. Sherman and Secretary of War Edwin Stanton attended services in the original building. Sherman had the Emancipation Proclamation read to Savannah citizens from the church steps. Nearly a century later, Dr. Martin Luther King Jr. gave his "I Have a Dream" sermon in this building before repeating it during the March on Washington in August 1963.

36. Frederick Ball House (c. 1814)—136 Habersham St. Ball was a master carpenter and built this wooden house as his personal residence.

37. Abraham Sheftall House (1818)—321 E. York St. This early 19th-century house has been carefully restored.

38. Judge William Law House (1855)—227 E. York St. Law, a Savannah jurist, rented this house when it was built as a pair with #39.

39. Gen. Alexander Lawton House (1855)—228 E. York St. Lawton served as an officer in the Confederate army and later as the chargé d'affaires to the Austrian Court in Vienna. Shortly before his death Robert E. Lee was a guest in this house in 1870 after a visit to his father's grave on Cumberland Island.

40. Marshall Row Buildings (1855)—236–44 E. Oglethorpe Ave. These grayish, brick townhouses are notable for their marble steps, porches, and other architectural details.

41. Conrad Aiken House (c. 1850)—228–30 E. Oglethorpe Ave. The well-known author lived at 228 as a child before moving to Boston when his parents died in a murder-suicide. Aiken returned to Savannah as an adult and lived at 230 during some of his most creative years as a poet and writer. In 1973, Aiken was named Georgia's Poet Laureate by then-Gov. Jimmy Carter.

42. Colonial Park Cemetery (1750)—E. Oglethorpe Ave. and Abercorn St. Savannah's second oldest cemetery, Colonial Park was opened for burials in 1750 and closed in 1853. Many pioneer settlers are interred here, including Declaration of Independence signer Button Gwinnett and the political opponent who killed Gwinnett in a duel, Gen. Lachlan McIntosh. The cemetery became a city park in 1896.

43. Lachlan McIntosh House (1770)—110 E. Oglethorpe Ave. While McIntosh never owned this house, he was a frequent visitor and guest in the home. It was built by John Eppinger as an inn and tavern and is one of the oldest brick houses in Georgia. The ironwork and the third story are 19th-century additions.

44. Joseph E. Johnston House (1821)—105 E. Oglethorpe Ave. Johnston, the commander of the Confederate Army of Tennessee during the 1864 Georgia Campaign, lived in this house after the Civil War.

45. Juliette Gordon Low Birthplace (1820)—142 Bull St. Designed by William Jay, this Regency-style mansion was built for Savannah mayor James M. Wayne. In 1831, the house was sold to William Washington Gordon, founder of the Central of Georgia Railroad. Gordon's daughter Juliette was born in the house in 1860 and married William Low here in 1886. Juliette was a long-time friend of Lord Baden-Powell, the Englishman who founded the Boy

Scouts. Building on the foundation of that organization, Low founded the Girl Scouts of America. In 1953, the house was purchased by the Girl Scouts of America and renovated with "pennies" donated from Scouts around the world. Now a museum, the house has been restored to the period of Low's childhood. *Hours:* 10 A.M.–4 P.M., Mon., Tues., Thurs., Fri., Sat.; 12:30–4:30 P.M., Sun. (Closed Wed.) (912) 233-4501. *NL*

46. Independent Presbyterian Church (1889)—Oglethorpe Ave. at Bull St. Organized in 1755, the original church on this site was erected in 1816 and burned in 1889. The present Georgian Colonial–style sanctuary is a duplicate of the original. Ellen Axson, daughter of pastor Samuel Axson, married Woodrow Wilson in the manse in 1885.

47. Chippewa Square (1813)—Bull and McDonough Sts. The square was named to commemorate an American victory in the War of 1812. At the center of the square is sculptor Daniel Chester French's monumental statue of Gen. Oglethorpe.

48. First Baptist Church (1833)—West side of Chippewa Square. Established in 1800, the church was designed in the Greek Revival Temple style by Elias Carter.

49. Champion-McAlpin-Fowlkes House (1844)—230 Barnard St. Designed by Charles Clusky, architect of the original governor's mansion in Milledgeville, this house is an excellent example of the Greek Revival style. The third story was an 1895 addition. Today, the house is headquarters for the Georgia Chapter of the Society of the Cincinnati, an organization of descendants of Revolutionary War veterans.

Walk B

50. Madison Square (1839)—Bull and Harris Sts. The square is named for Pres. James Madison. The monument in the center of the square is a statue of Sgt. William Jasper, a hero of the Battle of Savannah in 1779.

51. Sorrell-Weed House (1841)—Northwest corner of Bull and W. Harris Sts. Designed in the Greek Revival style by Charles Clusky, the house was built for prosperous shipping executive Francis Sorrell. His son Moxley Sorrell served as Gen. James Longstreet's chief of staff in the Confederate Army of Northern Virginia and was profiled in historian W. Southall Freeman's *Lee's Lieutenants.*

52. Green-Meldrim House (1853)—Bull St. on the west side of Madison Square. Built for English cotton merchant Charles Green, this John Norris–designed house is considered a masterpiece of Gothic Revival residential architecture. Especially notable are the parapet, oriel windows, and wrought-iron porch. Following Savannah's capture by Union forces in 1864, Gen. Sherman,

389

at Green's invitation, used the house for his headquarters during the city's occupation. In 1892, the house was purchased by Judge Peter W. Meldrim, former mayor of Savannah and one-time president of the American Bar Association. In 1943, the house was acquired by St. John's Episcopal Church for use as its Parish House. The house is frequently opened to the public. (912) 233-3845. *NR*

53. St. John's Episcopal Church (1853)—14 W. Macon St. Noted for its beautiful stained-glass windows, this Gothic Revival church was designed by architect Calvin Otis. Gen. Sherman and his staff attended Christmas services in the church in 1864.

54. Gen. Francis Bartow House (1842)—126 W. Harris St. This large, frame house was once owned by Bartow, a Confederate general killed at the First Battle of Manassas in 1861.

55. Pulaski Square (1837)—Barnard and W. Harris Sts. The square honors Polish-born patriot Gen. Casimir Pulaski, killed in the 1779 Battle of Savannah.

56. Savannah College of Art and Design (1893)—Bull and Charlton Sts. south of Madison Square. This main building of the school's complex was built as an armory by the Savannah Volunteer Guards, the oldest military unit in Georgia. In the early 1980s, the structure was renovated

for use by the college. Today, the old armory houses classrooms, studios, gallery space, and a shop featuring student's works. *Gallery hours:* 9 A.M.–5:30 P.M., Mon.–Fri.; 10 A.M.–4 P.M., Sat.; 1–6 P.M., Sun. (912) 525-4950.

57. Andrew Low House (1848)—329 Abercorn St. This site of a Revolutionary War–era jail was later acquired by English trader Andrew Low. British author William Makepeace Thackery was a guest in the home during two visits to Savannah (1853 and 1856). Gen. Robert E. Lee was honored at a reception at the house on his last visit to Savannah in 1870. The house was inherited by Low's son, William, who lived here with his wife, Juliette Gordon Low. As a widow, Mrs. Low founded the Girl Scouts here in 1912. Her niece "Daisy" Low was the first girl enrolled, and the nation's first troop headquarters was located in the carriage house. In 1928, the house was acquired by the Georgia Chapter of the Colonial Dames of America as their headquarters. It is open to the public as an antebellum period house museum. *Hours:* 10:30 A.M.–4:30 P.M., Mon., Tues., Wed., Fri., Sat.; and 12–4 P.M., Sun. (Closed Thur.) (912) 233-6854.

58. William Battersby House (1852)—119 E. Charlton St. Battersby, Andrew Low's business associate, built this house. A notable feature is the walled garden.

59. Lafayette Square (1837)—Abercorn and Harris Sts. This square honors the Revolutionary War hero, the Marquis de Lafayette.

60. Cathedral of St. John the Baptist (1898)—Abercorn and E. Harris Sts. Organized in the late 1700s, this is the oldest Roman Catholic congregation in Georgia. The original church building on this site, erected in 1876, was destroyed in a fire. The present church sits on the foundation and duplicates its Gothic Revival design.

61. Hamilton-Turner House (1873)—330 Abercorn St. An excellent example of the Second Empire style of architecture popular in the latter part of the 19th century, the house was built for Samuel P. Hamilton, a banker and Savannah mayor. Today, the home, which was prominently featured in the best-selling book *Midnight in the Garden of Good and Evil*, is an elegant bed-and-breakfast inn. (888) 448-8849.

62. Flannery O'Connor House (c. 1880s)—207 E. Charlton St. This simple row house was author Flannery O' Connor's childhood home.

63. Abraham Minis House (1860)—204 E. Jones St. Built in the style of an English townhouse, the structure is notable for its Egyptian-influenced doorway and cast-iron moldings.

64. Massie Heritage Interpretation Center (1856)—Southeastern corner of Abercorn and Gordon Sts.

The Massie School, one of Georgia's oldest educational institutions, is housed in a beautiful Greek Revival–style building designed by John Norris. The main building was completed in 1856 and the wings were added in 1872 and 1886. The Heritage Interpretation Center houses exhibits on the history of the school and on Savannah architecture. *Hours:* 9 A.M.–4 P.M., Mon.–Fri. (912) 651-7380. *NR*

65. Wesley Monumental United Methodist Church (1890)—Abercorn and E. Gordon Sts. Built to honor Methodism's founders, John and Charles Wesley, the church is an excellent example of Gothic Revival architecture.

66. Comer House (1880)—2 E. Taylor St. This house was built by Hugh M. Comer, president of the Central of Georgia Railroad. Former Confederate Pres. Jefferson Davis was a guest in the house in 1886 when he came to Savannah to celebrate the centennial of the Chatham Artillery.

67. "Cranes" House (1852)—4 W. Taylor St. This attractive brick house is notable for the two wrought-iron cranes guarding the front entrance.

68. Monterey Square (1847)—Bull and Taylor Sts. The square was created to commemorate the American victory at Monterey during the Mexican War. At the center of the square is a monument to Revolutionary War hero Gen. Casimir Pulaski.

69. Temple Mickeve Israel (1878)—Bull and E. Gordon Sts. Home to Georgia's oldest Jewish congregation (and the third oldest in the nation), the temple was established by a group of German and Spanish Jews who arrived shortly after the colony's founding. The Torah that was brought from Europe remains housed in the synagogue. The present building, designed by Henry G. Harrison, is the only Gothic Revival–style synagogue in the U.S. A small museum tracing the history of the congregation is located at 20 Gordon St. *Hours:* 10 A.M.–12 P.M., Mon.–Fri.

70. Oglethorpe Club (1857)—Bull and Gaston Sts. Built as the residence for British Consul Edward Molyneux, this Classic Revival–style house was later expanded and adapted for use by the private social club.

71. Forsyth Park (1851)—Gaston St. between Drayton and Whitaker Sts. Named for Gov. John Forsyth, this 20-acre park was once a drilling ground for the Savannah militia and has been a popular gathering place for more than seven generations of Savannahians. Notable features of the park include the elaborate fountain erected in 1858 and the Confederate Monument sculpted by Canadian artist Robert Reed in 1874.

72. The Georgia Historical Society (1875)—501 Whitaker St. Founded in 1839, the society is one of the oldest organizations of its kind in the nation. This building, known as Hodgson Hall, was built in honor of Savannahian William B. Hodgson, a scholar and one-time U.S. consul to Turkey. Funds for construction of the hall were donated by many local citizens, including members of the Telfair and Hodgson families. Today the hall houses the society's collection of historical documents and rare artifacts. *Hours:* 10 A.M.–5 P.M., Tues.–Sat. (912) 651-2125.

73. George Armstrong House (1920)—Northwestern corner of Bull and Gaston Sts. This home, constructed of bricks made from marble dust, was designed for Armstrong by architect Henrik Wallin. In 1935, the house was given to the city for use as a junior college. In 1964, it became Armstrong State College (now Armstrong State University) and relocated to a suburban campus. The house now serves as attorneys' offices.

74. Dr. Charles Rogers House (1858)—423-25 Bull St. Rogers, a wealthy planter and Presbyterian clergyman, had this double-house built. The wrought-iron work is notable.

75. Gen. Hugh Mercer House (1870)—429 Bull St. on the west side of Monterey Square. Designed by John Norris, work began on this Italianate-style house before the Civil War but was not completed until

1870. The house has gained great notoriety in recent years as the home of James Williams, a local antiques dealer who shot and killed his housemate Danny Hanseford in the house on May 2, 1981. The story of the murder and subsequent trial was captured by author John Berendt in the best-selling book *Midnight in the Garden of Good and Evil.* In 1997, the book was made into a movie directed by Clint Eastwood.

76. Gordon Row (1853)— Southeastern corner of Gordon and Barnard Sts. Stretching a full block, these 15 4-story row houses have been carefully preserved and restored.

77. Savannah Civic Center (1970s)—Orleans Square at Montgomery St. This modern structure is home to the Savannah Symphony and Ballet companies. The center also hosts a variety of events, from music and theater to three-ring circuses. *Information:* (912) 234-6666.

NOTES

CHAPTER 49

Melon Bluff Natural Heritage Preserve

LOCATION

✦ Melon Bluff is located about 35 miles south of Savannah via I-95. Take the Midway-Sunbury exit (exit 76), and travel east on Islands Highway for about 3 miles. The preserve's visitor center is located in a frame building on the right side of the road. *Information:* (888) 246-8188; www.melonbluff.com.

PARKING

🚗 There is an unpaved parking area adjacent to the visitor center.

BACKGROUND

📖 Just a short distance from busy I-95, Melon Bluff Natural Heritage Preserve is a land

apart. Here, centuries of human history have left faint traces on a rugged, almost primeval landscape of live oak and pine forests, marshes, and meandering tidal creeks. A walk along the preserve's miles of footpaths is a journey back in time.

More than 10,000 years ago, the first Paleo-Indian settlers came to coastal Georgia. They fished in the sounds and tidal rivers, gathered clams from the marshes, and hunted game in the dense forests. They were nomadic people who left behind little evidence of their centuries on the land. Today, only the occasional discovery of an ancient shell tool or a small oyster midden (trash pile) marks their long-vanished presence.

In the 16th century, during the earliest European explorations of the Georgia coast, this was the home of the Guale people, a Muskogean tribe who were ancestors of the powerful Creek nation. The Guale lived in permanent coastal villages from present-day South Carolina to the banks of the Newport River on the Georgia coast.

The Spanish were the first to colonize the area with the founding of St. Augustine in northern Florida in 1563. Choosing to subjugate the

Melon Bluff Natural Heritage Preserve

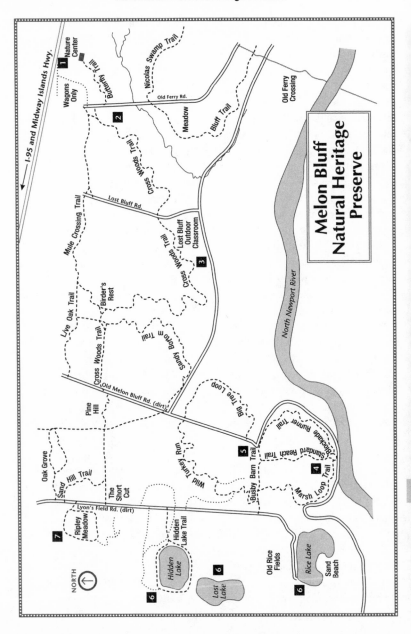

natives with "crossbow and cross," the Spanish built a series of Catholic missions, populated by both priests and soldiers, near the coastal villages of the Guale. The principal mission (and the only one yet found through archaeological excavation) was located adjacent to the Guale capital village on St. Catherine's Island, Georgia (Santa Catalina). The mission, Santa Catalina de Guale, was established in the late 1500s and lasted for nearly a century before being abandoned.

While conversion of the Indians to Christianity was one reason for building the missions, for Spain a more important motive was to solidify its military position in Georgia against expansion from the Carolinas by its hated enemy, the English. It was to counter this threat that the British crown granted a charter to Gen. Oglethorpe for the establishment of the Royal Colony of Georgia in 1732, and the first permanent English settlers arrived at the future site of the city of Savannah in February 1733.

Anticipating hostilities with the Spanish, Oglethorpe moved to build forts and establish towns as far south as Cumberland Island. Archaeological evidence still remains of garrisons and settlements on St. Simons Island, outside Darien (Ft. King George) and Midway (Ft. Morris), and elsewhere. In 1742, the Spanish made a last attempt to drive the English from Georgia by mounting a military invasion from St. Augustine. After burning farms and plantations, the Spaniards were soundly defeated at the Battle of Bloody Marsh on St. Simons and forced to retreat to Florida. They never seriously threatened Georgia again.

A decade later, a small religious group—descended from Puritans who landed in Massachusetts in 1630 and later moved to South Carolina—purchased 32,000 acres of land about 30 miles south of Savannah. The property, situated between the Medway and Newport Rivers was a mix of lowland marshes and rich alluvial uplands, both extremely fertile soils for the cultivation of rice and cotton respectively.

The first settlers arrived in 1754 and immediately built a log church for worship services. They christened the area St. John's Parish, and the surrounding community was called "Midway," possibly for its proximity to the Medway (Midway) River, about halfway between the cities of Savannah and Darien. The town never grew to have a population beyond a few hundred, but the richness of the surrounding land made many of the citizens extremely wealthy as owners of prosperous plantations covering many thousands of acres.

The crude log church was replaced by a sturdy wooden sanctuary in 1757 and served the growing congregation well for the next 21 years. As hostilities grew between Britain and the colonies, the fiercely independent families of Midway earned a reputation as the "Cradle of Revolutionary Spirit in Georgia." Among the church's congregation were two signers of the Declaration of Independence (Button Gwinnett, then the owner of St. Catherine's Island, and Lyman Hall), and two military heroes of the Revolution (Gen. Daniel Stewart, great-grandfather of Pres. Theodore Roosevelt, and Gen. James Screven, killed in fighting against British troops just a short distance from Midway in 1778).

When English troops occupied the coast in 1778, they burned the church to the ground and ransacked many of the surrounding farms and plantations. This destruction failed to dampen the temperament of the people, and when the State of Georgia was established during the Revolution, they quickly adopted Liberty as the name for their new county.

After the war, the settlement again prospered. A temporary church replaced the burned structure in 1784, and this was supplanted by the present Midway Congregational Church in 1792. In keeping with the congregation's Massachusetts roots, the structure's design is more akin to a New England meeting house than to other Southern churches.

For more than 60 years, the area thrived with the cultivation of rice in the swampy lowlands and cotton in the uplands. During the peak of slave-dependent antebellum agriculture, the black population of Liberty County outnumbered the white population by nearly 10 to 1, as the Puritan religious heritage of the people of Midway did not prevent them from owning slaves. Nor did they call for an end to the institution (as did the Puritan descendants who remained in New England and became outspoken abolitionists). Instead, they believed the slaves to be their wards to whom they had an obligation to provide "moral welfare and religious instruction."

One of the most ardent supporters for the moral and religious education of the slaves was the Rev. Dr. Charles Colcock Jones, a man often referred to as the "Apostle to the Blacks." Jones, born on a coastal Georgia plantation in 1804, attended school at Sunbury Academy before being apprenticed to an accountant in Savannah in 1819. There, he caught the eye of several local leaders and was nominated for appointment to the U.S. Military Academy at West Point. However, shortly before accepting the appointment, he became a member of Midway Church and was influenced by its pastor to study for the ministry instead.

After receiving his theology degree from Princeton in 1830 and marrying his first cousin Mary Jones, Charles Jones served for a time at the Presbyterian Church in Savannah. Within a few years, Charles and Mary became joint owners of three large Midway-area plantations: Arcadia (1,996 acres), between Midway and McIntosh; Montevideo (941 acres), south of Riceboro; and Maybank (700 acres) on Colonel's Island east of Midway. A large part of the present-day natural heritage preserve is composed of lands from Maybank Plantation.

Charles chose to give up his church work and return to Midway to manage his family's plantations. For the remainder of his life, he devoted much of his energy toward supporting Presbyterian mission work and providing religious education to slaves, even authoring two books on the subject. Jones was an active member of Midway Church and fostered friendships with many other notable congregants, including naturalist John LeConte and his sons John and Joseph (scientists in their own right and, later, cofounders of the University of California); Pastors Abiel Holmes (father of poet Oliver Wendell Holmes) and Jedidiah Morse (father of inventor Samuel F. B. Morse); and fellow plantation owner Roswell King, who went to northern Georgia in the 1830s to found a textile mill and town that still bears his name.

For the remainder of the antebellum years, through the Civil War (Dr. Jones died in 1863), and beyond to the difficult times that followed the South's defeat, members of the Jones family were devoted correspondents. Their thousands of letters, compiled in the book *The Children of Pride*, offer an extraordinary, first-hand account of life on a Georgia plantation.

Another large portion of the preserve, and the source for its name, was Melon Bluff Plantation, developed by Bartholomew Busby in the early 1800s. While the choice of name is obscured by time, it is thought that Busby may have grown melons on at least a part of his property. Melon Bluff Plantation was located on the banks of the North Newport River, a waterway that offered a deep, but swift and tortuous, channel running from Riceboro to Sapelo Sound. Schooners could navigate the channel, enabling the plantation to ship goods destined for Savannah, Brunswick, and beyond from its dock at Busby's Landing. A ferry also operated on the river, connecting the port town of Sunbury with the upriver community of Riceboro. A primitive road connected Trade Hill Rd. from Sunbury with the ferry landing, and today, the old ferry road is one of the hiking paths that crisscross the preserve.

Shortly after the outbreak of the Civil War in 1861, U.S. Navy ships blockaded the Southern coast. Many area families fled inland, and rivers like the Medway and North Newport became hiding places for Southern blockade runners attempting to run the gauntlet of naval ships to bring in much-needed supplies.

After the war, Melon Bluff was divided into smaller parcels of land. Many of these tracts were given to freed slaves in compliance with Gen. Sherman's Field Order No. 15. (Sherman proposed that freed slaves be allowed to establish their own separate nation on Georgia's coastal islands. The proposal, however, was not adopted by the government.) For nearly 50 years, a few small farms occupied parts of the once-vast plantations, but much of the land was simply abandoned. By the turn of the 20th century, most of the former rice fields had been transformed into forests filled with 40- to 50-year-old pine trees that were ideal for construction timber.

Beginning in the 1920s, intensive logging began. Narrow-gauge railroad lines transported downed trees by the thousands to portable sawmills. Following the tree cutting, Melon Bluff was again planted in annual crops, notably rice. Then, in the late 1920s, John Porter Stevens, a wealthy shipping magnate from Savannah, began buying land and reassembling the old plantations. Stevens, a native of Liberty County, had grown up in the area and loved the natural beauty of the forests, tidal marshes, and islands. He devoted his life to managing the tree harvests at Melon Bluff, restoring the ecological health and natural beauty

of the land, and preserving it as a wildlife habitat. By the time of his death in 1969, Stevens had conserved nearly 10,000 acres of land, stretching from a point just east of the town of Midway to Dickinson Creek and Colonel's Island.

The Melon Bluff property passed to Stevens' daughter, Laura Stevens Devendorf. She, along with husband Don and daughter Meredith, returned to Midway from California in 1972, to oversee the family property. In the mid-1970s, Melon Bluff was split by the construction of I-95, but one positive result of the project was the building of five spring-fed, freshwater lakes, three on the eastern side of the highway and two on the western side. From 1972 until 1997, the Devendorfs managed the property as a sustainable-yield tree farm committed to careful stewardship of the land. Though approached by developers interested in suburban or resort development, the Devendorfs chose, in 1997, to designate nearly 5,000 acres of the property as the Melon Bluff Natural Heritage Preserve. Here acres of salt marsh, forest, swamps, tidal creeks, and lakes serve as both a rich wildlife habitat and outdoor classroom, where visitors can enjoy an irreplaceable vestige of Georgia's vanishing wild coast.

On the remaining 5,000 acres, much of it stretching along the banks of Dickinson Creek, the Devendorfs maintain their own home and operate

399

two historic properties open to overnight guests. Another guest facility, the Ripley Farm, is a 2-bedroom cabin located at the western end of the nature preserve.

TRAIL DISTANCE AND TERRAIN

More than 12 miles of primitive roads and trails span the preserve, and the highlighted route traces an approximately 8-mile round-trip from the visitor center. Visitors are welcome to bring mountain bikes for use on the trails, or to rent them from the center.

The terrain is sandy, flat, or gently rolling, and in most areas heavily shaded by pines and live oaks. The forest and marsh are prime habitats for wildlife including more than 300 species of birds, white-tailed deer, raccoons, armadillos, alligators, and other creatures. The forest is also home to Eastern diamondback rattlesnakes so hikers should be observant, especially in warm weather. Pumps of fresh well water are located at various points in the preserve, as are outhouse-style restrooms and picnic shelters. Comfortable walking shoes are a must, and hikers should carry rain gear, as storms may pop up along the coast with little warning.

SIGHTS ALONG THE WAY

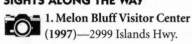 **1. Melon Bluff Visitor Center (1997)**—2999 Islands Hwy.

This unobtrusive wood-frame building contains information and exhibits on the area's natural and human history. The second floor serves as a classroom for educational programs. There is a nominal fee for access to the preserve, and maps are available at the center. *Hours:* 9 A.M. –4 P.M., Tues.–Sun. (888) 246-8188.

2. Old Ferry Road (c. 1800s)— Carved from the woods in the early 1800s, this primitive road once led to the Newport River ferry landing located about 2 miles south of this point.

3. Lost Bluff Outdoor Classroom (1997)—This spot's name comes from the site's scenic beauty, which was unknown, or "lost," until the trail was blazed here in 1997. Today, the outdoor classroom overlooks the marsh and river. The marsh evolved from abandoned, antebellum rice fields. The line of cedar trees in the distance to the south marks the location of old rice dams.

4. Busby's Landing (c. 1800s)— A modern dock marks the spot where Bartholomew Busby shipped his plantation goods downriver. The Confederate blockade-runner *Standard* was scuttled near this site in 1863. Locals say that, during periods of low water, the wooden-ribbed skeleton of the ship is still visible in the murky river.

5. Busby Barn (1997)—This shelter may be used for outdoor

Dock at Busby's Landing

education programs, picnics, or a place to escape an afternoon storm. A freshwater well is located nearby.

6. Rice Lake, Hidden Lake, and Lost Lake (1970s)—These three freshwater lakes were created during the construction of nearby I-95. Today, they offer habitat for many species of animals and birds.

7. Ripley Farm and Meadow (c. 1930s)—Dorchester Village Rd. at the preserve boundary. This cozy, 2-bedroom cabin is operated as a guest accommodation by the preserve.

NOTES

401

CHAPTER 50

Brunswick

LOCATION

Brunswick is located about 75 miles south of Savannah via I-95. Take exit 36 onto US 341/GA 25 (Newcastle St.) and travel south to downtown. Turn left on Gloucester St., then left again on Union St. Travel to G St. and park along the square of the Old Glynn County Courthouse. The walk begins on the courthouse grounds. *Information:* Brunswick–Golden Isles Visitors Bureau, (800) 933-2627; www.bgislesvisitorsb.com.

402

PARKING

Curbside parking is permitted on the streets adjacent to the courthouse, and commercial parking facilities are nearby.

BACKGROUND

Shortly after the founding of Georgia in 1733, Capt. Mark Carr, one of Gen. James Oglethorpe's military officers, was awarded land grants along the colony's southern frontier and Oglethorpe Bay. These grants included acreage near Midway and along the Turtle River below the garrison at Ft. King George and the village of Darien. In 1738, Carr constructed a tabby plantation house and began cultivating tobacco on more than 1,000 acres of sandy soil. Carr called his plantation "Plug Point," possibly in reference to the "plugs" of tobacco he sold for export back to Great Britain.

In 1770, the Colonial Council, meeting in Savannah, recognized the value of the natural harbor of Oglethorpe Bay and decided to establish a port city on its shores. Carr was given land elsewhere in exchange for 385 acres of Plug Point land on the peninsula between the Turtle River and the Atlantic Ocean marshes. The village of Brunswick, named for the ancestral German home of Britain's King George III, was chartered in October of that year.

The city plan, a grid marked by broad avenues, squares, and commons,

Brunswick

was similar to Oglethorpe's plan for Savannah. Streets and squares were named for members of the royal family, other prominent British families, and supporters of the colony. The first land lots were sold in 1772, and the village grew slowly.

Settlement of Brunswick ceased altogether with the outbreak of the American Revolution in 1775 and the evacuation of most civilians from coastal communities. With the end of the Revolution in 1781, people returned and, unlike their counterparts in many other communities in the new United States, the people of Brunswick did not rush to affix "more patriotic or American" names to their streets and parks. As a consequence, the historic streets of Brunswick still bear their original names from colonial days.

Brunswick slowly rebounded from the effects of the war, serving the rice, indigo, and tobacco plantations that spread along the coast. A major advancement in education occurred in 1788 with the chartering of Glynn Academy, today the second-oldest school in continuous operation in Georgia. A year later, development was further spurred by the legislature's selection of Brunswick as a state port of entry and the relocation of the county seat from Frederica on St. Simons Island (now a national monument) to Brunswick.

Despite its excellent port, Brunswick was isolated from the plantations of the Georgia interior. The cotton from these lands could be shipped to the coastal city of Darien, just north of Brunswick, by the navigable waters of the Altamaha River. But Darien did not have the deep harbor waters necessary for ocean-going ships, so goods then had to be transported overland from Darien to Brunswick.

In the early 1820s, several prominent Brunswick citizens initiated an effort to build a canal connecting the Turtle and Altamaha Rivers so that goods could be shipped directly from the plantations to the port. The project went bankrupt, and in 1834, a second attempt to build a canal began, this time in conjunction with building a railroad. Anticipating the prosperity the canal and railway would bring, the city of Brunswick was granted incorporation by the state in 1836. That same year, work began on construction of the Oglethorpe House, an elegant hotel that would rival the finest accommodations in Savannah. In the aftermath of the Financial Panic of 1837, however, the local economy faltered, even reaching the point where the city's charter of incorporation was returned to the state. The bank closed, businesses shut down, and work on the canal project was again abandoned.

A decade later, the city was slowly recovering and money again flowed into the canal project. On June 1, 1854, the Altamaha Canal opened,

404

and, two years later, the city was rechartered. The following year, the U.S. government purchased land on Blythe Island for construction of a Naval shipyard, a project that marked the beginning of a long relationship between the port of Brunswick and the U.S. Navy that has only been interrupted by the Civil War.

By 1860, Brunswick's population topped 2,000 people, and the port was bustling with activity. But storm clouds hovered on the horizon, and in January 1861, Georgia seceded from the Union and joined the Southern Confederacy. By December 1861, the U.S. Navy was effectively blockading Southern ports and Brunswick was suffering both from an inability to ship goods to markets and from a lack of provisions for inhabitants. Anticipating Union attacks on the port, civilians were ordered to evacuate the city and take refuge in Georgia's interior. As the Federal blockade tightened, Confederate troops withdrew from the city, burning the railroad depot and the wharves as they left. Unfortunately, the fire spread to the elegant Oglethorpe House and it too burned to the ground. Federal troops occupied Brunswick on March 10, 1862, and held it for the remainder of the war.

After the war, citizens slowly returned and began restoring Brunswick. The task was difficult, as much of Georgia was in ruins from both the economic consequences of the war and the physical destruction rendered by invading and occupying Union troops. The city was still in the midst of rebuilding in the mid-1870s when it was struck by a devastating Yellow Fever epidemic that sickened and killed hundreds of citizens.

Again, the region's rich natural resources facilitated the city's recovery. Heavy demand for the long-fiber Sea Island cotton brought tens of thousands of acres of this profitable crop into cultivation, much of it being shipped through Brunswick's now-bustling harbor. At the same time, southeastern Georgia's vast timber resources were being tapped for lumber and naval stores, and a fledgling seafood industry was becoming established along the city's wharves.

Brunswick was also becoming a tourism destination. In the 1870s, poet Sidney Lanier journeyed to the coast to treat his tuberculosis with doses of the fresh salt air. Gazing across the seemingly endless ocean of grass separating Brunswick from the sea islands, he was inspired to pen his most famous poem, "The Marshes of Glynn." By the 1880s, Brunswick's population swelled each winter as Northerners flocked to the Georgia coast to escape the harsh winters back home. In time, with the development of St. Simons Island and Sea Island as resort destinations, Brunswick became the official gateway to what came to be

405

known as "Georgia's Golden Isles."

During the affluent period of the early 20th century, much of the city's Victorian-style downtown, the old city hall and county courthouse, and many elegant homes in Old Town were built. After the First World War, though, prosperity faltered. Boll weevil infestations crippled the cotton market, and nearly a century of lumbering had depleted the longleaf pines that were the foundation of the naval stores industry. In 1929, on the eve of the Great Depression, Brunswick was struggling once again.

One bright spot was the influx of Greek and Portuguese fishermen who came to the area in the 1920s to harvest the bounty from the rich local waters. Soon, fishing and shrimping were major local industries, turning Brunswick into a national mecca for seafood. Today, Brunswick boasts of being the "Shrimp Capital of the World."

In early 1942, only weeks after the Japanese attack at Pearl Harbor brought the U.S. into World War II, massive convoys of ships were departing American ports bound for England with millions of tons of weapons and supplies. German U-boats (submarines) prowled America's coastal waters, and hundreds of merchant and naval ships were torpedoed and sunk. In an effort to safeguard the convoys, the Navy opened the Glynco Naval Air Station in 1943. For two years it was home to

both fixed-wing aircraft and fleets of slow-moving, lighter-than-air dirigibles (blimps) that proved ideal for antisubmarine reconnaissance work. By war's end, Glynco was the largest blimp base in the world.

In addition to this reconnaissance work, Brunswick was one of 16 cities chosen by the U.S. Maritime Commission to build new, light, and fast cargo ships for the hazardous convoy duty that was providing the tenuous lifeline to Britain. The J. A. Jones Company brought 16,000 men and women to their shipyards in Brunswick to construct these vessels, soon to be known as "Liberty Ships." The keel of the first Liberty Ship was laid in January 1943, and over the next two years, the shipyard operated 24 hours a day, 7 days a week, to produce an astounding 99 vessels. These efforts are commemorated in a 23-ft. scale model of a Liberty Ship on display at the Mary Ross Waterfront Park by the harbor.

Brunswick is again prospering as a major port, and the city is hard at work preserving and restoring its historic commercial district and nearby residential neighborhoods. With its rich history and convenience to coastal tourism destinations, the city is a popular stop for beach-bound travelers.

WALK DISTANCE AND TERRAIN

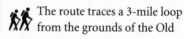 The route traces a 3-mile loop from the grounds of the Old

Mahoney-McGarvey House

Glynn County Courthouse, past the boat docks, through the heart of downtown, and along nearby residential streets. The terrain is level, with sidewalks in the downtown area and an abundance of shade trees along the entire walk.

SIGHTS ALONG THE WAY

 1. Old Glynn County Courthouse (1907)—701 G St. Before construction of the courthouse, this was Magnolia Square, one of the commons in the original city plan. The stately Neoclassical-style building, designed by the New York firm of Gifford and Bates, presents an identical entrance on all four sides. Since construction of the new courthouse, this building houses county offices. *NR*

2. Glynn County Courthouse (1991)—Across the plaza from the old courthouse. This red-brick and masonry building complements the architectural style of the older courthouse. The two buildings are connected by a plaza shaded by massive live oaks.

3. Mahoney-McGarvey House (c. 1891)—1705 Reynolds St. Designed by J. A. Wood, architect of the elegant Oglethorpe Hotel, this house is a superb example of the Carpenter Gothic style popularized during the late Victorian period. The Mahoney family bequeathed the house to the McGarvey sisters, who were early leaders in Brunswick's historic preservation movement.

4. Ritz Theater (1898)—1530 Newcastle St. Constructed by J. G. Conzelman as Brunswick's Grand Opera House, the building was converted to a movie theater in the 1930s and renamed the Ritz. Like many downtown, single-screen movie

407

houses, the theater closed in the 1970s and remained shuttered and in jeopardy of demolition. In 1990, the city offered the building to the Golden Isles Arts and Humanities Association and assisted in its restoration as a performing arts center. Today, the theater hosts performances by local and visiting artists. The lobby houses a visitor center offering local tourism and cultural events information. (912) 262-6934.

5. Mary Ross Waterfront Park—Bay and Gloucester Sts. An open plaza overlooks the docks where visitors may watch fishing vessels and shrimpers return with their day's catch. An open-air pavilion is the setting for a variety of community events, and the nearby farmers market draws shoppers for fresh produce. The park is an excellent spot for watching spectacular sunsets.

6. Old City Hall (c. 1888)—1229 Newcastle St. This rough-stone and brick, 3-story building is an excellent example of Richardsonian Romanesque, a style of architecture popularized by architect H. H. Richardson in the late 19th century. This building was designed by Albert Eichberg and is notable for its arched entranceway, elaborate use of terra-cotta (including gargoyles and angels), interior woodwork, and other details. Built at a cost of $33,000, the building was constructed to house city government offices and the public library. It now serves as headquarters

for the Old Town Brunswick Preservation Association and the Main Street Program. The building is undergoing renovation.

7. Burroughs-Hazlehurst House (c. 1870s)—8 Hanover Square. Designed by a Dr. Burroughs, the house, with mansard roof and arched woodwork porch, is representative of the French-inspired Second Empire style.

8. Wright House (1900)—905 Union St. Designed by J. B Wright, this Queen Anne–style house is rich with the ornamental details made popular by architect Charles Eastlake (intricate woodwork and stylized elements like balustrades, posts, porches, etc.). This house has a mirror-image twin next door facing Prince St.

9. Lott-Parker House (c. 1900)—827 Union St. Designed as a mix of Colonial Revival and Queen Anne styles, the house is notable for its semicircular front portico and complementary second-story bay window. The house was the work of J. J. Lott and is still owned by his descendants.

10. DuBignon-McCullough House (c. 1869)—811 Union St. One of the oldest structures in the historic district, this Second Empire–style house was built by Henry Riffault DuBignon as a wedding gift to his bride, Alice Symons. DuBignon died a short time after occupying the house, and it was later sold to John McCullough.

11. DuBignon-Lockwood House (c. 1896)—721 Union St. Built by

John DuBignon, this Queen Anne–style house is notable for its large, wraparound front porch and conical turret. The house has the only full basement in Brunswick.

12. DuBignon House (c. 1890)—716 Union St. This 2-story Folk Victorian house is notable for its detailed woodwork and second-story gabled porch. It was built for, and owned by, several generations of the DuBignon family.

13. Major Downing House (c. 1886)—825 Egmont St. Designed and built by John Baumgartner for Maj. Columbus Downing, this large, brick, 3-story Queen Anne–style house took two years to finish. The large front porch is not original. The house is now operated as the Brunswick Manor Bed and Breakfast Inn. (912) 265-6889.

14. Baker House (c. 1896)—902 Halifax Square. This Queen Anne–style house is notable for its palladian window, detailed woodwork in the porch gable, and the large front porch.

15. Captain Lamb House (c. 1895)—1110 Prince St. Lamb, a sea captain, built this house as a gift to his new bride. He is credited with importing the first camellias to Glynn County. The house is representative of the plain, Folk Victorian style.

16. Lover's Oak—North end of 800 block of Albany St. According to local folklore, this centuries-old live oak was once a secret meeting place for Native-American warriors and their maidens.

17. Nightingale-Hughes House (c. 1875)—900 Carpenter St. An example of the Eastern Stick style of Victorian architecture, this clapboard house was built for N. H. Nightingale and remained in the family for nearly 80 years. The original kitchen house still exists as a rear extension of the house.

18. McKinnon House (c. 1903)—1001 Egmont. L. T. McKinnon, owner of a large lumber company, was one of Brunswick's wealthiest citizens. This large, Queen Anne–style brick home with elaborate detailing reflected his status in the community. Today, it is the McKinnon House Bed and Breakfast Inn. (912) 261-9100.

19. Scarlett House (c. 1890)—902 Wright Square. The birthplace of Federal Judge Frank M. Scarlett (for whom the local Federal building is named), this Folk Victorian–style house remained in the Scarlett family until 1970. The original cookhouse is connected to the main structure by a "dog trot." The Atkinson house at 802 London St. is nearly identical in design.

20. Burford House (c. 1887)—1017 Egmont St. Built by Dr. John Burford in the Queen Anne style, the house is notable for its second-story sleeping porch. Dr. Burford had his medical office in the house, and patients would enter from the door beneath the porticoed entrance on the right side.

21. Aiken House (1908)— 1015 Union St. Built by Frank Aiken, a local banker, the low-pitched roof and porch reflect elements of the Prairie style, while the stucco finish and red-tiled roof offer a hint of Spanish influence.

22. Murray House (c. 1896)— 1112 Union St. This symmetrical Queen Anne–style house is typical of many tidewater houses constructed along the Atlantic coast during the latter part of the 19th century.

23. McKinnon Houses (c. 1910)— 1201 and 1203 Union St. Notable for their unusual gambrel roofline, these twin houses in Queen Anne style were built by L. T. McKinnon.

24. Glynn Academy (1889–1930s)—Mansfield St., between Egmont and Albany Sts. Founded in 1788, Glynn Academy has been a fixture in Brunswick for more than two centuries. The first building on this campus was constructed in 1840 and used until 1915, when it was replaced by a new Classical Revival–style structure on the south side of Hillsborough Square (now the prep school). The school expanded again in 1923 to include a building that housed classrooms and a large auditorium. A third building, designed in the Georgian style, was completed in the 1930s. The oldest building on the present campus is the Annex, a Richardsonian Romanesque–style structure constructed in 1889.

25. Marlin House (c. 1890)— 1325 Egmont St. Designed and built by L. C. Marlin, this wood-frame house is notable for its 2-story wraparound porches.

26. Lissner House (c. 1907)— 1319 Union St. Built by J. J. Lissner, this 2-story house features elements of the Prairie style (low front porch, use of natural materials, and floor-to-ceiling granite fireplaces). The threat of destruction of this house by the Georgia Department of Labor in the 1970s mobilized local preservationists and led to the founding of the Old Town Brunswick Preservation Association.

27. Brunswick History Museum (c. 1900s)—1327 Union St. This early 20th-century building is under renovation to serve as the headquarters for a museum of local history.

28. New City Hall (1901)— 601 Gloucester St. Although nearly a century old, locals still refer to this imposing Georgian Revival building as the "new" City Hall. Originally built to house the U.S. Post Office and Customs House, it was converted for use as the city hall in 1964. An interesting characteristic of the building is the mix of glazed and unglazed bricks.

CHAPTER 51

Jekyll Island Club Village

LOCATION

Jekyll Island is located about 85 miles south of Savannah via I-95 or U.S. 17. From I-95, take exit 29, SR 520/U.S. 17 (Jekyll Island Rd.), and travel east to the Jekyll Island Causeway. To reach the Village Orientation Center from the island toll-booth, travel north on Riverview Rd., then east on Stable Rd. The center is ahead on the right. *Information:* (877) 453-5955; www.jekyllisland.com.

PARKING

There is an unpaved parking area by the orientation center and another adjacent to the Jekyll Island Club Wharf. Parking around the Jekyll Island Club Hotel is reserved for hotel guests.

BACKGROUND

Caressing Georgia's 150-mile-long coastline is a string of barrier islands rich in scenic beauty and human history. Known as Georgia's "Golden Isles," Ossabaw, St. Catherine, Sapelo, St. Simons, Sea, Jekyll, and Cumberland Islands—separated from the mainland by blue-water sounds and golden marshes—have drawn people to their shores since the dawn of recorded time.

Geologically young, these islands were formed by shifting sea levels during the Ice Ages 35,000 and 10,000 years ago. The first known inhabitants were nomadic people of the Archaic period (8,000–1,000 B.C.E.) who fished in the shallow waters and hunted game on the islands. Except for a few spear points and shell mounds, these people left little evidence of their history in the shifting sands.

No island in the chain has a history more colorful than Jekyll. When the first European explorer, French navigator Jean Ribault, landed in 1562, the island was inhabited by the Guale people, natives of the Muskhogean tribes of the Creeks, who called their island, "Ospo." Ribault made no attempt to colonize the area, and his

411

claim of the island for the French was soon challenged by the Spanish, who controlled the nearby colony of Florida. In 1566, Spanish soldiers accompanied Catholic priests to the island to establish the Mission San Buenaventura, determined to convert the Guale to Christianity and thwart any French return. The priests, who found the Guale to be reluctant converts, ultimately abandoned their missionary efforts and returned to Florida.

Though there were occasional raids by ocean-going pirates, including the infamous Edward Teach (Blackbeard), the Georgia coast remained unsettled by Europeans until the mid-1700s. Then Great Britain, which already had established colonies in the Carolinas, chartered the new Colony of Georgia to serve as a buffer between its prosperous holdings to the north and its historic antagonist, Spain. After Gen. James Oglethorpe founded the settlement of Savannah in 1733, he quickly moved to build forts along the coastal islands to protect the settlers from attack by the Spanish. By 1736, the fortified village of Frederica on nearby St. Simons was filled with soldiers and settlers determined to protect their nation's interests and carve a livelihood out of the coastal soils.

Oglethorpe named the island just south of St. Simons for his friend, supporter, and member of the English Parliament Sir Joseph Jekyll. A grant for land on the northern end of the island was issued to Maj. William Horton, who arrived on the island in 1736 with plans to grow food crops for the settlers at Frederica. He constructed a 2-story house of tabby (a building material composed of sand and crushed oyster shells) on the island (the ruins still stand about a mile north of the village), as well as a barn and several other buildings.

The Spanish governor in St. Augustine soon sent emissaries to the island to meet with Oglethorpe and Horton about the two countries' rival claims on the land. Oglethorpe had arranged for his soldiers at Ft. Frederica to create the illusion of great military strength by firing cannons and marching along the beach on the southern end of nearby St. Simons Island while discussions with the Spanish were under way. The visitors were evidently impressed, and the two delegations agreed to allow the English and Spanish royal courts to settle the dispute. This decision so angered the Spanish government that the colonial governor of Florida was recalled home in disgrace.

But the peace was short-lived. An armed conflict between England and Spain, known in the colonies as the War of Jenkins' Ear, broke out in 1742. On July 17, a fleet of Spanish warships delivered troops to the southern end of St. Simons Island for an attack on Ft. Frederica. While marching north toward the fort, the

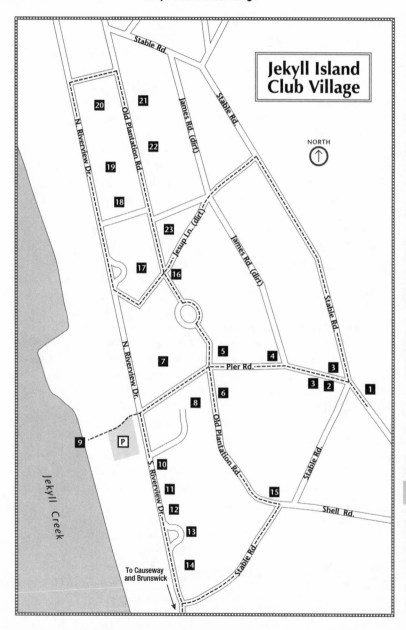

Spaniards were attacked by the British garrison at a place known today as Bloody Marsh. The Spanish were routed with heavy casualties and forced to flee across the sound to Jekyll Island, where they burned Maj. Horton's plantation before escaping back to Florida.

With the Spanish threat diminished and the colony more firmly settled, Oglethorpe returned to England for good. Horton, now in command of the troops in Georgia, set out to strengthen coastal forts and to rebuild his Jekyll Island home. Unfortunately, he died in 1748 before the work was completed.

In 1765, King George III granted Jekyll Island to Clement Martin, a strong loyalist, who held the property until the outbreak of the Revolution. His claim was forfeited after the war, and the new State of Georgia awarded the island to Richard Leake.

In 1794, the island was sold by Leake to Le Sieur Christopher Poulain DuBignon, a monarchist fleeing the horrors of the French Revolution. With several other French émigrés, DuBignon also acquired an island to the north which he named "Sapelo" for the ship that had brought him to America. (Sapelo was sold to Thomas Spaulding in the early 1800s.)

DuBignon restored and expanded William Horton's decaying tabby house for his large family and set about earning a sizable fortune cultivating more than 11,000 acres of high-quality Sea Island cotton. He died in 1825, but his family remained in control of the island for another 60 years.

Jekyll Island made national headlines in 1858 when the merchant ship *Wanderer*, carrying an illegal cargo of African slaves, beached on the island during a storm. The importation of slaves had been illegal since 1807, and the ship's owners were arrested, tried, and convicted in Savannah after a highly publicized 1860 trial.

When Georgia left the Union in 1861, the fledgling Confederate Army set up gun batteries on Jekyll and neighboring islands to protect access to the port of Brunswick. After hostilities began at Ft. Sumter, the Federal Government established a naval blockade of the Southern coast, and eventually the Rebel soldiers were ordered to abandon their positions. In March 1862, U.S. Marines from the USS *Mohican* came ashore and raised the Stars and Stripes over undefended Jekyll.

When the DuBignon family returned at war's end, they found their property in ruins. For 20 years, Poulain's great-grandson John Eugene DuBignon struggled, with modest success, to restore the family's fortunes. Then, in 1886, he was approached by a group of Northern businessmen with plans to purchase the island for use as a private winter retreat. DuBignon accepted their offer of $125,000 and a partnership in the exclusive Jekyll Island Club, opening what may be the most colorful chapter in the island's long history.

Within a few years, the barons of American business and industry created an idyllic, secluded paradise set amidst lush, landscaped grounds carved from the semitropical forest. *Munsey's Magazine*, a popular periodical of the day, described Jekyll in a 1904 article as "the richest, most exclusive, the most inaccessible club in the world."

Financier J. Pierpont Morgan, whose yacht *Corsair* was so large it could not dock at the island's wharf, was a member. So were publisher Joseph Pulitzer, for whom the literary prizes are named; tobacco magnate Pierre Lorillard; William Vanderbilt, brother of steel tycoon Cornelius Vanderbilt; Edwin Gould, son of railroad mogul Jay Gould; scion of New York society Vincent Astor; retailer Marshall Field; and William Rockefeller, younger brother of the famous oil baron. His elder brother John D. refused to join the club. America's first billionaire considered the $600 membership fee to be too expensive.

The club season ran from New Year's Day through Easter. Members arrived by private yacht or by train to Brunswick, where they could board the club's steamer for the short ferry trip to the island. Most guests stayed at the luxurious, rambling, Queen Anne–style clubhouse completed in 1889, while a few of the wealthiest members built private residences, mansions known as "cottages," on the grounds. Nonmember guests, called "strangers" by members, were limited to a maximum two-week stay at the resort.

Business and politics, twin passions of many club members, followed them to Jekyll. In 1899, presidential candidate William McKinley came to the island for a meeting with several club members to plan his campaign. The Federal Reserve Act was drafted at the club in 1910, and in 1915, American Telephone and Telegraph Company president Theodore Vail participated in the nation's first transcontinental telephone call from the island. Vail was at the club recuperating from an illness and ordered a thousand miles of telephone cable run to the island so that he might participate in the historic event, which linked him with Alexander Graham Bell in New York, Bell's assistant Thomas Watson in San Francisco, and Pres. Woodrow Wilson in Washington.

The Jekyll Island Club prospered through the "Roaring 20s" but suffered a decline during the Great Depression as many members saw their fortunes dwindle. Others, whose wealth remained intact, began traveling to newly developed winter resorts further south in Palm Beach and Miami, Fla.

With America's entrance into World War II in December 1941, club management decided to close indefinitely following the 1942 season due to shortages of supplies and staff. The war years took their toll. Gardens turned to weeds, while wooden buildings suffered from termite infestations, salt air, mildew, and vandalism.

At war's end, the remaining club members chose to delay reopening. In 1947, they accepted an offer from the State of Georgia to purchase the island and all the club's structures (including the private homes) for $675,000. The state had grand plans to convert the longtime millionaires' retreat into a public playground for the enjoyment of all. In 1954, a causeway and bridge connected the island to the mainland, and tourism boomed. (The island was so popular as a winter retreat for Canadians that, for many years, local merchants accepted Canadian currency.)

Most of the club compound remained closed to the public. Then in 1978, the Jekyll Island Club was designated a National Historic Landmark, and active restoration began in 1984. The state-initiated program, one of the largest preservation projects ever undertaken in the Southeast, has been remarkably successful, with the conservation of more than 30 buildings. The crowning achievement was the $19-million restoration and 1987 reopening of the clubhouse as a luxury hotel, just in time to celebrate the building's centennial.

Today, the Jekyll Island Club bustles again with activity as "strangers" browse in quaint shops, tour magnificent homes, or take "high tea" in the solarium of the elegant hotel. A stroll around the landscaped grounds offers a glimpse back to a time when America's richest families claimed a small island off the Georgia coast as their own "Golden Isle."

WALK DISTANCE AND TERRAIN

A stroll around the village is about 2.5 miles. The grounds are level with a mix of sunny lawns and live-oak shaded lanes.

SIGHTS ALONG THE WAY

1. Museum and Orientation Center (1897)—Stable Rd. Club members often brought horses and carriages to the island, and this building was constructed to serve as stables. It originally contained 45 stalls and storage space for carriages, tack, and feed. Restored for use as a visitor center in 1985, the building houses exhibits tracing the history of the club, a video theater, and a small gift shop. Motor-tram and horse-drawn carriage tours of the historic district begin here. *Hours:* 9:30 A.M.– 4 P.M. daily. (912) 635-2762.

2. Boat Engineer's House (c. 1900) —Pier Rd. west of Stable Rd. This was the residence of the engineer responsible for maintenance of the club's small fleet of ferryboats and pleasure craft. It is now a gift shop.

3. Dining Room Servants' Quarters (c. 1900)—Pier Rd. These modest frame structures are representative of the housing provided to the hundreds of staff who attended to the needs of club members. They now house a variety of shops.

4. Commissary (c. 1900)—Pier Rd. Staff could draw their personal supplies from this club-owned store, now also a gift shop.

5. DuBignon House (1880)—Pier Rd. at Old Plantation Rd. Built by John Eugene DuBignon when his family owned the island, this Queen Anne–style house served as the residence of club manager E. G. Grob for several years. It was later used as a guest annex. The house was moved

here from its original site to make way for construction of the Sans Souci Apartments in 1896. Today, the house displays exhibits of life on the island during the club era.

6. Morgan Indoor Tennis Court (c. 1900s)—Old Plantation Rd. In its earliest days, the club had outdoor tennis courts, but this cypress-shingled building housed an indoor court, possibly the first in Georgia.

7. Jekyll Island Club Hotel (1887) —Old Plantation Rd. at Riverview Dr. Designed by Chicago architect Charles Alexander, the large, rambling Victorian building opened in time for the club's 1888 season. The clubhouse contained all the most modern features of the day, and innovations were added as they became available— telephones in 1898, electricity in 1903, an elevator in 1916. Through the

417

Jekyll Island Club Hotel

years, the building was expanded many times to accommodate more guests, and the swimming pool was built in the 1920s. The grand dining room was the social center of the island, and chefs came from some of New York City's finest restaurants to work at the club during the winter season. Now recognized by the National Trust for Historic Preservation as one of the Historic Hotels of America, the dining room, café, and bar are open to the public. *Information*: (800) 535-9547.

8. Sans Souci Apartments (1897) —Old Plantation Rd. and S. Riverview Dr. Developed by a syndicate of members led by William Rockefeller, the apartments offered larger and more luxurious accommodations than were available in the clubhouse. When built, Sans Souci (which in French means "without care") had six apartments. Today, they are touted as the nation's first "condominiums." None had a kitchen or dining room so that guests would be encouraged to take their meals in the club's restaurant. The building presently serves as an annex of suite accommodations for the adjacent hotel.

9. Jekyll Island Club Wharf (c. 1887)—Pier Rd. at S. Riverview Dr. Nearly all club members arrived by ferries from Brunswick or aboard private yachts that moored at this wharf. Some of the larger vessels, such as Morgan's *Corsair*, anchored in the

deeper waters of Jekyll Creek. Today, the pier houses a restaurant and gift shop and provides moorings for water taxis, charter boats, and private craft.

10. Indian Mound (1892)— S. Riverview Dr. The name of this large, shingle-sided house was drawn from an ancient shell mound that was once in the front yard. Originally a small cottage built for Massachusetts inventor and industrialist Gordon McKay, it was purchased in 1903 by William Rockefeller, who expanded it to its present 25 rooms. After Rockefeller's death in 1922, the house was acquired by his son-in-law Marcellus Hartley Dodge as a residence for his aunt, Helen H. Jenkins. The interior (opened for tram-tour participants) is notable for its small elevator, cedar-lined safe, and stained-glass window on the stairway landing. An exhibit outside the house, erected by the Telephone Pioneers of America in 1965, commemorates the first transcontinental telephone call.

11. Mistletoe Cottage (1900)— S. Riverview Dr. This Dutch Colonial–style house was designed by Charles A. Gifford for locomotive manufacturer and U.S. congressman Henry K. Porter. In 1926, the house was purchased by John Claflin, an executive with Lord and Taylor department stores. Today, the cottage contains museum exhibits, and a sculpture gallery on the second floor displays the work of local artist

Rosario Fiore. The house and galleries are opened for guests on the tram tours.

12. Goodyear Cottage (1906)— S. Riverview Dr. Built by Frank H. Goodyear, a lumber (not rubber) executive from Buffalo, N.Y., the house was designed by Thomas Hastings. Today the cottage serves as a gallery featuring the works of local artisans. *Hours:* 12–4 P.M., daily.

13. Moss Cottage (1896)— S. Riverview Dr. Built by William Struthers, a Philadelphia businessman who was an early member of the club, this shingle-style house was typical of some of the earlier cottages built on club grounds. In 1910, the house was purchased by George Macy, president of the Atlantic and Pacific Tea Company (now A&P grocery stores).

14. Site of Pulitzer Cottage (1897)—S. Riverview Dr. at Stable Rd. An historical marker notes the site of the cottage built by newspaper publisher Joseph Pulitzer. After Pulitzer's death, the 26-room house was purchased by coal company executive John Albright. The house was lost in a fire, but some of the bricks were salvaged and used in construction of the Old Dunes Golf Course clubhouse.

15. Club Infirmary (1891)—Stable Rd. at Old Plantation Rd. Designed in the shingle style by owner-architect Walter Furness, the house originally stood on Riverview Dr. In 1896 it was purchased by Joseph Pulitzer, but he found it too small and immediately began work on constructing the house described above. In 1929, the Goodyear family purchased the house and had it moved to its present site to serve as the club's infirmary. From 1930 until the club's closure, the facility was staffed during the season by doctors and nurses from Johns Hopkins Medical School in Baltimore, Md. Today, the building is a bookstore.

16. Faith Chapel (1903)—Old Plantation Rd. This elegantly simple wooden church replaced an earlier, smaller sanctuary. Inspired by early Gothic-style rural churches of Britain and Colonial America, this interdenominational chapel has two exquisite stained-glass windows. The altar window, by Maitland and Helen Armstrong, depicts the "Adoration of the Christ Child," and catches the morning light. The large window on the west end of the chapel, set to glow in warm afternoon light, was the work of Louis Comfort Tiffany and is one of only five existing windows in the world that bear the artist's complete signature (look in the lower right corner). The chapel underwent an extensive restoration in 1991 and is a popular site for weddings, baptisms, and seasonal church services. It is open daily from 2–4 P.M.

17. Crane Cottage (1915)— N. Riverview Dr. This large house was built by Richard Crane Jr., son of the

419

founder of the Crane Company, manufacturer of plumbing and fluid-control equipment. Not surprisingly, the house contains 17 bathrooms—all with Crane fixtures. The Italian Villa–style structure was designed by David Adler and was the largest and most expensive ($500,000) private residence on the club grounds. Today, this house and nearby Cherokee Cottage are undergoing adaptive restoration as bed-and-breakfast accommodations managed by the hotel.

18. Chichota Ruins (1897)—N. Riverview Dr. Built by New York businessman David King, the house was sold to Edwin Gould in 1900. Gould's additions to the property included a private dock, bowling alley, and an indoor tennis court. Following the death of their youngest son in a hunting accident on the island, Gould's wife, Sally, refused to return to Jekyll. The house fell into disrepair and was torn down in 1941. Today, all that remains are the foundations, the courtyard swimming pool, and two stone lions that silently guard the entrance of the long-vanished cottage.

19. Hollybourne (1891)—N. Riverview Dr. Engineer and bridge-builder Charles Maurice worked with architect William Day on this Jekyll Island cottage. An innovative house that draws on Maurice's knowledge of structural strength, this is the only building at the club made from tabby, a native material made from sand, oyster shells,

lime, and water. The house has undergone extensive restoration.

20. Villa Ospo (1927)—N. Riverview Dr. This Spanish Colonial–style residence was one of the last houses built at the club. Designed by architect John Russell Pope for Standard Oil Company executive Walter Jennings, it is the only cottage in the district with an attached garage, as automobiles remained a rarity on the island until construction of the causeway after World War II.

21. Gould Casino (1913)—Old Plantation Rd. Built as part of Gould's estate, "Chichota," the casino housed the bowling alley, indoor tennis court (which remains), gymnasium, and greenhouse. The building was converted for use as an auditorium in the 1950s. It has undergone restoration.

22. Villa Marianna (1928)—Old Plantation Rd. Built by Edwin and Sally Gould's son Frank, this was the last cottage built at the club. Today it serves as residential quarters for Jekyll Island Authority staff.

23. Cherokee (1905)—Old Plantation Rd. An excellent example of the Italian Renaissance style, Cherokee was built by Edwin Gould for his in-laws, Dr. and Mrs. George F. Shrady. Shrady was physician to Presidents Ulysses Grant and James A. Garfield. Today, the building is being remodeled to serve as bed-and-breakfast accommodations.

CHAPTER 52

Cumberland Island National Seashore and St. Marys

LOCATION

Historic St. Marys, the gateway to the Cumberland Island National Seashore, is located about 100 miles south of Savannah via I-95 and GA 40 (exit 3). The island is accessible from St. Marys by National Park Service ferry or by private charter. *Information:* Cumberland Island National Seashore, (912) 882-4336; www.nps.gov/cuis. St. Marys Tourism Council, (800) 868-8687; www. stmaryswelcome.com.

PARKING

Curbside parking is available in downtown St. Marys and at lots adjacent to the National Park Service visitor center and ferry dock. There is no automobile access to the island.

BACKGROUND

Cumberland Island

By the numbers, Cumberland Island is the southernmost and largest of Georgia's nine barrier islands. It is 16 miles long and 3 miles across at its widest point. The seaward side is remarkable for its miles of nearly unbroken beach, while the lee side, toward the mainland, is almost continuous marsh. Behind the high dunes and above the marsh is the lush, vibrant forest dominated by stately live oaks.

A number of distinct, yet inter–related, environments make up a barrier island. The salt marsh is a sea nursery that is critically important to the health of the world's oceans. An ideal time to explore the marsh is at low tide when fiddler crabs run helter-skelter from their burrows in search of food and birds like clapper rails, snowy egrets, and Louisiana herons peek out from among the tall grasses. Cumberland is a stop along the Atlantic Flyway and many migratory waterfowl winter on the island, making birdwatching especially popular.

The island interior is typical of what botanists call a maritime climax forest. Even on the brightest day, sunlight struggles to penetrate the

421

interwoven arms of the Spanish moss-draped live oaks. The understory is filled with laurel oaks, red maples, sweetgums, and other trees. Where storms, fires, or previous timber harvesting have destroyed the dominant trees, the areas have filled with fast-growing, sun-loving loblolly pines. Beneath the canopy are a mix of smaller trees and shrubs, including sycamores, American hollies, magnolias, and the pointed fans of the saw palmetto. (Note: Be alert around palmetto thickets; they are a popular denning site for the island's diamond-back and canebrake rattlesnakes.)

Wildlife abounds here, but quiet patience is essential to capture a glimpse. The woods are home to the island's many native white-tailed deer (smaller than their mainland cousins), curious and sometimes pesky raccoons, and bobcats reintroduced by the Park Service in the 1980s in an effort to restore a natural predator to the island. Also present is the nine-banded armadillo, one of nature's true curiosities. These reclusive plant and insect eaters seem indifferent to human presence and will often pose for a snapshot.

Cumberland boasts more than 100 resident species of birds including cardinals, summer tanagers, painted buntings, Carolina wrens, pileated woodpeckers, wild turkeys, red-tailed hawks, and great horned owls. Two feral (non-native) animals have been introduced. The wild horses that some believe are descendents of those brought to Cumberland by the Spanish in the 1500s are more likely descended from horses used by antebellum and Victorian-era landowners; and hogs are the wild descendants of domestic pigs from the 19th-century farms and plantations that dotted the island. The National Park Service schedules controlled hunts of the deer and hogs to keep their population in balance, but the horses are protected and allowed to roam freely.

While fresh water is not plentiful on the island, there are low areas or "sloughs" where years of rainfall and runoff have collected to form shallow ponds that, with the lands around them, form a distinct plant and animal habitat. The largest freshwater pond is Lake Whitney near the north end of the island. Willow Pond, Johnson Pond, Lake Retta, and a few smaller pools are located near the center.

The pond communities support otters, frogs, fish, and water snakes (including the poisonous cotton-mouth), and serve as rookeries for herons, ibises, and woodstorks. Also present is the secretive American alligator. It is a nocturnal hunter (something to remember if you decide to go for a moonlit stroll near the ponds), so the more time you spend sitting quietly by a pond at dawn or dusk, the greater your chance of spotting one of these endangered reptiles.

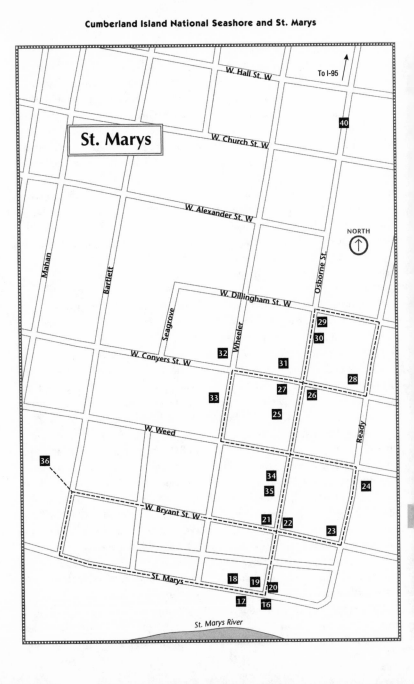

Whether swimming, shell collecting, or simply strolling, visitors usually spend much of their time on the island in its beach and dune environment. Few places on earth are as inhospitable and ever-changing as the shore of a barrier island. Waves constantly scour the ground with salt water, and there is little protection from the relentless summer sun or powerful winter storms. High tide differs from low; and the wildlife that shares the beach with you during the day is markedly different from the creatures that scatter from a flashlight's beam after dark.

For more information on the complex ecology of barrier islands, we recommend Stephen Swinburne's *Guide to Cumberland Island.*

Visitors to the island may be treated to glimpses of three of the world's rarest creatures: the Loggerhead turtle, the Peregrine falcon, and the Northern right whale. The huge loggerheads (their shells may reach four feet in length) spend their lives in the oceans, but return to the beach each spring and summer to deposit their eggs in pits along the high tide line. Sadly, commercial development on many barrier islands has taken a heavy toll on habitat, making protected areas like Cumberland Island vitally important to the turtle's survival.

Wintering on Cumberland, far from their summer homes along the Arctic Circle, small, sleek, and graceful

peregrine falcons ride the winds above the island in search of prey. With dazzling speed they dive from high altitudes to attack a hapless crab or other victim. Finally, a few miles offshore are the breeding grounds of the Northern right whale, a species that has been driven to near-extinction by centuries of hunting (now illegal). These large, gentle mammals travel the world's oceans in family groups, called "pods," and the waters off the Georgia coast are popular springtime calving grounds for the newborn whales. Sightings are rare, but a glimpse of any of these exceptional creatures would be a treasured memory from a visit to Cumberland Island.

Human beings are relative newcomers to Cumberland, yet we have had a profound and lasting impact on the land. Since prehistoric times, people have been drawn to the world's coasts, and even today, the bulk of the world's population resides on or near the ocean. At sites on Georgia's coastal plain, scientists have found evidence of human habitation in this area for at least 12,000–15,000 years. Today, all that remains for us to see are small oyster-shell middens (trash piles), scattered burial mounds, and an occasional bead or shell tool.

European explorers touched on these shores in the 1500s, and in 1565, the Spaniards claimed the island and

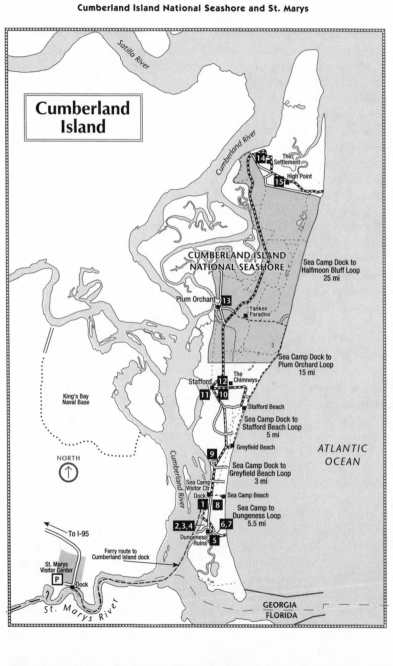

Cumberland Island

Satilla River

Cumberland River

The Settlement
14
15 High Point

CUMBERLAND ISLAND
NATIONAL SEASHORE

Sea Camp Dock to
Halfmoon Bluff Loop
25 mi

Plum Orchard 13
Yankee Paradise

Sea Camp Dock to
Plum Orchard Loop
15 mi

Stafford 12 The Chimneys
11 10
Stafford Beach

Sea Camp Dock to
Stafford Beach Loop
5 mi

Greyfield Beach
9
Sea Camp Dock to
Greyfield Beach Loop
3 mi

ATLANTIC
OCEAN

King's Bay
Naval Base

NORTH
↑

Sea Camp
Visitor Ctr.
Dock 1 8 Sea Camp Beach
Sea Camp to
Dungeness Loop
5.5 mi

To I-95

Cumberland River

2,3,4 6,7
Dungeness 5
Ruins

Ferry route to
Cumberland Island dock

St. Marys
Visitor Center
P
Dock

St. Marys River

GEORGIA
FLORIDA

named it San Pedro (St. Peter). The natives they encountered were the Timucuan, a tribe of the Creek Nation who called their island "Missoe" (sassafras) for the medicinal plant that grew there in abundance.

Jesuit priests, under the guidance of Fr. Baltasar Lopez, aggressively set out to convert the Timucuans to Catholicism, creating much unrest. After several instances of bloodshed, the Jesuits were replaced by Franciscans who were more willing to blend native culture and Christianity. The mission at San Pedro survived for about a century until the Spanish, at odds with their enemies the English, pulled back from the frontier to their strongholds in Florida. While historians believe the mission was near the present site of Dungeness, no firm evidence remains to tell us the story of the trials and hardships of mission life on the island.

When the English established the Colony of Georgia in 1733, two of the forts they built for protection were on Cumberland Island. The origin of the present name for the island comes from Oglethorpe's visit to England with Tomo-chi-chi, chief of the Yamacraw, who had befriended the English general. Accompanying Tomo-chi-chi on the ocean voyage was his nephew, Toonahowie. While in England, Toonahowie made friends with the son of King George II, William Augustus, Duke of Cumberland.

As the story goes, the young Indian asked Oglethorpe to name the island after his new friend.

Oglethorpe visited the island on several occasions and built a hunting lodge on its southern end. He dubbed his rustic lodge "Dungeness" after the English city that was the seat of the County of Kent.

In the years prior to the American Revolution, several prominent Georgians held royal grants for land on Cumberland Island, but little effort was made to farm or harvest the island's rich stands of timber. One of the few visitors to the nearly uninhabited island was naturalist William Bartram, who paused on Cumberland during his mid-1770s journey across the South to collect botanical specimens.

Following the Revolution, Gen. Nathanael Greene received several large parcels of land on Cumberland as settlement of a debt and began construction of a summer home. Greene died of sunstroke in 1786, years before his house on Cumberland was completed, but his wife, Catherine, with their five children, continued the work and occupied the home in 1803. Because the 4-story, tabby house was located near the site of Oglethorpe's old hunting lodge, Catherine called it Dungeness. After moving into the house, Catherine married Phineas Miller, her children's tutor, but Miller died shortly afterward.

Catherine and the children remained at Dungeness, where she enjoyed entertaining friends and visitors. During the War of 1812, Catherine entertained American troops stationed in the nearby village of St. Marys. She died in 1814, shortly before the British attacked and occupied the town. Catherine's daughter Louisa and her husband, James Shaw, continued to live at Dungeness.

In January 1818, a schooner bound northward from the West Indies anchored off Cumberland to bring ashore the gravely ill Gen. "Light Horse" Harry Lee, a longtime friend and comrade-in-arms of Louisa's father, Gen. Greene. Lee died at Dungeness and was buried there. In 1913, the state of Virginia had his remains removed and reinterred next to his son, Robert E. Lee, in Lee Chapel on the campus of Washington and Lee University in Lexington.

The antebellum period was the era of large plantations, Sea Island cotton, and slavery on Cumberland Island. Records indicate that in the 1840s, the population was 36 whites and 400 black slaves. With the outbreak of the Civil War, most plantation owners evacuated the island, leaving overseers and slaves to continue working. In 1862, Union forces finally occupied Cumberland and sent the slaves to Amelia Island, Fla. Following the war, a few freedmen and their families returned and established a small village at the north end of the island near Half-Moon Bluff.

Many white families never returned to the island, and the empty Dungeness burned in the 1870s. In 1880 Thomas and Lucy Carnegie (possibly after reading an article in *Lippencott's Magazine* about the deserted island) visited Cumberland for the first time. Lucy immediately fell in love with the island and convinced her wealthy husband that it would be a marvelous place to raise their five children.

Thomas was the younger brother and business partner of steel magnate Andrew Carnegie, one of the world's richest men. Within a few years, he had purchased 90 percent of the island.

The Carnegies demolished the crumbling ruins of the Greene-Miller Dungeness and began construction of their own, eclectic 40-room mansion on its foundations. The stone and brick structure became the centerpiece of a huge estate encompassing more than 40 buildings and employing a staff of 50.

Like Greene before him, Thomas Carnegie died before his Dungeness was completed, but Lucy and the children moved into the new home in 1884 as planned. There they lived in grand style, hosting politicians, diplomats, dignitaries, and celebrities at lavish parties, polo matches, and other high-society events. As Lucy's children grew, she gave each of them portions

427

of the estate on which they could build homes for their own families.

After Lucy died in 1916, Dungeness was shuttered except for rare occasions, such as a large family wedding in the 1920s. By the late 1950s, the main house and estate had been unoccupied for more than 30 years. In 1959, Dungeness caught fire (possibly set by poachers after a confrontation with the caretaker) and burned out of control for several days. The flames rose so high that the glow could be seen in Brunswick, nearly 40 miles away.

Within a few years, several family members, some infrequent visitors to the remote island, sold 3,000 acres to a developer. This triggered a battle both within the Carnegie family and with conservation organizations that hoped to keep the island intact in its natural state. In 1972, most of the property owners donated their land-holdings to the Federal government (with retained rights giving them access to homes and properties on the island for a period of years) for the purpose of creating a national park. Encircled and outnumbered, the developer finally gave in and sold his property to the government, also. Later that same year, Congress passed legislation establishing the Cumberland Island National Seashore.

Visiting Cumberland Island:
Because of the fragile nature of the island environment, visitation is limited to a maximum of 300 persons (including overnight campers) per day. There are five campgrounds on the island, and reservations, which may be made no more than 6 months in advance, are essential, especially in the fall and spring. Sea Camp, the largest, is adjacent to a ferry dock, while four back-country campsites are from 3.5 to 10.6 miles north.

Most visitors reach the island at either the Sea Camp or Dungeness docks following a 45-minute ride from St. Mary's aboard the Park Service ferry *Cumberland Queen.* The ferry schedule varies by season. Island information is available by calling (912) 882-4336, 9 A.M.–4:30 P.M., daily. Reservations for both the ferry and campgrounds may be requested by calling (912) 882-4335 between 10 A.M. and 4 P.M., Mon.–Fri.; or by faxing a request to (912) 673-7747 (24 hours a day).

St. Marys

A visit to Cumberland Island is incomplete without a walk around its mainland gateway, the village of St. Marys, whose history is linked to the islands and to its namesake river. During the colonial period, the St. Marys River marked the disputed boundary between the Spanish Colony of Florida and the English Colony of Georgia. As the two nations vied for control of the coast, this area remained a mostly deserted and dangerous place. Spanish and English soldiers clashed along the frontier, and pirates used the nearby islands and inlets as hideouts and smuggling dens.

The village of St. Marys was founded in 1787, when Jacob Weed, a grantholder near a place called Buttermilk Bluff, sold shares in his land to a group interested in establishing a new settlement. Surveyor James Finley laid out the streets in 1788, and his plan remains intact within the boundaries of the historic district. By the early 1800s, St. Marys was thriving as a center of shipping and commerce for the surrounding coastal plantations.

During the War of 1812, the British captured the town, occupying it for a few months until word arrived in the winter of 1815 that the war had ended. Four years later, in 1819, the region finally enjoyed a period of peace when Spain ceded its lands to the United States, creating the new State of Florida. No longer was the southern bank of the St. Marys River a hostile country.

During the Civil War, many citizens moved inland, and after the war, the village settled into nearly three-quarters of a century of tranquility as a backwater fishing port.

Prosperity returned with the construction of the Gilman Paper Company mill on the edge of town in the 1940s, an industry that drew heavily on the area's rich fields of timber. This was followed by the creation of the Cumberland Island National Seashore

in 1972, drawing thousands of visitors to St. Marys as the starting point for the journey to the remote island. Most recently, the construction of the U.S. Navy's enormous King's Bay Nuclear Submarine Base at nearby Kingsland has brought thousands of sailors and civilians to the region to work at the sprawling facility. It is a special treat for visitors to get a glimpse of the conning tower of a submarine as it glides through Cumberland Sound.

Locals are quick to point out their fervent belief that Savannah-born composer Johnny Mercer, a visitor for many years to St. Marys, drew on the tranquil beauty of the river and the marsh as inspiration for his Academy Award–winning song, *Moon River*. Gazing at a spectacular riverfront sunset, it is easy to capture that same sense of wonder that may have moved Mercer to pen the famous tune.

Today, St. Marys' old historic district, listed in the National Register of Historic Places, retains the small-town atmosphere that makes it an ideal place to slow your pace before or after an escape to Cumberland Island's natural paradise.

429

WALK DISTANCE AND TERRAIN

🚶🚶 *Cumberland Island*

Miles of sandy lanes and trails crisscross the island, offering nearly endless possibilities for hiking. While the terrain is flat, the distances between sites, especially toward the

Dunes along Cumberland Island's eastern coast

northern end of the island, make a day trip to see them very difficult. Possibly the most popular walk for day visitors, it traces an approximately 5.5-mile loop from the Sea Camp dock southward along the River Trail to the Ice House Museum, on to the ruins of Dungeness, past the old cemetery, across the dunes, then north along the wide beach back to Sea Camp and the ferry dock. An additional loop to Little Greyfield Beach will add about 3 miles and to Stafford House and beach, about 5 miles. The round-trip from the Sea Camp ferry dock to Plum Orchard is nearly 15 miles and to the old African-American community at Half-Moon Bluff, more than 25 miles.

Much of the walk in the interior of the island is beneath a thick canopy of live oaks, while the dunes and beach are exposed to wind and sun. When crossing the dunes, it is essential that walkers use only the designated paths. Consider the seasonal temperatures and humidity when planning your hike. Also, water sources on the island are limited, so it is very important to carry enough water. National Park staff are happy to offer tips and answer questions about exploring the island in any season of the year.

Note: Day visitors must remember that the last ferry of the day leaves the island at 4:45 P.M. If you miss it, you are required to charter a boat to take you off the island.

St. Marys

The walk through St. Marys is a pleasant 1.5-mile loop among live oaks and past elegant old homes and buildings. A side trip to Oak Grove Cemetery will add about a half-mile to the route.

SIGHTS ALONG THE WAY

 Cumberland Island

1. Sea Camp Dock and Visitor Center (1970s)—Originally constructed by Charles Fraser to serve as the sales office for his Cumberland Oaks resort development, the complex was converted for use as an island orientation center when the National Park Service acquired the island.

2. Ice House Museum (c. 1880s)—Built by the Carnegie family to store the large blocks of ice carved from northern lakes and brought to the island by barge, the building now houses a museum tracing the natural and human history of the island.

3. Dungeness Ruins (1884)—Built on the foundation of Gen. Greene's 1803 home, this massive mansion was once one of the largest private homes in America. Even in its deteriorated condition, the scale of this enormous house remains staggering. Visitors may walk around the ruins but climbing on them is prohibited (they are unstable and home to rattlesnakes).

4. Tabby House (c. 1800) and Gardens (1880s)—The 1-story Tabby House was built by the Greene family as a temporary residence while their main house was under construction. When the Carnegies purchased the property, this house was restored for use as the estate manager's office. It is now a museum featuring displays of life on the island during the days of the Greenes and Carnegies. The adjacent gardens were a favorite place for Lucy Carnegie and her children.

5. Dungeness Cemetery (c. 1800s)—It was in this small cemetery overlooking the marsh that Revolutionary War general "Light Horse" Harry Lee was buried with full military honors in 1818. His remains were moved to Virginia in 1913, but the tombstone placed over the grave by his son, Robert E. Lee, remains.

6. "Ghost Fleet" of Dungeness (1930s–50s)—These rusting automobiles once belonged to Dungeness staff and members of the Carnegie family. They have not been moved since the 1950s.

7. Dungeness Out-Buildings (1880s–1910s)—This complex includes a stable, garage, dormitories, dining hall, maintenance sheds, and other structures essential for the support of the massive Carnegie estate. Most of the buildings have been stabilized. A few are open to the public, and others are used by the Park Service as maintenance and storage facilities.

8. Sea Camp (1975)—Located a half-mile east of the ferry dock, this campground is the largest and most popular on the island.

9. Greyfield (1901)—Built by Lucy Carnegie for her daughter Margaret, the large house is the centerpiece of a 1,300-acre private compound within the park. It has been converted into an elegant inn by Margaret's daughter, Lucy Ferguson. *Information:* (904) 261-6408.

10. Stafford Cemetery (c. 1850s–1910s)—Established by the Stafford family, who owned a large antebellum plantation on the island, the burial ground contains remains of several generations of family members.

11. Stafford House (1901)—Built on the foundations of the old Stafford Plantation house completed in the 1840s and burned during the Civil War, this house was built for Thomas and Lucy Carnegie's son William. The house and surrounding property remain privately owned.

12. The Chimneys (1840s)—Rows of chimneys are all that remain of the Stafford Plantation's slave cabins burned by overseers in retaliation for the aborted uprising in 1862.

13. Plum Orchard (1898)—Second only to Dungeness in elegance, this grand Georgian Revival–style mansion was built by Lucy Carnegie for her son George. Among the large home's many amenities were an indoor swimming pool and an elegant ballroom. The house remains much as it was when the Carnegie family vacated the property in the 1960s.

Plum Orchard's future has been the subject of continuing controversy. While the Park Service stabilized the old structure and used a portion of it for staff housing, preservation advocates urged a complete restoration and possible reuse as an artists' retreat, gallery, and conference facility. However, the house sits adjacent to the Cumberland Island Wilderness, whose supporters opposed any restoration that would draw more people into the fragile environment. In 1999, a compromise was reached: Funds were committed for restoration; island visitation remains capped at 300 people per day; foot and boat access to historic resources at the north end of the island will be improved; and a National Park Service Advisory Board will monitor implementation of these plans and oversee Plum Orchard's future. Currently, there are tours of Plum Orchard on Sundays.

14. The Settlement (1860s)—This small village was established by the freed slaves who returned to the island after the Civil War. Many earned their living fishing, working for the Carnegies, or working at the luxury hotel located in nearby High Point from the 1890s to the 1920s. The Cumberland Island Museum in one small building is dedicated to archiving and preserving artifacts for scholarly research, but does have a small exhibit area open to visitors (Hours vary. Information: P.O. Box 796, St. Marys, Ga. 31558). The village's small church was the scene of the 1996 wedding of the late John F. Kennedy Jr. and Carolyn Bessette.

15. High Point (c. 1890s)—The rambling Cumberland Island Hotel was built here in the 1890s, offering wealthy tourists luxurious accommodations along the coast. It prospered until the 1920s, when a bridge was constructed to nearby St. Simons, making that island much more accessible. The hotel eventually closed, and the complex was purchased by the Candler family of Atlanta for use as a private retreat.

St. Marys

16. St. Marys Port Pavilion (1977) —Osborne and St. Marys Sts. This public pavilion overlooks the shrimp boat docks, commercial wharves, and the wide St. Marys River.

17. Cumberland Island National Seashore Visitor Center and Ferry Dock (1970s)—107 St. Marys St. Occupying a central location along St. Marys' waterfront (once the southernmost port in the United States), the center is the starting point for ferry trips to the island. *Hours:* 9 A.M.– 5 P.M., daily. (912) 882-4335. (At the time of this writing, the Park Service is constructing a new visitor center

and museum on Osborne St. north of the Riverview Hotel. It is scheduled to open in 2001.)

18. St. Marys Submarine Museum (1996)—102 St. Marys St. Taking advantage of the proximity of the Kings Bay submarine base, this old movie-theater-turned-museum offers exhibits on the origins and history of submarines and features a working periscope. *Hours:* 10 A.M.–4 P.M., Tues.–Sat.; 1–5 P.M., Sun. (912) 882-2782.

19. Riverview Hotel (1916)— 105 Osborne St. Built as a small resort hotel, the Riverview's second-floor balcony is a popular spot for watching activities on the waterfront. The hotel's Cumberland Landing Restaurant and Seagles Tavern have been St. Marys' fixtures for many years. *Information:* (912) 882-4187.

20. Cannon (c. 1800s)—Osborne St. median. This old cannon barrel is believed to have been taken from a British ship during the War of 1812.

21. Bank of St. Marys Building (1836)—Osborne and Bryant Sts. Built when St. Marys was a thriving commercial port, the bank relocated to Columbus in 1843. The building was purchased by the local Roman Catholic congregation and was used for many years as its church. It continues to serve as a parish community center, and there are plans to restore the steeple removed more than 50 years ago.

433

22. Spencer House (1872)—101 E. Bryant St. Built by William Spencer, U.S. Customs Collector for the port of St. Marys from 1871 to 1873, the large 3-story frame house is now a bed-and-breakfast inn. (912) 882-1872.

23. Frohock House (c. 1907)— E. Bryant and Ready Sts. Lester Frohock combined two smaller 19th-century houses to create this large home.

24. Capt. Samuel Flood House (c. 1800s)—Built by one of the many sea captains and river pilots who made St. Marys their home, this house is one of the oldest structures in the village. The large pecan trees behind the home were planted by Mrs. Flood.

25. Orange Hall (c. 1829)— 303 Osborne St. This house was built by planter John Wood as a present to his daughter Jane and her husband, the Rev. Horace Pratt, pastor of the nearby Presbyterian Church. Jane died before the house was completed, so it became home to Pratt and his second wife, Isabel. It is considered one of the finest examples of the Greek Revival style of architecture in Georgia. Today, the ground floor houses the St. Marys Welcome Center, and the upper floors are furnished as a period house museum. *Hours:* 9 A.M.–5 P.M., Mon.–Sat.; 1–5 P.M., Sun. (800) 868-8687. *NR*

26. Archibald Clark House (c. 1801)—Osborne at Conyers St. The oldest standing residence in St. Marys, this house was built by a Mr. Jackson and purchased in 1802 by Clark, who served as customs collector under seven presidents, until his death in 1849. Clark entertained several dignitaries in this house, including Aaron Burr, who stopped here after killing Alexander Hamilton in a duel in Washington, and Gen. Winfield Scott, who visited on his return from the Indian wars.

27. Washington Oak and Pump (c. 1800)—In the Osborne St. median. On the day of Pres. George Washington's funeral at Mount Vernon in Virginia (Dec. 18, 1799), the citizens of St. Marys carried a ceremonial casket from the wharf and buried it here. Six oak trees were planted around the grave. The last tree died in 1987, and its wood was given to the U.S. Navy for use in repairs to the USS *Constitution* ("Old Ironsides"). Today, the withered stump of one tree remains. The pump is for one of the town's half-dozen freshwater wells dug nearby the year Washington died.

28. Methodist Chapel (1858)— Conyers and Ready Sts. Established in 1799, this is the oldest religious congregation in the city. During the Civil War, the chapel was used by occupying Union forces to store supplies. In 2000, the small congregation gained nationwide attention when it was surprised by a multimillion-dollar bequest from the estate of a local businessman.

29. St. Marys City Hall Complex (1991)—414 Osborne St. This low-profile, modern facility, designed to blend in with the older surrounding structures, houses the St. Marys Tourism Council. *Hours:* 8 A.M.–4:30 P.M., Mon.–Fri. (912) 882-6200.

30. Toonerville Trolley (1928)—Osborne St. just south of City Hall. This small bus was adapted for use by commuters on the railway line connecting St. Marys and Kingsland. The trolley was made famous by cartoonist Roy Crane, who featured it in his popular 1930s comic strip, *Wash Tubbs & Easy.*

31. First Presbyterian Church (c. 1808)—Conyers and Osborne Sts. Built with public funds as a non-denominational church, Horace Pratt (see #25) was ordained here by the Presbytery of Georgia in 1822. The sanctuary was incorporated as the Independent Presbyterian Church in 1828 and rechartered as the First Presbyterian Church in 1832. It is the oldest standing Presbyterian church in Georgia. Many of St. Marys earliest settlers are buried in the church cemetery.

32. Gillican House (c. 1800s)—Conyers St. west of the Presbyterian Church. This house once served as the Rev. Horace Pratt's library and as quarters for his servants. A hole in one window frame is said to have been caused by British shelling of the town in 1814.

33. Episcopal Church (c. 1900s)—Wheeler St. between Conyers and Weed Sts. The first church on this site was built in 1812. The second, built in 1845, was burned during the Civil War.

34. Bacon-Burns-Stucki House (c. 1830)—Osborne and Weed Sts. This simple 2-story house was extensively remodeled in the 1880s.

35. Sandiford-Goodbread House (c. 1884)—209 Osborne St. Built by Ralph Sandiford and later owned by excursion boat captain Walter Goodbread, the 2-story cottage with open porches has been restored as a bed-and-breakfast inn. (912) 882-7490.

36. Oak Grove Cemetery (c. 1780s)—Bartlett St. between Weed and Bryant Sts. Older than the town, this burial ground dates to plantation days. The oldest marked grave is that of Richard Gascoigne, interred in 1801. One section of the cemetery contains tombstones inscribed in French, graves of a few Acadian settlers who came to the Georgia coast after being forced from Nova Scotia by the English. Most of the Acadians (Cajuns) settled in Louisiana.

January

- Bluegrass Music Festival (Jekyll Island)
- Martin Luther King Jr. Holiday Parade and Celebration (Savannah)

March

- St. Patrick's Day Parade and Festival (Savannah)
- Spring Tour of Homes and Gardens (Savannah)
- Arts Festival (Jekyll Island)
- Garden Club Tour of Homes and Flower Show (Jekyll Island)

April

- NOGS (North of Gaston Street) Tour of Hidden Gardens (Savannah)
- Sidewalk Arts Festival (Savannah)

May

- Seafood Festival (Savannah)
- Spring Tour of Historic Gardens (Savannah)
- Harborfest and Blessing of the Fleet (Brunswick)

July

- Old Fashioned Fourth Celebration (Brunswick)
- Independence Day Celebration (St. Marys)
- Red, White, and Blues Festival (Savannah)

October

- Oktoberfest (Savannah)
- Rock Shrimp Festival (St. Marys)

November

- Memorial Service for Submariners (St. Marys)
- Downtown Illumination and Christmas Open House (St. Marys)

December

- Christmas Tour of Homes (Savannah)
- Christmas on the River (Savannah)
- Plantation Christmas at Hofwyl-Broadfield State Historic Site (Brunswick)
- Old Town Victorian Christmas Tour of Homes (Brunswick)
- Candlelight Tour of Homes (St. Marys)
- Holiday Lights Community Celebration (Jekyll Island)
- New Year's Eve Celebration at City Market (Savannah)
- First Night (Savannah)

Atherton, Elizabeth and Rambo, Meredith. *A Selection of Nineteenth Century Homes in Historic Marietta, Georgia.* Marietta, GA, 1976.

Atlanta City Directory. Atlanta, GA: Atlanta City Directory Company. Various publishers, 1870–1992.

Bender, Steve. *Callaway Gardens, Legacy of a Dream.* New York, NY: Callaway Editions, 1996.

Blumenson, John J. G. *Identifying American Architecture, A Pictorial Guide in Styles and Terms, 1600–1945.* Nashville, TN: American Association for State and Local History, 1977; 1981.

Bollinger, J. Mark and Landrum, Brenda G., eds. *The Story of Andersonville Prison and American Prisoners of War.* Eastern National Park and Monument Association, 1987.

Boney, F. N. *A Walking Tour of the University of Georgia.* Athens, GA: University of Georgia Press, 1989.

Boyd, Brian. *The Chattooga Wild and Scenic River.* Conyers, GA: Ferncreek Press, 1990.

Brown, Fred and Jones, Nell, eds. *The Georgia Conservancy's Guide to the North Georgia Mountains.* Marietta, GA: Longstreet Press, 1991.

Coleman, Kenneth. *Georgia History in Outline.* Athens, GA: University of Georgia Press, 1978.

Cozzens, Peter. *This Terrible Sound— The Battle of Chickamauga.* Urbana, IL: University of Illinois Press, 1992.

Dickens, Roy S. and McKinley, James L. *Frontiers in the Soil: The Archaeology of Georgia.* LaGrange, GA: Frontiers Publishing, 1979.

Drummond, Margaret C., ed. *Guide To The Appalachian Trail in North Carolina and Georgia,* 7th ed. Harpers Ferry, WV: Appalachian Trail Conference, 1983.

Ehle, John. *Trail of Tears: The Rise and Fall of the Cherokee Nation.* New York, NY: Doubleday Books, 1988.

English, Thomas H. *Emory University 1915–1965, A Sesquicentennial History.* Atlanta, GA: Higgins-McArthur and Co., 1966.

Fancher, Betsy. *Savannah—A Renaissance of the Heart.* Garden City, NY: Doubleday and Co., 1976.

Freeman, Ron. *Savannah: People, Places, Events.* Tallahassee, FL: Rose Printing Co., 1997.

Fretwell, Mark E. *This So Remote Frontier—The Chattahoochee Country of Alabama and Georgia.* Tallahassee, FL: Rose Printing Co., 1980.

437

Georgia Conservancy. *A Guide to the Georgia Coast.* Atlanta, GA: The Georgia Conservancy, 1985.

Georgia Humanities Council. *The New Georgia Guide.* Athens, GA: University of Georgia Press, 1996.

Grady, James. *Architecture of Neel Reid in Georgia.* Athens, GA: University of Georgia Press, 1973.

Harshaw, Lou. *The Gold of Dahlonega: The First Major Gold Rush in North America.* Asheville, NC: Hexagon Co., 1976.

The Heritage Tour of Albany Homes, Albany, Georgia. Thronateeska Heritage Foundation, Inc., 1975.

Historic Savannah Foundation, Inc. *Sojourn in Savannah,* 8th ed. Savannah, GA: Printcraft Press, 1990.

Homan, Tim. *The Hiking Trails of North Georgia,* 3rd ed. Atlanta, GA: Peachtree Publishers, 1997.

Key, William. *The Battle of Atlanta and the Georgia Campaign.* Atlanta, GA: Peachtree Publishers, 1981.

Lenz, Richard. *The Civil War in Georgia—An Illustrated Traveler's Guide.* Watkinsville, GA: Infinity Press, 1995.

Linley, John. *The Georgia Catalogue—Historic American Buildings Survey, A Guide to the Architecture of the State.* Athens, GA: University of Georgia Press, 1982.

Logue, Frank and Victoria. *Georgia Outdoors.* Winston-Salem, NC: John F. Blair Publishers, 1995.

London, Bonnie. *A History of Georgia.* Montgomery, AL: Clairmont Press, 1992.

Martin, Harold. *Georgia—A Bicentennial History.* New York, NY: W. W. Norton and Co., 1977.

Martin, Van Jones and Mitchell, William R. Jr. *Landmark Homes of Georgia 1783–1983, Two Hundred Years of Architecture, Interiors, and Gardens.* Savannah, GA: Golden Coast Publishing Co., 1982.

McCash, William B. and June H. *Jekyll Island Club Historic District.* Jekyll Island, GA: Jekyll Island Authority, 1995.

Miles, Jim. *Civil War Sites in Georgia.* Nashville, TN: Rutledge Hill Press, 1996.

Miles, Jim. *Fields of Glory—A History and Tour Guide of the Atlanta Campaign.* Nashville, TN: Rutledge Hill Press, 1989.

Miles, Jim. *To The Sea—A History and Tour Guide of Sherman's March.* Nashville, TN: Rutledge Hill Press, 1989.

Mitchell, William R. Jr. and Moore, Richard. *Gardens of Georgia.* Atlanta, GA: Peachtree Publishers, 1987.

Pfitzer, Donald F. *The Hiker's Guide to Georgia.* Helena, MT: Falcon Press, 1993.

Reiter, Beth Lattimore. *Coastal Georgia.* Savannah, GA: Golden Coast Publishing, 1985.

438

Rhyne, Nancy. *Touring the Coastal Georgia Backroads.* Winston-Salem, NC: John F. Blair Publishers, 1994.

Schoettle, H. E. Taylor. *A Field Guide to Jekyll Island.* Athens, GA: University of Georgia Sea Grant College Program, 1990.

Scruggs, Carroll P. *Georgia During the Revolution—A Bicentennial Edition.* Norcross, GA: Bay Tree Grove Publishers, 1975.

Scruggs, Carroll P. *Georgia Historical Markers.* Valdosta, GA: Bay Tree Grove Publishers, 1973.

Sears, William H. *Excavations at Kolomoki: Final Report.* Athens, GA: University of Georgia Press, 1956.

Spector, Tom. *The Guide to the Architecture of Georgia.* Columbia, SC: University of South Carolina Press, 1993.

Strock, G. Michael. *Andersonville National Cemetery.* Eastern National Park and Monument Association, 1998.

Vanstory, Burnette. *Georgia's Land of the Golden Isles.* Athens, GA: University of Georgia Press, 1970.

Woodworth, Steven E. *Chickamauga—A Battlefield Guide.* Lincoln, NE: University of Nebraska Press, 1999.

ABOUT THE AUTHORS

Ren Davis is a native Atlantan and a graduate of Emory University with a degree in history. He earned a master's in public health from Tulane University. He has also written articles for the *Atlanta Journal-Constitution, Georgia Journal, Atlanta Magazine,* and *Tennis.*

Helen Davis is a native of Lewistown, Pennsylvania. She received her bachelor's degree from Ohio State University and her master's degree in education from Georgia State University. She has taught in the Atlanta Public Schools since 1980.

Ren and Helen are avid walkers, hikers, and backpackers, as well as award-winning photographers. The third member of their team is Nelson Davis who, at age seventeen, has grown up exploring Georgia with them.

Ren and Helen were coauthors of *Atlanta Walks, The Insight Guide to Atlanta and Savannah, Fodor's Pocket Guide To Atlanta,* and *Fodor's Cityguide—Atlanta.*